AMERICAN
RAGE

AMERICAN
RAGE

Rick Huffman

AMERICAN RAGE

iUniverse books may be ordered through booksellers or by contacting:

iUniverse
1663 Liberty Drive
Bloomington, IN 47403
www.iuniverse.com
1-800-Authors (1-800-288-4677)

ISBN: 978-1-4917-9930-7 (sc)
ISBN: 978-1-4917-9931-4 (hc)
ISBN: 978-1-4917-9929-1 (e)

Library of Congress Control Number: 2016909243

Print information available on the last page.

iUniverse rev. date: 06/02/2016

Contents

Down the highway, down the tracks, down the road to ecstasy
I followed you beneath the stars hounded by your memory
And all your raging glory.

I been double-crossed now for the very last time and now I'm finally free.
I kissed goodbye the howling beast on the
borderline which separated you from me.
You'll never know the hurt I suffered, nor the pain I rise above,
And I'll never know the same about you,
your holiness or your kind of love,
And it makes me feel so sorry.

Idiot wind, blowing through the buttons of our coats,
Blowing through the letters that we wrote.
Idiot wind, blowing through the dust upon our shelves.
We are idiots, babe.
It's a wonder we can even feed ourselves.[1]

—Bob Dylan

---

[1] Bob Dylan, 1975, "Idiot Wind," on *Blood on the Tracks,* Columbia PC33235,
33⅓ rpm.

Chapter 1

Alprazolam Morning

Speeding on a winding, tree-lined road, Leo Rickenbacker drives up a vertical embankment. His car rolls back, somersaulting and then crashing. The first person on the scene rushes over and peers inside the car, only to see the driver who, much to the would-be rescuer's surprise, is seconds away from lighting a cigarette. Of course Leo, hanging upside down from his seat, his air bags deployed as gasoline drips from his car, would try to light a cigarette. That's what he does, as he has no regard for any life, not even his own. The responder, looking nervously at the lighter, says to Leo, "Man, relax."

Leo replies casually, "I am relaxed. Just waiting to be rescued."

Leo can't afford to have anything happen. He is too far wedged into his plans. In a rush of momentary panic, he realizes that much of what he wants to accomplish rests in the hands of his own suicidal tendencies. Leo is a man without fear of consequence or moral interruption, but he is also a live wire who cannot be trusted to care about his own life, much less to carry out the grand plan he has set in motion.

"Let's get you outta here," the responder says frantically.

"Ready when you are." Leo smiles back. He does not know what to expect. He only knows to be prepared because from here on out there are no rules.

The perfectly coiffed lawn and majestically manicured landscaping explode from around the central brick mansion that is set atop its perch on the hill. Trees, plants, and flowers in a vibrant array of colors, shapes, and sizes dot the property and are spread out across the vast yard, providing shade, privacy, and stunning beauty. Red maples, nutgall oaks, and poplars provide the shade; holly trees and Carolina sapphires ring the home for privacy; and magnolias, dogwoods, and cherry trees provide the feel of Georgia Southern hospitality and charm. The tree-lined tunneled entryway drive is among the most spectacular and impressive in Atlanta.

Ben, Felix, and Dwight have the ground duty today for Elite Lawns and Landscaping, the lawn and garden company that provides weekly maintenance for the Marvel estate in Buckhead. They've been regulars on this account for years, knowing every blade and leaf like the back of their hands. They've been pruning, hedge trimming, mowing, grading, irrigating, aerating, and fertilizing the Marvel plot together for the past five or so years. The Marvel account was the company's largest, and the three amigos, as Ben, Felix, and Dwight were referred to around the office, were the caretakers of this exclusive property.

Ben, the job lead, is a tall, leather-skinned, very large black man who has spent the better part of half a century doing yard work with dozens of contract lawn services. He once ran his own yard cutting service, but unfortunately he surrounded himself with unsavory types who took advantage of his lack of business acumen and slowly drained his accounts. After he lost his business, he decided that he'd rather work for the Man than *be* the Man. He hooked up with Elite about the time they got the Marvel property, and immediately took ownership of the vast estate. He clicked with the Marvel mansion's matriarch, Christina Marvel, and developed the kind of business partnership with her that has blossomed through the years. He understands her expectations, and she completely entrusts her glorious home and exquisite surroundings to his ample hands.

Felix is a young man in his early thirties, skinny and hyperactive, a Venezuelan transplant who landed in Atlanta when Hurricane Katrina destroyed his home in New Orleans. He brought his wife and four kids to Atlanta for a temporary move until their land back home could be cleared and rebuilt. The family liked their new city. And since Felix and his wife's only real ties were back in Venezuela—all four of his children had been born in the states—they decided, like so many other Louisianans did poststorm, to stay in this new town of hope and dreams. Felix's yard work and landscaping skills are reliable and consistent, nothing more, but he is a hard worker who never misses any days or botches any assignments. Felix is nothing if not resourceful. He supplements his income with some small-time weed dealing on the side. He also isn't beyond an occasional act of larceny if an opportunity presents itself. But as far as his work as a landscaping engineer, as they like to be called, goes, he is solid.

Dwight is a young black guy and is sort of a surrogate little brother to Ben, who watches over him like a papa bear trying to keep his cub out of trouble. Ben, knowing the temptations that are readily available to his crew, is on a personal mission not to lose Dwight to the downward spiral of drug abuse and petty crime. Dwight is an okay worker, tries hard, follows directions well, and is a quick learner. He's just working to please Ben and keep his head above water. He has got a couple of kids with different baby mamas, but—following Ben's lead—he still tries to be a part of their lives and not be an absent dad.

❋ ❋ ❋

Ben and Dwight are busy off-loading the yard equipment from the back of the work trailer as Felix parks his car across the street and drags himself out. He slowly walks toward the guys as they struggle to roll out the large riding mower.

Felix looks terrible. Landscapers and lawn workers don't try to adhere to dress codes—or basic hygiene, for that matter—but he is in especially bad shape this morning. It was bad enough that he had to drive his own car to meet up with the guys instead of riding along in the truck.

"Shit, man," Ben says as Felix reaches them at the trailer. "You lose a bet?"

"I was in a car accident last night," Felix explains. Ben and Dwight stretch around Felix to look at his car. He notices them checking it out. "My wife was driving. Had the accident in her car."

"You okay?" Ben asks.

"Oh yeah, I'm fine. She T-boned a car after it blew through the signal. It was a newly married couple driving back to their hotel after the reception. It was bad. There was rice and cans and whipped cream all over the road. The groom came out and was screaming at me—losing his mind while yelling at and threatening me. He just wouldn't shut up. I told him to calm down and said that we could exchange insurance info and call the cops, mentioning that none of his hysterics were gonna bring his wife back."

Ben and Dwight are stunned.

"You killed her?" Dwight asks.

"Well, *I* didn't."

"So what happens now?"

"Nothin', I guess. Wasn't her fault. I guess we'll have to go to court or whatever, but the cops told us we weren't gettin' a ticket or charged. Just a real sad thing. It was an accident." Felix pauses for a moment and then snaps back—alert and seemingly ready to go. "So sorry I'm late."

After relaying his story, Felix helps Ben and Dwight off-load the trailer. They take the equipment and set up their staging area at the side of the main house, where they sort out the various tools for the variety of services they'll be performing that day. As they arrange the equipment, an Elite service van pulls up the main driveway to the house. Pat McLaren, the president and owner of Elite, steps out of the van with one of his assistants, Creep Sipotora.

Pat approaches the trio, who are busy working on getting the workday started, and calls Ben over to the side. As Ben approaches Pat, Creep comes out of the service van and joins them.

"You have the full outline for today's work?" Pat asks Ben. Ben nods and pulls a rumpled sheet of paper out of his back pocket.

"Good," Pat says, as he starts pointing out spots around the property that need extra care or landscaping enhancements. The lawn crew needs to make sure the work is pristine. This is the last "cleanup and beautify" opportunity for the Marvel mansion before the grand holiday party the Marvels are hosting on Saturday. "They're gonna want everything perfect for this weekend."

The Marvels have a history of hosting real throw-down parties. In addition to their annual holiday event, they also offer their home as part of a rotation of Atlanta-area mansions owned by wealthy, privileged, and influential families for hosting adult-themed parties. These are highly restricted invitation-only functions that have no limits to the excess and debauchery that may occur within the walls. They are "silent" events, talked about only in hushed whispers, and with lots of winks and nods, among the people who host and attend these wildly uninhibited parties.

"I'd like to have a cut of all the money they spend on the booze that'll flow here this weekend," Creep says as he joins Pat and Ben, who are reviewing the morning orders. "Or any day of the week for that matter."

"Dropped that years ago," Ben mentions. Pat turns and looks at him.

"Dropped what? Booze?"

"Yes, sir." Ben smiles. "I have a problem with the strong stuff."

"So you don't drink anything?"

"Nothing with alcohol." Ben nods. "I'm an alcoholic."

Ben and Creep both lift their heads when they hear Ben's announcement.

"Oh, true confessions," Creep says.

"Nothing like that. I'm just okay talking about it. It's not a problem anymore."

"Yeah, well, they say it's a disease, right?" Pat asks.

Ben nods. "Yeah, that's what they tell me. But it's the only disease where you can have a *great* buzz all the time." He laughs and immediately breaks through any uncomfortable vibe with his hearty chuckle.

"So you can't have even *one* drink?" Creep asks.

"If I had one beer right now, by four o'clock this morning I'd be finalizing plans for running guns to Nicaragua." Ben laughs out loud again, this time joined by Pat and Creep. Pat taps Ben on the shoulder and smiles.

"Keep up the good work," he says. "That's tough. You should be proud."

Ben smiles and turns to head back over to the work truck.

As Ben leaves, Pat leans over to speak with Creep.

"I didn't know that."

"Why would you?"

Pat shrugs his shoulders. He and Creep start up the front walkway toward the main house.

"Had the sex talk with my kid yesterday," Creep begins. "In this day and age, with all the easy free-porn access, it's a little trickier than I'm guessing it was when I got the talk from my dad. I had to find out just how much he already knew, and then I figured I'd take it from there. It's the new reality, right?"

"How did it go?"

"I asked him if he's ever seen porn, and he said he has. So I asked him if he had any questions."

"Did he ask you anything?"

"Yes." Creep pauses. "Things I absolutely knew nothing about. Some wild shit."

"Good talk then?" Pat laughs.

Creep shakes his head.

"Wait till you hear the questions when he turns eight."

"Jeez."

As Pat and Creep get to the door, Christina Marvel is opening it. She nearly runs into them as she bursts out.

"Oh," she blurts out, flustered. "Sorry, guys. I was just heading out. Do you need anything?"

"No," replies Pat, who is a friend and has known and worked with the Marvels for years. "Just wanted to check in and see if you need anything beyond what we've already discussed."

"I think we covered everything."

There's a brief moment of silence as the three stand at the doorway, looking at each other.

"Then we'll get to it."

Pat, Creep, and Christina all walk back down the pavers of the path to the front circular driveway. At the side of the house, Ben and Dwight are laying out the equipment and prepping the area. Christina and the guys look over to watch Ben and Dwight doing their work.

"Why are they looking at us?" Dwight asks.

"Take a look around," Ben says. "Who would you look at?"

❊ ❊ ❊

Yard work in the early morning hours of the fall and winter seasons can be quite pleasant. It's quiet, the winds whistle through the trees, and you can hear the distinct clicking sounds of the leaves and branches snapping together. The air is thin and cold, and the fog from your breath folds out of your mouth with each exertion of energy.

"We need to make sure this place is perfect when we leave today," Ben reminds Dwight. "This place needs to look like the cover of a magazine. If their party is crap, it won't be because of the yard and landscape. I've never been a scapegoat, and I've never sacrificed anyone to save myself. This place is not where I'm gonna start."

Dwight laughs and looks up to see a young, beautiful blonde girl sitting on a lounge chair next to the pool, which is behind the house. Despite the cold weather and chilly breezes, she is stretched out and absorbing the bright morning sunshine in a slinky one-piece bathing suit.

"Damn, take a look at that over there sunning in this weather."

Ben looks up. "Haven't seen her before. Must be a friend or relative in town for the party."

"I don't know about that," Dwight replies, fixated on her. "She has the kind of look that can turn a bald spot into a part." He shakes his head. "She is sweet. *And* she looks bored." He shifts his position and moves his head around, trying to get a better view. "God, look at her. I do love a pretty girl by the pool."

"She's not *that* beautiful," Ben offhandedly remarks.

"You don't think she's a babe?" Dwight says, more of a statement than question. "Fine, you can jack off to someone else." He faces Ben and grins.

"Like you'll ever be in a position to turn her down." Ben smiles back.

Before Dwight and Ben realize it, Pat and Christina have walked to where they are sorting the equipment. Ben sees Creep standing down at the street, talking to Felix by the van.

"His voice looks like it's putting his face asleep," Ben says about Creep. They both laugh as Pat and Christina walk up.

"How's it going, guys?" Christina asks in her most effusive voice. She seems to be happy, but the underlying anxiousness in her tone hints at her concern for throwing the perfect party. She demands that all aspects of her home and the "show" are flawless.

"Not too bad, Mrs. Marvel," Ben says. "We'll make sure everything is to your liking by the time we're done. It'll be perfect." Pat smiles as he stands behind her, happily listening to his crew leader reassure his client. "How is everything coming along with your plans?"

"Oh, things are starting to come together. I think it'll be a wonderful night—no small thanks to you and your team. You guys do such beautiful work. What would I do without you?" She smiles. "Now, unfortunately, I have to meet the AAA people where I left my car. I need to have a flat tire changed."

"We can take care of that," Pat tells her. "Where's your car?"

"I left it where I had the flat. Thanks for the offer, but I took a cab back here. I'm going to drive back to meet the guy and get it taken care of."

"You don't know how to change a tire?" Pat asks jokingly.

She laughs and rolls her eyes. "Never learned."

"Your dad never taught you?" Ben asks. "Just in case of emergencies?"

"Nope."

"It's simple," Ben continues. "You just take the jack out of the back, lift the car, turn the nuts off the bad tire, slip it off, put on the spare from the trunk, tighten up the nuts, lower the car, and you're off."

"Yes, well I just have one question." She grins. "How do you keep your hands from getting dirty?"

They all laugh with various levels of sincerity. She smiles.

"I guess I should have learned growing up. With me being from a small town and all, you would have assumed I'd learned a few basics along the way. But I'm a mess when it comes to this kind of thing," she says.

"I thought you were originally from Atlanta," Creep says.

"No, I grew up in Skunk Boone, Tennessee—just a tiny burp of a town about an hour east of Memphis. The sign at the city's entrance says, 'Population 2,658.' I'm not sure how they arrived at that number, but that's the way it stayed for as long as I can remember. Probably still there now."

"Heck, I grew up in a building with at least that many."

"How's that?"

"Courtesy of the county," Dwight says. "I spent a lot of my growing-up time in juvenile detention with a bunch of other dudes."

Christina, seemingly genuinely interested in his story, says, "Really? Tell me about it."

"The last time it was for a drunk and disorderly charge when I was seventeen, about ten years ago. I learned my lesson from that place. Had an angel with me ever since."

"That seems kind of harsh for being drunk, even when underage."

"Well, I kissed a cop during a traffic stop."

"My God, where did you kiss him?" She doesn't catch herself in time and immediately blushes. "Oh my ... never mind." They laugh again.

"Some people get the doughnut hole; some people get the crumbs," Ben adds.

"I don't know what that means," Christina says. "But I do know when you feel the wind in your face, it's just God whispering in your ear, 'This is your moment. Take it.' It comforts me to feel that way. It's letting the spirit live inside you."

"Yes, ma'am," Ben agrees, just humoring her because he can't roll his eyes. He knows she can start off on religious tangents, as he's been a captive audience to her faux preaching before. Christina somehow feels like she can redeem herself with every soul she thinks she reaches with her spirituality. "And the winds are speaking today."

"It is a beautiful morning, isn't it?" She turns to Pat and nods. "I've got to run. You men have a great day. I'll be back this afternoon. You know that if you need anything, just run inside and the housekeeper can help you."

They exchange good-byes. Pat walks with her to another Marvel family car as she gets in and starts the engine. From the side of the house, Ben and Dwight watch from atop the slight hill they're standing on. Felix joins them as they see Creep and Pat talking down by the street.

"When you cut the grass, you see the snakes," Ben comments.

"What's the best thing about being rich?" Felix asks Ben as they watch Christina pulling the other car out from the long driveway.

"Rich lets you walk away," Ben tells him.

They reorganize and spread out with their equipment, machines, pruning shears, bottled water, hoses, fertilizer, trash bags, and all the other tools they'll be using throughout the day.

Felix and Dwight walk around to the back of the house, beyond the pool area, where they can work and watch the action on the deck as a distraction.

"You know," Dwight says, "I think I've sold weed to every house in this neighborhood. There's lots of spoiled, entitled rich brats looking to score."

"I would have figured by now this place is way past grass," Felix says. "Most of these kids are scoring smack or oxy these days. Weed and booze are what they use to come down."

"I need to expand my inventory."

After Dwight and Felix set up their areas, Creep approaches, checking to make sure they have everything they need. Once finished, he starts to walk back down to the van. Before he leaves, he turns to Dwight and Felix.

"You know, I heard he pays to watch black dudes fuck his wife." Creep says referring to Marvel's husband John, and waits for their reaction.

"Jesus, that's messed up," Felix says.

"Yeah, that's, like, slave shit."

"I also heard," Creep continues, "that she used to be an 'exotic dancer' at one of our more exclusive gentlemen's clubs before her husband scooped her up."

"Ah, strippers." Dwight sighs. "One of the things Atlanta does best. Brisket, Coca-Cola, fried chicken, peach pie, and strippers."

"Just what I heard." Creep laughs as he goes down the walkway, soon meeting up with Pat, who is standing by the van reviewing worksheets.

"That guy is not funny," Dwight says, referring to Creep. "He thinks he's funny, but he's not. Not even close." He looks at Felix. "Have you ever talked to him? Ever heard him tell a joke? I have. It sounds like he's nailing a parakeet to a block of wood."

"That's all you got out of that?" Felix asks, dumbfounded. "That's one strange dude."

They head off to their respective areas around the house and begin working their magic on the yard.

Chapter 2

Screaming Fidelities

John Marvel is wrapping up his morning, watching *The Today Show* on TV and sharing the box of Honey Nut Cheerios he's eating from with his dog. The happy, tail-wagging terrier sits fixated on his owner, carefully waiting for one of the sweet treats to be handed over. John gets up to put away the cereal and looks at his dog, who is staring and following him around right under his heels. He almost trips over the dog as he walks toward the kitchen cabinet.

"How many times do I have to tell you?" he says to the dog. "You're gonna kill us both one of these days. You *can't* be walking around between my feet. We're both going to fall and get hurt." The dog just stares up at him, tail still flapping around. "No more cereal. When I'm done, you're done. See how that works?"

Marvel puts away the cereal box and starts taking off his boxers and T-shirt on his way upstairs to the bathroom. He walks into the bedroom naked. Christina is standing next to the bed, folding clothes and getting ready to leave the house.

"I'm gonna jump in the shower," John says to his wife. "You wanna do something with this first?" He points down at himself and smiles.

She looks at him and frowns. "As enticing as that sounds … no."

He reaches in and turns on the shower. He stands outside the shower stall door, waiting for the water to heat up. "I feel like you never take the initiative anymore when it comes to anything involving sex. If I don't start it, it doesn't happen, and when it does happen, I don't really feel like you're into it. Then I come to the realization that this is the way it is now. And that's really what it's all about. Sometimes I feel more like a roommate than a husband, part of your day's inconvenient itinerary."

He steps into the stall and begins showering, still keeping up his conversation with Christina. She's heard this all before and usually just ignores him. If she actually acted on one of his spontaneous requests, he'd probably be too flabbergasted to perform on command.

"You have a way of making your demons seem downright consumable." She laughs. "You know, I miss your impersonations. You know which one I like best? The one where you impersonate a normal guy; that's my favorite." Her bite is sarcastically tinged.

John continues with his shower routine, taking sneak peeks at himself in the shaving mirror mounted to the side of the stall. "I'm thinking of having some work done to lift my neck," he says while looking in the mirror, and then groans to himself. "Christ, never thought I'd say that."

The fifty-something couple often discuss ways to fight the scourge of aging and sometimes look into the different methods of fighting back. Their denial is as transparent as their need.

"You don't have any problem with your neck or anything else," she says, moaning back at him. "Stop looking at yourself."

"My issues are different. I'm dealing with a delicate, vulnerable mentality that's susceptible to turbulent vibes and pressures."

"And what's that supposed to mean?"

"It means I'm sensitive to criticism."

"You know what they say: one man's delicate, sensitive mentality is another man's insecure inner prick," she says with a laugh.

"Your problem is you don't know how to take a compliment," he says through the steady beat of the shower.

"And you do?"

"I don't know. I've never been complimented."

"Oh, poor baby," she whines sarcastically.

She leaves the bathroom and walks back into the bedroom. He finishes up with his shower, pulls the towel over from the rack outside the stall, and begins drying his hair. He steps out onto the floor mat and faces the bathroom mirror.

"Every so often," he says, towel wrapped around his waist as he studies his face, "you need to be reminded that our past mistakes needn't rule our future. We're all capable of growth."

"And you think getting your neck done is growth?"

He pauses after staring at his face. "Not exactly. I'd say that would be more transcendence than growth."

She steps back into the bathroom to face him. She gives him a nasty look that he immediately picks up on. It's the kind of look you get after you've said something that doesn't sit well with your audience. John gets this look from his wife a lot. And after so many years of marriage, it's part of the daily routine when he speaks.

"I know what you're trying to do," she says.

"What?" He feigns ignorance.

"You're making fun of Herman Zoo."

"Hey, I wasn't the one who invited him to our party. You're the Zookeeper. That's your business." Zookeepers are what devotees of Herman Zoo's Ministry call themselves.

"I thought it would be a good opportunity to *cleanse* our house."

"A crime scene cleanup team couldn't cleanse this house."

"You know," she says with a rising irritation in her tone, "you don't always have to be so dismissive of him. He's helped me through some difficult times, but you just make fun of him. The older you get, the more you only exist in your routine. If you don't like him, don't ask."

Herman Zoo is a strange mix of charismatic preacher, evangelist, spiritual master, and all the other titles bestowed on faith healers. Christina has embraced his ministry.

"I don't care." John turns and, seeing her standing in the doorway, says, "I just like to know what makes people tick. And I can't figure him out." He pauses. "All I know is that he seems to be just another religious zealot charlatan who talks people out of their money so they can go to heaven."

"So you know what makes me tick?" she asks.

"Of course."

"What is it?"

"I can't tell you." He smiles. "That would destroy my advantage."

She rolls her eyes and walks back into the bedroom. He turns back to the mirror and rubs his face with his hands, debating whether or not to shave.

"Didn't you learn anything from him?" she asks.

"I learned what I always learn. People are fools." John decides to shave. He hates the necessary evil of shaving. "Well, that and the only thing Jews are good for is covering shifts for gentiles who don't work on Christmas Day."

"That's an awful thing to say. You didn't get that from him," she barks back from the bedroom. "He has taught me to value more the daily laughter and joy you find and share in a place that feels like home."

"That sounds like something from one of his pamphlets."

"It's his philosophy."

"He's just a clown with props and a fairy tale, winking at his audience and worrying about who's the coolest person in the room."

"I'm not going to discuss this with you anymore. You're just looking to pick a fight over him."

"Am not," he says like a little kid who is pointing out someone else to blame. "*You* invited him to our home for our biggest party of the year. I'm sure having a spiritual presence spouting religious swill and condemning our lifestyle will make *everyone* more comfortable about enjoying themselves." His sarcasm is not subtle. He continues speaking while shaving. "He embodies intimidation and calmness in the same person—towering over his subjects, becoming this all-knowing and all-powerful being who garners the worship and love of anyone he meets. I've been watching him. He's quite the showman. His variations between friendship and dominance of all you Zookeepers are nuanced in a brilliant way. It's actually quite the remarkable performance. It makes me wonder if I—if I'm not careful—could fall for the same trick. I have to keep reminding myself how tragically sad and desperately cruel people like him really are. He's a man who deflects his own pain by causing it in others. And it's all that preaching from him that makes you more toxic than just the silhouette of a blind loyalist that you really are."

"You'll be sorry you said that to me when I'm gone," she says.

"I'm already sorry."

"I take what I need from him, and it helps me," she continues. "I think that's pretty much the human condition. You wake up and try to live your day in such a way that, once you go to sleep at night, makes you feel okay about yourself. You should be happy that he makes me happy."

John finishes shaving and washes his face with splashes of warm water. "If you feel good about yourself, then that's all that matters. From what I can see, when he gets lemons, he just gnaws on them all day."

He takes off his towel, pulls on a pair of boxer shorts, and walks into the bedroom. Christina finishes putting away laundry as he stands next to the bed getting dressed.

"It just bothers me," he adds. "Like people who feel compelled to take pictures of their food at a restaurant before they eat it. It's annoying."

"That's why what Zoo represents is so important for our times," Christina says, still trying to make her point. "The human race should recede into oblivion. We're a failure. He's trying to change our course."

"If by failure you mean the most successful species to have ever walked on earth, then I agree. Survival of the fittest. Darwin ... evolution ... we won."

"You've obviously never been to the Marietta DMV," she jokes.

"I just don't want our Christmas party to turn into something our guests will find"—he pauses to find the words—"difficult to navigate. We'll all have bowls of religious fervor sitting in front of us, and there really won't much choice about whether we're hungry or not. We are, or we'll *pretend* to be, because nobody wants to deal with the consequences of saying, 'Oh, um ... please, no more. ... I just ate and I'm stuffed. You got anything other than religious fanaticism to snack on?'" John picks up his wallet and watch from the dresser. "I bet you he has friends he hasn't even used yet, like those little kids they always trot out for the white-guilt crowd in order to get donations and sponsors. All that shit goes right into his pockets."

"My faith is to improve myself and our family. I'm looking to overcome the mistakes from my past," she counters.

"The past will never leave you alone," he says. "But only the weak allow it to call the shots. Every new day tells us to shed our old skins and fears so we can start anew. Most of us can do that. Remnants of past errors or traumas may linger in this or that way—guilt or nightmares or self-destructive habits—but healthy people move on. We've all done things we're sorry for. But you have to try to forgive yourself and try to grow into a better person. That's what the message should be."

"If you just listen," she says, "you'll see that what he says is true. The light at the end of the tunnel is just the world on fire."

"All the pain and misery he causes in the name of faith—it's all there right in front of us. It's almost begging us to do something to stop it. How else could something spiral so out of control and take over lives in the name of good and right? If he's not stopped, he'll swallow up real decency."

"He *is* decency. If you are in trouble, regardless of the reason—maybe you're working through some internal demons or substance abuse … whatever—if you ask someone close to you, 'Please don't give up on me,' all you're really telling them is that you don't have the will or desire to stop doing the destructive behavior on your own. You're letting them know not to give up on you even though you're not ready to work on yourself. Zoo fills in that desire to improve."

John ponders her response and decides he's had enough of combating the influence Zoo has on his wife. Like so many other things she's sampled and experimented with in their years together, he's aware of her proclivities. But if John's plans work out the way he's visualizing they will, Zoo will either become a major player in the Marvel money-laundering operation or suffer the consequences for refusing to participate. His tax-protected church cover is perfect for hiding funds.

Christina finishes up and steps out of the bedroom, but she stops after a few steps and turns around. "I almost forgot," she says bluntly. "Are you fucking the housekeeper?"

"No," he replies nonchalantly.

"Good," she says. "She's messing up everything. I can't deal with her anymore. You fire her."

"Okay."

She begins to leave again, and then turns back once more. "One last thing. There's something floating in the pool by the steps. I think it's some kind of dead animal. I didn't get close enough to look."

"It's a dead rat on the top step. I saw it this morning."

"Well, why didn't you get it out?"

"I paid for the house," he says. She stares at him, shakes her head, and shuts the bedroom door behind her as she leaves. He grins, listening as she walks downstairs. He can almost hear the irritation in her strut.

❋❋❋

Ben and his crew are cleaning up and loading the equipment back on the truck after having worked their magic on the Marvel homestead. Ben opens the garage door and drags the garbage cans out to the front for pickup after putting the bags of trimmings and clippings on the truck. Today is garbage pickup day.

"Hey, Ben," says a neighbor who lives across the street and is conducting the same morning ritual. The neighbor also uses Elite for his home yard work.

"Hey." Ben nods. After a pause, Ben continues looking at the neighbor. The man has a confused expression on his face. "You know … you're not wearing any pants."

The neighbor looks down to see his baggy T-shirt hanging down, barely concealing his naked bottom.

"Yep, thanks," he says to Ben with only a hint of embarrassment. He turns and walks back to his house as Ben shakes his head and returns to close the garage door.

❋❋❋

Felix and Dwight throw the last few bags of grass and clippings into the trailer. They walk around to the cab of the truck and start playing rock, paper, scissors while they wait for Ben. They're not shooting for money or anything in particular; they're only looking to kill time before leaving the work site.

Ben finishes up at the garage, secures everything, and walks back to the truck. He sees the two playing the game and notices that Dwight is throwing scissors every time. After a dozen or so games, Felix notices and starts to throw a rock each time to win. This happens for a few more games, with Felix obviously winning each round, his rock crushing Dwight's scissors.

"Why do you keep doin' scissors?" Ben finally asks.

"Improves my odds of winning," Dwight replies as he continues to lose each throw.

"How do you figure?"

"Because if he changes his throws, I'm sure to either tie or win two-thirds of the time."

"That's not true," Ben argues.

"Yes it is." Dwight pauses. "It's all math."

"But you keep using scissors. He'll just keep using rock and win."

"But I may change it up."

Felix and Dwight throw again—Felix with rock, and Dwight with scissors to lose again.

"But you're not," Ben says after watching a few more scissor losses by Dwight.

"But you don't know that."

"He's still winning," Ben observes.

"Only until the odds kick in."

Ben shakes his head. "I don't think you know how math works."

"You'll see."

After watching Dwight's several more losses to Felix, Ben grunts and walks to the back of the truck.

"You guys don't believe me," Dwight says. "You're both underestimatin' me."

"Is that right?" Ben asks with a sarcastic grin as he secures the back gate and blocks the machinery to keep it from sliding during their drive to their next stop.

"You know what I did during my last half hour in high school before I graduated?" Dwight asks.

"Smoked pot?" Felix offers.

"Jerked off?" Ben adds.

"That's what you think about me?" Dwight says with a look of disappointment on his face. "Screw you guys. I read books and poetry that weren't even a part of my classes. I cared. I studied during my time in school. I was no flop. It always meant something to me that I was smart. I wasn't like the other kids who were just passing time. I want to be remembered when I'm gone."

"No offense, but that's stupid," Felix finally adds. "Once you're dead and gone, all that's left of you is a face in some old pictures and in the blurry memory a few people."

"You can't start a sentence by saying 'no offense' and then say something like that."

"Okay, then take offense."

Ben comes forward before things get argumentative between his two workers. He just wants to get through the day without any unneeded hassles. "Get in the truck," he says to Dwight.

"I don't wanna sit in the middle," Dwight says with a moan.

"Get in." Ben laughs. "You get the bitch seat. You can practice shooting your scissors on the way to our next stop."

The guys pile into the truck. Ben starts it up, and they drive off.

Chapter 3

The Parallel Medium

The usual flush of tension rises steadily in the waiting room—now a gathering of his team's support staff, the program's technical advisors, venue coordinators, and sycophantic pay-for-backstage-pass privileged groupies. The dozens of people crowding the preshow area are scattered about aimlessly. Most had been hoping for a brief encounter with the man himself, but they had to settle for the subtle rush of occupying the same space and sharing the same oxygen as their spiritual leader. The stage manager, exercising her best frantic, delirious antics, barks commands and waves her clipboard to position the onstage talent. The eight-piece band is now in place, standing on their darkened marks and waiting to open the extravaganza. The familiar buzzing hum of the audience—shifting in their chairs, making light small talk, and rising in anxious anticipation of his appearance—provides a comfortable soundtrack for the quietly intense moments before the headliner steps onto the stage.

Herman Zoo breathes in deeply and deliberately, cleansing his lungs and refreshing his mind. Zoo is a self-described spiritual warrior who has built an empire on his speaking tours, self-help books, and new age philosophy of religion and God. He is at once an evangelical Holy Roller, a psychologist, a snake-handling healer, and for many, a charlatan of the highest order. He also conveniently deals in some of the more unscrupulous affectations of his cash, credit, and check business—funneling off large chunks for himself and laundering dollars through his organization that shelters many of his less-than-holy partners.

But among his fervent followers, he's a piece of a mystical nirvana that speaks to their fears and hopes. He commands huge crowds who worship at the altar of his podium and buy up his supplemental books, guides, podcasts, and DVDs.

Zoo speaks in grand themes of familial rivalry and ambition, of talent and jealousy and egotism, and discusses how much we despise the weaknesses in others that we fear we ourselves display. He talks like he's giving a eulogy for the destructive power of the myth of individual spiritualism, and as if lofty ideals can become perverted by the agendas of subconsciously terrified imaginary foes who struggle to silence his message. He has much in his hands. He wields great power and demands unconditional loyalty, but his corrupt dealings behind the façade of faith and redemption do little to justify his greatness.

"I think they're ready," the stage manager whispers to Zoo. She is still a tightly wrapped bundle of nerves, hoping to present an incident-free, rousing performance. "I think we've got them where we want them."

Zoo glances back at her, his stern eyes wary of her arrogant comment.

"Things don't always work out the way we want," Zoo tells her. "That's what happens when we grow up. We are not children anymore."

"I'm sorry," she says, trying to recover but stumbling over her words. "I didn't mean to imply anything—"

Zoo interrupts, not wishing to hear her rebuttal. "We're always judging. That's inherent in people. We judge. We're always judging everyone around us. Perhaps we judge our close friends and family a bit less, but that's only because we've judged them so much that we don't have to anymore. When you look out upon any gathering of people who have given their personal time and energy to come hear what you have to tell, there is no judgment. There is acceptance and an understanding that when people seek you out for help, there's a promise implied between the audience and the speaker. It's like a contract we've entered into. They come freely to hear what they think they need to hear, something that can help them make sense of their lives. They listen and use their free will to choose or reject the logical as well as the illogical when it comes to what makes humankind human and what waits for us when living in this existence ends. It's our desire to find the answers, wanting our needs fed, our lust fulfilled, and our happiness restored, that makes us live."

He pauses, taking a last look at the filled convention hall space. "They are here today to find those answers or, at the very least, to find out where to start looking."

"I understand," the stage manager replies. She's not a follower of Zoo and his doctrine; she's just trying to get the show off in time without disruption.

Zoo looks past the stage manager and spots his wife, Beverly, mingling amid the not-so-distant backstage confusion, a shadowy and combustible sentinel monitoring the activities from inside the domineering shell she calls a personality. If Herman is the voice who interprets the message from God, then Bev is the voice who tells the Lord when to speak.

"Have you ever played by all the rules, followed every direction, adhered to all the guidelines, and *still* ended up profoundly unhappy?" he asks the stage manager in a tone of self-preparation, psyching himself up like a closer stretching in the bull pen and tossing a couple of warm-up pitches before entering the game. "When that happens, there's a piece of that aimless existence in each of us that wonders what would happen if we dramatically altered the way we lived and decided *not* to follow the rules anymore."

He looks at her reaction, which is muted and expressionless. She's too nervous about putting on a good show to listen to his pregame assessment.

"You may still be able to do what you love, but it might require you to reassess what it is you *should* love. You live each day attempting to present the appearance of control, even when you have none. You should have had it all figured out by now, but you don't. You find out you don't have the tools to be the person you want to be." He pauses and turns to step out onto the stage. "That's why they come to me."

The band begins their slowly building intro music. As the driving bass beats rumble the chairs in the auditorium, a disembodied voice welcomes the guest to the stage. "With a message of hope and deliverance liberated from the gates of promise and paradise. … Ladies and gentlemen, Herman Zoo."

As Zoo struts confidently out to face the adoring, rapacious crowd— music swelling and pulsating throughout the hall—the stage manager allows herself a quick exhale. She is surprised for a moment when Beverly Zoo suddenly appears by her side.

"Well, it's off," Bev says.

The stage manager watches the crowd, noting their ridiculously over-the-top reception and the swirling vibe that has taken control of the auditorium. She is overwhelmed, because the reaction of the audience is clearly more deafening than she had anticipated. She feels compelled to pay attention to the proceedings.

She looks at Bev as they watch Zoo work the stage, sturdily gliding from side to side, pointing to people in the audience, whooping up the frenzy, and getting his minions primed for the coming pronouncements. It is one part ministry, one part charisma, and a heaping dose of Brother Love's Traveling Salvation Show.

"He's an amazing prophet," Beverly observes. The stage manager cringes a bit, happy that Beverly didn't just refer to him as a showman, as she was just about to. She politely nods.

"You know," Bev continues as they both watch Zoo calming the crowd to begin his formal presentation, "they say when you're sleeping, if you die in your dreams you die in real life." The manager doesn't know how to respond.

Bev looks directly at her as she tries to avoid eye contact. "Have you heard that before?"

The stage manager nods.

"What's the first thing that comes into your mind when you question that statement?" Bev inquires in a manner that's partly lighthearted yet partly deeply serious. "That is, assuming, of course, that you would even question it."

After barely considering, the stage manager says, "How would they know what you were dreaming when you died in your sleep, I wonder?"

"What do you mean?" Bev asks with a broad, insincere smile stretching across her overly made-up, painted face. It was a knowing smile, a menacing smile meant to force a validation of character, the kind of smile an enemy might offer before the implements of torture are revealed to the captive.

"Well," the stage manager explains, "you may have been dreaming about puppies and Christmas and then had a massive heart attack. I guess everyone who dies in their sleep was probably dreaming about something. There's just no way to know if what they were dreaming had such an effect on them that they died because of it."

"Huh." Bev keeps beaming. She claps at one of her husband's onstage comments, following the response of the crowd.

"What's your name?" Bev asks the stage manager.

"Christina Marvel." She extends her hand to Bev. Yes, Christina Marvel has managed to secure herself a spot just offstage for the proceedings, using her vast influence to cop a key position.

"Beverly Zoo." They shake hands as Beverly continues. "And why do I know that name, Christina? Ms. Marvel?" She turns now to face her. "Not Christina Marvel of the Marvels who are helping to sponsor this stop on our tour?"

"The same." Christina smiles. "My husband, John, and I are big supporters of your ministry, and I personally"—she lowers her head, and with a prideful whisper adds—"I consider your husband's message the moral confirmation that gives me a purpose and helps me to a more fulfilling and meaningful path."

Bev stiffly stands upright with a grin. "Well, darling, you sound like you could be on one of our partners-in-faith promotional mailers." They laugh. "And that means you are the very same Marvels who will be hosting the party we'll be attending this weekend." She hesitates for a moment, and then continues. "It is an absolute pleasure to meet you. I feel so embarrassed that this is our first encounter. I feel I know you so well already." She gives Christina a polite hug.

"Well." Christina laughs, returning the cordial hug. "I know we've missed a few opportunities to meet face-to-face. I'm so happy we have a chance to spend some time before the party. I was hoping we could get together."

"So I'm a little puzzled," Bev says. "You work here at the auditorium?"

Christina laughs. "No. Well, not technically. I'm not the actual stage manager. I'm just assisting." She moves in closer to Bev as if she's letting her in on a secret. "We're *very generous* supporters of the theater, and with our sponsorship sometimes I get little *perks*. I wanted to be right on top of the action."

Beverly takes a step away from the glowing Marvel. She becomes instantly wary of this now meddling woman. She knows the Marvels are an influential, very high-profile family with a big stake in Atlanta's A-list community, and she also knows what a manipulative couple—especially and almost singularly Christina—they are, fully capable of wielding their wealth and considerable political power to *persuade* people to let things go their way. The fact that this is the two women's introductory meeting is due solely to Christina's avoidance of Beverly at previous events and scheduling private time exclusively with the latter's husband. Beverly could feel the obligatory tentacles of this woman tightening around her. She knew *all* about her and how she wanted to help steer the direction of where her husband planned to take the ministry. She had been ambivalent about going to the Marvels' Christmas party before meeting one of their organization's biggest scheming donors, and now the thought positively revolted her.

"I think playing around behind the scenes like this is fun," Christina says with an exuberant smile.

"Glad you're having fun, and happy you have the chance to join us onstage," Bev politely says through her gnashed teeth. "I hope the secrets of putting on the show aren't too mundane."

"I find it all exciting, but it is what it is, I guess." Christina shrugs.

Beverly gives her a thorough, yet subtle, inspection. "It isn't what it is. It's never what it is." She returns to the comfort of her evil smile. "It is what it can be made to look like."

✺✺✺

The crowd—and for Zoo's purposes a *multitude*, his flock, if you will—sat with otherworldly determination and resolve, hanging on to his every story, metaphor, and reference, mesmerized by each example he so vibrantly illuminated. They were being taken on a spiritual journey, Zoo's mystery tour through the very thunder of heart, mind, and soul. The rattling of the faithful quaked throughout the thin walls of the auditorium.

Herman was prowling each side of the stage, shadowing every corner, and playing for maximum effect like a possessed rock star. His tone rose and lowered as needed to make his point. He tried to bring a fair amount of humor to his message, finding that some of the heartier laughs came when he poked fun at himself and his empire. His support team, the backstage crew, and all the stagehands were riveted to his performance, if not for his lecture, then to make sure their stake in the success of the show was ensured.

Zoo returned to the center podium, dragging the imagery of his tale out with prolonged silences, pausing to take a sip from the bottle of water that was sitting on a stand. Large digital display screens simulcast a loop of images from Zoo onstage or pictures and videos of accompanying materials and graphics. Two of the monitors were on either side of the stage, and a larger one was set up higher above the platform and bandstand, behind the performers. State-of-the-art lighting and quality stage effects boosted the production and helped rouse the house at the appropriate moments—as directed, of course, by Zoo and his deftly relayed signals and commands.

In this moment, Zoo's tall, thin body has a pale glow that is sketched beneath a full head of coal-black hair that sprays flashes of embers around the stage when the deep red fluorescent spots bounce off it. He has certain obvious physical characteristics from his father's Chinese heritage, but his mother's sun-bleached Southern California–chic sixties vibe unmistakably influences his manner and sound. His voice ranges from light and airy to ominous with foreboding peril, sometimes manifested in the Southern Baptist evangelical affectations of fire and brimstone, but usually in a nonthreatening, minimalist lure that hints persuasion over coercion. Sweat and raw energy radiate from his hands, often channeling the charlatan impulses of a Springsteen–Swaggart offspring showman at his best. As if admonishing himself, he wags his pointed finger as he continues his story while delivering his followers from evil. At times he waves his wireless mic around like a saber; at other times, during a somber shift in tone, for example, he holds it closely to his chest to help bring home an emotion.

"As half of a childless couple," Zoo embarks, "a certain young man was telling me, 'We don't like how much of our tax dollars go to public schools.' And he's arguing with me, very upset, running very hot. 'It doesn't serve me. My wife and I don't have kids—are never planning to,' he tells me. 'So for my money,' he says, 'I'm getting nothing.' And he's mad." Zoo pauses to let the argument lie in the air. "He thinks, and maybe he's right. We can't judge that just yet. But that man believes that he gets nothing in return for his tax dollars."

"Now he's spittin' mad," Zoo emphasizes, using a conciliatory tone in his voice, "and I don't want to be the one who is going to tell him he's wrong." Zoo smiles and chuckles. "I don't want to get into a fight over this. I'm not *that* reckless, you understand …" He coaxes the audience along. He puts his hands on his hips, steps around the podium, moves to the front of the stage, and ponders. "Well, I guess that implies I'm a little reckless." He scans the audience, who respond with laughing and cheering as his eyes glaze over their respective section of the auditorium.

"But you get my point," Zoo says, returning to his story. "I tell him that he's not really making the persuasive argument as he thinks he is. I try to reason with him, so I say, 'Hey, kids today are bad enough as it is. Believe me, you don't want them running around any less educated than they are already. Let the schools have the money." Zoo laughs. "I don't know, ladies and gentleman," Zoo says complainingly, shaking his head. "Sometimes trying to get some people to understand is like explaining a cell phone to a cat." He chuckles along with the audience and returns behind the podium to glance at a few notes before stepping back to the side. "But paying property taxes is nothing more than an insurance policy against something awful happening. And that's what our faith provides us. It's nothing more than an insurance policy against everlasting damnation."

"You know, folks, I've got all these freckles now that I'm getting older. They're all over, and there's nothing I can do about it," he shares, sighing as his followers laugh. "But I just connect the dots and hope it spells out a message to Satan." His voice begins to quiver as it rises in both volume and depth. "More ridiculous things happened and the good people, those commited to fight Satan's evil, for them it's kind of like watching someone drop a beautiful marble statue down a hill. After the first hit, you've already seen enough to know what things are going to look like by the end."

He stomps with fiery determination to the front of the stage as the crowd rises in response to the intensity in his voice.

"The problem with life today"—he slowly bastes his delivery, finding a deliberate way to convey his message with a simmering urgency—"is our profound loss of a parallel medium." He once again institutes a momentary silence, allowing his message to percolate. "It's not that I stand here proposing that I know you better than you know yourself." He holds the microphone to his side, tilting his head as the crowd reacts with light laughter and shouts. "But I *do* know you better than you think I know you." The crowd cheers. "I also know that one of the biggest problems we face today with everything surrounding our lives is the overload of programmed fear we are subjected to each and every second. Whether it's on television; in the social media on Facebook or Twitter or Instagram or whatever the latest app is; in the movies Hollywood makes today; in the corrupt messages in our books, or the naked filth and perversity on magazine racks; or in the endless loops of degradation on twenty-four-hour news and entertainments shows—" He pauses. "And each one of those outlets, those direct lines to evil—those are there to raise your anxiety, to heighten your terror, and to break down your faith in God and in the security that only truly comes to you through your personal convictions and love for yourself. And we are beaten down daily by a million people with a million different thoughts, opinions, and expert analyses on whatever incident happens to be the event of the day. So we get to hear these perfect strangers give us their ideas on something they weren't present for, formed by 'news' gathered from their favorite biased sources, which is further warped by their own prejudices." He takes a long break to gauge the crowd. He brings his voice down to almost a whisper, pulling the audience slowly into the conversation. "All the world, all the talk-talk and blah-blah, everything *they* use to suck you in—the good stories, the fun stories, the human interest stories, the stories of death, of war, of terror, of confusion, of the apocalypse—everything you hear all day, every day, is all meant to appeal to just one overriding human trait, the one trait that every single actualized organic life presence on earth is innately trained to exploit."

The crowd is silent, waiting for the revelation. Zoo rewards their patience with a slow and denigrating condemnation.

"Your unfailing and complete devotion to consumerism."

The audience's buzzing merges in sounds of hushed agreement, at the same time embarrassed and humiliated, sometimes forming in gasps of self-realization. Some people nod in bobbleheaded agreement as if they've suddenly realized for the first time that they blindly follow the story line on whatever they're spoon-fed and ultimately throw a whole lot of money away by buying all the wrong things. The irony of this gathering and the fact that its bottom-line message is so utterly embraced and yet so completely lost on the participants is almost unfairly transparent.

"But that's not our problem anymore," Zoo assures his followers. "Because we know where our journey is going to take us. We know that our leader, our Lord the Father and his Son, Jesus Christ, will illuminate the path before us. Because, you see, we all face two choices. Every single moment in our lives, at every crossroads, amid every life-altering decision we encounter, there is what I call the parallel medium. Think about that for a minute: the parallel nature of our lives. And with the safe route—well, *safer* anyway—the parallel medium still must try to avoid crossing paths with the parallel monster that dwells on the other side. We are constantly presented with choices, with options, and we always have at least two ways before us." He raises two fingers into the air, extending a *V* sign extended to the crowd, stops by the podium, takes another sip of water, wipes off his brow with a cloth napkin, and begins to walk the entire expanse of stage to explain his message of the parallel medium (his philosophy) and how to incorporate it into daily life.

"Two choices. And, good people, am I right when I tell you that two choices can sometimes be two *too many?*" he shouts to the roar of the crowd. "Good Lord, I don't *want* to make the choice." He begins now mimicking a talk with God. "Don't present this temptation in front of me. Please, Lord, you decide for me. That's why I praise you, God. Do you remember, Lord, that part in my prayer each night about thanking you for watching out for me during the difficult times? That part's in there to cover the whole making-a-decision thing. That falls under my 'difficult times' category. I put that in there so I don't have to make these tough choices." Zoo chuckles under his breath while telling the story; the audience laughs along.

Zoo gathers himself and stands tall and stately, commanding the stage. "But that's not really the way it is, and that's not really what any of us expect from our faith. God wants us to grow. He wants us to face the parallels we confront and use the dual nature of our lives to strengthen our resolve and to teach us how to face the next encounter with more understanding gained through the experience of our trials and temptations." He pauses, places the handheld mic back on the podium, and adjusts his hands-free lapel microphone. He clasps his hands together and brings them slowly to his lips, appearing to ponder this quandary.

"We all know what I'm talking about here." Nodding, he opens his arms and extends them toward the audience in agreement. "We're all trying to coordinate our real life with that life running right alongside, the parallel medium that's always beside us, holding our spirituality and beliefs. It's the second of our parallel lines. You see, our life—yours and mine, the one that we're living—well, that's one line, our lifeline, if you will. But there's the parallel line that journeys right with us every step of the way. That's what I call the parallel medium, because I see it as our subconscious—sort of the angel on one shoulder and the devil on the other as we strive to maintain some kind of *medium* course. We try to stay on that medium, but there are passengers on that line who are always trying to take over steering—and that's what can take you on detours where you never know what may happen. That's one of the crazy parts of *free will*, I suppose, because that parallel line holds all the excess, has all the danger, and houses the temptations and seductions that have a strong calling. It's where we store the more base and prurient nature of our soul. It is surely the parallel line that we can easily cross *over*." He stays calm, and very matter-of-factly explains to the now quiet group, "That's what we all have, and that is why we are here today: to learn the tools for how to deal with your parallel lines, how to identify the red flags that can get in your way, and how to better understand and allow the parallel lines of your real day-to-day life to coexist with the life you live for yourself in your head."

"So today should be an expression of your joy," Zoo exclaims, raising his arms. "Explore your dream life. Parallel lines exist in life between what we are (or what we have become) and what we dream and fantasize for ourselves. We wonder about the parallel line tracking along the same course as our own lives. Does it stay separated from us for eternity? Does it only tease, or do our two lines ever converge? Can two people living parallel lives that only intersect occasionally ever find travel on the parallel medium? What are the consequences when you begin to envy the parallel line not taken? And perhaps most importantly"—Zoo again masterfully draws out his big reveal—"what do you do when you think you've reached the parallel medium and then realize how unhappy you are? Can you survive in a world where envy and disappointment are both a part of your chosen resume?"

Zoo picks up the microphone again and steps to the front of the stage. "I will help you," he says quietly, sincerely. There is a genuine humanity in the way he begins phrasing his assurances. "This is a contract … what we have, a promise between us—a promise to explore our fears and find out about our options. I am here to help guide you to your parallel medium, and to make sure it holds for you all the keys to your happiness. I want to make it work for you." He holds his hand up in a halting signal, indicating a stop. "I won't fix you," he emphasizes. "I'm not here to do that. But I will help you. I won't presume to change you or fix what's wrong with your kids or your marriage. I'm not here to get you promoted or help you pick the winning lottery numbers." The audience laughs. "No, I'm just here to help navigate the parallels in your life, to differentiate your options, to help guide you along the parallel medium so you can better face the temptation and seduction of the parallel monster. You will learn that God's plan for each of you has many stops on both lines. Which you choose to explore and which you avoid carry great importance."

He pauses as the house lights go dim. A single red spotlight is then focused on Zoo at center stage; rotating gold and green lasers form a triangle around him. "What is the right way to live?" he implores. "And would you live that way if you thought there was no punishment in this life or no reward in the next?"

The band crashes into a thundering crescendo of musical energy, bringing the audience members to their feet as they cheer and yell. Zoo's people, his tour entourage and promotion aides, come running from offstage. They pass through the side doors, into the auditorium, and onto the floor to greet the attendees. They begin pairing up with guests to take them for scheduled tabletop exercises, to attend side conferences and lectures, or—between events—to browse the temporarily fashioned bookshop and gift store.

Zoo accepts his devotees' adulation, smiling, waving, and then clasping together his fists, clenching them in a victory thrust as he promises his return to the stage after the attendees' obligatory—and pricey—workshops and buffet lunch. As the crowd is escorted out of the main auditorium through the wafting haze of smoke, the flashing lights, and the still pulsating musical score, Zoo sweeps offstage with a swagger befitting a warrior, a spiritual slayer of our internal demons and dragons that are battling for control of our souls across the lines that blur the parallel between our medium and our monster.

Chapter 4

The Parallel Monster

Snake handlers refer to Scripture as evidence that God has called them to engage in this practice in order to show their belief and faith in him. Their devoted misguided exercise is drawn from the book of Mark 16:16–18. "And these signs shall follow them that believe: In my name shall they cast out devils; they shall speak with new tongues. They shall take up serpents; and if they drink any deadly thing, it shall not hurt them; they shall lay hands on the sick, and they shall recover." Therefore, in a very real biblical sense, snake handling is indeed a calling. However, as seems to be the case during biblical discussions, verses are so ridiculously open to interpretation that their true meanings can be twisted into acts and implications not necessarily intended literally. This is how "they shall speak with new tongues" becomes speaking with an almost hysterical fanaticism in different, previously unknown languages or even gibberish, instead of perhaps the intended meaning of teaching and preaching with a new or different approach and argument. It is how "take up with serpents" becomes snake handling and not learning and discovering the ills and lives of the less fortunate and how an individual can help to make things better. Instead, that verse is read to mean that one should actually pick up deadly reptiles. It seems that "taking up with serpents" could be a metaphor for living among others in order to find out the causes for their plight. The verses convince the true believers that laying hands on the sick so they can recover is easy, as if the laying hands on a cancer patient's body will cure the person, not realizing that maybe those verses mean using expert hands trained in the science of medicine to heal the sick. And in the end, it all leads to repairing the soul—which, for a quasi old-school fire-and-brimstone preacher, yet very much a practicing contemporary who stays current with the taste of today's audience, is the only thing that really matters. However, for someone like Herman Zoo, modern-day Pentecostal minister, a spokesman for God, the very mouthpiece for declarations of spiritual warfare of the *new age*, the finances of waging the war are all that matter. It is a stark lesson in the ends justifying the means, although ultimately no one ever reaches the end. There is no end. There are only the means, and Zoo makes that fit whatever particular endgame he is currently playing.

Herman Zoo practices the art of snake handling. He was raised among a large family of Pentecostal extremists who followed this charmed and preordained "blessed" lifestyle. Zoo watched his own father die at the age of forty-one after a rattlesnake bit him during one of these revival services. The incident didn't come close to fazing him. He accepted it as a condition of belief and as his father's entry into the eternal afterlife of paradise. If anything, it made his faith grow stronger.

Herman's father lived in agony for three days after the painful bite was left untreated and in God's hands. When he was bit, he said he wanted to die in the church. Three hours after he was bitten, his kidneys shut down. After that, the group that had congregated to pray for him waited. Time passed as they waited for his heart to stop. Herman hated to see his father go, but knowing he died for what he believed in comforted the boy.

"I know it's real; it is the power of God," Zoo told friends who tried to console him after his father passed. "I had to continue on with his works. If I didn't do it, if I'd never gotten involved, it'd be the same as denying the power and saying it was not real. I'm seeing something that was always hidden."

Herman Zoo, smart as he was—shrewd businessman, great showman, brilliant sales and marketing instincts—still had the family's completely unhealthy obsession and was invested in the practice of snake handling, not to the extent that he believed the display of faith was more important to the Lord than raising money, but he was a little more genuine in his faith than some of the other, obvious charlatans who steal from the desperate and lonely. And he knew snake handling wasn't the true path to the endgame.

Rick Huffman

"Once you no longer have to prove anything to anyone," Zoo would warn his critics, "you become a different person. You no longer *need* to be the person you were. Anybody can do it that believes it. These signs shall follow those who believe. This is a sign to show people that God has the power."

Chapter 5

We're Not That Old Anymore

John and Christina Marvel are a part of the historic Old South elite, part of the generations of mythmakers that have the privilege of old money. They possess the customarily famous charm and grace. They have the fabulous mansion on the hill. They present the finest parties on the Atlanta social scene, introducing the latest cultural touchstones and showcasing the newest and grandest toys, personalities, and gadgets—whatever item, person or idea is hot at the time—specifically to bring even more attention and praise to their already lavish lifestyle.

Christina has been singularly focused on her latest obsession: to show off at the Marvels' upcoming Christmas party extravaganza. She is driven to become an influential part of the Herman Zoo Ministries and has spent much time, money, and energy to make it happen. She was so taken with his personal appearances, his television specials, and the network he created to spread his message that she felt compelled—her version of a calling—to support the cause. John's conviction isn't deeply held or even relevant, but his backing, although not quite as enthusiastic, was critical to fostering his wife's faith and her standing as a significant and ultimately persuasive financial sponsor, while at the same time helping to cement Zoo's position as somebody Marvel can work with in his alternative business ventures. The financial loopholes given to IRS-sanctioned churches held great promise and opportunity.

Christina has been carefully cultivating her partnership with Zoo's organization. Although she has many personal reasons to find salvation, most of the spirit behind her spirituality is self-serving and has the primary purpose of enhancing her social status. John's interest, other than helping to provide his wife with a hobby and to aid her in her pursuit of social one-upmanship, is to exploit what opportunities might lay within the broadcast structure and capabilities of Zoo's network and how he might be able to leverage Christina's influence with his own ambitions.

"We have to get moving," John calls out to Christina, who is still in the master bathroom getting ready. As usual, he is ready to go and waiting for her to finish.

"It takes a lot of work to look like this whenever I leave the house," she answers back.

"You don't *have* to look like that," he says to himself, getting impatient with her fine-tuned primping and buffing. He's getting clearly irritated by the delay, so he takes a seat on the couch to wait. Then he calls back, "You look at life in terms like 'once upon a time,' and I am all about 'wouldn't it be nice if ...' I think that's the biggest difference between us."

Christina, of course, is paying no attention to her husband's comments from the other room.

"Wait till I tell everyone at work tomorrow that you're actually cooking dinner now!" John jokes.

"It's none of their business what I do or don't do," Christina tells him.

He says under his breath, "They already know what you *don't* do."

John Marvel had a strangely dramatic life, and he managed to come out on the other side of what could have been just a case of survival when he probably shouldn't have survived. That was in an era when many didn't make it. For John, it was not just the drugs, and the excess and laziness that comes from family wealth. It was also his endless string of scams, broken love affairs, betrayals, hidden agendas, and "just go with it" recklessness that comes with unearned, unlimited wealth and boredom. Sure, he had a bit of a head start with Daddy's money, but that didn't last. He learned to take what little he had left and turn it into lucrative, if not exactly legal, enterprises.

He is not about repentance, but his willingness to follow his wife's best efforts at consciousness and redemption is noble in a way John usually doesn't demonstrate. He seems happy and satisfied with his life and his marriage. Christina can be a challenge, as she skips around causes with varying degrees of commitment to the different fads, trends, and latest indulgence, but he knows there are different chapters and different battles at different moments in one's life. He knows when he has to make peace so he can take on new, more important battles.

John is most happy when his wife is happy. The key to her happiness is making sure she is busy. Christina needs to be working on *something*, anything. She has to be doing something, making something, planning something—it's always something. She's not one to sit around; it's an incomprehensible notion that her mind isn't working on something. To be idle would be a waste of her precious time, every moment of which must be filled with a form of stimulus that keeps her running until she passes out at the end of her day—whenever that happens to be.

Christina steps out of the bedroom and walks down the hall. She greets her husband, impatiently waiting.

"Okay, ready when you are," she proclaims with buoyancy. He looks her over, up and down, with a wolfish leer.

"Wanna fool around?" he says matter-of-factly, not expecting a response.

"Not yet."

He hesitates, puzzled by her answer.

"Not yet?" Her reply now has his interest. "What's that mean?"

She looks back at him, smiling, teasing.

"If you'd said 'not now,'" he continues, trying to explain his confusion, "I could understand that. 'Not at the moment.' Even 'not ever.' But *not yet*? Doesn't make sense."

"I have no idea." She laughs.

"You're much better at indignation than passion."

"Darling," she woos in her finest Southern seductive voice, "I've spent our whole life together telling myself you were conceited or selfish. Turns out you're both."

"Hey, but I'm just playin' devil's advocate here," he confesses.

"What's in it for me?" she asks with a devious grin.

"Anything you want," he jokes. "I won't ask again for another three months."

"You know," she replies smartly, "you can't just keep using that as an excuse every time you make some bombastic request." She exaggerates while mimicking his voice. "I'm *just* playing devil's advocate."

"Sweetie, I can talk a honey bear out of a honey tree."

"Okay, hotshot." She smiles. "Get your mind off the hedonic treadmill already, and let's go."

"That is *not* how I thought that would go." He laughs.

"How *did* you think it'd go?"

They walk out the door, get into their Escalade, and drive away to the appointment. John and Christina Marvel have convinced themselves that what they are doing is "soul refining," a cleansing search, when really all they are buying is a shady-at-best spiritual path to their empire-building illusion. Their souls don't need refining; they need purging.

※※※

One of the religious rogues had told the Marvels that they needed to rid their bodies of demons as her group of followers gathered before dusk one Saturday around a small fire near the base of Kennesaw Mountain. They should cut their skin to let the evil spirits out, the holy pretender told the couple. Then she told them that they needed to cauterize the wounds to ensure that those spirits would not return. It was at this point that the Marvels moved on to their next experience.

In their next encounter they found a rather unique individual in a man who took a decidedly anti-higher-power approach to his healing. In fact, his beliefs were contrary to every other organized religious group or evangelical sermonizer the Marvels had previously encountered. This man summed up his worldly beliefs in a very simple, easy-to-embrace way.

"What you believe in about the afterlife is what actually happens to you when you die," the minister intoned. "For example, if you believe in reincarnation, you'll be reincarnated. If you believe in heaven and hell, then if you're saved you'll go to heaven, and if you're a sinner you'll go to hell. If you believe in nothing, that's what happens: nothing. You get buried. You rot."

Clearly, this wasn't a biblical approach to the afterlife—unless, of course, you already believed in this man's doctrine—so it was more of a customized fit for most people. This turned off the Marvels. They wanted to find someone who had deep-rooted beliefs, someone who could not be shaken from the faith he or she lived by and preached.

The Marvels have reached the stage of life wherein they might think, *Our life is fine, but the really good years are more or less over in terms of career, good money, decadence, travel, and general excitement, so henceforth we're looking at a kind of slow, steady-as-she-goes downhill slide.* True, their spiritual serenity and life wisdom are peaking now, and that's beautiful, but the Marvels' days of real electricity and occasional triumph are over. At least they have their laurels, their mansion, and their highly regarded reputation to rest on. But they know they don't have it all. One day they'll wake up and find it isn't enough. It isn't the nourishment they crave. They are terrified that it will all be over much too quickly.

Aging is rough business. It's good if you have someone there to help you through it, but otherwise, when you're staring down the neck of that terrifying final bow, it's enough to make you want to turn back and find any outlet to sustain yourself. In the end, all the Marvels want is to do it all over again: watch their young ones grow up, and see their peers drop away while new young ones become ready to take their place. Slowly they realized that they would fade away themselves, and it occurred to them that life is terrifying. Isn't that why religion was invented in the first place?

Eventually they found themselves at a Herman Zoo revival.

"It is going to be a homecoming like the old days. Whether you were raised in the holler or running the mountain ridges, the Holy Ghost–filled speaking-in-tongues believers will help you find your path." This was Zoo's promise at the beginning of the barnstorming sermon.

John and Christina were in attendance. Before it had started, John leaned over to one of the other attendees, apparently a regular follower.

"Why is this Herman Zoo guy so popular?" he asked the starry-eyed zealot.

"Because he's a god."

"A god?"

"He's not *actually* God; he's a god. He's a tool God uses to speak directly to us."

"Why was he chosen?" John asks, genuinely interested in the hysteria that surrounds a Zoo revival.

"Because he's so cool."

"Cool? That's the criterion?" John ponders the answer. "What makes *him* so cool?"

"He's cool because he has no pretense of cool. He just is."

"That's it?"

"Think about it," the young man continued. "It's amazing just to be here, to be honest. What are the odds of us being alive? Whichever way you look at it, it's pretty amazing to be here, to be alive, to be able to communicate, to be able to laugh, fall in love, observe nature, read, travel, watch our children grow. … Life gives us a lot. I'll take the heartbreak and the agony when it comes, and I'll swallow it. It's all part of the process. We're all heading to the abyss eventually anyway."

The difference was, as John thought, *Even though we may all be heading to the abyss, let's have a hell of a journey along the way.*

Talk about a crowd that's a sucker for a certain not particularly distinctive style of inverted sentimentality. A man stands before the crowd, screaming spiritual passages and waving serpents around, while the assembly falls into a trance that becomes the genesis of an energized mission. Zoo *owned* these people.

In the end, John Marvel chose not to adopt the Herman Zoo mission, but Christina became such an advocate that the connection was inevitable. Besides, Zoo made such a powerful impression on the couple that they felt compelled to invite him to their Christmas holiday extravaganza. Zoo was just as thrilled to find a new, affluent, captive audience. John Marvel was just as thrilled, but for more distinctively selfish reasons.

Herman Zoo had *big* plans for the Christmas send-off. Having a presence at the "party of the year," with all those high-profile movers and shakers of the greater Atlanta well-heeled community in tow, well, the proverbial sky was the limit for conversions. And even if he couldn't bring converts into the fold, he could certainly find hefty donations and put on a show they'd never forget.

Chapter 6

The Pirate of Las Olas

Leo Rickenbacker stands at the counter, holding a bag of dog food. He stares down at his dog, Flagler, who is undividedly staring straight back at him with eager anticipation. He takes the bag and walks over to the corner of the kitchen, where the dog's food dish awaits.

Flagler follows impatiently, step by step, clocking Leo's every move.

"Don't worry, girl," he says to the dog in his sweetly hushed kiddie-voice dog tone. "Fuck everyone, right?"

He begins to pour some of the dry mini chunks of dog food from the bag into the dog's dish. As he leans over pouring, he tells the dog, "I don't care what anyone says, I don't think you're getting fat." He continues pouring a little more, and then closes up the bag and sets it back down on the floor of the pantry.

❈ ❈ ❈

Leo sits quietly in the corner of the driver's license bureau, layered in a gray wool coat pulled over his green and yellow plaid sweater. It is very cold in Atlanta, thanks to a Canadian front moving down across the North American plains and pushing the Midwest and Tennessee Valley weather patterns across the north Georgia pine-filled hills. The culmination of rain activity hanging in the clouds had brought the unexpected subfreezing temperatures, and had dumped enough snow across the suburban strand of homes that the proud Southern city came to a blizzard-like standstill.

He picked up a cheap old used car to replace the freshly totaled Toyota he rolled. He had come out of the accident relatively unscathed—a few bruises and aches, but nothing serious. It was more of a general inconvenience than anything else.

Slumping in his chair, waiting to hear his name called to renew his driver's license, he fell dreamily into thoughts of what it must be like in a warmer climate. South Florida, perhaps? He read in the paper that Miami was enjoying sunny skies and midseventies temps. He always fantasized about South Beach and imagined himself on the white-hot sand beaches that lead to gentle waves of cool, refreshing ocean waters. Given the icy cold and soul-numbing freezes, he could only imagine that if somewhere in the world was experiencing seventy-degree weather, then it was surely a gemstone type of conspiracy perpetuated by the government to further dismantle the minds of US citizens. *Why would the government want to subject us to such teases?* Leo wondered to himself. He reached down to pick up the now-cold cup of coffee sitting on the floor next to his chair, took a sip, and grudgingly swallowed.

He once took a trip to the Bahamas for a long weekend. That seems like forever ago now, especially with the cold winds bristling outside and the daily chore of rising from bed and trudging to find work every day. He remembers not liking the islands, the swarms of small children paralyzing his travels through the town by inhibiting each step, grasping at his legs and begging for money. The beauty of the warm breezes couldn't dissuade him from his immediate dislike for the locals and the miserable malaise that seemed to fog the islander mystique.

The only reprieve he's had in the past weeks was when he shuffled downtown to Centennial Park and joined the small gathering of miscreants who were trying to organize Atlanta's homegrown minor league version of the Occupy Wall Street-type protests. It didn't matter to Leo that he was participating in something that might have started as a noble and maybe even reasonable counterpoint argument to what's been happening in today's economy but that has deteriorated into a collection of unemployed, sometimes drug-addled, usually criminally minded rabble-rousers looking for TV airtime, handouts, and unchallenged dissent.

Although he could drive himself into moments of great despair, Leo would often let his mind wander to the continuous factory line of obligatory Christmas parties, gatherings, and events that would inevitably take over the social season of the community. These "clash of the fashions" spectacles were a regrettably unnecessary part of the elitist networking rotation. Nothing irritated him more than watching the glammed-up ladies flaunting their social stature and struggling to outdo their neighbors with bigger parties, more elaborate food offerings and entertainment, and increasingly sophisticated lighting and holiday displays. Leo would obsess about these events and be amazed by the expanded level of transparency among the spiffy guests and well-heeled homeowners. He hated the hypocrisy of watching, as people of a certain social stature feel compelled to go out of their way to be nice just because the hostess with the fifteen-hundred-dollar dress is serving courses that cost five hundred dollars a plate.

His contributions to the Occupy mob—it was actually more like a small, but vocal and defiant, pack—amounted mostly to holding signs and cheering wildly when one of the group's designated speakers whipped up the thin crowd of curious onlookers and disinterested naysayers.

Although the insight and motivation to act or react to any progovernment, capitalistic monarchy was lost on him, what *was* intriguing to Leo was carrying out his own little surprise wake-up call to Atlanta's pseudoroyalty. He could barely contain himself when he thought of all the mayhem and messy inconvenience that a well-executed subversive plan could play in this morally counterfeit town. *I can't get the phrase* 'active shooter' *out of my head,* he thinks while awaiting his turn at the counter. *It just sounds*—a glazed look comes over his face—*so cool.* And its effectiveness in disrupting the routine of life appeals to him.

While running a plan over and over through his head, Leo finds his vision being shoved aside by the man sitting next to him. The man is nudging Leo's arm after seeing that his number is being called.

Leo looks at his ticket, stands up, and walks over to the counter. A particularly irritable, nasty-mugged, young female sits with the disgruntled look of pure antipathy and loathing.

"Can you take your license out?" she says, groaning, as he approaches. "Can't you read the sign?" she snaps, pointing to the wall.

"I can read," Leo cracks back. "Just didn't happen to see that particular sign, so I missed it. Besides, I was looking for the warning sign."

"What warning sign?" the nasty young woman barks.

"The one that reads, 'Bitch on duty.'" Leo grins.

He stands without incident for the remainder of the ordeal while producing all the documents necessary to process his renewal. During his entire time there, Miss Happy Pants keeps staring at him with evil; he *knows* it is her best voodoo curse. What she doesn't realize is that her demeanor simply provides more power for him to harness in building the hatred for what he sees as civilized life crumbling around him.

＊＊＊

Leo stands looking at himself in the mirror. He's not so much disgusted as he is disappointed. He is uncertain. The look on his face doesn't match the words of praise coming from his mouth. He's heaping unconditional praise on himself while staring back bluntly and dispassionately.

"You are smarter than most people. You are a hard worker. Once people get to know you, they think you're a pretty nice guy. You refuse to admit defeat." He pauses and rubs the palm of his hand across his cheek and chin, feeling the abrasive stubble. When he returns to his one-on-one with the mirror, he strangely changes his affirmations to the first person. "I like to do nice things for people in need. I try to treat people with the respect I expect in return. I am always successful in everything I try. I earn a good living and try to live right. I believe that parallel justice is a defensible response to the inequalities between people. I know that I must mean something to someone."

He shakes his head and exhales deeply.

"Face it," Leo says candidly to himself. "If you were as great as you say you are"—he pauses—"you'd be better."

Chapter 7

Oak Wilt

Oak Wilt is one of the most serious tree diseases in the
eastern United States, killing thousands of oaks each year
in forests and landscapes. The fungus takes advantage of
wounded trees, and the wounds promote infection. The
fungus can move from tree to tree through roots or by
insects. Once the tree is infected, there is no known cure.

The old red brick building that houses the business offices for Pat
McLaren's Elite Lawns and Landscaping was declared a national
landmark in a ceremony decades ago. The structure, originally built
in the early eighteen hundreds, was initially an outpost for the Dahlonega
territory gold miners and wilderness explorers. It eventually became a train
and transportation depot before it was a central booking station for travel
routes throughout the Southeast and destinations north and west.

"I know what you're trying to do," snaps Karen, Pat's terminally
eccentric, vaguely beautiful wife, in her *Real Housewives of Atlanta* kind
of way.

"I hired a new girl to help with the all the paperwork and sorting
around the office," Pat explains sheepishly. "It's been a mess. We can really
use the extra help to get everything in order."

Karen and Pat walk in together. A beautiful, shapely young blonde
woman is leaning all the way over at the waist, with her rear end facing
them and her slim, sexy legs crossed as she bends over to pick up some
papers from the floor.

"That's the new girl," Pat says delicately.

Karen blasts him with the obligatory stare-down.

"Sherry," he calls to her as they enter the room. He turns to Karen. "This is Sherry Turnquest."

She stands up and turns around, flashing a beaming white smile and a cutesy pout.

"Hi, Mr. Mac," Sherry says enthusiastically.

"Hey, everything under control?" he asks before pointing at Karen. "This is my wife. You'll see her around from time to time." He pauses. "Anything she says, run it by me first."

"Nice to meet you." Sherry waves. She says to Pat, "Mrs. Devlin called you back. She said you have to call back in morning."

"In *mourning*? Like, is she sad or grieving? Or do you mean in *the* morning?" Karen grimaces as she makes these comments. "Use your articles. Jesus."

Karen huffs and walks past Sherry. She moves down the hallway and goes into her husband's office. He follows her, turning to Sherry to make a remark as he passes her desk.

"She can be the greatest asset in the world, or she can just be absolutely an impossible pain in the butt, sabotaging everything in her wake. Don't let it bother you." He steps into the office and closes the door. Karen is already sitting in his chair behind the desk. He grabs himself a cup of coffee from the pot sitting on his office counter.

"Want some?" He holds up the coffeepot.

She shakes her head and starts rummaging through some of the stuff he's got on the shelves behind his chair.

"Look at all this junk," she says while picking things up, inspecting them, and putting them back in their places. "When was the last time you dusted this crap?"

Pat ignores her, as is his habit whenever her whiny commentary begins.

Suddenly Karen sits upright in the chair and pulls a box from behind a stack of files. She turns and confronts him with a box of condoms. "What are you doing with these?"

"They're not mine."

She stares at him.

"Really?"

He says to her with a frowning, dismissive look on his face, "Are you crazy? Do you honestly think I'd try to hide a box of condoms in this office? I have a hard enough time hiding the weed from you."

"You're wasting your time explaining any of this to me," she flippantly says. "You'd have more luck explaining it to a shoe. And the shoe would be more interested in what you have to say."

He looks at her and shakes his head. "And probably understand it better," he barks back, annoyed.

She takes the box of condoms and begins to put it into one of the drawers in his desk. "At least keep them off the shelf." She spins back in the big chair. "Jesus."

"Will you not put …?" he says, straining to stop her. "Don't put them in my desk. I told you, they're not mine." He takes the box from her hand. "I'm sure they're one of the guys. I'll find out and give them back."

"Why don't you just put them in the men's room for everybody's easy access?"

"So do you have plans for the day, or you just wanna sit here and torture me?" Pat asks, ignoring her snide comment and obviously growing more irritated by her presence in the office.

"I've got a few errands to run. I need to finish up Christmas shopping and then pick up a hostess gift and get a new pair of shoes for the party." She hesitates, grabs her purse, and then remembers something. "Hang on, got your smokes here." She reaches into a pocket in her bag, pulls out a pack of cigarettes, and hands them to Pat.

"Thanks." He takes the pack.

"The clerk at the pharmacy really pissed me off," she says bluntly. "I go in there to buy them, and the old lady at the counter says to me, 'Did you remember to get your flu shot? People our age need to get one every year.' People *our* age! I wanted to slap her."

"Ah," Pat replies. "The parties, the presents, the people—all the charms of the season to bring out the best in everyone. If we survive Christmas this year, we'll never have to prove ourselves to anyone. In fact, it'll be like we cheated death. We can then probably do all kinds of extreme stuff without fear of injury. We'll be predisastered, like Bruce Willis in *Unbreakable*."

Pat and Karen McLaren are an interesting couple. One might even confuse them for a fun couple. They've been married for over a quarter century and have come to live in that aggravating place where the slams and snide remarks to each other come fast and easy. Their attacks on each other are well-crafted darts, honed by years of overlooking the annoying and otherwise irreparable damage their actions instigate. Nevertheless, what sometimes seems to be playfully biting banter on the outside doesn't do much to conceal the very real antagonism going on inside during most of their hostilities. After all these years, though, they have figured out a way to make their relationship work.

Because they're not acting here, their marriage has the outward appearance of a dolled-up face, when actually it's a portrait of torrential contradictions. They're nodding and going "Yes, dear" and "Whatever you say," but it's obvious they're not there. Pat is tired of the meaningless, exhausting nitpicking, and Karen is quietly livid because she's finally begun to understand that her life is being really and truly misspent.

Karen is an even more impenetrable person than her husband is. The unfortunate thing is that the couple don't take a chance and make use of their actual talent in some way. But like with so many of their peers who flit from function to function with the sole selfish intention of outdueling their cohorts, the McLarens are the way they are because everybody lets them be that way.

"We're not perfect, but at least we're not perfect together," Pat once said, and then quickly retracted it. "Okay, that didn't sound right at all."

And it's the only way they've ever known.

"So this party isn't an option?" Pat says to Karen as she steps toward the door in his office, ready to leave. She shakes her head emphatically.

"It's the *Marvel* Christmas party. No, it's not an option. We have this discussion every year."

"I love the guy, but I can't stand him during the party. He changes when he's hosting. He becomes a show-off and has a pretentious attitude with that 'look but don't touch' vibe. He seems all right until he opens his mouth. Like, I get the whole laid-back, square-jawed rural-dipshit thing and how it's all folksy and charming, but he is *exactly* the sort of guy you meet when working or drinking at an above-average local bar and you think, *Huh! This guy seems cool.* Then he starts talking and the *real* stuff comes out. He says something offhanded about 'the coloreds' or 'the faggots,' and you snap back to reality. It happens just like that." He snaps his fingers. Nothing happens, just resounding silence. "That should have popped. It loses the impact without the pop." He returns to his point.

"So then you remember, *Oh, right. In real life, these people suck.* And you pretend to be interested in what they say while most of them wrap this entire underground orgy of excess in praising the Lord and giving blessings in *his* name while their tolerance is *zero.*

"It's because of people like the Marvels that every day this country slips further behind the rest of the civilized world in terms of the stuff that actually matters. There are diseases going uncured, inventions going uninvented, science going unresearched, and important social changes going unmade because a substantial portion of this country believes like them—without a hint of irony—that such progress is forbidden by a line of text from a centuries-old book of campfire stories about an invisible man who lives in the sky."

Karen stands still, stoically listening to Pat's little outburst. When he finishes, she exhales, pulls her sunglasses out from her purse, and puts them on. She looks exasperated.

"All this ranting and raging—and he's one of your friends. Would hate to hear you go on like that about an enemy." She begins to step out. "All right. I'm leaving. Don't let your new chick and her ginormous butt work too hard on her first day."

"Sherry." He rubs his nose and adds, "That's her name. And for the record, I hate when you think it's cool to use 'hip' words like *ginormous*." Pat begins an animated description of his point. "Sure, it might be in the dictionary now, but that's only because a bunch of wavy college coeds made it up and everyone started overusing it—everything's 'ginormous.' So now we have this funky *cool* new word."

"Let's quit while we're ahead." She pauses and turns before sulking out of the office. "And we're not that far ahead."

"Hey while you're out, can you pick me up a—" His voice trails off as he sees her flash him the twisted-psycho-killer look he knows all too well. It's a very different look from the one he's used to—the bewildered, confused stare. "You know what, nothing that can't wait." He waves her off. She marches out.

Pat listens to the sound of his wife's footsteps on the hallway floor outside his door. His issues with Marvel, Zoo, and all the others getting overly involved in his business are beginning to become a problem that he'll have to figure out a way to resolve. His lawn company also serves as the face of his marijuana distribution business and provides a means for laundering the cash operation. Marvel is screwing his lawn guys over on the distribution split, but he isn't aware that McLaren knows all about it. Zoo is screwing Marvel over by blocking or rerouting distribution, something Marvel doesn't know about, while he's also squeezing McLaren on percentages. Some fancy showbiz doctor, because he lost his daughter to Zoo's movement, has his hands in the pot by running a business to deprogram Zoo's cult followers. Zoo's step daughter OD'd while in the doctor's care. Marvel is trying to launder drug and kickback money through Zoo, who gets it back as payments to the doctor's clinic and outreach programs.

Everywhere he looks, Pat sees nothing but arrogance, betrayal, and disappointment.

Karen is already home and settled when Pat drags himself back in from work in the midevening. She is propped back on the sofa, lazily playing games on her iPad and half watching a rerun of *Law and Order*. Karen is used to his working late nights; it's the nature of landscaping and lawn service work. He had made sure the office had all the daily receipts and service orders, checked that the books were balanced, and confirmed that the following day's schedule was set and the shop's four large trailer trucks were routed correctly. Once he confirmed that all his territories were covered, the workday was done. Then there was the matter of whatever reconciliations he had to do with the side business.

"What a day," he says throwing down the backpack he uses as his briefcase. "When I was driving back home, the car next to me was the same exact car as mine, only in white," he says as he steps around the living room table. "I won." He walks into the kitchen and takes a bottle of water out of the refrigerator. "Although I don't think the other guy knew we were racing."

He looks at Karen, who is sitting quietly, unmoved, and looking down at her iPad.

"So I finally called back Mrs. Devlin. You know her family—real rich, lives in La Vallée Tendre Abondante. Huge woman, giant pain-in-the-ass customer, and one of our bigger accounts," Pat says. "She's always threatening to sue. This time it's because she claims we didn't finish removing the exposed tree roots pushing away from the beds near her driveway. Doesn't like the way my guys leveled them off with sod to match the rest of the yard.

"And having to talk to her." He grimaces. "Her voice is like an oil tanker trying to warn smaller boats out of its path."

He looks at Karen and chuckles a little. She shows no emotion and just keeps playing on the iPad. He waits a quick moment for any reaction.

"Are you there?"

"I heard you," she says calmly.

He looks at her and then into the air. "Right, forgot." He says matter-of-factly. "That's code for 'Tell someone who gives a crap.'"

"Why don't you just dump her? She's been a headache for years, from the first day you got that contract."

"There's only one driving motivation, and if you can't guess what it is, then there's a good chance this is the first time you've heard of the economic system referred to as capitalism."

"Then deal with it. That's your choice." She looks up. "When did you start thinking things were gonna get fair?"

"If we had a dog and it could talk, he'd say something like that."

"I just think you need to hang on to the really good customers. They're worth the extra attention. Sometimes you have to deal with their BS, but she's been a longtime customer and we *always* get paid."

Pat jerks up, animated and energized, with a giddily accusatory snap.

"You just contradicted yourself." He points at her. She sits unruffled, composed, as he rants. "Not forty seconds ago you just said the exact opposite. Just then." He points backwards repeatedly, as if to indicate that the time when she uttered the statement was lurking behind him. "Not *forty seconds*. You completely reversed your position in less time than it takes to complete the first measured, named unit of collected time in seconds. In less time than one minute—the milestone marking that first unit of time—you contradicted yourself." He pauses, pleased with himself. "Unbelievable. It's amazing to me that anything a man might do completely confounds a woman. But still, we're amazed after watching your little preparation displays or after watching you spend a solid forty-five minutes trying on a dozen different tops until you settle for the first one you tried on."

Karen finally perks up a bit and, without moving her iPad, replies firmly. "Then maybe you should figure it out for yourself, or with one of those little pop-tart divas you seem to be hiring at work now."

Pat stands down and lowers his previously flailing arms. "Okay, well, I don't think you get the point," he says quietly to himself. "So like I was saying"—he redirects his attention back to Karen—"just another typical day. Nothing out of the ordinary." Then he adds with a smart-ass snarl and snicker, "And I haven't been hiring pop-tart *divas* here. She's the first. If anything, she's probably just the beginning of a *trend*."

He watches as his wife returns her concentration to Facebook, or eBay, or an online game, or Pinterest, or whatever other current site that's captured her attention. He steps over to the sofa and walks past her, flirting with her as he passes by.

"Honey, I've got a present for you."

"Really?" she says hesitantly.

"I'll give you a hint. It's hidden under my clothes. And it's not a Dremel." He stops, looking at her with a devilish smirk, making reference to the variable-speed rotary tool he bought Karen for her last birthday.

She looks up, trying to conceal a breaking smile beneath her composed countenance. She sighs. "Really?"

"If you don't want to, I'll just go into the bedroom and enjoy myself."

"No you won't," she informs him, now ready to chuckle. "I know you better than that."

"Yes I will," he says defiantly. He walks into the bedroom, mumbling under his breath. "Wow, apparently *that's* one thing I've been able to keep secret."

Chapter 8

Elk Horn Gate

Wednesday night is John Marvel's night out with a couple of his closest confidants, including Pat McLaren, an associate with whom he's had a longtime client–customer lawn and landscaping relationship and who is a fellow member of the Community Small Business Council. John and Pat's third-wheel friend is a freelance entertainment and event director—a fancy self-appointed title for party planner—named Francesco Fitzwilly. Strangely enough, he's never been called Fitz or Willy, or Frank or Franco, or something that would seem a more appropriate nickname to highlight such a colorful name. But they call him Biz—as in Lord Biznez, his performing stage name, the one he uses to DJ, play host, and MC at local clubs, private parties, and convention events, or when any person or organization hires him for music and entertainment services. Biz is straight up, doesn't have a problem speaking his mind, and can fall comfortably into any situation. He's tall, thin, and fashionably sharp, with an upwardly focused professional business sense. There's the too-wide smile that crinkles his eyes and then slowly falls into a tight-lipped smirk when he's telling a story. His sandpaper voice cracks whenever he increases the volume too quickly, like a dam holding back a wave of emotion that's about to crest.

Francesco Fitzwilly can adeptly shuffle his personal act between smooth-as-cream young, sharp-dressed business associate and the sometimes outrageous posture of a black man—dangerous and a hint of intimidation, with his slicked back hair and his flair for the dramatic. He caters to all levels of clientele, so he rarely refuses special requests from his guests, regardless of how excessive the creative demands can be. The deeper the pockets, it seems to Biz, the more he finds himself arranging ethically interesting and morally ambiguous acts in venues from bizarrely themed party mansions to rented-out abandoned warehouses. He sometimes finds himself squarely in the middle of some wholeheartedly messed-up situations, trying to escape the images of some scary visions that cannot be erased from the mind. Years of these experiences have pretty much screwed up the way he views his world approach and what it takes for him to accommodate and cater to some of the more functionally fucked-up things he finds himself involved with. Lord Biznez is ready for anything, all the time.

The trio makes for a fascinating group of strangely symbiotic creatures, given the nature of their backgrounds, beliefs, and personalities, but they are linked by strong business partnerships, some very prurient and excessively selfish plans, and a little subsequent bonding with some of the significant others. They certainly remain guarded in some ways and aren't immune to keeping secrets from each other. Regardless of the formula or the common interests that binds them, these nights out together are Marvel's one secured, guaranteed moment of complete abandon. They can go out, talk serious shop, and get hammered while figuring out how to sort out this messed-up world they find themselves nefariously, but cautiously, scamming. They would be great guys to run into. You wouldn't want to make plans with them, but if you bump into them, grab ahold and hang on. You might have one helluva night.

Tonight they are at the Elk Horn Gate, a beautifully rustic, elaborate cabin with a good old-fashioned bar full of unfinished lumber alongside ornate woodcarvings. Appointing the walls of the high ceiling enclosure are paintings reflecting the outdoor hunting and fishing lifestyle. Adorning the walls is a wide array of guns and other weapons mounted alongside the result of their respective intent—so many trophies of nature's prey displayed everywhere around the different rooms. It isn't a neighborhood haunt or a sports bar; there are only a few TVs that no one is paying attention to, an outer room, and a main area with a lone bar offshoot. Customers don't come in wearing shorts or sneakers; this is more the after-work business crowd, and they expect to be treated with that level of attention and deference. The later it gets, of course, the friendlier the place becomes. Elk Horn Gate doesn't have a completely unwarranted reputation as a place where consenting adults who share common interests can usually find a way to close the deal.

The three men take a circular booth in one of the more quiet side rooms, away from the noisier main "great hall" area in the center of the lodge. There is a nice medium-length wooden bar set back, with a few customers sitting and drinking at the counter. Another four or five tables have customers coming and going, so the atmosphere is steady but relaxed.

Immediately after the three men settle into their booth, their immodestly clad young server is upon them, her glistening boobs happily cheering and nearly popping out of her tight top. She has a pretty face, a megawatt glow in her smile, and the I'm-so-typically-adorable perky personality that accompanies the type.

"Good evening, gentlemen." She sparkles. "My name is Julep. I'll be your server this evening."

"What's your name?" Marvel asks her to repeat.

"Julep."

"Like the drink," Pat says.

"But not the mint." She giggles. "My mom *hates* mint."

"That's cute." Marvel smiles at the annoying syrupy voice.

"So to start things off, do you know what you'd like to drink?"

"I have a question that maybe you can help me with," Pat begins. "I need some good female advice. Maybe you can help me out, Julep."

"I'm happy to help." She beams. "I'm helping out a friend now who's just had a bad breakup. His girlfriend broke up with him and he's hurting."

"Oh, it's not that kind of advice," Pat says. He hesitates before saying, "What do you know about love anyway? You're just a kid."

"I'm just trying to get him through having his heart broken."

"You can't help someone get over being dumped if you've never been heartbroken yourself. And you don't seem like the kind of gal who ever lost a guy you didn't want to lose."

"Maybe I've had my heart broken. How do you know I've never been hurt?" she asks with just a hint of irony.

"For starters, you don't seem like the kind of person who would carry around all that emotional devastation. You still look pretty happy, and that's not usually a trait that follows heartbreak."

Julep laughs nervously and pivots back to Pat's question. He is staring at her, taken by her petite sexiness. "What did you want to ask me about?"

"Can you just go ahead and repeat whatever it is you just said again? Because, I gotta tell you, I didn't hear a word."

She purrs. "Silly."

"I don't suppose you've had many life-altering events yet. You're still young and working as a waitress. Life hasn't gotten too messy yet."

"I'm not a waitress. I'm your serving hostess." She smiles.

"Just keep the vodkas coming, honey, and you can call yourself an astronaut."

Biz speaks up. "I'm ready to order a drink."

The table refocuses, and the men place their drink orders. What they order is not important. What is not unimportant, however, is the fact that they are out and starting up that nice foggy state of mind that comes with drinking away the day's stress with good company in a welcoming place.

Julep returns with the drinks and asks if the men are ready to order any food.

"They have a great brussels sprout appetizer now. I had it last time I was here and it's fantastic," John tells his companions.

"I hate brussels sprouts," Pat tells him.

"You haven't tried them like this before: crispy on the outside, tender and spicy when you bite into them."

"I've had them boiled, steamed, sautéed, fried, deep-fried, flash-fried, stuffed, baked, grilled, roasted and au gratin. Know what I don't like? Brussels sprouts."

"Okay," John says to Julep, "I think we're good for now. Maybe in a little bit."

"Wait," Lord Biz says. "Let's get an order of grilled octopus, and toss in an order of those brussels sprouts too. Thanks." He looks at Pat and shrugs. "They sound good to me."

Julep smiles and nods as she leaves the table, telling the men she'll be back in a little bit to check on them.

The men each take an obligatory sip from their drinks. There's a brief down moment before John breaks the silence.

"You know," he begins, "you're more likely to experience a higher level of stress when your favorite restaurant closes than if you lose a finger. Your brain has coping mechanisms that help you deal with physical tragedy, but you're on your own when trying to find a new place to eat—one that always makes your food exactly the way you like it, and where the staff know your name and have your drink ready for you when you're seated. Psychologically, that's a lot more stressful to overcome than the loss of a finger. Same theory applies to pain. You can handle losing your finger better than you can deal with a stubbed toe. The doctor can give you painkillers for the lost finger, but you're not so lucky with a stubbed toe. Your stress levels are much higher for stubbing a toe than for losing a finger."

"Well, you certainly put the *k* in 'what the fuck,'" Biz comments sarcastically.

"Since we're talking about stress and loss," Pat says, laughing, "what's up with cryonics?"

"Cryonics?" John asks. "When they put bodies into deep freeze?"

"Yeah, you never hear about it anymore. When did all the hype about that start? It's been like forty or fifty years now. Don't you think that by now some of those frozen bodies would be ready to come out of deep freeze so they can be treated for the illnesses that were going to kill them? That was the point, right, to stay frozen until technology got to the point where they could find a cure for your disease? Certainly they've found cures to diseases these people had back in the sixties or seventies. Isn't it time to bring back Walt Disney? I'd try it out on him first."

"Okay, two things," Biz counters. "First, that's all batshit crazy. Storing frozen bodies? It's just another big moneymaking scam for nutjobs who have too much disposable cash. Second, I heard that Walt Disney isn't frozen. His body is being held captive by Captain Nemo in the storage compartment of the *Nautilus*."

"It's nice that you feel you can share that with us," Pat jokes. "Once you open up and are completely honest with people, you won't have a lot of friends—but at least they'll all be the *right* friends. That's why I like you. I'd rather have someone tell me the truth than tell me what they think I want to hear." He takes another drink from his glass. "And almost everything you say is something I don't think I want to hear."

"I can't stand being bipolar," Biz says with a wink. "It's so awesome."

Julep comes back to the table with a platter filled with different sushi rolls and a sampler tray of snacks. "Here, guys," she says as she sets the tray down at their table. "Compliments of the bar. We're trying out some new items, so we're giving away a free sampler as a teaser. Let us know what you think. I'll be back with your order soon."

The men nod their approval and say thanks.

"My wife eats the sushi, but not the rice," Pat comments. "Thinks it's too fattening—unnecessary carbs or some other psychotic nonsense. She leaves these little ring holes of rice with the insides eaten out of them. Looks positively alien when she's finished."

"I guess I can see that," John adds.

"No, it doesn't make sense. It's too much. One of nature's inexplicable phenomena."

"You make her sound like the human embodiment of the aurora borealis. It's not stunning and mysterious; she's just cutting calories. Sounds like she's dieting."

"When is she not?"

"Same with Christina," John says. "Always dieting."

"Yes, and she looks fantastic," Biz notes. "I noticed she lost some weight the last time I saw her. She looks really great. You know how she did it?"

"Yeah. She cut out fried foods, alcohol, and carbs."

"Sounds like lunch," Pat jokes.

"We really got her at Thanksgiving." John starts chuckling. "We had a lot of family over for the holiday, and I cooked a Cornish game hen along with the turkey. When I brought it out and started carving—I had hid the hen under the turkey—I pulled out the hen and told her the turkey was pregnant. She really lost it. I guess it wasn't very funny." He pauses, still smiling as he recalls the story. "Really fucked up the rest of the day though. She was pretty pissed off after that."

"Well, you embarrassed and humiliated her in front of your guests."

"It was still pretty funny."

"And you wonder why you have to beg for sex." Biz laughs.

"Nope, we've got a system for that," John replies. "She says she now only wants to have sex when it's spontaneous, which is code for only when *she* wants to, which is code for rarely."

"They have their own world and set of rules, don't they?" Biz says, talking about the women. "And we are always looking for the operations manual."

"They're at their best when they're together," Pat adds. "Karen loves her weekend getaways. It's just the girls sitting around the resort pool, more glammed up than they need to be, chatting about their husbands, jobs, kids, and projects, and spending all the time gossiping endlessly about all the women not there."

"Bored housewives aren't getting enough," Biz says. "They read those books and watch those fantasy movies, and then they don't understand why their husband or partner isn't more receptive, adventurous, and *dangerous* in bed. Or worse, when we try to be those things, they freak out and want to know why we're being so *weird*."

"This is coming from a man who sleeps with a different woman every time and doesn't need to bother himself with these trivialities." John raises his glass to Biz. They all drink.

"I've been through all that marriage stuff before. I just can't do it. Doesn't mesh with my DNA." Biz pauses. "I had a marriage there once, but the emotional disconnect was glaring. My ex-wife and I were really nothing more than semicompatible roommates. Everything a marriage is *supposed* to be about was missing."

"That's what a whole lotta days feel like," Pat agrees.

"You remember how bad my marriage was," Biz reminds his friends. "All that drama with her ex, and then he dies in that car accident. That was like the end of the world for her. Couldn't snap her out of that funk, so I finally had to say, 'Looks like you lost the real love of your life, darlin' … so see ya.' Jesus, that whole thing messed her up." Biz gets annoyed just thinking about it. "And half his shit is still being stored in my garage."

"That sucks," John says. "I remember her. That wasn't a good time for you."

"Thank God for alcohol." Biz smiles. "It's always been there for me like no woman ever has."

"Amen."

"Started as a kid," Biz adds. "Once I found out there was something I could take legally that would alter my reality, I was all in. Hooked. My reality wasn't all that great, so booze was a perfect fit."

"I guess we're all junkies when it comes to something," Pat says.

"People need escapism," John says. "They want to experience spectacles and magic and enough feel-good moments to serve as a distraction from the fact they are slogging through a tough marriage, raising difficult kids, taking shit from their bosses, and seeing death lurking right around the corner."

"Those feel-good moments don't cut it," Pat adds. "Raising kids is hard. Our job isn't to just keep them alive until they're legally allowed to get the hell out of our house. It's to pass along as much knowledge as possible to ensure that they have a fighting chance of being successful when they're on their own. And this is all done under an extremely tight deadline. We're cramming thirty-plus years of our own experiences and lessons into a tiny decadelong window between the age when the kids are actually old enough to listen and the age when they're old enough to shut us out."

"My parents didn't have a lot of rules," Biz says. "I was smoking and drinking and doing all kinds of shit that would have freaked my parents out, but God forbid if I was caught eating sugary cereals. We were not allowed to have them in the house when I was a kid. I remember the first time I went to a friend's house and they had Captain Crunch. I thought it was Christmas. I wanted them to adopt me."

The men take a little breather while they call Julep back to the table for refills. She returns with the appetizers. After taking the drink order, she returns to the bar.

The lounge area and tables are now nearly completely filled. The noise level from the various conversations around the room has risen, and the atmosphere has taken on a livelier, more relaxed mood. It's the time of the evening when people seek out answers to life in the company of others and with the soothing charm of the alcohol in their glasses. They dwell on the mundane day-to-day, finding comfort in the miseries of others. There are two ways to dwell on life. The first is through self-reflection, analyzing your thoughts, feelings, and actions to learn how to get better. The second, which is much easier but far more desensitizing, is through self-infliction—which amounts to endlessly focusing on all the ways you've messed up. Either of these choices should ultimately lead to self-awareness, which really just means that you have full knowledge of your own failings.

Hopefully you'll be self-aware enough to realize that the scars are from a self-inflicted wound.

"So what do you wanna do with this guy?" Pat breaks the momentary silence and gets directly to the point.

"I want control of his *empire.* I want to expose the charlatan and take over his operation. I want him on the ground looking up at me and begging for salvation," John announces.

"That's it? Sounds easy enough," Biz says sarcastically. "You don't care for this guy much, huh?"

"Something like that." John nods.

"You know, rage without vision is a problem," Pat tells him. "You can lose focus, miss your opportunity."

"I understand," John agrees. "That's why this is a team effort."

"So what do you really know about this guy?" Biz asks.

"Well, as you know, he operates his ministry out of Atlanta, has the local-access Christian cable TV station shows, and runs a side business called Sounds from Heaven, or some such shit, that's supposed to help people connect with their loved ones in the afterlife. ... He controls every aspect of this operation, and believe me, it's a cash cow."

"Don't underestimate the desperation of people trying to buy their way into heaven," Biz adds. "Shit, just let them enjoy a couple of hours of preaching and hallelujahs, and people carrying the cross of Jesus while beating the shit out of Satan and evil with no moral gray areas. Fear, bitterness, selfishness, and hysteria motivate religion, so why not, I suppose? Those are all the ingredients motivating most of us now anyway. Religion has always just been a way to understand death. Somebody had to figure out a way to deal with it."

"If you can't even bring yourself to contemplate death, then you're not ready for it. And that's okay, because most of us aren't," John says. "But if you're always avoiding thoughts of death, it's doubtful you are really ready for life, and that's something you cannot run from without looking like a fool. These people turn to this guy to lead their charge to the pearly gates."

"I guess I believe in some kind of afterlife," Biz adds. "Even though it doesn't make any sense logically, I guess people still need something to grasp at. Lots of crap doesn't make any sense, but there it is, so why not?

Maybe it's better to believe in something than in nothing at all. We're not nihilists." He looks at his friends. "Not much."

"I'm going to become an evangelical environmentalist," Pat jokes. Then he preaches: "I believe I will be held accountable by God if I harm, destroy, or willingly interfere with the natural life flow of nature's ecosystem. I'm a steward of the earth. I sacrifice as a calling by God. Conservation requires sacrifice. We don't own our planet, our surroundings—God does. We are accountable to him in the ways we treat the earth, cultivating the natural and organic healing herbs—the very land he blessed us with to live on and populate and create as an offering to his glory."

"Jeez, as if we aren't accountable for enough shit already, huh?" John laughs.

"Although Pat's rarely correct," Biz says, chuckling, "he's *never* in doubt."

Julep returns to the table with the refreshed drinks.

"Everybody good?" she asks.

"I think so," John says as he grabs a spiced piece of smoky grilled octopus and pops it in his mouth. The spices are a bit too strong; he begins to cough at the heat. His face contorts from the sting.

Julep sees his reaction and frowns. "I'm sorry. Too spicy?"

John shakes his head and waves his arm, indicating that he's okay, but he's still not able to say words, as he's still recovering from the first taste.

"All right, I'll bring some water to the table. I should have done that first thing. Sorry." Julep rushes away to grab a pitcher of ice water.

John takes a long gulp from his drink and exhales the heat. "Whoa, that was hot." He shakes his shoulders and regains his composure. "Okay, that was a kick." He finishes his drink and grabs a chunk of the crusty bread to help vanquish the spice. "So where were we?"

"Religion, heaven, and appetizers," Pat says before continuing with his topic of discussion. "I saw a picture of heaven, one of those 'artist's renderings.' It showed the fluffy, puffy clouds, and angels flying around, and people in robes walking the lush landscape. There were dogs and cats and animals roaming around. All I could think about was the animals. Are these our pets in the afterlife? Are they animals that live in heaven, or are they there because they died and that's where they landed?" Pat pauses.

"Do we eat the cattle in heaven? Are they there for our food supply? Do we even eat in heaven? The picture was very confusing."

"This guy has an empire ripe for the picking," John announces enthusiastically, changing the subject back to the audibly unmentioned topic of Herman Zoo. "I know because we're already using him with the donations and some of the lower-level dealings we run funds through. He's a genius, the way he perverts people so he can be taken more seriously. He happily takes all the money while exploiting the same fundamental human tendencies that lead people to search for answers. Then he gets on a stage and enlists his 'magical thinking' seminars to the public." John pauses before continuing. "But now he's got some TV celebrity doctor on his ass who has been trying to expose him. Obviously," he says with a sneer, raising his eyebrow, "we also invited him to the Christmas party. He'll be there. Apparently his game is to bring former members who've left the church and then reprogram them, or whatever they call it. It's a real bitch fight. Anyway, I'm just thinking with all the business we have going on, and with the increased revenue along with some of the problems we've run into, we'll need another place to launder money and run the business through. That church can be used for a lot of cleansing. It's quite the scam. Of course, in matters of faith, they all are."

"I've never been down with organized religion," Biz says, "not even when I was a little kid and it was forced on me every Sunday. I hate to sound like a snob now, I but always thought those who are *true believers* have limited individuality or sense of self."

"Yeah, and prosperity theology is fake," John adds. "And he's all about the prosperity. He's got one overriding purpose, to spread the gospel throughout the world across his cable system, satellite transmitters, computers, and smartphones—and his little army of thieves and con artists keep his machine fed. One giant swindle to make sure the faithful keep the money rolling in." He pauses and sighs. "I still can't believe Christina has bought so deeply into all this shit and I'm playing along with it. Makes me sick."

"I still can't understand some people," Pat says. "And how this guy just strolls through the people who go broke by sending him money. They are wasting their lives. He feeds off them at each of his tour stops or after every TV spot. It's worse than criminal—especially when his prey is the weak and the frightened."

"The weak and the frightened are always the easiest prey. It goes all the way back to survival of the fittest. The weak always suffer." Pat collects his thoughts. "I mean, I don't know about Christina, but you just don't know what the trigger is. People have to try things to find out if it's for them. And it got us in. Maybe that's the good that is supposed to come out of it."

"I think when you have people rushing to serve your every whim and need, critical thinking goes out the window," John says. "It's just too seductive a set of circumstances for an insecure person not to give in to it. And then you bow to this charismatic leader who himself is an explosive combination of narcissistic ego and complete insecurity."

"You really have it in for this guy," Pat states. "Bad."

"I've had Herman Zoo lined up for a while now. Ever since Christina lost her soul to his *word*, and her money and time to this guy and his *vision*, I've been trying to figure out a way to either get in on his action or bring him down," John says. "It's like she's in a cult when she gets rolling on it." He pauses. "Scary. I'm also pretty sure she's shared more with him than just donations."

"This makes more sense now." Biz nods.

"I'll deal with *that* after I figure out what the deal with Zoo is going to be," John says, resuming. "So here's what he's all about. He's got a four-star diamond organization. When I say four-star, I mean he's bringing in money on basically four different fronts. The lines of cash may come from a lot of the same fans or supporters, whatever you call them, the faithful, but from different buckets. He's got the church—that's the first and the most transparent. It's hard walls with live bodies, cash money, and pledges. Special donations and charity drives. They run day cares and church camps. Second base is his TV ministry. Huge bucks, faceless donations, growing international audience. He takes missionary cruises and excursions to the Holy Land for Bible study. All travel supplied and paid for by the ministry. The third diamond in his crown is Sounds from Heaven or Messages with God. I don't remember the exact title, but it's a service that promises to connect the living to their loved ones in the afterlife. It doesn't fall under the precise spiritual message he preaches, so it's operated separately. It catches some of the cattle who don't follow his shows or his preaching thing but who have a weird fixation on the dead. It captures more of the psychic loonies: spook-hunter types, séances, crystal ball shit, all the other flak—that business. It all still falls under his umbrella."

"Covering all the bases." Pat shakes his head. "He's got a lot going on."

"Wait, then there's home base, the fourth diamond—the ace." He smiles. "He began opening addiction rehab centers specializing in substance abuse rehab, marital counseling, and something called productive reenlistment—which entails sessions that are used to reorient members back into the fold if they've left the church for any reason. I hear that it's more of a kidnapping and brainwashing." He stops to take another drink. "Anyway, you can imagine how much money *that* operation makes. He's cashing in from the church regardless of allegiance—coming and going and coming back." He looks at his partners across the table, who are listening carefully and are duly impressed. "And it's even covered by insurance."

"Damn." Biz smiles. "And you've got a tap into this?"

"I think so." John nods. "It's all about parallel lines. That's the theme for his current road show—parallel lines—and it has a spell over Christina. It's the latest fashion at our house. It's all she talks about anymore, always figuring out ways to work it into examples around the house."

"What's it mean? How's it figure into this?" Pat asks.

"Parallel lines—that's his philosophy about life and how we travel through it. He uses different examples to show that for every choice we make there's always an alternate, but parallel, path that continues alongside us. It's the route that mirrors what our lives might have been. It's off on a different direction, some other zone or level. It's all a distraction to what is really happening in front of you. It's his bait and switch, the ploy he uses as a diversion to raise your curiosity. It's simple deception, really." He pauses. "It's classic misdirection, the same thing all televangelists use. I think it's only fitting I follow the same formula for Zoo."

"The same trick, you mean," Biz says. "Karma for the televangelists"— he pauses—"and for all the other magicians."

"Know what's funny?" John says with a chuckle. "He doesn't like being called a televangelist. He thinks it's demeaning and cheap. He doesn't think of himself as just a minister but as a therapist, a mass psychologist, and a healer."

"Brainwasher."

There's a stir at the table for a moment as the men refresh themselves, grabbing bites of the snacks and taking a sip before resuming.

"So what do you have planned for Warren Moon?" Biz asks, mocking the name.

"Zoo? I'm keeping it simple," John tells his partners. "Teddy Roosevelt said, 'Speak softly but carry a big stick.' I say that if you speak loudly enough, you don't need a stick at all."

"Offer-you-can't-refuse deal?" Pat asks.

John nods. "Something like that. I'm reserving any judgment about what is going on between him and Christina until I see how favorable our arrangements are. No point in setting up a profitable venture if the face of the franchise succumbs to his ultimate reward prematurely. We wouldn't be following his prosperity model."

"That's focusing on the ends by sparing the means." Biz laughs. "Very patient of you. And you said we all stop learning."

"I didn't say we ever stop learning. I just said I can't be *taught* anything anymore." He takes a second to look at his friends. "You know the strange thing?" He pauses and shrugs. "This guy, his preaching at least, doesn't seem all that bad. He's a cheat and a fake and no better than a two-bit grifter making his latest play, but some of the things he preaches about— they're good things. They make a lot of common sense. Most people would be better off if they tried to live with some of the values he talks about."

"And at the same time he uses his missionary work in Mexico to move weed through his churches," Pat says, admiring what Zoo has accomplished with his underground businesses. "We have dealings with a lot of the same places and people who—off the books anyway—roll up under some of his business interests. His wife, Bev, she runs most of that side, from what I've heard. His involvement is very low-key, obviously, so most of what we hear is just that: hearsay. But that's where I would want to apply the pressure. It's the best cover for laundering I've seen. Even businesses that are red-flagged for unusual activity are almost never hassled. The courts know the bullshit legal implications they have to wade through. The religious freedom fights they have end up with their having to deal with all the nuisance lawsuits—it's a built-in shield. It's constitutional law versus religious allowances. Eventually it wears you down."

"Well, it took some planning, but we'll have the latest mouthpiece of God in my humble home in celebration for the birth of our Lord." John smiles. "It's going to be a wonderful occasion, our best Christmas party yet."

❋❋❋

Herman and Beverly Zoo had been invited to the Marvels' Christmas party. It was an interesting turn of events that brought an invitation to this blasphemous holiday affair into the hands of Zoo. Christina Marvel was searching for spiritual answers to a series of negative events in her life that caused her to reach outside her comfort zone. Her search led her to invest time in a variety of eccentric and unconventional methods of spiritual healing involving close-up cleansings with Zoo. John has been dutifully playing along with his wife's affection for Zoo and his attendant spiritual movement, waiting for the opportune moment to begin his hostile takeover.

John's exposure to Zoo only confirmed his belief that everything in society is a glib advertisement for the immaculate sexiness that comes from being famous, wealthy, accomplished, and well-dressed. That was certainly part of Zoo's appeal. You can't very well throw your allegiance and faith into the arms of a slob. But Marvel still feels that there is something so incredibly cool about being wise and hardworking and accomplished and not necessarily placing all the credit on some otherworldly being. His wife, to his sincere disappointment, fell in face first—eyes wide open but glazed over thanks to her alcohol and alprazolam mornings.

Her visits to the church were pretty decent at first, cordial anyway. She viewed the church with some hesitation at first, but eventually she settled into a victim reality she created for herself, like a bubble she now surrounds herself with to ward off the perceived negative energy that she feels is brewing—and that, let's face it, she loves. She only finds some type of self-satisfaction when she's putting down others, so this newfound revelation of spreading joy and happiness is on the wrong side of her tracks—at least in her mind. But her greater understanding of evil in the world helps her perpetuate the notion that it's everyone else against her.

She used to engage in mind games with her elitist friends just to maintain some type of control over their perceptions of her—a kind of Munchausen syndrome played out for adults. She really loves to be invited to an event and then turn down the invitation and tell others why she made that choice so as to discredit the function. She tells everyone she wants to go here or there, but then she doesn't show, always offering some kind of incredibly warped story to explain her absence. She's as stubborn and fixated on being miserable behind a happy face as her husband, John, is fixated on engaging in deception and illicit activity behind the false face of legitimate business. There's nothing anyone can do about Christina's demeanor; they can only consider what can possibly be done to make her happy. But then they find that there's nothing that makes her happy. Even when the Marvels packed up the entire extended family and went to St. Augustine Beach for a holiday week, John *knew* it would turn out badly. And even if it didn't turn out badly while it was happening, he knew that her after-stories would be brutal.

The only peace Christina has been able to find is in the works, and maybe the arms, of Herman Zoo.

John believes that if you can convince a person who doesn't really think much of you to do a favor for you—even a small one—then this tricks him into suddenly believing that he now likes you. All you need to do is remember to thank him enough and remind him often of the favor he did. It's not as effective a ploy the other way around. If you do something nice for the other person, do him a big favor or take care of an annoying problem, he might appreciate it, but that's the end. If the other person feels like he's in your debt, then you've lost him. But if you can get someone to do something for you, then it's like you're in *his* debt—and people *love* that. *That's* control. They'll be drawn to you and won't really even know why. John believes that's the real profit of deceit.

❉ ❉ ❉

Julep nods to indicate "thanks" and "good-bye" while walking away from the table after settling the check. The guys are just finishing up, taking a few more minutes to decompress before heading home.

"The only thing I like better than something good happening to me is something bad happening to someone I don't like," John says. "So I'm floating."

They laugh. "Why is that?" Biz asks.

"Because I'm petty and insecure?" He smiles.

What John really thinks is that Zoo is dangerous and eventually will need to be stopped. He knows things are ultimately just things and only have the weight we give them. But for Zoo, and now Christina, everything's a ritual, everything's a symbol—and once Christina accepted that, she didn't feel as beholden to the idea of being true to any singular institution: her family, her home, her town, her county, her faith, or her religion. Once you've accepted that you can distance yourself from these matters, you can make tough decisions that are ultimately good for your own development without concern for anything or anybody other than the person guiding you to your enlightenment. You are able to make choices without regard to your loved ones or your relationships. That is why John began planning for Zoo's time on earth, his occupying of his mortal-being vessel, to be only temporary.

"I already have someone that'll be there on the inside for us," John says, "working the party for me—a part of the catering company—and with ties to the church. Kind of the conflicted-type mentally, but it'll be fine if and when we need someone. He'll be ready."

"So you have a crazy guy waiting?" Pat asks.

John hesitates. "I guess crazyish. I think this is part of the professional help for his personal issues, so there's that." He grins. "Besides, who am I to tell an impulsive psycho with a gun that he's making a bad life choice?"

Pat clears his throat and starts to slide toward the end of the booth, readying to leave. "I've gotta head out," he says. "Should probably hit the road while I can still clearly see the accident coming. Didn't work out so well last time."

John and Biz look at each other, not sure what Pat is talking about.

"What happened last time?" John asks.

"Got into an accident with a newly married couple," Pat explains. "There was rice and stringed cans and whipped cream all over the road. The groom came out of the car, and he was screaming at me—completely enraged. I told him to calm down. I said that we could exchange insurance info and call the cops, but none of that—or all his yelling and crying—was gonna bring his wife back."

They groan.

"I always thought that was a funny joke." Pat laughs. "No, there was no accident. But when I got home, I told Karen I was happy to have made it back. I kept nodding off while I was driving home. It was a tough drive. She told me I should've called to let her know I had too much to drink, and she would've come to pick me up. I told her it was okay, that driving was the only thing keeping me awake."

"You should have called her."

"I made a mistake."

"You don't make mistakes; you make choices," Biz tells him. "You make a decision and then you deal with the consequences."

"Life is gonna happen either way," Pat replies. "Driving to work, picking up some things from the store late at night, flying to visit friends or to meet people for a business trip—hell, walking your freaking dog—you make the choice to do something, and if it's gonna happen it's gonna happen. It's really out of our hands once we set the course. It's like punching in your destination on your GPS. The path has been preprogrammed. What happens the rest of the way is up to you."

"Someone once said," John adds, "I would rather die ten years too early than ten minutes too late."

They collect their few items and rise from the table to leave. They've programmed their intentions and now only have to plan the details. The choices have been made. Now only the consequences wait.

"I know a writer, a friend of mine from Savannah," John says with a smirk as they leave the lounge. "He could turn this into a helluva story."

Chapter 9

Modern Rage

Leo is sitting in his therapist's office. He is slumped back in the corner of a couch that is carefully positioned across the back window of the fourth-floor office. The view overlooks the man-made office park lake with the obligatory cosmetic fountain spraying water spouts high into the air. He's casually staring at his doctor, Jeremy Peacock, who is seated across from him in his large leather-bound captain's chair. Leo is recounting a recent incident, a fairly pedestrian textbook example of just one variation on a number of psycho stories that many psychiatric patients bring with them into a therapy session.

"So he says, 'Gimme your wallet,'" Leo says, generously using his hands to illustrate the story. "'Gimme your wallet?' I say to this piece of shit." He pauses for effect. "I don't think so.

"He looks right at me, exactly like you'd expect someone to look after he's just been told something he doesn't expect. 'You're kidding, right?' he asks me. I just smile and say, 'Nope. I'll give you the cash, and you can even have the credit cards, but no way will I give you the whole wallet.' Do you have any idea what a pain in the ass it is to get your driver's license replaced?"

Peacock just listens. He has no expression on his face, and he takes no notes.

Leo continues. "Then he says back to me 'Okay, forget it, man. Just hand over the cash.' I manage to get a closer look at the guy and ask him, 'Do you even really have a weapon?' He looks back at me with a kind of nervous twitch and says, 'Yes,' in this shaky voice, and then he tells me he has a gun in his jacket pocket. Now I know he's bullshitting me, but I say, 'Fine, whatever, no big deal.' And I hand him the cash." Leo takes a brief glance around the office, wondering if there's anything different from his three previous visits.

"Why did you give him the cash?" Peacock asks.

Leo shrugs his shoulders. "What would have been the point of doing anything else?"

Peacock smiles and tilts his head. It was not the response he was expecting from his hyperaggressive and seriously angry patient. Leo balked at the opportunity for confrontation—a strange choice coming from a man so filled with rage that he wants to carry out an active-shooter scenario while quietly contemplating his possible targets.

"Do you think you're a tough guy?" Peacock asks.

Leo takes a moment to consider the question. "Tough guy?" He shakes his head. "Nah. The way I see it, there are just two types of tough guys. One kind wears a shirt that says, 'I'm not a guy you wanna fuck with,' and the other kind wears a shirt that says, 'Don't fuck with me.' The difference may seem subtle, but think about it. You know what I found out?"

Peacock waits without expression for Leo's answer.

"That I don't look good in either shirt."

"So you don't think of yourself as a bad guy either?"

After a moment, Leo concedes. "I'm serious," he deadpans, "but not dangerous. At least not to myself." His deadpan sulk curves into a smirk.

"You sure about that?"

"The whole good–bad thing … I'm not sure. If you break it all down, the whole world comes down to good versus bad. Law-abiding citizen*s* against the lawless. Patriots versus terrorists. It's the fundamental question, isn't it? Who's the good guy and who's the bad guy? It's the first immediate judgment we make when we meet someone for the first time or encounter a new situation. It's human nature. Figuring what's what with people certainly seems to be obvious to our eyes. But is it the same in their eyes, the bad guy's eyes? We just figure that the bad guys *have* to know they're bad, right? But it doesn't work that way. The KKK, al-Qaeda, and ISIS believe they're the good guys too."

Leo's little adventure with being mugged reinforced his dismally absurd view of people and their inherent stupidity. How most of them somehow manage to make it through their worthless and pathetic days confounded him. It may be a frivolous distaste, but it was present with him always. He simply did not *like* people, not having either the patience or the empathy to care about them one way or the other. They were dull, dim-witted organisms who have been placed carefully in his way, creating obstacles and roadblocks, making impossible his simple plan to get through life with minimal aggravation and angst. They were just part of the drudgery he has to face every day when he walks out the door.

Even within the "safe" confines of his home, Leo still found it necessary to deal with the scummy bacteria clouding his waters. Ranging from customer service representatives in Gurgaon, India, speaking educated but unintelligibly accented English to the could-not-possibly-give-less-of-a-shit operator at the cable television dispatch desk, Leo thought himself to be surrounded by the inanity of human beings. It was shock-and-awe bombardment on a daily basis.

Leo wasted hours sitting idly in front of his TV, staring sluggishly at the screen, getting his media-fueled injections of cynicism, apathy, and chaos. His perception that everything is futile thrived in this environment. Nothing survives, he believed. His instant conclusions about every TV talking head would fall somewhere along a simple sliding scale. Careerist. Soulless. Self-absorbed. Next.

"Watching these guys, all I see is the *intensity of audacity* shouting back at me. The level of assholery is just amazing," he says now, moaning to himself as he leans in to catch all the talking points. After a couple of hours of engaging in this alienating process, Leo catches himself and tries to focus on his therapy and the exercises he was taught to rely on when his mood began to sink. *Okay,* he tells himself, *that's just like you and how you go about perceiving everything around you. Perceived impression leads to negative projection, which leads to dangerous oversimplification followed by a snarky "fuck off."* He takes a deep breath. *Shake it off, dude; you've been carrying that bag around long enough. Time to kick it to the curb.*

No sooner had he fallen into the blanket of his head-soothing therapeutic exercises than a blaring television commercial began issuing a raving testimonial about a new pill to battle low-T.

"Doesn't matter," he says to himself. "Low-T, no-T, lifeless dick, high cholesterol, diabetes, raging blood pressure, heart disease, cancer. It's always *got* to be something. We can't live in this society without looking over our shoulder."

He watches the friendly, upper-middle-aged man bemoan the consequences of low-T while singing the praises of the miracle pill that can fix it all. He's calmly strolling along a beautiful lake pathway draped in colorful flowering trees and absorbing his surroundings while the voice-over lists detailed descriptions of the awful side effects. Leo thinks, *I'd at least like to know who's gonna wipe me.*

※ ※ ※

Dr. Peacock shifts his weight and rests his elbow on the right-side arm cushion of his chair. Leo reaches over to the coffee table separating the two and takes a sip from a bottle of water he brought with him to the session. After the drink, he twists the cap back on and plops back into the comfort of the couch's inviting cushions.

"Now you took off for a long weekend last week—a break for you," Peacock says. "Was it a vacation or just an extended getaway for a few days? Did you get a chance to relax and have a bit of fun?"

"I met a friend in New Orleans," Leo says, recalling his weekend trip. "He was staying at a dump called the Come On Inn or something—a trampy, cheesy name like that. It's located inside a cluster of warehouses, small businesses, and two ugly-ass gas stations. I'm pretty sure a lot of those places are on an armed robbery rotation list that gets passed around the neighborhood. They get hit all the time. Not a five-star location according to Yelp, if you know what I mean."

"Lovely. So what did you do?"

"Well, I had this friend stopping in New Orleans for a weekend layover, so I met up with him there. Figured we could catch up and maybe do a little drinking, a little gambling, party to a little jazz, whatever trouble we could find. So we are at this dive of a hotel, disgusted at the rooms, the bad location, and all. Now, mind you, this is based not only on what we saw, but also from the warnings of the desk clerk when my buddy checked in. We decided since we probably wouldn't be spending too much time in the room anyway, what difference did it make? Our room, which was a few doors down from the office on the main floor, was very small and run down. It was so moldy smelling that it *had* to be unhealthy. I mean the pillows, bed linens, and mattress all had the same strong moldy smell. The wallpaper was stained and ripped, and in the bathroom it was stapled onto the wall. The bathroom vent was filthy and rusty, the tiles and woodwork were stained, and a decrepit air conditioner was stuck in the wall. The AC unit was poorly maintained and rusted. It took about an hour, but we changed rooms and moved to one on the second floor. The new room wasn't much better, but the mildew smell wasn't as suffocating."

"Not an ideal start to a weekend getaway."

"Just the beginning." Leo squirms. "As soon as the bags were in the room, I stepped outside and breathed in that Cajun night air with the idea of going for a walk and maybe hitting the Quarter. But down in the parking lot, there were two Asian-looking girls making out, and every time I went out on the patio, they saw me looking. Finally, they turned around and gave me this look that yelled, *Are you gonna stare all night, perv, or do we get a little privacy here?* Shocked the shit out of me. These girls had put the stake in the ground and claimed the parking lot for themselves. Eyeballing intruders were not welcome. They were not quite as big as the Samoans you usually see. So in addition to the trashy hotel, the surrounding area was ruled by territorial Polynesian alpha lesbians."

"You can't say it wasn't an interesting way to start."

"While I was watching the two Samoans—and believe me, as intimidating as their eye lasers were, you can't look away when two women are making out—I wondered why all women aren't lesbians, or at least bisexual, on some type of convenient, casual level. Think about it. Most men are disgusting jockish greaseballs and are generally fucking repulsive. We're either overly competitive, narcissistic, fucking inaccessible, social-climbing assholes or comparative losers who don't have enough energy to get up to grab another beer or bag of Doritos from the kitchen during a football game. How do women, whether they're nineteen or sixty-five, look at some sweaty fucking *dude* and not say, 'Eh, I'd rather be with the hot skinny chick in the T-back G-string sunning by the pool'? Seems like a no-brainer." He pauses to grab another drink from his water bottle. "And men themselves have zero self-awareness. Go to a convenience store at 3:00 a.m. and you'll see some greasy-haired, forty-three-year-old, sun-scorched, backwoods, sandal-wearing, tweaked-out redneck trying to flirt with a young girl with absolutely no shame, no self-control, and not a thought in his head like, *I am ugly and uncool, and this chick thinks I'm a dickhead for hitting on her.* I guess it's better to kiss somebody's ass in the shade than to pick strawberries in the sun."

"Interesting metaphor," Peacock notes.

"Yeah, my gramps told me that. He always had a throwaway line. He used to tell me, 'Keeping the blinds drawn doesn't stop the sun from shining somewhere else.' Sometimes it seemed like he was the only person I knew growing up who made any *real* sense."

"Did he have a hand in raising you?"

"He was around a lot. My dad was a no-show most of the time, so it was mostly up to my mom. She dropped me off with my grandparents a lot. She'd split most every night to go out and make money." Leo looks squarely at Peacock and cautions, "Don't ask—at least not right now. Sometimes Gramps would come to the house to cook dinners and try to keep a clean place. He was a disciplinarian too. I didn't mind so much, although I sure had to take a lot of shit from him. He was never really happy with where he was in life. I guess sometimes he'd take it out on me and my sister."

"How?"

"When we were kids, if we didn't finish our dinner, he would take the plate and whatever was left over and dump it on our head at the table."

"That's extreme," Peacock says. "When I was a kid, if I or my siblings didn't finish all our dinner, my parents would put it in the refrigerator and make us eat it for our next meal the following day. It was awful but not humiliating."

"I'd rather have it dumped on my head than have to eat it the next day. At least it would be over with. I can't imagine it gets any better tasting the next day."

"That's very true."

"So what was I talking about?" Leo asks.

"You were telling me about your weekend in New Orleans."

"Right." He collects himself and continues. "So eventually we left the hotel, decided to go into the city, and, you know, cruise the Quarter and check out what was going on. It was a Saturday night, so things were bound to be a kick."

"Did you get into any adventures?"

"Oh yeah," Leo confirms. "I found out my friend wasn't exactly on the up and up, so I had to skirt a few situations that might have found me in a bind otherwise."

"For example?"

"Well, we took his car into the city. Along the way, he suddenly decides to stop at a sub shop to pick up a sandwich. Okay, I wanted to get going, but hey, I figured he was hungry and needed to put something in his stomach before we started drinking seriously."

"What happened?"

"We go into the place, and he orders a shrimp po'boy. 'It Ain't Me, Babe' by Bob Dylan is playing on the shop's radio. My buddy starts talking to the cashier when she sees him humming the song. The cashier says, 'Ya can't beat Johnny and June's version.' He says, 'No, can't beat the original.' They laugh, although I can tell he was kinda irritated that she thought a different version was better. Anyway, he takes his sandwich and we walk back to the car after kidding around with the clerk for a few more minutes. She was a cutie." Leo pauses to visualize the cashier. "So we get to the car and he opens the trunk. There's this young girl lying in the back. Big smile on her face. My friend tosses in the sandwich and says to her, 'Here, now be quiet.' He casually closes the trunk and gets in the car to drive off."

Peacock, shocked at this change in events, leans forward and starts blurting out a steady barrage of questions. Leo lifts his hand to put a stop to the interrogation. He then goes on to explain.

"It was some girl he hooked up with before we got to the hotel. Think he met her at the airport, something like that, but it was really messed up. Anyway, he didn't want to just *spring* her on me, so he made her stay in the trunk until he thought it was the right time to introduce us."

Peacock sighs and sits back in his chair. "That's one of the oddest things I've ever heard. I hope this gets better for all parties involved. Was she hurt or tied up? He kidnapped her?"

"No, nothing like that. She was cool with it. I told him to let her out and asked him what the deal was. He gave me the whole story. He said that he was embarrassed, but he wanted to know if it was okay for her to stay in the room. I didn't give a shit. I was just there to get out of Atlanta and forget about everything for a couple of days."

"What was she like?"

"She got out of the trunk. She was pretty hot—hot in body temperature because of being in the trunk, not *hot* hot—and was dressed more like a trashy white girl from some cold, industrial northern city, like Detroit or Pittsburgh. She also had a fake Goth thing going—lots of black makeup and some kind of tint in her hair. She was in her midthirties, a little past the expiration date for *that* look.

"She had a couple of black-ink tattoos that looked like prison-scribbled amateur hour, and a mildly attractive shape. She had short hair and was wearing a tank top with some slogan written across it—I don't remember what it said. She wasn't a shapeless lump."

"What was her name?"

"All he ever called her was A-Cup," he says.

"As long as it all turned out fine."

Leo hesitates, and then uncomfortably switches his position on the couch, leaning forward with his elbows and forearms resting on his knees, his legs propping him up.

"So our next stop is a convenience store. My buddy goes in through the store's front door after saying he'll be right back. As he goes, A-Cup tells me they've been prepping this job since they met earlier that day. *They are planning to fucking rob the place!* It's one of those fancy superstore minimart gas stations. So now I'm sitting in this car knowing that my buddy is about to rob the place. I don't know if he's got a gun. I don't know what the plan is. The only thing I'm pretty fucking sure of is that I'm sitting in the getaway car." Leo pauses. "I said it would be a kickin' Saturday night. Apparently he had *much* bigger plans than I did for the weekend."

"That's remarkable."

"Wait, not finished. So when he gets near the checkout counter, there's a guy in line standing in front of him. So get this: the guy in front of him in line robs the place before my buddy even gets the chance to."

"Then?" Peacock is intrigued.

"Then A-Cup and I jump out of the car and run toward the store. We can see my buddy knock the robber over the head with a large, heavy drink cooler. You know, those big metal ones that sit on the countertops with cold drink bottles—Dr. Peppers or energy drinks. Anyway, he really pounds the guy with this thing. The robber falls to the ground, barely conscious."

"I'm gonna hit him again," my buddy is screaming. He's completely caught up in and hyped by the moment. He's like in this adrenaline-fueled rage rush."

"No ... why?" I say. "You hit him. He's out."

"I want to make sure he doesn't wake up and go crazy," he says to me. Then he says, "Let me hit him again so he'll stay out longer."

"He's already out," I tell him. "I don't think it works that way. I don't think hitting somebody once they're out keeps them out longer unless you jump right to coma or death, and we don't wanna go there."

"So what did you do next, get out of there?"

"Nope. This will really blow your mind." Leo sits back again, obviously more relaxed and using his hands and arms to punctuate his points. "Because my buddy never got the chance to begin robbing the place himself, he was just like some innocent bystander who acted under pressure and subdued the bad guy. Like a Good Samaritan. The store manager was ecstatic; he couldn't have been more thrilled and appreciative. I guess he's been robbed, like, half a dozen times in the past couple of months. Bottom line: my buddy was a big hero. At the scene the cops were patting him on the back. He was shown on the local news, and the story spread across social media there. Everyone who was standing around gave him a round of applause when we left. The manager gave us a night on the town in the Quarter on him. It was great. Check that—it was decadently great. It was fate. I mean, how does *that* happen?"

Leo had a glint of madness in his eyes as he recalled the night.

"So let's try and tie this whole thing back to the good–bad discussion we were having when we started," Leo says. "I guess that bridge between good and bad still needs fixing. I didn't stay out of trouble."

"My first thought was that this is the answer to your prayers."

"How do you figure that?"

"Sounds like every one of the different things you ran into that night had nothing to do with you," Peacock explains. "You didn't start anything, you weren't an accomplice to the various acts, and in a strange twist of fate you ended up standing side by side with a circumstantial hero. Sounds like a reasonably successful weekend, if only because all of the things that happened were out of your control—but they all managed to fall your way. There's never a bad time for luck to pass your way."

"Fifty years and *this* is the prayer God finally decides to answer?"

"Still," Peacock adds, "it sounds like something was looking out for you that night."

"I don't think it works that way for me. I went to confession once and ended up in an exorcism." He snarls and widens his eyes to appear possessed.

"Do you ever just think about what's best for you?"

"Why, is somebody else thinking about it for me?"

Dr. Peacock chuckles. "It's important to remember that putting yourself first isn't a sign of vanity or an indicator of any lack of humility. In many cases, it's your most basic survival instinct coming forward to prevent you from entering something potentially worse and more damaging."

"You know what, Doctor," Leo begins, straightening up in his chair, wagging his finger at Peacock, "I admire how you bring everything back to the message. It reminds me of a story I first heard as a kid. There's this hunter. One day he gets a new rifle and decides to go hunting with it. He goes on a trip out to the woods and eventually comes upon a nice-sized black bear, so he takes his gun and shoots it. Then he feels a tap on his shoulder. The man turns around and sees this huge black bear, who says to the hunter, 'That bear you shot was my wife, so the way I see it you got two options: either I have sex with you or I maul you to death.'

"Now, the hunter doesn't want to die, so he lets the bear have his way. Afterwards the man goes home and doesn't tell anyone about what happened. When hunting season comes the next year, he goes out and comes across a brown bear. He gets his gun and shoots the bear dead. Then he feels a tapping on his shoulder. The man turns around and sees a huge brown bear, who says, 'That brown bear was my wife, so the way I see it, either I have sex with you or I maul you to death.' Again, the man doesn't want to die, so he lets the bear have his way. Then he stumbles home, not telling anyone. When hunting season arrives the next year, the man goes out and eventually finds a grizzly bear. He takes his gun and shoots the grizzly dead, and then he feels a tap on his shoulder. The hunter turns around and finds an enormous grizzly bear, who says to him, 'Let's be honest, you don't come here for the hunting, do you?'"

A wide grin crosses Dr. Peacock's face. "Well." He smiles. "I never thought about it that way."

"Old too soon, smart too late." Leo starts to get up, anticipating the end of the session, and then adds sarcastically, "I haven't felt this pumped since I got my first belt." He catches the look on Peacock's face.

"Whoa, you blinked first—twice," Leo says. He smiles, pointing at Peacock. "Or you blinked last first. Either way."

They both stand. Leo begins walking toward the office door to leave. As Leo reaches for the doorknob, Peacock drops a quick question.

"Any particular topic or issues you want to discuss next time? Something to prep for? I have business in Phoenix next week, so it'll have to be for the week after."

Leo pauses for a moment and then quietly replies. "I hate Phoenix. I think of it as a place where they send people to wait until a spot opens up in hell." He turns and takes a step toward Dr. Peacock's desk.

"I fantasize that I have a series of detonators fixed to explosives I've spread throughout different locations around the properties where I work, catering parties. I, armed with a semiautomatic assault rifle, stalk the grounds of a grand estate to dispense justice. As the injured and dying lie screaming and bloody on the ground, reaching for me as I step over their bodies, I realize they're finally waking up to see the world as it is." He smiles. Backing out of the office, he adds just as he closes the door behind him, "Have a pleasant evening, Doctor. Maybe I'll see you in a couple of weeks."

"But what have they done, all those people? Why do they deserve that?" Peacock yells out as the door slowly reopens and Leo peers into the office.

"At this point," he replies, "you often can't really tell. What's behind this sort of thing?" He pauses. "The nice thing about social justice is that it doesn't matter whose goal you kick the ball into. And when they dissect the event, the real reasons never matter or have any real impact on the national conversation. It all comes back to impotent arguments about mental illness and gun control. Maybe once, just once, people should take the reason the shooter gives at face value. It might frighten you to learn how often you find that you share the killer's very same beliefs."

Peacock stares at the door and takes a breath. He shakes his head as Leo leaves, writes a few notes on the pad that is lying on his desk, and picks up the phone to check on his next appointment.

Chapter 10

You Can Throw Out Everything Else

P at McLaren was sitting at his desk in the Elite Lawns and Landscaping office, sorting through the different work orders he had lined up for the day. It was a little after ten o'clock in the morning. His work trucks had already been dispatched a few hours earlier. The workday ahead was officially on.

He was finishing up in the office and getting ready to go out on the road to check on his trucks when one of his supervisors, Creep Sipotora, happened to walk past his door. Before he passed, he poked his head in. Creep was Sipotora's nickname, given to him by his parents when he was just a small child because of his proclivity to creep and move proficiently around the house. Of course later in life, Creep would have some difficult times trying to explain to people who didn't know him that his name wasn't associated with the deviant pervert to whom you'd normally assign the label.

"Hey, boss." Creep waves.

"Hey," Pat replies. "What's up?"

"Glad you're still in the office. Don't forget, I'm outta here next week."

Pat sets down his paperwork and sits back in his chair. "That's right, I forgot. You've got a vacation coming up. Any plans?"

"We're going camping." Sipotora is obviously excited about his upcoming vacation. "Try to get in a little camping and hunting."

"Really? I hate camping," Pat says dryly. "I hate the outdoors."

"Strange choice of work considering that every aspect of your business is based on the outdoors," Creep observes with a smile. "Why?"

"Because nature is full of terrible things that can easily hurt, kill, or eat me."

"It's not that bad."

"Yeah? Ever notice a deer's head is made of weapons?"

Creep laughs along with Pat, who chuckles.

"Never seen you turn down the meat and sausage I bring back."

"Yes, that's true," Pat smiles as he shakes his head. "Very true."

"Listen, I checked in early this morning at the Marvel place," Creep tells him. "After the job yesterday and the event scheduled tomorrow night, I wanted to make sure they didn't need any last-minute things.

"Right, how was it? I was gonna check in on that later. Everything good?"

"Seems to be. They have our numbers if they need us. Mrs. Marvel's not afraid to call when she wants something."

"And if there's anything they really hate, I'm sure I'll hear about it at the party tomorrow."

"Okay, I've gotta run. I'll swing back by at the end of the day. I need to take care of a few things here before I leave next week."

"Sounds good. I should be here later today." As Pat finishes his sentence, Sherry blasts into the office looking a little disheveled—not her usual perfectly coiffed figure.

"Hey, I'm really sorry," Sherry begins explaining as she enters, interrupting while Pat and Sipotora are still talking.

"You okay?" Pat asks her. She appears winded and flustered.

"I'm fine. I'm really sorry I'm late." She takes a deep breath and sits down in the chair in front of Pat's desk. "I was detained for shoplifting." She might as well have said, "I stopped to get a drink of water," as it was that straightforward, reserved, and uneventful in tone. Sherry certainly knew how to push the minimalist perspective.

Sipotora, upon hearing this news flash, stops in his tracks before leaving the office. He turns to listen, intrigued.

"You were arrested for shoplifting?" Pat tries to clarify.

Sherry nods her head. "Well, detained. Wasn't actually arrested and processed. They let me go after questioning."

"What did you do?"

"It's a long story, but basically I have contracting work on the side hosting recruits during college visits to the schools. Pays pretty well." She pauses and stands up. "Can I grab a quick cup of coffee? Haven't had any caffeine all day." She walks over to the back counter of the office and pours herself a cup, adds a healthy dose of sugar and cream, and then returns to her seat. "Where was I?"

"Detained for shoplifting and hosting college recruits."

"Right." She pauses again to take a sip of her coffee. "Cute guys too. In *great* shape."

"So what does hosting the recruits involve?" Sipotora asks. The tone of insinuation is in his voice.

"I ..." she stumbles a bit on her words. "I sort of provide them with a special service. It seems to help them relax during the recruiting. I guess it can be a very stressful process. The school looks at this as a tool to bring in talent."

Pat and Creep look at each other, both immediately realizing what she's probably referring to. Pat shakes his head, still confused as to how getting detained for shoplifting has anything to do with blowing college recruits.

"So why were you detained for shoplifting?"

"Well, I was leaving the school's admin offices after meeting with one of the recruits. When I walked through the bookstore on my way out, a rent-a-cop guard grabbed my arm, saying he saw me stuff a T-shirt into my shorts."

Pat and Creep looked over Sherry carefully. She is wearing skin-tight, frame-hugging shorts, mid to high length on the thigh, leaving very little room for malfeasance. They look at each other with a knowing smile, each thinking the security guard must have spotted an unsavory opportunity to take advantage of a cute little thing.

"Did he find what he was looking for?" Sipotora asks, trying to tone down the noticeable sarcasm.

Sherry looks baffled when he asks her the question. She doesn't seem to know how to respond. After a moment, she answers. "Of course not." Her attitude and manner get more serious. "I had to practically undress for him in the security office to prove I didn't have anything."

"Sure," Pat says, unfazed. "That makes sense." He looks at Creep. "Makes sense to me."

"Seems reasonable," Creep adds.

"Well," Sherry continues, "I didn't think it was appropriate. I mean, look at me." She stands up and turns. "Where the heck am I gonna put anything?"

They both take a long look.

"Yeah," Creep says. "He should have known better."

"So," Pat begins slowly, "I think we need to discuss the meaning of the word *appropriate*. For example, it was not appropriate for the guard to accuse you of shoplifting with no proof. Check. It was not appropriate for you to undress to show you didn't shoplift anything. Check. And this is just me throwing another one in the mix here: it's probably not appropriate for you to be performing sex acts with college recruits."

After a few uncomfortable moments, Sherry speaks up. "Are you really mad?" She tilts her head and offers a pout. "You're furious with me."

Pat shakes his head. "I'm not happy."

"You don't seem that upset."

"I was upset before. I'm over it now. How long do you want me to be upset?" He pauses and looks at her. "You must be a calming influence."

"That's good." She seems relieved after hearing this.

"Not necessarily," he counters.

She stares at him, pursing her lips. "I'm not going to lose my job, am I?"

Pat looks back at her, thoughts swirling through his head. He suddenly is a little troubled and mystified at this young woman. Is she as naïve as she's acting? She *must* know the ulterior motive of the guard. She *has* to know that what she's doing with the school recruits is wrong. He wonders if the college is compliant with this whole situation. And he's beginning to think he just hired a little ball of fire and energy who's about to turn everything in his efficient office upside down.

"No, you're not going to lose your job. I guess I'm just concerned and a little disappointed." He leans back in his chair. "That's quite a story."

"Do all your days begin this way?" Creep asks with a laugh.

Before she can answer, Pat jumps back in. "Listen, we'll talk about this later. Firstly, Sherry, is there anything you need to do with the school or the police or whomever to make this right, or is the matter settled now?"

"I think it's settled."

"Fine. Then let's just forget about it for now and get back to work." He gets up from his chair. "Unfortunate incident. Just keep me in the loop with *anything*—something to tell the grandkids."

Sherry gets up from her chair. She and Pat follow Sipotora out of the office. They walk to the reception area. Creep waves good-bye as he heads out to his truck to hit the road.

Pat starts to collect his things to go out and make his rounds. Sherry corners him before he leaves.

"I'm so sorry about all this. I'm so embarrassed. The whole thing should never have happened."

Pat looks at her again, not sure whether to agonize over her or empathize with her. He takes a rare serious boss's tone with her. "Being ignorant isn't the same as being curious."

She nods and returns to the front desk to start her day at the office. He takes his stuff and heads out the door to begin driving the territory and checking on his workers. He wonders to himself how someone can have such disregard for her job that with barely a few months in, the drama has already begun.

"I wonder what surprises I can expect next," he mumbles to himself as he gets in his truck and drives off the lot.

Chapter 11

The Talented Dr. Brooksby

D r. Emerson Brooksby's path to his status as King of Recovery began years ago when he took an apprenticeship with a newly founded addiction recovery center in Palm Beach, Florida. He received his doctorate in psychiatric medicine and studies from the Los Angeles University Center for Health Services back in 1990 and immediately bonded with a bounty of Hollywood A-list movie stars and top-of-the-charts pop acts and rock bands. Unfortunately for Brooksby, that bonding was a result of his services as doctor to the stars, the doctor who was available to supply any and all forms of drugs. It didn't hurt that he was also able to bypass a few federal and state regulations, which enabled him to hand out prescriptions for medical marijuana as if they were pizza coupons.

It didn't take long for Dr. Brooksby to start taking a little too much of his own medicine. A careful dealer always knows not to dip into the product. Needless to say, Brooksby wasn't careful. What began as sampling the supply from time to time quickly turned into a full-blown addiction. His habitual Percocet suddenly became oxy with a side of meth and a cocaine chaser. His sloppiness and cantankerous craving for the fast life and the spotlight raised red flags across numerous law enforcement agencies, stretching from LAPD's drug enforcement task force to investigators for the IRS, with another half dozen in between. They were all keeping a very close eye on him.

If this wasn't enough pressure for the flamboyant doctor, he was also starting to hear grumblings from a number of investors who had given him large sums of money. Brooksby was trying to raise funds for his effort to build an addiction recovery center somewhere along the Southern California coast. Details were sketchy, but he had a hot reputation as an insider with the celebs and paparazzi, so it was easy for him to find willing sponsors. The money kept pouring in. Brooksby's lifestyle reflected his blushing wealth. Add some high-stakes gambling to the mix, and he was a combustible comet soaring around the Hollywood Hills while driving in the latest model high-performance vehicle.

It was no surprise that this drug-dealing, Ponzi-scheming doctor found his way into the hands of the authorities. He worked backroom deals with some of his partners, patients, and clients and was successful in paying back a reasonable amount of the money he had taken from investors. In return, he served five years on a twenty-year sentence and kept his mouth shut. While in prison, he was the stereotypical changed man. He used his medical background and practice in psychiatry and addiction recovery, as well as the experience with his own personal demons, to create a rehab program in prison. He followed that by developing a very popular extensive post-rehab recovery lifestyle program to keep the patients sober. They met daily, organizing tasks and taking steps toward becoming contributing members of society again.

He was released from prison with some acclaim and fanfare among the inner circle of the entertainment industry. Shortly after his return to town, the same people who had called themselves friends and patients, however, turned a cool cheek toward him and refused to welcome him back into their fold.

Eventually Brooksby took his now aged and more weathered lived-in profile, his street smarts and media savvy, and what little money he still had, and made the cross-country trip to Atlanta, where he parlayed his still-hot reputation into a regional state-of-the-art reengineering center he named the Brooksby Reengineering Institute (BRI). After a few years of operation, the BRI became nationally known as one of the premier addiction recovery facilities in the country. Dr. Emerson Brooksby's innovative "reengineering" programs became a phenomenon, and the good doctor found himself exactly where he wanted to be. He was an industry pacesetter, a leader on the cutting edge of addiction recovery through his reengineering techniques.

One of the more controversial methods he employed was to combine different types of addiction treatments into the same program, although most of the problems would seem to require different approaches. This meant that the different reengineering sessions were made up of addicts from any suitable compulsion, dependence, obsession, or need. He became a talking head on every cable news show whenever related topics would come up as news stories. It was now part of his weekly routine to appear on television. In so doing, he collected a substantial number of fans and devotees. He is now embarking on a new project to find an even greater audience on television through his new pilot program.

The group of patients for his latest reengineering sessions includes a handful of B-listers and no-listers, but these people collectively have a distinct sense of personality that producers think will make a good addition to the current roster of shows that are already popular in the world of reality TV, which covers recovery, rehab, intervention, addiction, and hoarding, among other things. Brooksby is determined to keep his show at a higher level than the similar programs already on the air that stretch the dimensions of reality with their semiscripted plots and structured episodes. He is going to try to forget about the cameras, have them be as unobtrusive as possible, and allow no professional stage direction or camera lighting or setups to be done on the premises of BRI.

Today is the inaugural meeting of the reengineering participants in this session's encounter. This is a get-acquainted introductory summit, an opportunity for each team member, as they're called during the course of the session, to tell the others about themselves and to learn a little about their colleagues-in-dependence. The opening ceremonies, as it were, generally start slowly until a level of trust and understanding can be established through a series of conversations and ground rules. The first gathering of team members can either be an exhausting drag or extraordinarily illuminating. With the eclectic mix of egos and wildly inflated personalities involved in this team, the participants promise to fall somewhere beyond the normal rehabilitation process. Dr. Brooksby is eagerly looking forward to bringing this team together and focusing on their recovery in front of a cable-ready TV audience and a network anxiously looking for ratings.

✳ ✳ ✳

The BRI has a very large plush and inviting central meeting area that is casual while maintaining a professional, restorative healthy vibe. In the center of the room is a series of three curved sofas that are spaced to make a three-quarter circle. Resting in the remaining quarter of the circle is a comfortable lounger, Dr. Brooksby's spot and home base during the sessions. It is from this chair that Brooksby moderates the discussions and performs his acts of sustaining sobriety among the chosen. And fortunately, even the nonchosen can be dried and enlightened if they can pay the tab.

Kip Balotta, a former child actor who achieved a fairly sizable measure of fame as "Scotty," the precocious youngster who, on TV before America's eyes, grew from an impish adolescent into a gangly teenager on the weekly sitcom *Sliced Turkey*, is at the BRI in his fifth attempt at rehab as a recovering alcoholic and a walking pharmacy of abused meds. The booze and pill problem provided a solid base for his hefty cocaine habit. He considered cocaine to be merely a habit, as his real problem, he believed, was his addiction to heroin.

At the end of the sofa, sitting nearest to Dr. Brooksby, Kip Balotta slides back and positions himself. He is wearing a white V-neck T-shirt with the name of some faded seaside bar written across the front and baggy, knee-length mustard-color shorts covered with a pattern of different-sized squares and triangles in various shades of red. His legs are crossed, and he's rapidly tossing his flip-flopped feet around nervously. Prior to finally taking a seat, he was bouncing off the walls and pacing around in a casually animated manner, undeterred by obstacles in his way. This was opposed to his more formal working pace, which is more staccato and firmly grounded. In simple terms, when Kip is in the vicinity, you could turn around at any moment, anywhere, and find him standing right behind you, watching. At work or in a more formal setting, you can hear him come stomping from a mile away.

Sitting next to Balotta is Karoleen Young, an attractive thirty-something airline flight attendant training leader and self-described sex addict. At first glance, Young appears to be a lovely, quietly introverted professional businesswoman. As you slowly strip away the protective layer of her defensive shield, she reveals herself to be a highly motivated, tough-minded, type-A personality with a penchant for using her sexual charm to unlock career paths. Her sexual appetite failed in its efforts to fulfill her insatiable carnal needs.

Next to Young and across from Dr. Brooksby sits Ned Symbol, a midfifties gay fashion designer who is at the institute for purposes of sexual reorientation. He is making an attempt to begin living a straight—that is, heterosexual—lifestyle. This controversial treatment is an innovative new program at the BRI and has many detractors. One camp maintains that the whole perceived process of changing one's sexual orientation is ethically flawed, while others say that a person can't alter the course of his or her life choices, that certain characteristics are innate and our traits are mapped from birth. Sexual preference is a God-given characteristic, these latter people believe. Ned, who is somewhat effeminately wired but struggles with his flamboyancy, is still at a psychological crossroads in his efforts to change. It's not that he necessarily *wants* to become straight. Nor would any change in orientation help his career. In fact, many would say it would hinder him in his chosen profession. It's more that as Ned grows older, he wants to make sure that he's been doing the right thing, so to speak, for all these years. Even around this circle of participants, he finds himself eyeballing the male patients more frequently than the he eyes the females. He would tell himself that this is because he finds fault with the men's clothing choices, not because the men ooze a certain sexual heat as opposed to the women, who don't excite him at all physically.

Parked next to Symbol is a man who clearly falls into Ned's sexual wheelhouse of broad-shouldered hunks whom he'd love to conquer— or be conquered by. This is Cliff Malomar. Malomar is a self-professed outdoorsman who hosts a hunting and fishing show on cable TV. He is in his midforties and is in exceptionally sound physical shape. On his program, he takes his guns and rods out into the natural wonder of our woods and waters, tracks down the critters for his human companions, and spends the first half of the show observing the animals, fish, and fowl in their habitat. He and his guests discuss the animals and their natural homes, where they dwell and how they live, and the various roles they play in contributing to the environment and circle of life. During the last half of the show, Cliff kills the animals. Cliff is at the BRI to deal with his anger management issues.

Finally, sitting next to Malomar is Mayra Vanity, the only true A-list celebrity in the group. Vanity is an international superstar recording artist and performer whose musically hot backbeats and wildly choreographed dance numbers captivate fans from around the world. Mayra, in her late twenties, is slim and exotically beautiful with a vibrant cocoa-shaded skin tone and a remarkably fit physique. She is trying to fix a lifetime of struggling with eating disorders and her weight and body-image issues. Just to add a little extra spark to her already life-sucking sicknesses, she has a hoarding problem.

It is quite an impressively disparate and eclectic group of patients. Within the personalities sitting around the circle in the meeting area were secretly hidden private demons and delusions that have rendered each of them powerless. Brooksby decided not to have any kind of formal introductions and wanted to avoid delving too deeply into each patient's personal history, career, and notoriety, or the circumstances that brought them to the institute. He wanted to try a different approach with this group by starting off by getting everyone together and just beginning a friendly discussion. He felt this method would help to open people up and make them feel as comfortable with the process as possible before they got into anything too heavy.

Brooksby knows that this is a very ego-driven, high-caliber group of people who are used to getting their way and walking on waves of praise and adoration. He also knows that in some cases, the slow demise of that adoration was a trigger for an escalation of the person's disorder. These aren't the happiest, friendliest, or nicest people to deal with. In fact, they are about as standoffish, rude, pouty, entitled, and spoiled as any group he can remember in his years of providing treatment. There were jealousies, withdrawals, detoxes, and insecurities too intensely prevalent among the group for Brooksby to game-plan for. He thought it best to simply get them together and let each find out about the little tics and surreptitious motives and secrets as conversation flowed and they slowly discovered what the others had stashed away in their closets.

Dr. Brooksby waits a few moments for each to settle with their coffee or bottled water, takes a deep breath, and makes a careful observational review of his patients. He takes a moment to look around the meeting center, makes a mental note of where the camera setup is located and where the TV show runner is standing, and makes sure there will be minimal distractions while producing these sessions for the cable broadcast.

He had dealt with difficult groups before. People recovering from addiction can generally be as complicated and tricky as petulant, stubborn children—and this assortment of patients promises to be as challenging as any he has encountered. It will be a survival test of wills. Inside, Brooksby is churning, excited and eager to explore the dynamics of this collective cast of demanding, self-absorbed eccentrics.

After everyone appears to be settled and relaxed, albeit anxious, the doctor eases back into his chair, crosses his legs, and with the ever-present notebook in his lap, begins the session.

"Welcome, everybody," Brooksby begins. "Now who would like to start us off this morning?"

Kip Balotta sits up on the couch and, smiling broadly, clears his throat and raises his hand. He begins to stand up when Dr. Brooksby motions for him to remain seated.

"We're not making any announcements here," he tells Balotta. "No need to stand. We're just talking."

"Okay." Balotta casually complies. "Where was I?"

"You weren't," barks Cliff Malomar. "So far all you've done is stutter and stop from standing up."

Balotta stares at Malomar for a moment, and then turns his attention back to Dr. Brooksby.

"High school was okay," Balotta tells the group. "Could have been better. Took a lot of shit from the other kids about my acting gig. I used to get teased and pushed around. My using really got bad. Drunk all the time. Drugs every day. Started turning myself into a tough guy to back all the assholes away from me. I wasn't that tough, but I acted like a complete lunatic whenever somebody fucked with me. It was the only way to escape school." He pauses, looking around at the others, who have no visible reaction. "*Now college*," he says with more excitement in his voice, shaking his head. "I fucking killed it in college. It was great."

The group don't seem interested in, much less impressed by, Balotta. He didn't exactly come out of the gate inspiring the others to exhibit openness and trust.

"At least you could have dressed a little nicer for everyone's first meeting together," Karoleen Young scolds him.

"It's a hundred and fifty fucking degrees in here." He looks to his side, where Karoleen is seated. "Whoever is in charge of the thermostat in this place is overcompensating for the cold outside. I'm burning up. You're lucky I wore *this* much."

"Are you finished?" Mayra Vanity, irritated and antsy, asks.

Balotta turns his sights on Vanity, who is glaring back.

"Jesus Christ," he barks. "I just fucking started." He is dismayed by the lack of patience within the group, and it shows. "I mean, c'mon. I. Just. Fucking. Started."

"Well, go ahead, nobody's stopping you," Ned Symbol says, adding his two cents.

"Okay," Balotta snaps, frustrated with the group already. "God damn, you can't swing a dead cat around this place without hitting a fucking jerk-off."

"Let's give Kip the opportunity to finish," Brooksby interrupts. "We just began the meeting. We all need to relax, listen, and maybe learn. We're not going anywhere. No one here's in a rush to go because they have other plans today." As he looks at the group, he can see the disinterest. The patients aren't responding to this talk-talk intro session of the program. "I know it's early, but we need to find a rhythm and show some respect and encouragement to our team members and to the process. So thank you in advance." He smiles and turns to face Balotta. "Please continue."

"Yeah, please continue, movie star, er, I mean ... what is it now? Bank teller, right?" Young snarls, showing her unexplained immediate contempt for Balotta. She looks at the others. "Don't fuck with him," she adds. "He'll have you audited."

"Shit," Balotta says under his breath, looking over at Young, who is sitting with a snarky, know-it-all smirk. "Either you are the one person in this whole facility who is virtually impossible to like or this is your way of flirting."

"So are you done telling us what you are doing here?" she asks, rushing to move things along.

"One question at a time," Balotta snaps. "The team can only have one quarterback." He looks at the group, points around the meeting space, and stops his hand when his finger is aimed squarely at Young.

"I noticed that no matter how bright a room is," he begins telling her, "you have the quality of sucking all the light for yourself." She uncomfortably shifts in her seat on the sofa.

"Your voice makes me itch," she comments, turning her head away from Balotta. "That's probably why you can't get back on TV."

Before Balotta can erupt back, Brooksby intervenes again.

"You know, Karoleen," Emerson starts his direct feedback to Young, "you have shown tendencies in the past of deflecting your anger at yourself and your simmering self-esteem issues by lashing out at others. This isn't your first try at rehab. If you want to succeed, you may begin by thinking about some of the other approaches that are available to you."

"I thought you were in here for sex," Cliff Malomar blurts.

"I am." She nods.

"So what did you do when you left rehab the first time? Just run around getting laid and giving blow jobs?"

"No," she casually replies. "I decided to try to keep things at home, in the privacy of my own room. So I started a website. Made extra money doing video-cam sessions. Lots of money."

"What's the site?"

"Online I use the alias Thai Trinity."

"Why Thai Trinity?" Brooksby asks.

"Yeah, isn't that a soup? It's got, like, lemongrass, coconut milk, and cilantro or something?" Symbol adds.

"You don't look Asian," Malomar observes.

"I think it has roots in Hinduism," Balotta guesses.

"So she doesn't eat cows either?" Malomar asks Kip.

"No, it means she uses three holes," Vanity flatly states with a grin.

Karoleen looks up at her with a knowing sparkle in her eye, points at her playfully, and beams. "Bad girl," she purrs while wagging a finger.

"Oh. I thought maybe it had something to do with a heroin-farming region you're from in Southeast Asia," Malomar says.

"Okay, well, I've learned that you each have vivid imaginations." Brooksby stops the banter, discouraged by the tone. He takes a long, deep, cleansing breath, looks into the eyes of each patient, and tries to get the group back on track. "I didn't think I needed to reiterate some of our basic principles. In addition to checking your ego at the door, our primary ground rule is to show respect—respect for yourself, respect for the others in the group. Please respect each other's time and what each of you has to share with the group. Interrupting or making side sneers or comments isn't an acceptable way to show how you're feeling about a person or what he or she has to say. It's inappropriate, and I won't tolerate it. Please watch yourself and what you say. If you have direct feedback you want to provide, wait for the proper moment before addressing that person. We want to have civil, positive, and constructive meetings."

There is a collective moment of silence in the group as Brooksby notes the expressions and body language. After a moment, Vanity sits up in her seat.

"But that's not what they want for TV," she observes.

"What are you talking about?" Brooksby faces Vanity in all seriousness. "What do you mean, 'not what they want'? Who are *they*?"

"The producers who picked us to be on the television show."

"Believe me," the doctor says. His voice already reflects his frustration with the group at this early stage. "The cameras are just here to capture the sessions and show how the process works. They're not meant to inhibit, and they're not meant to draw otherwise unrealistic responses either."

"When my people spoke with the cable station, they tried to tell them all about my issues and why I wanted to check in somewhere that might help me. The TV producers were set on me getting treatment and having it aired on the show. I explained it, and it went right over their head," Vanity explains.

"I don't know what that is," Brooksby comments.

"It means she didn't get it."

"No, I didn't mean the 'over their head' comment." Frustrated, he tosses off his sentence in midexplanation. "What I meant was … never mind." He sighs.

"Can I tell the group about one of my recurring dreams to see what interpretations everyone has?" Ned Symbol jumps in to get the ball rolling again. "Wouldn't this be the perfect place to discuss dreams and the meanings behind them?"

"Sure." Malomar groans. "I bet you have some *fabulous* dreams," he says, mocking Symbol. "I'd push a small child down a stairwell to get a chance to talk about your dreams."

"Great!" Symbol continues undeterred, ignoring Malomar's comment. He looks at Brooksby for validation. The doctor nods his approval.

Ned begins, not looking at anyone in particular, his attention now focused on the recounting of his dream. He is quietly animated, flowingly re-creating moments in his story with subtle turns of his hands and facial expression. It is like a Shakespearean soliloquy.

"This beautiful pup was frolicking outside in the smooth, soft grass, jumping and yelping with joy. Nearby lay the largest, most blubberingly disgusting bull toad I'd ever seen. The toad was sitting back and clocking the eager pup with what looked like an evil grin. I grabbed the ant and roach killer and began furiously spraying the toad in an effort to kill it. The toad looked right into my eyes, the eyes of his attacker, and leaped menacingly toward the pup. I lifted the spray can and began frantically hosing down the toad as it leapt. It landed a few feet away from the dog and stayed only an instant before jumping again and clinging to the side of the house wall. The dog came running over to join in the excitement, and the toad turned to position itself toward the dog. It had a sinful, maliciously wicked look on its bloated, excreting face, preparing to leap at my cheering pup below. The pup jumped high into the air. The entire scene faded into slow motion. I was reaching for the dripping toad. The toad snarled and puffed itself to twice its size, preparing to attack. The two locked eyes and jumped toward each other, facing certain death, when suddenly I dove into the mix with the ant and roach spray in one hand, and a pool-skimming net in the other. I thrust the net in front of the toad, catching it in the mesh. I took the handle of the net and slammed it down into the grass, capturing the toad. I then proceeded to douse the toad with the spray until it twitched and died."

"Well, that was freaking trippy," Balotta says. "What the fuck is that supposed to mean?"

"That's what I'm waiting to find out from hearing what each of you have to say about it," Symbol says. "We just said that ... interpretation of dreams. So ... any thoughts?"

"Yeah," Cliff replies. "I think you're fucking crazy."

"That's not productive," Brooksby interrupts, annoyed by Malomar's insensitive comment.

"Sorry," Malomar says, feigning remorse. "I didn't really mean that."

"Now that's a positive step," Brooksby recognizes. "Apologizing for something hurtful is a major inroad to successful recovery."

Malomar nods and then adds, "But there's no way. There's no amount of therapy or reorientation that's gonna keep this dude from being anything other than a homo." He looks at Symbol and tilts his head. "Sorry, just sayin'."

"Don't worry about it," Ned responds. "I'm still wondering about that myself."

Karoleen has the group's rapt attention as she continues with her story. She speaks slowly, carefully designing her tale with a sinewy seduction that draws in every bit of the group's interest and concentration. They can barely take a breath between the shallow moments when she stops to pause in her recollection.

"Then he gently put a light cotton pillowcase over my head and tied my hands together in front with silk scarves," she says, continuing with her tale. "He carefully put his fingers in my mouth through the fabric of the pillowcase. I remember the feeling was coarse at first. It felt dry and unpleasant. But as he slowly inserted his fingers and pulled back, I could feel my body writhe to the rhythm of his motion. The excitement moistened my mouth, and I yearned for him to continue. When he pulled away and stopped, I reached for more. He started teasing me as he explored other parts of my body. I was beginning to feel how my entire body began to glisten with a smooth layer of perspiration in expectation of his next move. With my head covered with the pillowcase, I had no idea what was coming next. The anticipation was driving me insane. Suddenly I could feel hands all over me—strong, rough hands would probe me one moment, and gradually I could feel softer, smoother feminine hands tickle me and stroke up and down along my defenseless, writhing, waiting flesh. I was completely helpless and vulnerable as many hands began touching me. ... I can't even tell you how many people were now in the room, their hands exploring me and driving me to the very precipice of release before they stopped, leaving me exhausted and frustrated, begging for more. I was crawling around the floor searching for their touch, reaching out with my bound hands to find them, to reciprocate my aching tormentors. It was the thirst for this purely physical, animal-like sex that left me hungering for any emancipation I could find." She makes a throaty, breathless sigh. "But I was just a toy. Their plaything." A calm smile reaches her face. "And I longed for all of it. Every. Single. Moment."

Karoleen looks around the room to see the group members leaning in toward her, hanging on her every syllable. She had played it straight throughout her entire account and knew now that she had them waiting breathlessly for her to continue her story. It was at this point that she selfishly decided it was *exactly* the time to stop.

Waiting just a moment longer, she looks over at Cliff and asks, "You hard yet?" He sits up uncomfortably and tries to shake his head as she immediately turns her attention to Mayra and announces with all the bravado and cockiness she can muster, "And it's okay if you want to make out with me. But I'm gonna keep my shirt on."

Ned Symbol tells the group he has something to say. Balotta turns and whispers to Malomar, "This oughta be rich."

"Go ahead, Ned," Brooksby permits.

"I was just going to say," Ned begins, stumbling uncharacteristically over his words, "that I think your story, Karoleen, really illustrates the fact that we all have these dark secrets and fantasies that we usually try to keep hidden away and certainly never share. I find it admirable that you're willing to reveal such a personal incident in your life to the rest of us, and I thank you for it. It's given me the courage to reevaluate where my head is at and reconsider what secrets of my own I'm willing to share."

"Jesus Christ, Symbol," Balotta says, groaning. "This is a recovery center. She's a sex addict. Seems to me what she's sharing is part of the program. We're supposed to be sharing. Why the hell are you so surprised?"

"Well, I didn't hear anything quite so lucid from you," Ned snaps back. "Karoleen is willing to give us such intimate details of this encounter, and I find it refreshing. It just shows that we all have these thoughts, and each and every one of us has thought about the more lurid side of sexuality."

"That's a very good observation, Ned," Brooksby says encouragingly. "And I agree with you. One of the most basic instincts that we always suppress is our feelings toward sexuality, especially when it comes to thoughts about what's not considered to be normal." He raises his hands to place air quotes around *normal.* "Sexually speaking, there's so much that's taboo when we discuss the topic. Even if we think about something that's out of what we consider to be the realm of ordinary sex, we become incredibly uncomfortable when it comes to verbalizing our thoughts. We automatically assume that people will judge us. We wonder if maybe we've said or shown an interest in something that we shouldn't have. But we know—or at least *should* know—that at some time or other everybody lets his or her mind wander and considers what it would be like to try something different. In that respect, Karoleen is only different from the rest of us in that she's comfortable enough to talk about the things that most of us would rather keep hidden away as part of our dark secret."

"If it's okay to discuss this kind of stuff," Symbol says, "then why is it always referred to as a 'dark' secret? I think when that kind of language is used to describe our sexual nature, it makes it all the more prohibitive and forbidden. It's what keeps these discussions in the closet."

"And you'd know a thing or two about the closet," Balotta says snarkily.

"Okay, stop that right there. I don't want to have to keep refocusing your attention on what's appropriate here," Brooksby says. "Now, do the rest of you agree with Ned's statement?" Brooksby asks.

"If a guy wants to stick his tongue or put his dick somewhere he never has before, somewhere he may always have thought of as taboo, even if he doesn't want to and probably never will, that doesn't mean the thought of it never pops into his head from time to time," Malomar explains. "It may suddenly occur to you during Thanksgiving dinner around the family table. There's nothing you can do to get it out of your head, and then you get that crippling fear that someone is going to find out and judge you. The friends and family whose opinions you care about will look at you like you're some kind of a twisted monster, and you'll have nothing to shield you from that terrible blow to your psyche. And it makes you and everyone else feel strange; it takes you to bad places sometimes. And really, what is it? It's just a thought that occurs to us. Like when we walk down the street and some asshole pisses us off and we visualize the ways we'd like to kill the prick. I mean, everyone else thinks that too, just like with our thoughts about sex, but we'll never get together and be comfortable enough to just voice any of these thoughts, and not just because that would be an awkward conversation for us to have, but because suddenly we might be viewed as weird or worse. And it's especially bad because you *know* everyone else has the same thoughts from time to time."

Karoleen pauses to think about his comment. "And you know it's not wrong, but it certainly feels like it is. So we just keep it bottled up inside, because it's just too dangerous to talk about." Young shrugs her shoulders. "At least on the first date."

"She's right," Malomar says with unexpected understanding in his voice. "I might think your feet are beautiful and sexy and attractive, but just keep them away from my crotch. But some folks are into that and all about anything that has to do with feet. Some of those same people will be open about that desire. Others, not so much. Deep, dark thoughts and desires are just that for a reason. They're dark because we're afraid of what they say about us, and we fear that they represent other aspects of our personality." He looks at the faces staring at him from the group and continues.

"I mean, you might just be sitting there drinking a diet Coke and reading the *USA Today* when all of a sudden you think—just completely out of the blue and for no apparent reason—*Hey, it'd be kind of awesome if someone tied me up, spanked me, and made me wear latex panties later tonight. Now pull my hair and call me a dirty, nasty pony boy.*"

The group members' faces take on a surprised gaze of unsure speculation, reinforcing the whole point of the discussion. They all begin collectively judging, proving the point of the argument.

Brooksby interrupts the few moments of uncomfortable silence to refocus the circle from their immediate group judgment of Malomar's statement. "Each of you have probably entertained one or two thoughts in your life, and you were shocked that it even popped in there for the two seconds you held on to it before you pushed it away. Or maybe you didn't push it away. Neither makes you bad; your mind is an incredible machine, and you're going to think all manner of random or out-of-bounds thoughts."

Karoleen speaks up after listening to the discussion that had been prompted by her story. "It's just bizarre that you and everyone you know will live your lives pretending that those thoughts never happen. If we acknowledged them, though, at the very least our conversations would be more fascinating over breakfast."

Vanity, somewhat annoyed that Karoleen seems to have stolen the interest and attention of the group, thereby blocking the former's spotlight, looks at Young dismissively. "No one plays a beautiful loser more beautifully than you, sweetheart," she announces cattily.

"Jealousy is an ugly look for you." Kip laughs as he admonishes Vanity.

"It's her 'look at me' moment," Vanity continues. "She's nothing more than a second-rate participant falling behind in the group with nothing to contribute, so these stories are her way of grabbing everyone's attention." She looks at Young. "If, after all you do, it blows up in your face, then all you can do is scrape off the gunpowder." She then turns to Kip. "Or in your case, snort it."

"It's people like you who need a reality show film crew following your every move and utterance," Young snaps back. "You use bogus credibility that you think only you own, making otherwise sensible people feel like they need to look like airbrushed princesses. You just float off the stages and magazine covers and TV screens until the rest of us lose all hope of having pride and self-respect because we can never live up to those expectations."

"No wonder the rest of us end up all fucked up and suffer from depression," Symbol adds, "and end up sharing with strangers in a room like this."

"Unfortunately, I think depression is, in many of your individual cases, a by-product of always being successful, of never having failed when you were young." Brooksby begins a more detailed and thorough analysis of the discussion. "It's a strange result, but it's right there. If everything always seems to work out for you, you have no frame of reference. Your mind starts creating scenarios of diminished self-worth and value. Everybody has always told you what a star you are and has hung on your every word, but you begin to question the world around you— and it's scary to see what's really out there. You try to find a place where you fit in, and not just on top of the world. You wonder if there will be a spot for you if, one day, you find yourself no longer on top. You begin to question yourself. You question the people around you. And then maybe something happens to trigger it all—who knows? Maybe you lose the girl. Maybe a truck runs over your dog. Maybe your new show doesn't get picked up. You're a failure for the first time in your life, and what you always thought you were entitled to is gone. Life becomes real life for the first time, and that trumps any success you might have had. Some people seek clinical help to find the source of how they feel and why they feel the way they do. Others self-medicate; they try to drink their problems away and look for outlets to channel what's going on in their head. Others end up here. But the wounds stay with you and mark every endeavor you chart. And when you see each step you take not bringing you any closer to happiness, you disappear into a haze of fear and self-loathing. You wake up one day and realize you're not the person you thought you were or wanted to be. And then there's no one around you to pull you up and straighten you out—probably something you needed from a very young age. Hopefully you can use the experience to find a purpose."

"They say that, ultimately, power is the final goal," Brooksby concludes, "the biggest prize. Once you've got money, and prestige and fame, power is all that's left. If you look deep down, that's not really it. All people really want is to finally have control of themselves and their time."

"How is that different from being a whore?" Balotta crudely counters.

"Are you selling yourself for money?" Symbol asks him.

"I've been selling myself for years," Balotta responds. "I just never made any money from it."

"Then what do you sell yourself for?"

"There's more valuable collateral than cash when you're dealing yourself as currency."

Symbol keeps looking at him, waiting for an answer. Balotta finally accommodates his question. "Sanctuary."

"What about you, Miss Vanity?" Symbol turns his attention to the showy queen. "You've been run through the public gauntlet a lot more than the rest of us."

"Expecting her to answer a question truthfully on the first try is downright negligent," Balotta quips, referring to Vanity. "People like to think that because you are stunning, you're just this torpedo, but I've got a feeling that you're *way* more complicated than that. Am I right?"

"Everything I've done," Vanity replies, "is a horrible guilty pleasure from which I've derived no actual pleasure."

"I just realized what you remind me of." Balotta lifts his head as if he's suddenly on to something. "Remember how, years ago back in school, when you ignored the hot girl it only made her more interested in you?"

"Oh yeah … that *always* worked," Malomar snips sarcastically.

"No, really," Balotta argues, "the girl who was always *all that* seemed to be fixated on the guy who wouldn't give her the time of day. Her only reactions were either to make fun of him and shun him and his friends or to seek to know more about him because she found his disinterest too fascinating to resist."

"You don't know what you're talking about," Vanity says in disgust. "That's a small price to pay to avoid having to deal with the real world. You think you can explain everything away with an insult or some condescending, snarky wisecrack. If I was really being honest with myself, I wouldn't wish me on anyone."

"Nailing down the cause isn't the point here," Balotta says, looking at Brooksby for reassurance. Getting nothing, he continues. "The whole point for a man is that we can be giving the eulogy at our own grandmother's funeral and if there is a girl in the front row showing cleavage, we will be imagining those boobs in our face. Our own dead grandmother is not five feet away, but suddenly that's what's on our minds. When that happens, when we get that aroused at the funeral, we get mad at the girl showing the cleavage. Because we, ourselves, our own rational personality that knows right from wrong and appropriate from inappropriate, knows this is a bad place to get aroused. So it comes off like cleavage-girl is *conspiring* with our sexual weakness to screw us over. But I have never explained this to a woman, especially one as self-centered as you, who didn't look at me like I was insisting that all men are secretly werewolves. And we try to conduct our everyday business like this. We have to live around the fact that we're trying to do little everyday things, like buy a coffee at Starbucks, with a talking pair of boobs."

"I think you are manifesting your anger with the abundance of a soul whisperer in nonspecific flights of brisk intentions," Brooksby says.

Symbol leans over to Balotta and whispers, "I have no idea what that means."

"Neither do I. Just nod and smile." Balotta smiles broadly at Brooksby and then whispers back to Symbol. "After all, he's a doctor."

✵ ✵ ✵

The cameras cut for the day and the group settle back into their respective rooms for private reflection and a heaping course of healthy snack food and reading material. Brooksby walks back to his office and tosses the files on top of his desk.

It is during these times that he wonders to himself how much good he is really providing these patients. He can listen to their problems, their bitching and moaning, and the abundance of neuroses that could fill shelves of books and study groups. He knows he is paid very well to facilitate these sessions, and although most of the people he sees will never truly be "cured" of whatever it is that seats their demons, he wants to find one person for whom he can actually make a difference. Until then his search, and his compassion, will have to be subjected to the proclivities of trying to reason with unreasonable people. Maybe one day he will actually find a *human being* who will respond to treatment.

That really would be a treat.

Chapter 12

A Relative Kind of Bad

Most of the work crew and office staff at Elite Lawns and Landscaping are in the office on a very bright and sunny, and very wintry cold, Saturday morning. It is one of those beautifully divergent days where a glorious blue-sky sun illuminates the chilled temperatures.

The landscaping teams are preparing for the day's schedule, and the bustle in and around the office is progressing in its usual hectic predispatch pace. Most of the office's key team members are finalizing the duties and running at full speed to get the crews out on the road.

Pat is overseeing the controlled chaos. Saturdays are always the most hectic, and there is lots of work to be done before he goes home to get ready for the big Christmas party tonight. He is joined in the office by his new assistant, Sherry; the dispatch manager, Corbie; Corbie's right-hand man, Creep; the landscape architect Georgie Imbesil—whose surname, which has caused him a lifetime of torment, confusion, and kidding, does not sound like *imbecile*; it's pronounced "Im-*bes*-il"—and, of course, Pat's wife, Karen. They are all multitasking while organizing the day's activities, but they're still finding time to carry on their random discussions and various takes on the world at large. Saturday mornings are always good for some rapid-fire talk before attacking the busiest workday of the week.

Creep steps into Karen's part time office looking for Pat. He is holding a clipboard and has a sour look on his face. She sees his expression and knows immediately that whatever he is about to say isn't going to be good. Before he can say a word, she stops him.

"You know not to bother him when he first comes into the office in the morning. He hates that, especially if you have bad news or a problem," she warns.

"What do you consider bad news or a problem?" he asks.

"Bad is relative," she replies. "It's whatever *he* thinks is either bad or a problem. And in the morning, *everything* you hit him with is either bad or a problem."

Before Creep can say anything else, McLaren comes out of the bathroom and sees Sipotora waiting for him. "I put the seat down for you."

Pat can also see that Creep has some pending issue hanging over his head that he's waiting to discuss. He relents with a heavy sigh. "What's the problem?"

"The Marsh account is upset that we're raising his cutting prices. When our guys got there, the husband and wife were at the door to complain. He wants to negotiate a new rate."

"What are we charging him now?"

"The base fee. We told him, 'Sorry, we gotta raise our fees.' We've been charging him the rate of $85 a quarter, and we let him know we're gonna have to raise it to $95."

Pat considers this for a moment. Earlier he had decided to implement an across-the-board rate increase for the standard cutting and trimming services. "What did you tell him?"

"We said, 'You've been at $85 for about eight years now, and we're raising everyone in the neighborhood, so ...'"

"What does he want?"

"He was upset. Actually, his wife was the one who was really upset. Wants to know what justifies more than a 10 percent increase."

"Shit. Marsh has been with us eight years?" Pat ponders aloud. "Maybe we should grandfather in the accounts who have been with us for more than"—he pauses, working out the situation in his head—"oh, five years? Cut a break for our longtime customers?"

Karen quickly jumps in. "We haven't had a standard rate increase in years, and we've already got different rates for so many different accounts. I think it's time we standardize what we charge. Besides, I don't see why a 10 percent increase is that unreasonable. We can get all our regular accounts on the same page. Half of our neighborhood customers have different rates because of your wheeling and dealing through the years. Now is the time to get those customers in line. Makes sense after all these years. Our expenses have gone up more than 10 percent in the past few years. Only seems fair."

Pat looks at Karen and laughs. "Honey, think of what we drop at the casino in a night."

"Yeah," she snaps back. "And why do you think we can *afford* to drop that much?"

Pat pauses and takes a deep breath as Creep stands waiting for a decision. "Okay," Pat says, "go ahead and charge what we've been billing them. I'll go see him and let him know." He looks at Karen and asks, "Didn't we send a notification letter out with the rate increase?"

"Yes," she responds firmly.

"All right," he says. "I'll talk to them. In the meantime, just let it be." He can feel Karen's disapproving headshake. "Anything else?" he asks Creep.

"Nope," he says, but before leaving he adds, "what about the other customers? I'm sure it'll come up again—and especially in *his* neighborhood. We service, like, every other home in that subdivision. Word will get around."

"Just deal with him for now," he snaps back, annoyed at this new can of worms he now has to deal with. Pat would just as soon avoid the conflicts involved with things like price increases, dissatisfied customers, and complaints. He hates the little confrontational things involved in running a small business, even though it's the basics of the operation. That's why Karen is so valuable to the shop. She is the enforcer and is always having to be the bad guy in business dealings, cleaning up some of the messes he creates. Pat knows this, which makes him appreciate her ability to take on that role. It also makes him cringe whenever she confronts him about his "nice guy'" attitude. Between the two of them, they are usually able to find a delicate balance of having a customer-friendly, mutually agreeable partnership with their clients and still somehow run a profitable, legitimate business.

Sherry steps in and excuses herself. She is somewhat self-conscious about having to interrupt the discussion, but she has an important customer on the phone.

"It's Mrs. Wilkerson. She wants to speak with you," Sherry tells him. He immediately begins shaking his head and sighs. He has known Wilkerson for fifteen years. She's become more of a friend than a customer. But he also knows the baggage that comes with the business partnership they've developed over those years.

"Do you know what she wants?" he asks Sherry, who shakes her head no.

"Only that she wants to talk to you." She pauses. "I don't think she's calling to tell you what a wonderful job we did," she adds with a note of sarcasm.

Pat reaches over toward the conference telephone and looks up at Sherry. She nods and says, "Line two."

He pushes the button and activates the speakerphone. As soon as the line comes alive, the room fills with the sounds of construction noise and a steady rattle of talking and clamor in the background.

"Ms. Wilkerson," he begins, "what can I do for you?"

"Pat," she says, her voice barely audible over the racket in the background. "Excuse the noise. I've got eight men here banging away."

The people still in the office conference room begin to laugh out loud. Creep and Sherry make a couple of snide comments that they think go unheard. Wilkerson obviously overhears the remarks.

"They're roofers, you idiots," she says after hearing the innuendos and remarks. "I was talking about the roofers."

"Sorry Mrs. W." Pat apologizes with a wide smile on his end of the line. "Is everything okay?"

"Would I be calling you if everything was okay?" she says. "I have a problem with one of your workers here. I asked to have some extra work done around the pool flower beds. The man you have out here just nodded as if he was going to do something, but then he just up and left. He didn't say if he was coming back and didn't even acknowledge that I had asked him to do anything. Just nodded and left."

"Okay, no problem," Pat says. "We'll take care of it. Who did you speak with?"

"I don't know his name. He was a sturdy black or Hispanic guy. Kinda balding. Spoke really poor English."

"I run a lawn service." Pat laughs. "That narrows it down to everyone."

There are chuckles on both ends of the call.

"Don't worry, Mrs. Wilkerson, I'll take care of it." She thanks him, and he disconnects the call. He looks at Creep, who reads the obvious message in his look.

"I'll handle it."

Pat smiles. As Creep steps out of the office, Corbie pops her head in.

"Noah Fuentes is here to start working. Said this is his first day, that you hired him last week?"

"Oh yeah." He pauses to think for a second. "Put him with Herbert's crew; he's shorthanded today."

"You hired a new guy?" Karen asks, realizing that Pat brought on yet another worker.

"Yeah, we need some temp help. He's on the books already. Sherry added him last week."

"Yep." Sherry nods, agreeing. "Cute little guy. Didn't think a midget could do this kind of work."

"You hired a midget?" Karen asks with some surprise in her voice. "I can't believe you hired a midget to work here."

"Yeah, what's wrong with that?"

"What does he look like?"

"He's a midget," Pat replies, flustered and exasperated with this talk of midgets. "He's the only midget that works here. What kind of description do you need? When you see a midget walking around, that's probably him." He glances around the room, seeing mostly grins on the other faces. "Sometimes I think your head is filled with that popcorn stuff ..." Pat starts snapping his fingers, grimacing while trying to find the word he's looking for. "Um, that ..."

The others begin shouting out guesses.

"Jiffy Pop ... Orville Redenbacher," Corbie yells.

"Carmel corn. Candy corn," offers Sherry.

"Why are you guys helping him?" Karen says with a disappointed frown.

"Shake and Bake?" shouts Corbie, who immediately covers her mouth, shaking her head while mumbling to herself, "No, not Shake and Bake." She looks up.

"Sorry, I'm all outta different kinds of popcorn."

"Me too," adds Sherry.

"Not the *eating* kind of popcorn," Pat says, groaning. "I'm talking about that Styrofoam packing popcorn stuff. The white foamy things you put in boxes when you ship something." He pauses. "Jesus."

The others nod. As they start to leave, Sherry remarks, "Ever mix M&M's with movie popcorn and shake it together?" She looks around to blank stares. "It's amazing."

Chapter 13

Bits and Pieces

Guests arrive at the long circular driveway in their freshly detailed, scrubbed and washed megamobiles, stepping out from the car doors looking every bit as cleaned up and vibrant as their vehicles. The party hosts have arranged for valet parking on the grounds of the Marvel mansion to make the enticement and anticipation of arrival more alluring.

It is a beautiful evening, filled with promise and uncertainty. The especially chilly December night has brought out a dazzling collection of gentlemen in tailored suits and ladies on display with the newest, most spectacular evening dresses designed to create fashion envy among their peers. As guests arrive and step briskly up to the enormous wooden front double doors, an elegant couple greets them. Each guest is presented with a crystal champagne flute filled with the bubbly relaxer and is then ushered into the magical occasion.

Once inside the massive home, guests are free to roam about the main house or wander off into the cold night to explore some of the property's guest cottages, the outdoor pool, and the patio deck area, or else they stroll along the natural walkways through wooded landscape, meandering creeks, and a small man-made lake.

Inside the house, the fireplaces are at full roar. The unlimited abundance of food and drink choices, and the obvious excesses in all manner of music, decorations, and exuberance, would make the Ghost of Christmas Present from Dickens' *A Christmas Carol* blush. The guests oblige by taking advantage of the house and grounds, fully embracing the atmosphere of the season.

❄❄❄

Maybe it just did not *seem* as cold as it had in years past. Maybe he was finally getting used to this despicable winter weather, unusually frigid now thanks to an aberrant heavy dusting that hit the city. Maybe with age his body has acclimated to its surroundings and environmental freezes don't have the impact they had when he was younger, leaner, and more eager to attack the outdoors. Whatever the reason, Leo finds himself huddled in front of his large floor-to-ceiling living room window, staring down from his sixth-floor apartment at the manic last-minute Christmas shoppers scattering about on the streets below, looking like cockroaches searching for cover when surprised by the sudden onset of light. He still can't help but feel contempt for the happy revelers who are hopping from store to store looking for bargains while carrying bags of coupons and newspaper clippings advertising the latest "door buster" deals available at the outlets. Why is he so angry with them? After all, it is their money and their time, and they are the ones being exposed to the elements. If they choose to waste their time engaged in this "festive" activity, then so be it. Not Leo though. Leo is determined to remain vigilant against this annual tide of commercialism and foolhardy overspending. His thoughts again wander to South Beach, where the bodies are hard and tanned and hot, the food is spicy and exotic, and the weather, well, the weather is simply superb. Was it too late for him to grab a last-minute ticket to fly down and enjoy a tropical holiday? Probably not. Was he going to go through the hassle of actually purchasing a one-way fare, packing his stuff, and grabbing a cab for the airport? Most definitely not. For now, it is destined to be another gray Christmas under the blanket of snow and ice, where even Santa's reindeer wouldn't holiday during their downtime. Oh well, another swig of Crown Royal Black certainly will help to shut the window on the brutality of the world. Leo is now slowly losing focus as the warming effects of the booze begin to wash over his body. Merry Christmas indeed.

The Buick swings around the corner and moves into the cul-de-sac leading to the large wraparound driveway in front of the mansion. The couple inside bypass the valet option, opting instead to park their car a few hundred feet from the home's main entrance in an open spot along the side of the entrance driveway. The couple throw open their respective doors, she jumping out like an expunged Pez candy, he like he is dragging himself out of a hospital bed.

He slowly lumbers over to meet up with his wife, who is already standing anxiously next to the trunk. With her foot tapping frantically, she is struggling to control her outrage.

"I can't believe you are this disorganized." She sighs while watching her husband fumbling around for the hostess gift he had haphazardly tossed in the trunk. "Hurry up. I'm freezing."

"Stop rushing me. Jesus, it's like I'm always in line waiting for ride at Disney World or something … hurry up and wait. Move a little … stop. Almost there … nope. It takes you forever to get ready, so I'm watching TV, and then you're finished—and *bam*," he barks back in frustration. "Time to leave, time to leave!" He illustrates his point by waving his arms in the air frantically. "Then all of a sudden *I'm* the one getting the stare. Hey, this is what you get, so take a deep breath and slow down. Besides," he adds, "you've known me a million years and I've always been this way." He turns after carefully collecting the awkwardly ornate gift-wrapped present, flinging it from side to side, trying to keep one of the numerous flowing ribbons from getting tangled in the trunk door, which he slams shut with his elbow. "What makes you think I'm gonna be any different now?"

"And all these years later, I still have to stop you from being late."

"Hey, all these years later, I don't tell you to stop being boring."

And this was the beginning of Pat and Karen McLaren's night out. They had arrived at the party rushed, irritated, and slightly ruffled. Karen was especially upset that her appearance upon arrival was not at all the way she had looked when they had left their home to drive to the event. The weather, and the usual pre-event bickering, all seemed to take out their anger on the pristine look she had spent hours creating for the social.

Their conversation in the car ride over had been rife with confrontational finger pointing. The back-and-forth accomplished nothing as they bickered about the tiniest specks of discontent.

"Nothing," he had told her in the car when she asked him to rub her leg to feel for hair.

"Sure, there's nothing on that leg, but feel the little stubbles here." She pointed out where she missed shaving. He glided his hand across her other leg and did not feel anything.

"Oh yeah," he stated sarcastically. "I'm sure all the girls will notice." He rolled his eyes.

"What is your problem?" she asked.

"Nothing. It just seems ridiculous that you're worried about something as insignificant as a little stubble on your legs, like anyone is paying attention or even cares. Honestly, I can't feel anything."

"*I* can."

"I'm sure you do. But that's because you're nuts. There's nothing there. Feels just fine. And, I repeat, *no one* is gonna look, care, or comment."

She shut him out and looked away in a huff, glaring out the window as they continued driving.

✳✳✳

Almost as if to fulfill some sort of upper-crust stereotype, a gathering of the guys stand away from the center of the action, holding their drinks while their obligatory chitchat dismisses whatever topic they happen to be pontificating about.

Matt, a detective for the Georgia Bureau of Investigations (GBI), is one of the men who are all standing around philosophizing and gossiping with each other like a cackle of teenage girls.

"One of the strangest cases I had," Matt says, beginning his story, "was when this guy murdered his wife by causing her to have a fatal reaction to penicillin. He started taking huge doses of penicillin until the amount in his system was so high that it resulted in lethal levels of it in his semen. Whenever he had sex with her, it was like delivering a shot of penicillin. It eventually killed her."

"Hmm," the man next to him says. "I wonder if that would work with a peanut allergy?"

The group chuckle. They stand. Almost in unison, each takes a sip from his glass, like they are all on a synchronized drinking team. One of the men makes an observation about one of the male guests who wisps by the group, apparently keenly zeroed in on his destination.

"I bet he's gay," says the guy.

"You think you can tell that just by looking at him?"

"No, he gave me a blow job in the bathroom about half an hour ago."

The group laugh at the crude remark. After another orchestrated drink, a different man in the group adds a new thread to the conversation.

"I'm sitting on the plane next to a gravel-faced meth head who is wearing a stained wifebeater and smells like stale cigarette smoke. He has bad hygiene and reeks like a brewery. I'm flying into town, and the pilot comes on the intercom speaker. Now, whenever I fly I like to hear the pilot come on and talk to the passengers. Makes me feel better. So he comes on and says, 'We're about to encounter severe wind shear ahead. Got to be honest with you, I've only ever flown through wind shear in simulator exercises, so you better strap in and be prepared to hold on.' No shit, he really said that." The man pauses. "All the passengers start looking at each other with the same terror, like, *Did we really hear what we thought we just heard?* It was something."

"So what happened?" asks one of the guests in the circle. The others look at the speaker with curiosity.

"We crashed into the side of a mountain," the man telling the story proclaims with a heavy dose of sarcasm. "What do you think happened?" he asks incredulously. "We landed. The point is that the pilot actually said that over the intercom."

"Well," the other man says, "at least he was talking to you. That's what you wanted."

The pilot-story man stands dumbfounded, takes a sip from his drink, and turns to face the other men in the circle.

"Yes, but they're supposed to come on to be the reassuring voice that settles our nerves. They're not supposed to heighten our anxiety."

"And what's with the three-hour-loop satellite graphic they're always showing on the Weather Channel?" the other says continues without missing a beat after his pilot comment. "I don't understand. Does it mean it's the weather from the last three hours, or is it the forecast for the next three?"

"Doctor, I have a question," says the other man mockingly. "What's considered stupider on the retard meter, idiot or moron?"

"I don't think that's a police-approved comment," one of the other men says with a smile.

"Sorry, not *stupider*. Should never use that term. … I meant *higher*."

"Take a look at what's standing over there by the Christmas tree," one of the men interrupts to say as he notices a particularly stunning woman in an excitingly low-cut purple dress. He motions in her direction as she flirts away with an interested younger man. "Wow, what a dress."

"Easy there, big guy. You're a married man."

"Don't worry about me," he replies. "Just looking. I have willpower, you know. If you have willpower, it just proves it conquers all."

"You mean that it just proves it *can* conquer all."

"Huh?"

"Willpower *can* conquer all. Doesn't mean it *always* will. But the possibility is there."

He looks at him peculiarly. "That's what I said."

"Nope. You said, 'Willpower conquers all.' What you meant was it *can* conquer all. It's not an all-encompassing, finite concept." He pauses to have a drink. "Just sayin'."

"Why do you always do that to me?"

"What?"

"You constantly question my comments, like you're the grand arbiter who judges every single syllable to come out of my mouth." He's getting worked up, but his faux anger is just idle chitchat to fill up talk time with the group. "It's a no-win situation. Like parenting. If you're a good parent, you aren't getting any ribbons. But be a bad parent and Nancy Grace starts banging at your door ready to toss your ass to the dogs."

"Calm down already," one of the men cautions with a smile. "Don't get so worked up about it. You need to step off the ledge."

"You mean step *away* from the ledge," the other man corrects him.

"No." The first man is adamant. "Step off the ledge."

"Wrong," the other man continues. "Step off would mean plunging to certain death. Step away and you don't fall."

"I think you're wrong."

"No, I really think I'm right."

The group pauses for a moment, and then the man states, "You know what? He's right about you. You *do* think you're like some great authority on speech correctness."

The group settles back into people watching and being obnoxiously critical. As the drinks continue to flow, the conversation buzzes, bouncing from topic to observation to opinion to reminiscing. The men are all comfortable with each other. Some of them are acquaintances, a couple are close friends, and a couple of others have been drawn in to kill time and socialize while the wives are off entertaining each other with their own brand of conversation and grapevine plucking.

The talk takes on various forms as the discussions continue, each member of the group trying to outtalk and outboast the others. The drinks have been emptied and replenished nonstop throughout the gathering, which contributes to the off-the-wall, topic-bouncing talk.

"I'm really going to enjoy myself tonight. It's my last chance before I get the honey-do list a mile long to finish up before Christmas. I've got a bunch of shit I have to put together for the holidays."

"If you need any help, let me know. I've finished up most of my chores."

"I have to dig up the instructions for most of the stuff I have left to do. Complicated shit."

"I never read the owner's manual," the grand arbiter boasts. "Guys don't read manuals to put shit together. Hell, I put together the gas grill without an owner's manual and still had six pieces left over."

They laugh, each knowing the drawbacks that come with winging it. Leftover pieces probably mean he'll blow himself up one of these days.

"Good luck with that."

"Sarcasm is the lowest form of irony."

"Bitching about sarcasm is the lowest form of criticism."

After a few more minutes, one of the men nods his head to the others and excuses himself from the group to go mingle, that age-old party adage for a phony but wholly engaged performance of interacting with strangers.

"I'm off, gents," he announces. "Gonna check out the rest of this castle."

"See you around the grounds. Stay on your best behavior; they've got cameras and microphones everywhere."

"All the world's a stage, but most of us haven't rehearsed."

"Where did that come from?"

"From the Bible. Straight from Jesus." He smiles as he messes with the guy.

"Well, for starters, Jesus didn't *write* the Bible. His friends did. And you know what dicks your friends can be."

"I don't think that's biblical," says the grand arbiter. "I think it's Shakespeare."

They all look at him with a condescending stare that needs no words to interpret.

✳✳✳

Pat and Karen McLaren managed to put just a little of their bickering aside long enough to achieve quite the accomplishment by making it to the party after their usual civil war at home. After putting down quite a few beverages, they are now festively mingling around the party and chatting it up with all the others, imbibing, rejoicing, and spreading Christmas cheer all over the goddamn place.

Pat walks delicately—a polite way of suggesting that staggering is pending, surely just a few more drinks away—over to a well-attired couple talking near the fireplace mantle. When he reaches the two, he stops and turns to face Karen, who is still standing back, by one of the Christmas trees.

"Hey," he yells to her. "C'mon … I'm over here."

Karen looks up in reaction to his summons. She begins her walk over, moving between and through the evenly spaced guests in the large living room. She reaches her husband, and he drapes his arm around her. Together they approach the couple he spied from across the room. Pat begins his spiel.

"Think your girl is sweet now? It won't be too long before she's a nagging, screeching frump of quadruple-stranded pearls and estrogen, with the emotional unavailability of Spock." Pat begins tilting his head, motioning toward his wife behind her back. The couple look at each other and then at Pat. "And yet she's *still* arrogant enough to think she's smarter than everyone else in the room when it comes to life."

"I'm sorry," the man politely says to Pat and Karen. "I don't think we've met." He extends his hand. "My name's Donald. This is my wife, Paula."

"Pat." Pat introduces himself and then again motions at his wife. "Karen." He shakes Donald's hand firmly. "I was just kidding about all that 'screeching frump' stuff. It was sort of an icebreaker."

"Yes," Donald replies cautiously. "It was"—he pauses—"interesting. Certainly broke the ice." He chuckles.

Pat lets out a hearty laugh and squeezes Karen. She bumps him away with her elbow and unhinges herself from his arm. Her piercing look is one of flippant contempt.

"Don't give me that 'look at what I can do' smirk," she warns with glib humor in her voice.

"Now you see." Pat hesitates, motioning toward Donald. "Am I right, Donald?" he asks.

Donald nods.

"See, Donald," Pat says, beginning his soapbox rant, "this is *exactly* what I was telling you not one minute ago. Remember? Just said it." He points at Karen and takes a couple of steps away to give himself room to move and pontificate. He focuses on the now curious couple. "Now, Donald, as you and I can both attest, every single male can remember the first time, oh … what? … four or five years old, maybe, that he showed his little johnson to a stranger and everybody started freaking the hell out." He takes a moment to look over at Karen and then says dryly, "When I said 'little johnson,' I meant penis." He looks back at Donald and Paula, and goes right back into his sermon. The couple watch him, visibly amused by his inebriated antics.

"Guys can remember the first time they got in trouble for hitting somebody, for taking a piss in public, and for trying to jump off some high tree branch or a wall or set something on fire. When we grew up"—Pat begins demonstrating pulling and churning movements with his hands and arms, his drink carefully balanced in his grasp—"we had all these hard-core, vile, *powerful* male urges, all evil and profane suggestions whispered to us by the devil on our shoulder, who was working with our little Captain Dick. And *that's* what gets us all in trouble." He looks over again at Karen. "Captain Dick, you know … metaphor." She sneers at him.

"Still with me, guys?" Pat raises his eyebrow as he asks his somewhat cornered audience. They smile, nodding their heads. "Okay, so anyway, we go through all these years of growing and adapting and understanding the world from what we learned from these *urges*. So when we start to get nostalgic for the fury of our past, we dress it up in some ridiculous *Gladiator*-type fantasy where everybody is shirtless and screaming and hacking things with swords. Or we hunt down the bad guys and take 'em out like Dirty Harry or Jason Bourne. We climb into starships and fight alien invaders from the skies, blasting away with weapons of destruction that only the imagination can invent. Boys are taught from an early age that this is how the world is or should be—all of these primal impulses we've been acting on that got us grounded, or sent to detention, or expelled, or even arrested from kindergarten till death. All of these things should not only be allowed but also be *celebrated*." He pauses to let his little lecture sink in and enjoys a long swallow of his drink. He looks at Karen and winks.

Donald seems to agree, or at least to acquiesce, and smiles. Pat smiles back, gesturing with his glass. "Am I right or am I right?" Paula seems a little uncomfortable, almost hesitant, as she anxiously awaits Pat's continuing speech. She is painfully aware that more is coming.

"And then at some point, women took it all away."

There is a brief moment of quiet that certainly feels longer than it actually clocks in at. The couple stand there, processing Pat's latest statement.

"And there it is," Karen declares. "Here comes the booze editorial."

"You know what I'm saying, Donald," Pat encourages, ignoring his wife. "That once great world of heroes and warriors and cigars and dirty jokes has been replaced by a world of grumpy female supervisors looming over your cubicle to hand you a memo about sending off-color jokes on company e-mail." He allows a minute for a comment or remark, but none comes. "I understand that might sound like a self-serving version of society and maybe a gross overexaggeration, but it doesn't matter. The result is going to be the same. We feel a combination of frustration, humiliation, and powerlessness that makes us want to get it back in the only way we know how—by being petty and immature. And yeah, there's some *meanness* that comes out. But all we really want to say is, 'Maybe next time you'll remember who has the *dick* in this relationship.'"

The previous temporary moment of brief quiet is now an uncomfortably extended silent period, passing without comment.

Finally, Karen speaks out again. She is both fascinated and embarrassed by her husband's speech. But the festive atmosphere and mounting toll of beverages seems to have her settled in and enjoying the banter.

"Are you certain you don't have some kind of head wound? I can't understand why you're not falling down more."

"That's why I love this woman," Pat quickly snaps back. "It shows the two sides of her fragile personality—one insecure, frazzled, and ragged-edged, and the other beautiful and serene." He pauses. "And *frazzled and ragged-edged*." He looks at his male counterpart for support. "But as we both know, Donald, the infuriating truth is that however much guys might want an emotionally stable, not-too-complicated, and positive-minded woman for a wife, before we marry we're more often drawn to the half-crazies. Part of it is because we are intrigued by just how to best use this craziness to our advantage. Another part of it is because, simply put, the whack jobs are *amazing* in the sack."

Before anyone can react or comment, another couple walk up to the group. They are younger, closer to late twenties or early thirties, as opposed to the fiftyish couples who are already discussing Pat's world according to alcohol.

The younger, athletic-looking man introduces himself simply as Jack. He also introduces his wife, Kristin.

"I hope you don't mind," Jack says with a guarded tone, "but I heard some of what you said and I have to agree. I mean, you don't have to be a genius to realize that we're all intertwined and vulnerable, sharing the same pulse—everything and everyone in ways that defy explanation. And we're all the same as little boys. It transcends generational differences. All you have to do is let it in. Without that upbringing, I never would have known what I know or, at the very least, *remembered*, for whatever that's worth. It was the way we learned to dream to be men."

"Totally on point," Donald exuberantly agrees, pointing to Jack while clinking glasses with Pat. "Nailed it."

"That was our blueprint," Jack continues. "Our youth had a relaxed, unpolished quality that made it feel very real—a peek at adulthood if you didn't follow all the rules. I went through some crazy shit—and some crazy ladies—myself," he whispers with a knowing smile, "and that spirit of being a boy and all the adventures that came with it. I know it got me through plenty of rough patches. Most important, it was all about making choices. That's what the best adventures of our childhood are always about, and that's what I remember most—the horror of realizing that eventually, sometimes sooner than later, your best years may be behind you, and only drudgery and self-disappointment lie ahead. It's paralyzing. But now I'm totally cleaned up, newly married, a new father, a home … all the trappings. I'm obviously in a better place—and good for that. Sometimes we have to go back to that place where our instincts were honed. Maybe there we were better at the game, or at least more creatively interesting. When our personal lives and lifestyles are less settled, that kiss of danger keeps us sharp. There's something about living a wild-ass life and wondering what and who the hell you are, going through the emotional upheavals, that seems to feed the right kind of creativity." Jack shrugs and looks at Kristin. "Or sometimes not."

"I have a little scale at home that I use to weigh my food going in and then coming out." Kristin breaks her silence to add an element of odd information to the conversation. Kristin is one of those women who appear to be on life support except for these brief instances when they break from being arm candy and speak, shattering any illusions of reality. She is also clearly fixated on her personal appearance and body image.

"What's that mean?" Paula wonders aloud.

"You weigh your feces?" Karen bluntly asks.

"As long as what went in doesn't exceed what comes out by more than 7 percent during a cycle, I feel okay about myself," Kristin explains. The others pause as they consider her bizarrely eccentric admission. Each clearly doesn't want to participate in furthering the discussion.

"Man, that is *a lot* of work," Pat finally observes.

"I always ask her why she's so worried about her weight." Jack giggles while telling this to the group. "She has the body fat percentage of a window."

Pat leans over and whispers in Karen's ear. "We're looking at a special kind of crazy here. If you ever come home talking like that, I'll immediately assume you have taken on a second job fucking Japanese businessmen for poker chips in Vegas."

❋ ❋ ❋

Leo is concerned with the fitting of his Santa costume. The bulkiness of the outfit makes his movements difficult and awkward, but he doesn't have time to fret about it. Considering it was a last-minute fitting change, he'd had to make do. He is just pleased that things worked out and that the talent-for-rent and catering company hired him part time during this holiday season, allowing him to check off another box on his plan's to-do list. Once on board, he persuaded his boss to put him on "Santa patrol duty" so he would be available to work parties in character during the Christmas season. He had carefully plotted and maneuvered his way onto the work manifest for the Marvel home Christmas party. The Marvel Christmas party wasn't exactly a secret. With a high-profile social crowd always included on the guest list, it was a very publicized and well-covered affair. Each year there was even a small local community TV film crew at the house filming in and around the party, interviewing guests and showing off the opulence. For attendees, making it known that they were invited to the event of the season was a very scheming way to flash their uninvited friends and competition.

Once Leo found out more of the details about the party plans from the order form and supply list, he began to put his plan together. It was these exceptionally beautiful people, the fashionably trendsetting crowd invited here to this extravagant palace, these vulgar creatures, whom Leo would show the true meaning of Christmas. And it sure as hell wasn't drinking eggnog under the mistletoe while calculating the retail value of the home furnishings, faux praising the over-the-top decorations, or drooling over other party guests' husbands and wives.

Leo arrived at the party with two other Santas in tow. They were escorted to the affair in the company limo, which was flanked by cars filled with the waitstaff—dressed as Santa's helpers, elves, and fairies—along with a service truck that held the equipment that the staff set up outside on the lawn to prepare the evening snacks and meals.

Leo's job, as it was with the other Santas, was to mingle around the guests, pose for pictures, proclaim a continuous stream of "ho ho hos," and hand out candy canes and peppermint gumdrops. The Santas were specifically assigned to different areas of the property so they wouldn't be bumping into each other and ruining the illusion.

On this evening, Leo was in the illusion-busting business. Under his bulky costume were strapped layers of explosives ready for him to place around the house so he could detonate as soon as he found the perfect moment for maximum impact and value. He also scored two AK-47 shaved-barrel assault rifles with a dozen backup clips, which were secured to his sides. While he waited for his time to arrive, he followed the Santa routine and mingled with partygoers, sneaking drinks when he could and making Christmassy small talk with festively inebriated guests.

Santa was the hit of the room whenever he entered. He was immediately surrounded by a bevy of dolled-up women begging their dates to snap pictures of them hanging all over the jolly fat man. Leo was only more than happy to accommodate all requests, secretly knowing that within a short time all this glamour and kitschy success would be brought down with explosive rage. He also was getting off a bit on the parade of sexy women who were being obvious in their "Santa groupie" sleazing and flirting. More than a few hinted at a Kris Kringle liaison in one of the many empty rooms.

Once he was able to move past the initial rush of photo ops, he strolled over to the same group of men who had established their territory in the corner of the main living room earlier. They welcomed him over to the group, good-heartedly humored by his presence.

"Hey, Santa," shouts the grand arbiter from before as he puts his arm around Leo when he approaches. "Settle an argument for us." He looks at the group of guys. "I think we can all agree to take Santa's opinion as the final word on this." They all nod in agreement.

"I hope I can help," mumbles Santa/Leo.

"Okay, here goes," he begins. "I think it's ironic that someone as deeply invested in his music and style as Bob Dylan knew he had to change to remain vital to himself, not to others. He did it so he could *feel*. It didn't mean he had to swerve from his message. You can stay on topic. You're just introducing it through new and different ways and formats. Because it doesn't necessarily appeal to his fans doesn't mean the message is any less critical." The man seems solidly committed to his position.

Leo pauses for a moment, contemplating the statement, and then says sarcastically, "That *is* ironic."

The rest of the group laughs as the man gives Santa a disappointed look and shrugs. "C'mon, Santa, you can do better than that. Back me up on this." He smiles. Leo looks at the man from behind his overgrowth of fake white beard and out from under his red cap, sneering inside as he visualizes what this idiot will look like with his intestines strewn all over the fancy interior design.

"You've got that look on your face," one of the other men says to the grand arbiter, "like the face a coed has when she walks out of a guy's dorm room, looks around, and realizes that she made a really bad decision."

"My daughter's done that a few times in college," another man adds. "Of course, she's never told me about any of her adventures in school. I always hear about it from her mother. I can only imagine what goes on that they *don't* tell me about."

"They say you always remember your first sexual encounter," one of the men says. "All I remember was the exchange of money."

"My son is starting to feel the changes and is realizing things will be very different now with college coming up. He's got a high school girlfriend—his first—that he's worried about leaving. They've been dating for a little over a year, but she's gonna be a senior in high school next year and he's leaving the state for college. It's gonna be a hard transition for them."

"Yeah," says another. "It's hard to make those kinds of relationships last. Once you leave high school and go to college, it's a whole different world. Your eyes really open up."

"Yeah, but it's hard to leave your high school girlfriend when you leave for college."

"I know it's tough," says another man with a son who started college the previous year. "My son was in the same situation." He pauses. "The hurt lasts about thirty-six hours."

The group laughs. Santa tries to remove himself from this self-absorbed team of drunken businessmen who are spouting off about their own importance, their admirable parenting skills, and the vital roles they see themselves carefully manipulating in front of the others. It was all about status, but more importantly it was more about one-upping your rivals. Leo's first few attempts at excusing himself were unsuccessful. This group loved having an audience with Santa.

"The world's tough today for everybody," says one of the men who had been silent and listening up to this point. "That's why I worry about my kids. Not that they'll have any big financial problems. We've all faced ups and downs through the years with money. That works itself out. I'm worried about their place in the world with this new social universe and the infrastructure created around social networking. Twitter, texting, sexting, skyping, Instagram, the porn and dating sites—all built on *avoiding* the intimacy required to nurture relationships. Personal private interactions are at an entirely different level now. The rules have changed so much for how people deal with each other today. And the rules change every day. I'm afraid those skills are being lost."

As the men pause to take synchronized sips from their drinks, the party's host, John Marvel, walks up to the group. The grand arbiter, obviously a friend of Marvel's, greets him as he emerges.

"Our host," he shouts, putting his arm around Marvel. Apparently, putting his arm around any guest who happens to walk by is a fairly common habit for him. "This is brilliant. What a beautiful turnout. And what a surprise—you managed to have this wonderful setting right in the middle of all this dreck." He laughs as he pulls in his host tighter with his hug.

"The dreck was my idea,' Marvel dryly responds.

"What about the flowers?" Marvel is asked. "All these fancy, stinky flowers covering every last spare spot in the house. Betcha those were Christina's idea. I *hate* flowers."

"Why?" Marvel asks, not really caring one way or the other.

"Reminds me of hospitals and funerals. The look, the smell. The memories. Awful."

They all pause for a moment before Santa/Leo calmly provides the last word on the subject. "I hate birds."

Leo excuses himself and tells the group he's supposed to be making the rounds. They give him a hearty *Merry Christmas* cheer as he hands them each a candy cane, bows, and slips away, backing into the rest of the crowded living room. He carefully avoids making eye contact with his "employer," John Marvel.

He quickly begins looking again for the perfect spot, perfect moment, and perfect opportunity for his yuletide surprise. Any night rescued from boredom is victory, he tells himself. It doesn't need to be any more complicated than that. It reminds him of when he was back in school himself, back when he had a future, when he had something to live for. He remembers the vengeful, confrontational fights he used to have with his boyhood neighbor and nemesis. The competition between them throughout school was keen. It was present among them when it came to track and field, baseball, final grades, getting picked for pickup football games, getting girls, and so forth. All of the victories coveted by school-age kids always seemed to be just outside Leo's grasp. They fell into the arms of his old enemies, except that one time when he finally found victory against his sternest competitor. He remembers standing atop the awards podium, looking down at his adversary after finally winning a race and medaling on the track field, and asking him, "Does *fuck you* sound different from up here?" It was a singular reward after years of coming in second and always watching what winners looked like from below.

Leo was like a cranky Persian cat who is always jumpy, thinking that all of humanity is out to pull his tail. This Christmas, his present would be to let *everyone* know he is a saber-toothed tiger who is imploring them to fuck with his tail.

✳✳✳

He held her tightly for a little while longer, savoring the feeling, absorbing the moment. He was breathing it in, squeezing every last drop of memory from it. He was not about to let one little piece slip away from the confines of this little cottage set just off the main house's east flank, nestled in the woods with a small backyard porch overlooking a small lake and a meandering stream.

"This is nice." *She* sighs.

He kisses her forehead. "Every day should be like this."

He thinks about what she said: that she didn't have anybody like him. It was true. And he is suffering from the same malady: there was no one like her. They shared different sensibilities and an understanding of each other that transcends the kind of connection someone has with a spouse, siblings, or other family and friends. You find it only once with just one person, and it's different from anything you have with anyone else. It's not better or more special, and it doesn't replace or dismiss what happens inside any other relationship; it simply compliments all the other things you may share with others. Even when time passes, what this couple share together is kept safe until they meet up again.

He gazes down at her. She is superb, so finely delicate and stunning. His thoughts remain with her, wondering about her innermost secrets. There's so much there and so much around her—and heaven knows so many wonderful things she's worked so hard for and deserves—but sometimes he wonders if she ever discovers that as comforting and safe as all of that is, she still enjoys finding the other her every once in a while. So while everybody else is stumbling around in their weekend get-together backyard parties, telling stories that get longer as their drinks get shorter, she surveys the landscape around her. She finds herself cringing—not all the time, but every so often—when she gets a peck on the cheek as she walks by her husband, which leaves her feeling empty like the good wife has just been *rewarded* and got the old attagirl pat on the back.

It's just that right now, all the hard work and trust and faith and time invested in the world they created for themselves—as satisfying, rewarding, and loving as it is, must be put on hold. This thing finds you and shakes you up. We find ourselves inspired with a renewed energy that's been missing as we've been waiting for a boost to knock us out of our comfort zone and remind us that we are wide awake.

It is what they have and share, and it's wonderful and scary and compelling—always new, exciting, and adventurous. That's why he was looking for the girl. That's why the girl was hoping he would find her.

And that's why they're both here now.

Slowly slinking, she turns to face him, easing her body with a slither onto her side. She makes circles on the bedsheet with her finger, coyly pursing her lips as she begins to speak.

"The TV people filming the party back at the house asked me if I want to be on camera and do an interview. I don't know if I should do it."

"Are they trying to get sound bites from all the guests?"

"I'm not sure. They're all around. They asked me once already." She pauses. "I think I want to do it."

"I think you should."

"I think you should do it with me." She smiles. "I'd like that."

"Nope."

"What if I asked you real nice?"

"I'd say 'no' real nice."

He leans over and kisses her cheek, lost in her dangerously mischievous smile.

"I think we should get back to the party."

❄ ❄ ❄

Leo finishes making the rounds, a full rotation through the main house, ensuring that he has mingled with as many people as possible. He uses this as an opportunity to stake out his prey. He has concealed four of his explosives. He isn't sure yet where he plans to unleash the other reindeer—his nickname for the explosive devices he had strapped to his torso—but he is closer to making a final decision. He had four remaining places and narrowed his choice down to the center of the house in the main reception hall or the grand living room as guests merrily gathered around the showcase Christmas tree. He decides to stroll outside and have a cigarette on the patio next to the pool.

The deck surrounding the sparkling blue pool is carved into ornate rockwork with wood trim along two sides. There are a few brave couples wandering around outside, trying to stay warm and taking in the chilly winter evening.

Leo follows a cobblestone path around the back by a gazebo and walks over to a wood bench nestled in the pine straw among the trees. It is secluded, but he can still hear the sounds of Christmas music playing from the house. He pulls out his pack of cigarettes, lights one up, and takes a look around the spot before taking a seat on the bench. He enjoys the hot taste of the smoke warming his lungs in the frigid cold of the night while extinguishing his lighter, holding it a good distance away from the still-strapped-on firepower.

He takes a long, careful look back toward the house, paying attention to every detail. He notices the guests' movements, where the flows of people seem to gravitate, and what draws them to the different parts of the property.

As he continues to study the house, he can hear a rumbling and the crunching sound of shoes on foliage. He turns to see a young woman who is bundled up with a heavy coat and wrapped with a scarf. She is making her way into the clearing near the bench where Leo sits.

"Mind if I join you?" the friendly young woman asks.

Leo takes a close look at her, seeing if he can recognize anything familiar in her face. She does a double take, looking at him as she gets closer.

"I know you," she says with a smile, taking her gloved hand out of her coat pocket to point at him. "Let me guess." She pauses, dragging out her next line. "Prancer, right?" She lets out an adorable giggle that she simply cannot contain. If Leo weren't so preoccupied, he would find it to be downright infectious.

This spontaneous outburst of sheer laughter forces even the stoic, reserved, and determined Jolly Old Saint Nick to break a smile.

Leo points his finger back at the young woman and winks. "You got me." He says.

"Actually I *do* recognize you." She plops down on the bench next to him. She keeps moving her head from side to side, checking him out. "I met you—well, walked by you—when you were picking up your Santa suit the other day at the office."

"Oh yeah," Leo replies, with no clue whatsoever and no recollection of the woman. He doesn't remember ever seeing her before. "Good to see you again."

"I'm over by the grills. I work setups for the food trays and put them on the serving tables." She pulls out her own cigarette. Leo takes out his lighter and fixes her up. "Glamorous, huh?"

"At least you don't have to wear an uncomfortable, sweaty, smelly suit."

"Hey, that looks pretty damn comfortable on a night like this," she says. "But I must say, your description certainly doesn't sweeten the pot."

"I guess it could be worse."

She takes a long drag from her cigarette. "So have you had a chance to enjoy yourself, or are they swarming you?"

"It hasn't been too bad," Leo curtly replies, now just wanting to be left alone with his thoughts. She can sense the irritated tone in his voice.

"I'm Maggie," she says.

"Santa," he deadpans.

She nods her head matter-of-factly and mutters under her breath, "Yep, glad I took a walk all the way out here to get away from the assholes."

He looks over at her.

"Hey," he blurts, disturbed by her comment.

"You a little stressed there, Kris Kringle?"

"Got a lot on my mind, so yeah, a little bit stressed."

"That's the thing the people here don't understand. They think you can cure stress with a mocha latte and bath bubbles. Much different in the *real* world, isn't it?" She explains, "They'll never get it. They're used to either getting what they want—no questions asked, no roadblocks—or stomping their feet, screaming and crying that the world isn't being fair."

Maggie takes another puff from her cigarette and blows a series of smoke rings into the frigid air. The tobacco rings flow graciously away with her exhaled breath, which is visible alongside the smoke.

"Working these events, it makes me wonder how some of these people ever made it to begin with. All this big money. A lot of it daddy money too, passed down along with the family business. Generation after generation leading the way, carrying the cultural and high-society torches for the community." Maggie pauses and then exaggerates a retching sound. "*Yech.* One of these days they are all gonna get a big wake-up call. The two economic collapses didn't change anything. The housing market crash and mortgage fraud exposure didn't change anything. We're all paying the tab for bailouts and golden parachutes and CEO perks. And *they* don't even pay attention to the people in the streets who are trying to get their attention through peaceful means." Maggie pauses after another puff. "Time for more meaningful wake-up call. Maybe they won't sleep through the next one."

"These days, my only interest in people is seeing what I don't want to become," Leo says, breaking his silence reluctantly after carefully considering her comments. They sounded like something he could have recited word for word.

"Lighten up, Santa. It's Christmastime." She tries to cheer him up, not knowing that the ticking time bomb—figuratively and damn near literally—is just waiting for the right moment to explode. It certainly wasn't going to happen here outside, though, while she is sitting with another loser from the catering and talent rental company.

"You keep Christmas in your way and leave me to keep mine in my way."

"Ah," she exclaims. "Scrooge."

"Yes, so ..."

"You know what your problem is?" Maggie begins, interrupting him. "You're like a wounded animal caught in a trap. When someone comes to the rescue, you fight it because you don't realize they're only trying to help." She waits for a reaction. He just sits quietly, taking another puff from his own cigarette. "I'm not the enemy," she continues. "I'm on your side. We work for the same boss."

"I don't need to be rescued," he says.

Maggie tosses her cigarette on the ground and presses it out with her boot. She stands up from the bench and turns to return to the catering grill area out back.

"Well," she says shyly, her original enthusiasm and laughter now stifled by the grumpy Santa. She had approached him in the spirit of the holiday season, open to lively conversation and perhaps even to making a new friend. She was leaving feeling that she had just lost a small piece of Christmas magic. "Thanks for all the holiday cheer. Have a merry Christmas."

Leo looks up at her from his seat on the bench and remains silent. Maggie walks away. He watches her slowly make her way back up the path as it disappears into a small cluster of trees around the corner of the house.

After a few minutes, Leo rises up from the bench and brushes the light snow off his coat. He pulls down on the sleeves and straightens the jacket before heading back to the house. He stops to take one last look back, in the direction where Maggie returned. The pathway is empty. He might have to find this woman inside, he decides as he makes his way back toward the house. *She sounds like one of my kind,* he thinks. Maybe it's time to find someone he could share his rage with.

"And the four horseman of the apocalypse say, 'Checkmate.'"

Chapter 14

The First to Go Next

From the outside, the guests at the Marvel party look like they are engaged in some kind of self-perpetuating cycle of unflinching reassurance and back patting, which is dangerous for the dynamics and creativity of a social event. It is worse than forcing the atmosphere in a vacuum; it's creating the swirl in a vacuum that elevates all ideas and opinions—and nothing needs to be edited or revisited or even questioned at all. It's one thing to take a position on whatever subject is being discussed, one with which you are comfortable and whose rhythms you understand. However, it's quite another to talk with a nodding mirror image of yourself that supports your every comment. Nothing is more irritating than a yes-man. Sometimes a disagreeing voice is one of the most valuable things to have in a creative, imaginative environment. It's a good way to keep one's head out of one's ass. Otherwise, the conceit takes all the spark and spontaneity out of the room. Every guest opining about every subject reaches the point where his or her limitations have been exhausted. *Your argument was great right up until it was terrible, and it was terrible right after you started making it.*

This is the attitude Pat and Karen McLaren took with them into the party. They agree on almost nothing, expect for their aversion toward the condescending, petulant revelers who are really only looking to promote the latest vapid events in their lives and to force their somewhat uninformed views on the more reserved guests. There was fresh chum in the McLaren shark-infested waters, and they couldn't wait to dive in and stir up the blood. And with the ever slowing trickling flow of the money from different side businesses being diverted or downright annexed by some of the people who are also at the party tonight, Pat is especially interested in clocking the various players. He is watching and waiting for an opening.

The McLarens are standing in the corner of the main living room watching the party unfold as they continue a running commentary that targets the other partygoers. No outfit, hairstyle, shape, size, weight-challenged body, or other attribute is exempt from their barbs.

"Why would someone invite their maids to a party like this?" Karen remarks after seeing some of the Marvels' housekeeping staff socializing around the house in their fancy party fashions.

"Some people are very close to their house staff. They become part of the extended family. They help take care of the kids, are around for all the holidays." He pauses. "I can see inviting them, especially if they are close. The housekeepers probably helped to set up and clean the place for this party, so why not let them enjoy it?"

"Then it would be fine with you to invite the pool cleaner, the bug-sprayer guy, and the lawn maintenance crew too?"

"You are a snob." Pat turns to Karen and sticks his tongue out, making a funny face. He then looks back at the assembled group of revelers.

"And before you forget, *we* are part of the lawn maintenance crew," he reminds her as she frowns. "Oh, man, this is gonna be a treasure trove of neuroses." Pat excuses himself from Karen and walks over to John Marvel. Pat and John go back quite a few years. Their friendship now extends to a business partnership. On the outside, they always project a professional and well-oiled front.

John made his fortune in an upper-crust, white-collar manner, whereas Pat started up his own small business and worked his blue-collar butt off to achieve his goals. The two had mutual friends such as Lord Biznez, were members of the same community council, and of course shared their weekly Wednesday night watering-hole getaways. It all began at an impromptu meeting during the "world's biggest cocktail party," a Gator Bowl tailgate party before a Florida–Georgia football game, years ago, and the two have been friends ever since.

"That's a really weird way to eat sushi," Pat tells John as he approaches. John is sampling a plate of sushi, carefully eating the insides of the roll, avoiding the wrapper and rice. "I'm sorry, that was dismissive of me," Pat admits. "I've been trying to get better about watching what I say. It's just that this is the second time I've discussed this peculiar habit of sushi eaters. It's like only eating the doughnut hole."

"Thank you for that." John acknowledges his admission and apology.

Pat pauses for a second and then continues. "That's a really fucked-up way to eat sushi."

John laughs. "There's the Pat I was looking for."

"What time you got?"

"It's a quarter to midnight," Marvel replies, looking at his Tag Heuer.

Pat looks at his watch. "It's a quarter to eleven." He lies about the time and then says boastfully, "Look at that. I've got a thirty-dollar watch and it's right, and yours there must have cost a couple of grand and it's wrong. Just goes to show that money doesn't always buy quality."

Karen walks over looking at her watch. "It *is* a quarter till midnight. Your watch is wrong. His is right."

"What do you expect from a thirty-dollar watch," Pat spouts before laughing.

Christina curls up behind her husband, sneaking up on the group from behind. She pops her head from around John's back as she arrives.

"Is everyone having a great time?" She beams. "I think this year's party has more personality than we've had in past years."

"Like the difference between a personality and a personality disorder?"

"Ha ha." Christina exaggerates her sarcastic comeback. "Cute. Do you always have to be such a snarky beast? Remember back when we used to discuss these kinds of things in a civilized, adult manner?"

No one responds.

"Yeah," she adds. "Me neither." She laughs.

"Karen," John says, "would you like to try the sushi? We have some yellowfin tuna that's top-shelf. It goes down really well with a cold shot of Ketel One. The wild salmon is amazing too."

"No, thanks," she replies. "I don't care for it."

"You don't like sushi?" Christina seems shocked. "Why not? You've at least *tried* it before, right? You're not one of those who doesn't try something because of the way it looks or because it sounds yucky." She makes an appalled face, pretending she's reacting to the offer. "Ew, raw fish. I'll *never* eat that."

"Sorry, no." Karen is ready to move on. "No reason. It's just not my taste."

"C'mon. Nobody dislikes something just for no reason. Preferences are guidelines of your personal prejudices. It's only food."

"Well then." Karen contains her distaste for Christina's pompousness. "I have a prejudice against eating a scaly, fishy animal raw that was swimming around in a toilet bowl of water somewhere earlier today." She pauses. "And it's more of a rule than a guideline. Cook it up—that's fine. But never raw."

"You're turning into a little old Jewish woman," Pat tells her with a laugh. "You're gonna end up sitting around playing mah-jongg with your little blue-haired Jewish old-lady friends, a gold chain holding your glasses around your neck while you're wearing a frock and a frown."

"Are you going to let him speak to you that way?" John jokes and laughs.

"It all balances out," Pat explains. "In our house, I get a vote and she gets the tiebreaker. You know why married men usually die before their wives? Because they want to."

They all chuckle.

"So what you are saying is you're married to a bitch. That's sweet." She smiles and playfully slaps Pat's arm.

"All you had to do was ask, honey."

"Listening to you is like waiting for a sneeze."

"Eh, she's getting too predictable," Pat tells the Marvels with a dismissive wave of his hand. "I remember when I was a kid; my favorite TV show was *The Wild Wild West*. James West and Artemus Gordon. Jim and Artie were the best. All the action and suspense and intrigue and love scenes and inescapable situations, it was mesmerizing to watch. So much fun. Not like the terrible Will Smith movie version. I'm talking the Robert Conrad, Ross Martin series. Now after all these years when I watch it on TV, I realize I didn't see it so clearly before. I never realized that every single show is exactly the same. Just plug in different locales and bad guys and love interests. It is so predictable, but I was just too young and in love with it to notice. Same exact story every time."

He pauses to take a drink and to look at Karen before continuing.

"She's *exactly* like that."

"Really? For example?" Karen snips back.

"All right. You always asked for my help to write our son's school essays. Always. But you never—*never*—used any of my stuff. I wrote great essays, but not once did you use them. This happened dozens of times through the years. But did I ever say anything about it? All the years of trying to help, I was just shrugged off, tossed away, and yet I never said a word. How nice of a guy am I?"

"So why did you bring it up now?"

"You asked for an example," Pat boasts.

"But why did you pick that one particular case for your example if you're so proud of yourself for keeping it such a 'big secret' after all these years?" She puts air quotes around "big secret."

"I was waiting for the opportune moment."

Christina's attention is distracted from the conversation as she recognizes one of her special guests wandering around the room with a few other friends.

"Oh, Emerson's here," she announces to her husband and the McLarens once she sees Emerson Brooksby walk through the room.

"Who is Emerson?" Pat asks.

"Emerson Brooksby. I'm sure you've heard of him. He's the latest craze in rehab. Relocated here from LA," she begins to explain. "He's been on TV a few times. He has this new approach to rehab for treating all kinds of problems. You know how it is; you can be addicted to *anything* these days. I read about him a few months ago and have been following him online. I thought that since he's in town, it'd be fun to invite him to the party. He has a special event here at the theater this month. I thought I'd attend."

"What are you addicted to?" Pat asks her dryly.

"Oh no, silly." She laughs and slaps his arm. "Not for me. It's about the process." She takes a sip from her drink. "I find it all so interesting."

Before Pat can reply, Herman Zoo and his wife, Beverly, approach the couples. Christina makes her usual big fuss as she greets her arriving guests and introduces them to Pat and Karen. The Zoos politely greet the McLarens.

Beverly is a shrill, obnoxious, awful, dreadful, vicious person who bathes in the riches her husband's ministry provides her. She has had a constant struggle with her weight. She is short and big-boned, which is polite way to describe someone who is fat. She could sometimes really sacrifice and struggle and drop a lot, and look really good, but then she gains it back with interest and looks frumpy and miserable all over again.

She is a grotesque, revolting human on every level. As a way to keep her husband in line, she attempts suicide by way of pill overdose anytime Herman tries to do anything against her wishes. She's even more of a true believer than Zoo himself. Given that she is a sadistic, domineering sociopath, the couple clearly have a poisonous relationship. And that's without the snakes. She is capable of seeing things through to their bitter, bloody conclusion, without much redemption for anyone involved.

After meeting the McLarens, the Zoos turn their attention to the Marvels.

"This is a lovely party," Herman tells the Marvels. "Or should I say gala?"

"You're too kind," Christina purrs. She has been spiritually attracted to Zoo and his philosophical teachings and ministry since she first discovered his fellowship. She was positively mesmerized by his snake-handling skills. She felt the instant attraction. Christina is very much that type of person. She gravitates quickly toward whatever the latest and greatest thing is, and then just as quickly she drops it. Nevertheless, she is never one not to have the latest fashion, trends, or fads as she primps around her estate during one of her events. This is why the local celebs, the socialites, the money people, the glam-slam poseurs, and Christina's newfound movers and shakers like Herman Zoo and Emerson Brooksby find their way to being invited. They are the latest and greatest on the scene, so they are must-haves at any affair she and her husband are hosting. And her recent conversion to more devoutly follow Zoo's ministry has certainly raised the stakes in her commitment.

Pat, an unapologetically unconverted adversary of organized religion and its leaders, is quick to step into a discussion with Herman. Zoo, surveying his flock from the lofty perch of his smooth confidence, is well aware of the charismatic preacher/hustler and the mountains of his followers' money that he built his empire on. Pat can't resist the opportunity to tweak the nose of such a hypocritical and arrogant asshole. He decides to start up a little innocent party chat to mess with Zoo and his abominably repulsive wife, Bev. He also figures it's a good way to start chipping away at the competition by prying from the inside. He knows Zoo isn't aware of what he knows. He figures that Zoo probably regards him as someone who barely has an inkling of the name. The two had certainly never met face-to-face before now.

"Can I ask you something, Herm?" Pat asks, showing an abundance of disrespect in addressing Zoo in both his tone of voice and his use of the clipped name.

Zoo nods. "Sure. But I prefer to be addressed as Herman or Dr. Zoo, if you don't mind."

"You're the preacher." Pat sidles up to Zoo and begins his story. "The other day, my wife here," he says, motioning indifferently toward Karen, who is standing next to him with a churlish grin on her face, "and I were sitting at this little outdoor café. We chatted for a while. After the food came, I got out my iPad to check my e-mail. After about ten minutes, I could feel this weird stare coming from across the table. While I was working and concentrating, Karen was just sitting there doing nothing. Really, she was just sitting there ... absolutely dead fucking nothing. Now I'm a live-and-let-live type of guy, but it started to bother me when I realized she was just plopped down and staring into space. Now I ask you, who just sits in a chair like a fruit platter and stares out coldly and emotionlessly? I mean, you must have *something* to do, no? Check your e-mails, write notes to yourself, or read a fucking newspaper article or a book. Take pictures of something or talk to the waitress or get up and use the bathroom. But do something ... right? You can't just fucking sit there." He glances at Karen, who shakes her head slowly as he tells his story.

"Anyway, I started thinking about divorce right after I noticed that. What does this person possibly have to offer me if this is what she does?" He looks at Karen, who reciprocates his smirk, knowing that her husband is running a little head game on Zoo. "So I ask you, is it me?"

"I understand," Zoo replies slowly, selecting his words carefully. "We park our cars in the same garage. I have my two golden rules. First, life is short and precious, but then we die and we learn our fate; and second, he who is not busy being born is busy dying. You have to be a dynamic force in this world. There are players and there are benchwarmers. I don't subscribe to *anyone* being a benchwarmer if there's still life left in his or her soul. You can't just sit in a chair and do nothing. Ever."

"See," Pat admonishes his wife. "I told you it isn't normal behavior."

"I don't understand what's wrong with just taking a moment to relax and reflect. Why does everyone have to be in some agitated state of perpetual motion?" Karen defends herself.

"I suppose," Zoo continues, "if you're sitting on a beach, let's say, or on a hillside overlooking a skyline, or watching the sun rise or set, or sitting at a park looking up at a full moon, then that's different because you've got something to look at. But just at a restaurant?"

"So what Karen is essentially doing while I'm answering e-mails and staying engaged, if I'm hearing you correctly, is waiting to die." Pat smiles broadly, knowing that Zoo has slipped into his trap of nonsensical argumentative logic. He also knows that Zoo is pulling the old magician's trick of trying to make sure he appeases everyone with his response and interpretation.

"I don't discount that she might have been thinking serene thoughts, but is that enough in this tap-tap-tap world of today?" Zoo chooses his words carefully. "So let's turn the other cheek and be open-minded and hypothesize that she wasn't just sitting in her chair. Let's say that she was praying or meditating. Whatever the reason for that time of reflection, it is comforting to know that maybe it helped the world in some way."

"He's got enough iron in his blood," Bev says, shaking her head with hearty approval, "to carry the whole world on his shoulders." With a hypnotic tractor-beam lock-in, she metamorphoses into a protective, nurturing maternal avenger. For such a disgusting creature, she seems almost soft for a fleeting moment, soft like a wolverine mother protecting her family.

John Marvel, who has been listening and watching the interaction intently, feels compelled to add his view on the topic. "Was she doing some kind of breathing exercise thing while she sat there?" he asks Pat. "Were her eyes closed? Was she engaged in what you were doing or just completely lifeless?"

"Still standing right here, John," Karen reminds her host, as the group seems to be talking around her while speaking *about* her.

"If she wasn't meditating or doing something productive," John adds, "then I think your instincts are right. I would dump her." He laughs loudly and pats Karen on the shoulder in a conciliatory gesture.

"Here's exactly what Karen was doing," Christina says, deciding to add her insight. "She was contemplating her exit strategy from a totally terrible relationship. She was telling him, in a passive-aggressive way, to get the hell on with it already. Shit or get off, right?" She looks at Zoo for validation and then blushes after realizing she cursed.

"Well," Zoo explains, ignoring the curse, "her point of view could very well have been, *What do I have to offer this relationship if he sits down with me and pays more attention to his phone than to his wife?* That would be reasonable to assume also."

"Holy shit. I'm right here." Karen finally confronts the group with her side of the story. "We were sitting there, and this jerk-face," she says, motioning gleefully toward Pat, "gets on his iPad and starts typing. I'm, like, sitting there with nothing to do because I don't have an iPad, I have nothing to check on my phone, and I'm not into always staring at the cell phone and texting, or updating or posting or refreshing constantly. So he's not the only one who's thinking about divorce. What he did was self-centered and rude. He is more interested in cultivating the perfect Facebook update than he is in having a conversation with his wife. That's the way I see it. So who's dumping who?"

"What kind of people sit at a table together and don't even try to talk with each other?" Christina asks.

"Married people," Karen replies.

"You know what? While I'm standing here listening to you talk," Pat tells his wife, "as entertaining and bizarre as it is, it seems to me like your version is like having a booth at the flea market. You flaunt your wares and make a sale, and it's all transitory bullshit. It seems to me that you'd want to say something more substantial before one of us drops dead waiting to hear you make sense."

"The undisputed fact is that most women are not always the heavenly reward most of the men in this town might imagine," John observes off-topic. "Rather, they're more like white blood cells smothering a virus."

"I hope you realize that the more you men speak, the deeper the hole you're digging," Karen announces. "There will be payback."

"You see that—the secret to a woman's power is that she can say no to us." Pat follows John's tangled tangential comment and Karen's not-so-veiled threat. "Until we can say no to women, men will never have any power. And the truth is, what they have to offer ain't all that great. And when it's over, we can't wait for them to split. Even married guys. Sometimes it's just too much work and hassle. Getting laid anymore is like some kind of great existential redundancy." He begins acting out. "I'd like to have the soul sucked out of me, and then after that I'd like to have the soul sucked out of me in case there are any remnants."

"That's one of smartest things I've heard all night." John chuckles. He offers to the group, "I always love to hear Pat's take on the spontaneous vacuum he calls marriage. It's quite a scale of extremes and issues. Very interesting how so many different dynamics are in play."

"Well," Pat says, "I'm already going to hell, but I'm shutting up now, 'cause I don't wanna go all the way to the seventh circle or anything."

"I know people who think the way you do," Karen says, about to throw him a zinger. "However, most of them don't own shoes." She pauses, still looking at her husband. "So if you had it to do all over again, you wouldn't marry me?"

"Hell no," he announces confidently. "I did that. Know what to expect. Why in the world would I do it again? It was kind of fun the first time around. I'm not complaining, mind you—but please. Again? No way."

"Then I should go ahead and dump you," Karen snips. "Leave you fat and happy with the dog, and your peace and quiet and your iPad updates."

"Hey, the dog is a great source of comfort and stress reduction," Pat counters to his wife. "Whenever she wants some lovin' or hugs and petting, she comes around and sits down next to me and stares right at me with those big eyes. Kinda like what you do when you're horny." He pauses and then looks to the rest of the group. "Only my dog comes around *a lot* more often."

Zoo feels compelled to add a comment, not realizing that he's fallen into the inimitable banter Pat and Karen have sucked him into. "Your husband is like that uniquely colored crayon in the box, silver, for instance, that you don't always use on every drawing but that you're glad to know is there."

Karen thinks for a moment and then replies. "No, he's more like raw sienna, that shit-brown color that no one ever wants to use and wonders why Crayola even bothered including it. Besides, it's the perfect hue for his verbal diarrhea. Too bad they don't have a color called drab."

"It's funny when you get so riled up that you have a hard time speaking correctly." Pat smirks while egging her on. "Do it again."

His comment breaks the flow of the discussion with a round of jokes and one-liners from the group. Herman and Bev Zoo seem a little relieved that the tone has eased up. They realize it's more of a light, fun conversation than a confessional. As they each take sips, or gulps as the case may be, from their drinks, one of the party waitstaff walks up with a tray of snacks.

"Oh, I love these little breaded shrimp bites," Bev says as she grabs one from the platter. "They taste just like the old Long John Silver's shrimp I used to eat as a kid and loved before I found out that food gets better than that."

As Bev grabs a handful more of the shrimp, looking more like a fat, spoiled, trashy moocher than the wife of a respected preacher, Emerson Brooksby finally makes it over to where they all are standing. John and Christina welcome him and take a few moments to introduce Brooksby to Pat, Karen, Herman, and Bev.

Pat takes a few steps over to Bev as she stuffs the coconut shrimp into her greasy mouth. He approaches her as she chews.

"I've actually lost a lot of weight," he begins. "I used to be over two hundred pounds. Lost over thirty pounds just by watching what I eat, no exercise at all." He pats his slim stomach arrogantly. "Try to stick around one sixty-five, one seventy most of the time."

"That's hard work," she comments. "Nice accomplishment."

"Thanks." He grabs one of the crab-stuffed mushroom caps from another tray and takes a bite. "How 'bout you?"

She looks strangely at him, confused by his question. "How about me *what?*"

"What do you weigh in at?" He pops the other half of the mushroom snack into his mouth and then gently dabs his lips with a little paper cocktail napkin. "What do you go, a buck fifty—maybe fifty-five?"

She straightens up, aghast at his inquiry, but not certain whether this line of questioning is in jest.

"Excuse me, but proper ladies don't discuss these private matters," Bev reminds him, gritting her teeth through a forced smile.

"Oh." Pat acts perplexed. "I always thought the boundaries were age and feminine hygiene products."

As Bev huffs, Brooksby begins socializing with the group, sensing a bit of tension.

"This is a magnificent home," Brooksby compliments his hosts. "I love the way it's decorated. Very Christmassy, very festive."

"Thank you, Emerson." Christina beams. She absorbs the moment, feeling completely fulfilled and bursting with smug self-delight at two of her prize acquisitions who are both enjoying her party. Having both Herman Zoo and Emerson Brooksby in attendance is quite a coup and is sure to be accompanied in the local What's Hot in Hotlanta sections of the city magazines by colorful photos and celebratory text. And why not? After all, Christina never fails to invite the Atlanta media—both print and local network—to all her functions. This ensures that her events are captured and publicized for historical purposes, a *must-have* on the list of any good Southern belle hostess. It actually means more bragging rights within the inner circle of the Atlanta power movers and shakers. She who boasts loudest boasts best.

"With such illustrious guests," Christina says, "I feel this burden—this weight on my back—to make sure everything is the very best! A lot of pressure." She laughs nervously.

"Oh, it's no big deal if the party is a dud, really." Pat takes the opportunity to rain a little on Christina's marvelous parade. Christina and Pat have always had a strained yet cordial friendship and relationship. "Just the guarantee that it would be the first thing anyone thought about when they looked at you, always, your entire life. It would be such an enormous calamity of an event that, regardless of whatever else you may accomplish, the fact you hosted this disaster would definitely appear at the beginning of your obituary. So it's only obituary-level pressure. You have lots of years before you have to start worrying yourself about that kind of stuff."

He smiles at her and sips his drink. She smiles back, concealing a sneering dismissal. She wanted so badly for everything at the party to go brilliantly, and she was feeling it on the inside. She had become overly sensitive to any little quip or comment. Pat was feeding on that and loved how uncomfortable he was making his hostess. In the back of his mind, though, he was also hoping Christina would realize he was just joking. He wasn't as close of a friend to her as he was to her husband, but he couldn't resist breaking through that smugness to give her a hard time.

"You know what," he says, deciding to test the limits of his luck with one more barb, "if it makes you feel any better, I've been at this party all night long and no one, *I mean no one,* has asked about you."

"Okay, easy." Karen jumps in. "Take your foot off the gas."

"I don't think he's even in the car anymore," Christina snaps back. The group chuckles, encouraging her struggling attempt at a comeback.

"He thinks he's the Messiah, doesn't he?" Karen continues. "Like *he* can never say or do anything wrong. He doesn't understand there's always cautionary tales behind the story we tell about ourselves."

"Luckily for you, Pat," John says, entering the fray, "we have the freedom to be wrong, the freedom to be ignorant, and the freedom to be assholes, and dammit if *you* don't embrace those freedoms every day."

"Emerson, you see what goes on here?" Pat turns his attention to Brooksby. "Can we talk a minute? Let me ask you a question. I have a friend who's gone for sex addiction treatment. I don't how to put this, man, but it's getting really bad." He pauses and winks. "Okay, you got me, it's not *really* a friend, you know. Anyway, so *he* had mad sex with the maid in my kitchen last night, and she's been working for us for twelve years." He looks and nods at Karen. She is standing with her arms crossed, an annoyed frown on her face.

"I'm not sure what to do about it," he continues. "He hasn't hit the bottom of the true bottom, but his bottom is exposed and I can hear the bottom calling his name." Pat stops and then leans forward to whisper. "Can you give me the name of a good clinic, or somebody who can recommend one?"

"Hey, ya know that whole 'cautionary tale behind the story we're telling' stuff your wife was talking about?" Brooksby flashes a knowing smile and winks. "Let's ignore the shit out of that."

The whole group collectively feels the playful vibe. Everyone laughs. They see the two special guests more at leisure, more human and approachable. As things settle, Brooksby turns to Zoo and begins a more serious-minded topic.

"Dr. Zoo," he begins, "I have a question, if you don't mind."

"Only if you call me Herman."

"Okay, Herman. It seems to me that we must face similar issues although we're not exactly in the same profession—or game, if you will. Being an addiction recovery specialist, I was thinking about the types of things I have in common with someone who is presumably a man of the cloth and in the business of salvation. What do you find to be the biggest challenges you face when you deal with someone with a stubborn reluctance to accept help or encouragement, or who lacks the reason to experiment with the tools that might make them a better person or bring them some measure of inner peace?" Although these two men have never met, Brooksby assumes that Zoo is aware of his daughter's story, although Brooksby covers up that knowledge at every turn.

"That's an intriguing question." Zoo is sparked with light-switch-on enthusiasm, eager to respond. "It's something I've thought about with great interest." The others gather around a little closer, leaning in to hear the great master's words. Instantly, the space becomes a symposium forum starring two clashing charismatics. "I've found that all forms of religion can attract and energize the cretins of the world—those who have some kind of primal need to process life in good versus bad, black versus white, and be-saved-or-be-damned terms. And in many ways, although we'd like to be able to believe we live in a just and fair world, reality shows us differently.

"I remember during one of my recent travels to Zimbabwe, I toured areas where entire generations of families live next to a garbage dump. They spend every day digging through trash for snips of food and bits of anything they can find that might be recyclable. And even after all that, it only pays the family something like a dollar a day. They've lived there forever, hundreds of them, living off the trash trucks, picking through the garbage with rakes and their bare hands. I was disgusted by the disparity I saw between this and the other stops on my tour, which included visiting the great plantations and mansions that were reserved for only the very rich and elite. I couldn't reconcile eating in a palace the day before and then witnessing such human suffering and inhuman disgrace. I thought about that visit a lot. It was sights and sounds and odors that burned inside of me and that now cannot be hidden from my thoughts and prayers. That stretching of my senses needs to stay with me forever."

Bev stares at her husband, exhibiting a rehearsed look of being in awe of his account. The others are all listening carefully, each appreciating that they were having a singularly distinct one-on-one with one of the world's foremost—or infamous—evangelists.

"After many nights of prayer and meditation about what I witnessed, I realized something very important. It was something that altered the course of where I was to take my message." Zoo continues. "You simply cannot feel bad for all these people. You can't take it all to heart and lose sleep over it and think there's anything in the world you could even begin to do about their plight. This is the way the world is, and that's it." He pauses. "If God doesn't care enough about them to help, then there's certainly nothing any of us can do about it."

Some in the group strain their heads to see him more clearly when they hear this. They hadn't been anticipating that Zoo's parable was going to reach that particular conclusion. They hadn't seen his story going there.

"I realized you can't save these people. You can pray for them, but to try to do anything else drains you of your ability to have compassion." Zoo has a firm resolve in his voice. "It's a struggle to not let that happen. You stop truly caring for the cause and can only think about the days until you've completed your commitment. It's like you're doing time in prison. Otherwise, you're very unhappy for a long time. You don't experience joy. At the end you only experience relief, if you're lucky."

Brooksby is nodding in agreement. "Let's face it," he says, concurring with Zoo, "sometimes being brave may be the act of somebody who is just too hungry and cold and tired to care anymore. We are basically being told in no uncertain terms that our lives are not our own, that we belong to some concept, some fictional utopia, and that we're supposed to be dominoes— that we are theirs to use as they see fit."

"I'm not sure what that means," Christina whispers to John, "but I enjoy thinking about it."

"There's an inherent need for us to believe, and there's the inevitable abuse by others of that need." Zoo was being critical of the inequity he observed, but he could just have easily been speaking of his role as a manipulator of faith. He continues. "It would be about the radical loneliness in all of us. About how relief from that loneliness is there, but only sometimes, and not always when you need it most. It's about the rise of a kind of spiritual cynicism that substitutes obedience for faith. I try to keep faith in its proper place. I'm not a *spiritual polluter* like so many of my brethren are. I just agree that we may be through with the past, but the past isn't through with us."

"I don't remember the past," Pat says.

"The past is all there is to remember," Karen argues. "If it's not in the past, then it's happening now, so there isn't any need to remember it. You don't appreciate a moment until it becomes a memory. It's only remembered once it's in the past." She takes a breath and sighs. "Things that happen to us when we're young just seem so much more important and meaningful because they're happening to us for the first time."

"I remember when I was a kid," Pat adds, "I used to go to bed at night—and this was when AM radio went off the air at midnight." He looks around the group and smiles. "Yeah, I'm old. Anyway, the last song they played every night before they went off the air was 'Good Night' by the Beatles. Ringo did the vocals. I used to listen with cheap little earplugs so my parents couldn't hear that I was still awake." He pauses. "If life keeps score," Pat announces to the group with a grin, "then I win."

Brooksby passes over this comment and refocuses his discussion with Zoo. "The things that you grow up with stay with you for life. You start off a certain way, and then you spend your whole life trying to find that certain simplicity you once had. It's less about staying in childhood and more about keeping a certain spirit of seeing things in a different way."

"I agree. I also believe we should do things we don't need to do and do them well," Zoo adds. "Eventually you'll realize you needed those things all along."

"I remember one night we went to a concert," Pat says, starting to submit his two cents, much to the chagrin of the two spotlight guests. "It was one of those they used to throw in stadiums, four or five bands playing the whole day and night. Anyway, the local radio station was giving away a metallic green Chevy Nova. They filled it with bags of marshmallows. You had to guess the number of marshmallows to win the car."

He pauses and takes a sip from his drink before continuing. The others are waiting to see if he's going to make a point. Karen, watching him in routine form, bored with it as usual, just shakes her head.

"In the parking lot," he says, "it started raining really hard. The rain was coming through the sunroof in our VW van. We had rainwater all over the place, and it leaked all over a box of cassette tapes we had in the backseat." He pauses another moment. "Remember, honey?" He looks at his wife, who stands there without confirming, just giving one of those looks. "One of them was *Ode to Billie Joe* by Bobbie Gentry." He begins humming under his breath, singing the title track: "Up on Choctaw Ridge, Billie Joe MacAllister jumped off the Tallahatchie Bridge."

He kind of chuckles to himself and takes another drink. The others are hesitant to say anything just yet, not sure if he's finished or holding out his story's payoff.

Finally, John speaks up. "So ... what ... did you ... I mean ... were you telling us about the Nova or ... I think I speak for everyone when I say that we're not sure." He is sketchy and tentative in his comment. The others are all shaking their heads in agreement. "Did you win the car, or what?"

"Nah. Didn't play."

"You know, there's something very wrong with you," Karen remarks. The group laughs.

"How would you know if there's something wrong with me if I don't know what something wrong is? Very subjective," Pat jokes. Then he ponders. "I think I want that on my gravestone."

"So you already know your epitaph. What about your eulogy?" John asks. "You've probably thought about that too."

"I think it's wise to look ahead. Start early—plan your funeral now." Pat is matter-of-fact in his assessment. "It's not a morbid thought, at least not as much as you might think. If you want something to happen in a certain way, especially the last thing in your life, you might as well do it right." He looks around. "Seems perfectly normal to me." As he sees the faces of the others, he detects doubt.

"Okay, maybe not normal, but—" Pat tries to explain. "None of us are *normal* per se. When I say 'us,' I mean not just us." He points with a circular motion to the group. "I mean *us*." He takes both hands and turns around to indicate everyone. "*Normal* is something you read about in a book."

"You intrigue me," Zoo says to Pat. "Don't get me wrong, I'm enjoying your stories. But it seems to me that you're reaching for acceptance. Not in the 'look at me' way, but in general—just the normal need to be liked and acknowledged." He nods at Pat. "I find that to be such a conventional trait among the people I meet. It's the need to be liked, to fit in, and to feel normal. It makes me wonder all over again about the influences of parenting versus environment in our experiences and upbringing."

"There's that word *normal* again," Pat replies, testy and unchained. "Well, my dad was a terrible navigator. When I was growing up, every one of our vacations ended with banjo music, rusty shotguns, and staying in motels operated by people who were missing teeth." He smiles, and then laughs with a tease, nodding to Zoo's comment. "Maybe you're on to something there. The whole nature–nurture thing."

"I'm not sure I agree with that," Brooksby interjects. "Wanting people to like you is nice, but I'm confident that there's always going to be many who don't," he says with a bit of gallows humor. "You'll always be able to hang on to that."

"Or maybe he's just a genius at misdirection," Zoo adds.

"I don't think *genius* is the word I'd use," quips Karen.

"Consider this," Zoo begins. "There's an argument that frogs are good bioindicators of our environment. Their absence, health, or sickness provides an indication about the general cleanliness and chemical balance of a given ecosystem. Since their skin is so permeable, they pick up pollutants readily and are an early warning signal of any problems in that microenvironment. Well, I have a little theory that people can be mapped in a similar way. Only this time, it's not slimy aquatic amphibians, but rather certain types of personalities. The overall 'health' of a given environment, in this example a party or gala if you will"—he motions around the room—"can be determined at a glance by seeing what's going on with these rare kinds of individuals. Much the same way frogs give an early warning signal, these kinds of people can signal a great party like a healthy population of frogs happily croaking the night away."

Zoo looks around the circle of guests, taking a pause from his anecdote. Karen, along with the rest of the group, is listening to Zoo, trying to see how this pertains to any of the discussions preceding it.

"And *that's* the genius of nature," Zoo concludes.

"It's certainly a strange way to show genius," Karen observes.

"I agree with Dr. Zoo," Brooksby concedes. "Geniuses roll how they roll. Geniuses make and live by their own rules. They don't play the game like obedient little mice. They're better off working on their own, being self-employed or doing something in the arts. Regardless, if you want geniuses to work for you, you're going to have to put up with their peculiarities and their crap. That's the nature of a genius personality.

"Of course," he adds, "most people are either unable to understand or refuse to understand this and are always trying to discipline geniuses for not playing by the rules and not behaving in a straight and narrow fashion. That's why they need the space and freedom to create, uninhibited and uncensored."

"Interesting," notes Zoo. "I'm not saying that's wrong, but genius isn't always some free-flowing seed best left to spread on its own. Sometimes, you need a few gardeners."

"What the hell are they talking about?" Karen whispers to her husband out of earshot from the others.

"Not exactly sure," Pat whispers back. "But I think I might be a genius."

She nudges him playfully in the side. They return their attention to Zoo and Brooksby, who are continuing their discussion in front of the group.

"Someday a *real* rain will come," Zoo says. "My beliefs can be compared with what Edna Mode once said: 'Never look back; it distracts you from now.' It gives me strength, encouragement, and focus. It makes me wonder if I really think I've given enough in my life already, that I'm exempt from having to do anything for myself again. Is it ever all right to become selfish?"

"Well," Pat announces, "isn't that just the perfect absinthe-soaked cherry on the cyanide-and-gravy sundae word to use, *selfish?*"

Zoo's face, which has been relatively agreeable to, if not accepting of, Pat's smart-ass comments up until now, has slowly transformed into one that broadcasts annoyance. There is perhaps even a shade of menace.

"I missed the part where that's *my* problem," Zoo contends.

"My point wasn't that it's *your problem*, which, by the way, is a pretty narcissistic way of looking at it." He surveys the room. "Okay, who is the first to go next?"

"Why don't we talk about the cheery things we have to celebrate during the holidays?" Christina says, trying to intervene and settle some suddenly elevated emotions. "All this serious talk when it's almost Christmas."

"Oh no, it's okay." Zoo puts up his hand to settle her concerns. "I've always encouraged others to question before they follow, to speak up with their fears, to ultimately follow their beliefs. I always enjoy hearing what others have to say about my work. I actually like to hear from the people who oppose my message."

"*Actually like the people who oppose my message,*" Pat repeats, mimicking Zoo. "Translation: if you back off and stop making fun of my little charade, you'll be the last put in a reeducation camp."

Zoo studies McLaren carefully. He's not sure what to make of Pat's insistent hostility. His carefully barbed remarks are out of place, as just a few minutes earlier everything seemed to be just good-natured innocent joking. Zoo's demeanor has now turned sour.

"We all know what's likely to happen," Zoo begins his response. His voice is now moving in with the hoarseness that comes with his sermonizing. "Have you ever watched those shows about wild animals? They get the cameras in the savannah and capture the ways of nature. Watch the next time they are observing a pride of lions. It's interesting." He pauses for a moment and then continues.

"The first thing a younger lion does when he takes over is to kill the older, weaker lions, and then he begins establishing his kingdom. He goes around and kills all the cubs, and then he goes to the lionesses and mates with them and produces cubs of his own." Somehow, through all the conversations and glancing jabs, Zoo is now commanding the floor, standing in the center of a circle made up of the original group and now a dozen or so more who happened by and stayed to listen. "I'm not saying all the nonbelievers are goners, but it would foolish to presume that everything will stay intact and the world will find equal justice."

He makes a complete turn in the center of the circle, looking upon the makeshift improvised congregation. He smiles, easily slipping into his evangelic persona.

"Forget it," he emphasizes with a wave of his hand. "One way or another, there will be a lot of roaring and growling and bared fangs. There will be pain and more snarling and blood on the grass. It's going to be traumatic. And it's going to be quick."

He pauses. Although a couple of guests look like they are about to say something, the group remains quiet and transfixed.

"I'm just saying, watch any nature documentary about lions," Zoo says in a softer tone, pulling back on the preachiness. "It's the clarity of purpose. It's the kind of clarity that only comes from absolute need. The clarity of mind that comes to a man standing on the gallows is astonishing."

"Which man?" Pat interrupts. "The one pulling the lever?"

Zoo stares directly into Pat's eyes. "Does it really matter?"

Pat smiles broadly and lets out a laugh. It helps to break the tension that is hovering over the group's increasingly large circle of observers.

"Well, that's very boring and very verbose," Pat announces, lifting his glass. He looks at Zoo, who looks back and smiles, also lifting his glass.

"Oh, that sounds like you, honey," Karen says, patting her husband on the chest. "Except not the verbose part. Just the boring part." The group laughs. She adds "Well, and yes, the verbose part too."

"You know she used to have a real romantic spirit," Pat says as he puts his arm lovingly around his wife. "She used to." Then he whispers to her tenderly as he holds her close. "And after all these years, God rewarded me."

Chapter 15

The Fabulous Marvel Mansion Mystery Tour

Christina Marvel is in flat-out, full-throttle, elegant-hostess-and-gracious-homemaker mode as she hastily gathers together a small group to stand around her in a circle. They huddle near a corner of the large audiovisual rec room, which is decorated tonight in heavy reds and greens with silver stars, lights, and sparkles. Inside the large home theater, a variety of Christmas movies are playing on a loop. For this event, each of the rooms are decorated to a theme with different colors and lighting. Each of the Christmas trees is uniquely adorned to match its room.

The Marvel mansion is part of a local insiders' club and is on the house rotation for themed parties each quarter. The Christmas party isn't a part of the usual club events. A small group of local businessmen, politicians, athletes, and other special invited guests convene quarterly to have a social. The usual goings-on at the quarterly socials are decidedly "anything goes" in attitude and activity. These gatherings are reserved for more decadent, sexually charged, and morally ambiguous hookups and depravity. It's not something you would expect when looking at the lives of these community leaders and business autocrats. It is a poorly kept, but tightly controlled, secret among the city's elite. You have to be a member and have a "house key" to join the parties and enter the homes in the hosting rotation.

The Marvels subsequently use their annual Christmas bash to cleanse away a year of sin and frivolity. Christina, with her reappearing contemporary Lady Macbeth complex, has found herself confounded by the internal struggles she faces regarding the incongruent actions of her life. She grasps at ways to make herself feel better about who she is and what she has become—a prime example being her overactive involvement with Zoo and his preaching. She doesn't have time to consider all her demons now, though. She has a showcase event to flaunt and pimp.

Christina is clearly excited about taking this small group around her home and can't wait to release her inner prideful self—a sure-to-be Southern sappiness sugarcoating all the venom behind the commentary. She'll be parading front and center, headlining the "gloat float," leading the tour.

"C'mon, everyone. Let me give y'all a cook's tour of the Marvel mansion," she proudly hails the group. "I like to think of this as a home that would make Margaret Mitchell proud."

"She refers to her house as the Marvel mansion?" Emerson Brooksby whispers to Jack, who is standing next to him and is somehow "fortunate" enough to be a part of this spontaneous walk-through of the home that "would make Margaret Mitchell proud."

He nods. "Yeah, and she's the more humble of the two. Wait till you get to know John better. Don't get me wrong. They're good, solid people—but you'll see. You can see it right away if you know what to look for. Little characteristics give them away."

Brooksby nods, encouraging Jack to continue.

"John's style of vanity is more manicured, sort of inherently more a part of his DNA in a genetic, haughty way. He always keeps that bogus, camera-ready smile working so he can appear to be everybody's friend, even though he's smug and arrogant, almost pompous at times." Brooksby listens closely, impressed with Jack's assessment and openness. "I think it's because John was *born* into the money. It's pure birthright. Christina, on the other hand, married into the bank account along with taking on the role of family matriarch. It's like a goddamn Lifetime movie or a late-night cable soap. Her ego is driven more from her sense of entitlement—what's *owed* her for her perceived sacrifices and for the referential way she was raised by her parents, who treated her like a deity. She can afford to be more eccentric. She can get away with it. It's almost *expected*. That's why you always see her as more of a snob. She becomes patronizing and dismissive.

At first glance, she looks as plastic as a Barbie doll. And you figure her for having a mannequin's brain. But don't sell her short for a second. She has a huge personality and hides the bite of a coiled viper inside, always ready to strike. That quality rules the roost. She's not the smiley-faced urchin who's always trying to see to it that everything's perfect." Jack takes a sip from his drink. "Real contrast, huh?"

Brooksby is genuinely impressed by the display of insight demonstrated by Jack's two-minute analysis. He had begun to formulate his own ideas about the Marvels but hadn't thought about it much until now. He extends his hand and shakes with Jack as they formally introduce themselves to each other.

"Okay, do we have everyone who's going on the tour?" Christina tries to reach the group without being overly loud or obvious so that others standing around won't overhear and want to join in. The tour group consists of Pat and Karen, Jack and Kristin, Emerson Brooksby, and Herman and Bev Zoo. It is being led by the hosts, Christina and John—Christina cheerleading the way out in front, pointing out elaborate home furnishings or one-of-a-kind pictures and knickknacks, and John containing the rear, ensuring the cattle stay with the herd.

The first route takes them out of the rec room, around a corner, and up a curling staircase to a second-floor hallway. As the women in the group and Herman stay close to the front with Christina, Jack, Brooksby, and Pat hang a little farther back with John. After a brief look around one of the kids' spacious bedrooms, Christina is on cruise control, chatting nonstop at this point with almost no regard for or knowledge of anyone who might want to offer a word.

"So what's really worth seeing?" Pat asks John as they stroll from room to room.

John shrugs his shoulders, laughs, and then deadpans. "How the hell should I know? You've been through this drill before. Why are you even coming along? How many times have you been here already? Shit, I never listen to what she says on these tours, so I don't know anything about this stuff. I just know I paid a helluva lot for most of it. If that's any indication for what's worth seeing, then everything is worth seeing." He breaks out with a bigger, heartier laugh. "No, these Christina Marvel little home tours are more a showcase for Christina Marvel than the Marvel mansion." He continues with his contagious chuckle.

"You have something, honey?" Christina yells back to John after overhearing his banter in the background.

"No, babe. Just answering some questions about the wallpaper," John lies, giggling with the guys as if he just got away with something in homeroom. Christina returns to her tour.

"Is Kristin going somewhere?" John asks Jack. "I heard you talking before and saying something about having to pick her up next week."

"Yep," Jack says. "I have to pick her up from the airport. She leaves tomorrow and gets in next Friday morning, taking the red-eye back from Denver. She's visiting her sister and her sister's kids for the holidays. Nieces, nephews, cousins—all that crap."

"Family, sure, I get it. It gives you some time off. That's nice every so often."

"Yeah, I need to take advantage of the time too," Jack agrees. "She doesn't really want to go. It's a family obligation type of thing, so she'll be in a pretty foul mood when she gets back. She always is after a family visit."

"You should plan a nice return for her," John suggests. "Schedule a romance day."

"Not very spontaneous," Pat warns.

"That's the closest we get anymore," John says.

"Are you guys kidding?" Jack laughs. "What part of 'foul mood' did you miss? I can tell you, she won't be peaches and cream getting off that plane. She'll have spent a week at a place she doesn't want to be and will have flown all night to get back. I can see her now trudging down the gate's exit with her carry-on, looking exhausted, miserable, and angry. Her first words will be, 'Let's get the fucking car.' It's not like in the movies when you meet up at the airport after spending time away from each other and you slow-motion run into each other's waiting arms. Yeah, I'll be back at work after I drop her off at the house." He pauses, shaking his head. "They've been trying to get us to move out there to help take care of her mom. Want us to buy a summer home or something so we can spend 'our share' of time taking care of everyone. That's not in the cards."

"Moving to Denver? You know what they have in Denver?" Pat says. "They have trouble breathing in Denver."

"I didn't know Kristin's family was from Denver," John says.

"Why would you?" Jack asks curiously. John shrugs without really thinking about it.

"Yeah," adds Pat. "Besides, I thought old people and retirees all move to Phoenix or Florida."

"Well, I could use a little beach time right about now," John says. "A secluded cabin on the Gulf, waking up to salty air, ocean breeze, and getting sand on my feet. Watching a nice sunset. That would work right about now."

"Yes," Brooksby adds, "Florida is a better place for a second home. It's not without its faults, but it has to be better than Denver. I still can't figure out why people live where it snows. But Florida has a whole different foreigner-immigrant thing going. At least in Miami. It's a lot like LA. I can start to smell the Miami exotic *feel* as soon as I hit the city. You start to feel that sort of rot in your bones—the traffic, the language, the *disconnect* with what you usually associate with American values. I'm not saying the place is bad, but it's just something that happens to you and you never really feel it happening. All of a sudden—boom—you're just *there*, and it sucks."

"I've always thought of it as the place you move to when you're ready to die," John says. "That's the joke, right? I love vacationing there, but I can't imagine living there."

"You're being irradiated from the inside out by a small but a constant dose of 'sunny and eighty-five with high humidity and a chance of afternoon thunderstorms' while the rest of the world goes on spinning around you in real time with real weather," Brooksby says. "And then suddenly it's six or seven years later and it only feels like a few weeks or months. You wonder where the better part of a decade of your life went. But at least you know it's still gonna be sunny and eighty-five tomorrow … banana republic status notwithstanding."

"My wife told me she'd leave me if I ever did one of two things," Pat says. "Cheat on her or pick up and move the family." He pauses. "I told her I *never* plan to move."

"How'd that go over?" Brooksby laughs.

"My sister-in-law is so overprotective as a mother," Jack says, jumping into the discussion. "We've known our niece and nephew from the day they were born. The youngest just graduated from college. It occurred to me that in the over twenty years I've known those kids, they've *never* answered a question I've asked them when their mother was with them. She always runs interference, intercepts the question, and answers before either of the kids can. It's completely psychotic."

"Sounds like you really need to have a spontaneous romantic getaway when you pick up Kristin," John says.

"Yeah, but not her style," Jack laments. "How did I end up with the only truly nonromantic woman in the world?" he asks. "Don't get me wrong, I can appreciate it. It's what drew me to her; she doesn't stand on pretense or fall into any conceivable female category." He pauses. "I like that."

"Hey, buddy." Pat puts his hand on Jack's shoulder. "It's a big club. You should know that by now. 'Nonromantic' is the latest and longest-lasting stage once you've been with someone long enough."

"But Christina." Jack looks to John for support. "She doesn't seem too inhibited."

"Whoa, slow down there, Speed Racer," Brooksby says, not wanting to wade into the waters of talking about each other's spouses.

"She's a good old girl." John laughs. "She has to be. She's from Kennesaw—a real Atlanta gal."

"I know her, John." Pat smiles. "She's not from Atlanta. She was born in New Jersey."

"She was born in New Jersey," John says. "She had no control over that. She *chose* Atlanta."

"How 'bout you?" Jack asks Brooksby, already uncomfortable with the fact that they're discussing significant others.

"I have an ex-wife and am currently unattached."

"That can have its advantages," Pat notes.

"My ex is a witch. That's why we got divorced," Brooksby explains. "And it wasn't like being married to a good witch—like Samantha from *Bewitched*—who can do stuff for you and blink things and get you out of tough situations."

"I think we can all relate to the *witchy* side."

"No, she was an actual witch. A Wiccan. She practiced nature worshipping, had candles and symbols strewn all over the place, cast spells—all that kind of wacky shit. I'm all for 'to each his own,' but it got a little ridiculous. I got out before she moved on to sacrifices."

"You still have to see her. Ya got kids together or anything?" Pat asks.

"Not anymore," Brooksby replies. The others are curious about his strange response. "That's a blessing, I suppose. Last time I heard anything, she was getting remarried. I tried to text out, 'Congrats on your engagement,' but the auto-correct feature changed it. I didn't realize until after I hit send that it actually read, 'Congrats on your enhancement.' Apparently she'd just had a boob job a few months before, so that didn't go over too well."

The guys in the back completely missed Christina's commentary about some of the attributes and points of interest in different upstairs rooms. The group heads back down a different staircase leading to the first floor. The men at the back dutifully follow.

"They say this house is haunted. I don't know about that, but it definitely has a spirit." Christina maintains her constant narrative as she leads the group downstairs and past a small library and workroom set up as a home office. They all step inside as she pauses and addresses the group. "Oh, and now you're in one of our 'ghost' rooms."

"Ghost room?" Pat's head is whirling with one-liners waiting to be delivered.

"Yes, our library is one of our more popular rooms. There have been numerous reports of paranormal sightings and strange ghostly sounds coming from this room. It's very special."

"Special? How is spending time in a haunted room special?"

"Most folks seem to like the idea. Makes for a spooky, fun evening."

"Well, are these ghosts friendly like Casper, or are we gonna get sucked into the TV by some deranged clown? That could be a problem."

"I don't know about all that, but I prefer to think of these things as the *challenges* we encounter when living in such a charming home with so much history and intrigue."

"By *challenge*, what she really means is *problem*," Jack mutters so that only Brooksby can hear, but Christina catches his comment.

She turns with a sneer. "No, we face challenges."

Now that she has engaged his mocking quip, he speaks up to the group.

"I didn't mean any disrespect, but the word *problem* has really changed since I was a kid. Problems used to be mathematical equations, or issues that arise that could be anything from a common annoyance to a real concern. Now we've subverted the word. *Problem* has become a very problematic word, if you will. A problem was just a problem and you dealt with it. Somehow, these days saying that something is a problem means either that somebody has a serious personality disorder or that some type of doom-and-gloom cloud is looming. It involves a situation that borders on devastation." Jack pauses, takes a sip, and continues.

"If you characterize someone by saying they have a problem, it doesn't mean things have taken a turn for the worse. Nowadays it means it's over for them. Problems have come to mean disaster. If someone tells me they have a problem, today it means they've wrapped up all that negativity and are bracing for the Stinger missile to hit the fuselage."

"And when exactly did 'No problem' take the place of 'You're welcome'? That doesn't work at all," Pat offers.

"Well, now we've morphed into 'What's your problem'—which always comes across as an aggressive attack," Jack agrees. "If there's a serious issue, it's not a challenge; it's a problem."

"I'll take *problem* over *challenge* any day. It's just more direct," Brooksby says. "If it's perceived to be negative, then so be it. The contemporary use of *challenge* is so innocuous and evasive. It's an acceptable euphemism for *problem* because of the corporate training mentality to dumb something down so it's less negative. 'Don't step on anyone's toes'; 'Don't panic people with incendiary words or terms.' 'Houston, we have a challenge.' A stupefying cultural shift."

"Well," Christina says, flustered by her guests' sidebar conversations about the proper use of *problem* versus *challenge*. She continues her tour. "The *ghosts* who reside here have long memories."

"What the hell does that mean?" Pat whispers to Karen.

Karen flips her hair and moderates her tone, mocking Christina quietly to her husband. "I think ghosts lack a certain je ne sais quoi."

Pat laughs at the impersonation, which draws Christina's attention.

"I'm sorry," she says disingenuously. "Did someone have a question?"

There's a little buzz among the group, but no one steps forward.

"Okay, we can walk down here to the projection room."

The party heads down the hall en masse, walking toward the home theater.

"How long did it take you to make all the improvements and additions to your home?" Zoo asks.

"Oh my." She stops and turns. "Let me think. We moved in fifteen or so years ago, and really … we've been adding and changing little things about the place all along. The theater and library are new additions—well, refurbishments actually. Most of the rest of the house is pretty much the way it was when we bought it. We brought in furnishings and little touches from around the world to add to rooms or put up for display. I think this will always be a work in progress. As long as I can keep coming up with new ideas, this place will constantly evolve."

"So most of the design elements are your idea?" Brooksby asks.

"Guilty," Christina gushes. "I wouldn't say I designed the layout and décor, but I certainly took a lot of what I've seen in my travels and adapted it for our needs and enjoyment."

"It can be argued," Zoo adds, overhearing Christina's prideful boast, "that *adapters* are the true geniuses of our society. Innovators just light the fuse, but when you look throughout history note and all of the great creations, you realize that it's the innovators who labor to find what works—but then the *adapters* come along and take that spark and turn it into something really practical. It's the difference between an artist and a designer. The artist creates something from a blank canvas or sheet of paper. It's the genius that comes to life from the mind of the creator. A designer looks at the world, takes the palette of the artist, and discovers things that can be made better. Great designers have a different set of skills but can leverage those to improve—or at the very least reimagine—parts of the world that were created by others who came before them."

Pat rolls his eyes and leans in to whisper to Brooksby. "Is it me, or is listening to him like the hallucinations that flood your mind when a toxic virus is in your bloodstream?"

Brooksby chuckles. "A lot of his vanity relies on some very fancy self-delusion."

"The guy walks around like he's Yoda or something."

"No one does emotional constipation better than he does."

Pat considers this for a moment and observes, "Can't imagine there are a lot of people competing to be the best at emotional constipation."

The group continues down the hallway to a second set of stairs that lead back down to the first floor and the garden and kitchen wing of the home, bypassing the theater. As they walk, Pat strides next to Zoo, distressingly interested in his particular brand of faith and religious conviction.

He turns to Zoo as they step down the staircase. "Hope you don't mind if I ask you a question about your practice."

"Not at all," Zoo concedes. "Anything."

"Why do you have to handle poisonous snakes? I mean, if the goal is to handle serpents, won't nonlethal types do?"

"The point of handling venomous snakes is to reinforce my beliefs. A strike or bite from a venomous snake strengthens my faith in God and my beliefs because he shields me from inherent danger."

"Have you ever been bitten?"

"Thankfully, the Lord has provided my shield."

"Thankfully?" Brooksby can't help but comment.

"Yes," Zoo replies. "He has been my protector."

"But if the point of handling poisonous snakes is to have no fear of being bitten because of the strength of your faith, then why are you thankful? It should make no difference whether or not you're bitten. The Lord is protecting you." They reach the bottom of the stairs and pause. "That's the whole point, isn't it?" Brooksby has a sudden contempt in his tone.

Zoo turns to face Brooksby. He has realized for the better part of the evening that Brooksby, McLean, and what is now a small but engrossed faction of his newfound, inebriated acolytes, have the potential to undermine him. He contemplates that Brooksby might become an outspoken nemesis to his faith. Zoo has had to dispatch these irritants to his enterprise before. He is used to laypeople trying to outsmart him, outwit him, and embarrass him. He's used to the attacks and cynicism. He's had a lot of experience in confronting people with a very defined vision of the world as a corrupt wasteland made by humans who are pure of heart and crazy of ass.

"The mere fact that the snake doesn't strike is a sign of God watching over my actions. It removes my humanity—and not humanity as an act of service or compassion, but humanity as defined as fear, full of hate and uncertainty. It guides my actions to rise above the type of humanity that promotes hatred and dissent. It strengthens my bond with the Lord."

"As a former Christian," Brooksby counters, "I have to say it's less about hate and more about doing whatever it takes to earn the favor of God and avoiding the consequence of sin. And because God doesn't communicate directly to us, he tasks his followers to rely on pastors, priests, spiritual heads, and fear to gain compliance. That can lead to some scary misinterpretations."

The group settles into a room decorated in bright fluorescent colors to continue their discussion. Most of the guests take this opportunity to refresh their drinks before carrying on the debate.

"Most people don't even bother to read their Bibles. It's easier to listen to and obey an articulate authority figure like you, because you seem—to your followers, anyway—to have your spiritual ducks in a row," Brooksby adds. "They see you as one of God's *anointed*. If they let you down, they let him down. That's where you pick up the pieces, and the donations—from the fear, guilt, and shame that come into play."

Christina Marvel has been stewing silently to herself all the while that Zoo and Brooksby have been taking attention off her and her home tour. The two continue to go at each other. Although it hasn't gotten too overtly nasty, the potential for escalation is simmering under the surface. She intervenes to diffuse the veiled hostility.

"It's Santa," she shouts, pointing at one of the jolly characters who is wandering the house and passing out candy canes. "Hey, everyone loves Santa! Kids, adults—" she stumbles over her words—"and whatever's between kids and adults!"

The rest of the group pause as they listen to her, and then immediately return to their discussion without missing a beat. She sighs in frustration and shakes her head as she approaches Santa. The discussion continues, the interlocutors dismissing her proclamation.

"Ultimately it's comforting to be part of something big that claims to have all the answers, provides meaning, and offers immortality. But if you keep asking questions, refuse pat answers, and travel enough to see how different people and their beliefs are, well, then it all starts to unravel." Brooksby hesitates before adding, "*You* start to unravel."

"Then what role does destiny have ready for you to play?" Zoo counters.

"Don't try spouting any insightful speculation as to how you would have made a decision in a situation that doesn't allow for that kind of speculation," Brooksby replies, intensifying his argument.

Christina, without subtlety, calls downstairs at some guests from her perch at the railing of the upstairs balcony. "You coming upstairs?"

"What's up there?" one of the guests yells back.

"The view," she proudly replies.

"The view of what … down here? We can see down here from down here."

She forces a smile and waves off the guest while mumbling, out of character, under her breath, "What an asshole."

Karen, having observed this little back-and-forth, steps over to a flustered Christina and rests on the railing next to her, watching the movements of the guests who are milling around on the first floor. It's a quietly chaotic scene—thousands of brightly colored lights flickering throughout the house that is oozing with Christmas decoration and charm as the guests inhabit their territorial space, only venturing away to engage in conversation or grab another drink.

"I know your problem," Karen tells her. "You had a dream when you were a little kid that one day you'd be rich, successful, and famous. Then you woke up one day and realized it all came true, but the years have passed you by and what you once dreamt about and prayed for isn't enough to make you happy." She takes a sip from her glass. "At least, it doesn't feel the way you expected it to feel at this age."

"How do you know that's my problem?" Christina considers indignantly.

"Because that's everybody's problem."

✳ ✳ ✳

The entire touring party reunites on the first floor and slowly disseminates back into the downstairs crowd. Zoo and Brooksby are still at odds in their philosophical head knocking, which is threatening to ruin the evening's otherwise pleasant vibe, what with the intensity of their arguments spilling over into the good time being had by all.

John Marvel joins Pat and Jack, who are standing not far from where the action is about to continue. They watch the two combatants circling for another round of pontification.

"Are they gonna keep this up all night?" John wonders aloud, concerned that if it continues, then eventually it may impact the upbeat tone of the party.

"Doesn't look like either one is ready to back down," Jack comments. "They're both such smug pricks that you're forced to take the opposite side of any argument they may have, even if you agree with them, just so you don't have to take their side."

"Yeah," Pat agrees. "It's great, but who do you root for? It's like watching a Nazi beating up a Klansman."

Zoo and Brooksby have taken up positions in the glass room—a gleaming, marble-floored room surrounded on three sides by level-controlled tinted-glass windows that offer beautiful views of the home's perfectly manicured and landscaped immense backyard. The glass room is the least holiday-adorned spot in the house, thus offering a more combative environment for the two.

"You don't have to be a Christian to understand that principles like treating others the way you want to be treated or choosing to live a decent life are probably pretty good ideas," Brooksby resumes as they step onto the glossy marble. "And you don't have to be an evangelical to understand that the notion of being born again could apply just as easily to a criminal who gets a lucky break and decides to redo his life the way it should have been done the first time. At its most powerful, beautiful level, Christianity, like all religions, is about the denial of the self for the betterment of others, about setting things aside and making the right choices to make the world a place that is slightly less inhospitable and cruel."

"How can you argue with that?" Pat whispers to John. They, along with Jack, feel like ring announcers for the big match.

"There's always only ever three choices you can make in life," Brooksby continues. "Go with the status quo, rebel against it, or make it work for you. That's what you do with the amazing way you work your groups. All your followers, those *disciples*, for lack of a better word, don't realize that all you do is help them into an expensive cascading sequence of personal meltdowns."

"And you," Zoo counters, "you convince your patients they need to confront some catastrophic psychosexual backstory. They pay you to unravel their lives. How is that any different?"

Pat decides once again to add his more loosely formed take on the subject to that of the two thoroughbreds. He interrupts their discourse. "We've been listening to you two go at this all night," he says. "Just so this whole thing passes the 'reasonable' test, let's put things in perspective. It's only common sense that as far as organized religion, cults, or any other spiritual movement is concerned, for true believers they are either *all* wrong or every single one of them is right."

Chapter 16

Everybody Knows This Is Nowhere

He, as we'll continue to know him from here on, was standing in the foyer of the grand entrance when the woman approached him. *She*, as we'll still refer to her, is a petite figure sheathed in a yellow-blue silk thigh-length casual evening dress, her dark hair pulled back from her determined forehead. She said hello—and nothing more—with an engaging confidence. He was absorbed in her simple greeting and found himself compelled by her engaging charm and easy manner. And that voice. And that face. Suddenly it wasn't merely just a beautiful face. It was a privilege just to behold. Her beauty is particular, distinctive. There is a timeless style behind it that reveals obvious self-assurance and character rising from the quirks and choices of the past.

And she was just as he remembered her. Deep down inside, beyond everything else she is or might be, she was still that adorable little girl with the alluring big eyes and the magical smile.

They hadn't seen much of each other in recent years, but they kept in touch and tried to stay relatively current with the seasonal twists of stuff in their lives. It was an opportune moment of fate that brought the two of them together this evening at the Marvel affair. They regarded the prospect of spending an evening together, even among the ornately wreathed and garish party guests, as a chance to share in each other. They've been able to revisit past choices and, after examining the spell they have over each other, felt the sting of the trials and temptations suddenly in their path. They got past that earlier in the night at the cottage, and now they were only trying to be happy party guests. To everyone else at the party, they were just two revelers who found each other in the night. But they knew their secret was safe between them.

It was an interesting place for them to be, not just finding each other together and alone, but also reconnecting after many years. He wonders about how a different ending to their story years ago may have changed the shape of things. It was a long time ago in a world so very different from the one in which they exist today.

It was important to reconnect with the people in his life who had helped to shape his path. It's so easy to let the years pass by when you embark on your journey and start navigating your way around life, finding your way to new friends and new adventures. Then, all too quickly, you lose contact with so many of the influences that brought you to where you are. One day you wake up and realize that you need to find that connection again, that you want to feel that rush of promise. You want to recapture the fresh innocence that always precedes exploration and discovery. And he discovered long ago that no matter how much time he spends with her, it will never feel complete.

He also knows that before the rest of their lives are over, they have to find a way to spend more time together, as a booster shot if nothing else. They exchange a knowing smile, having already shared a brief intimate moment. And throughout this evening, they'll have the opportunity to reconsider those trials and temptations once more. But first, they have to gracefully navigate their way through the crowded rooms of festive and talkative partygoers.

They embraced when she greeted him after they bumped back into each other after their cottage encounter. They had each carefully made their way from the empty loft via separate routes and staggered the times before reconnecting downstairs. They walked together through the clutter of people, orienting themselves and dispersing to different parts of the mansion. They found what they thought was more of a secluded spot just adjacent to one of the main living rooms, but a very brief moment of privacy was quickly interrupted by two of Brooksby's more outspoken TV patients, quasi celebrity Mayra Vanity, and flight attendant–sex addict Karoleen Young. They were the true spitfires of Dr. Emerson Brooksby's therapy group and weekly television rehab reality show. Their onscreen infighting to grab the televised spotlight made for some of the show's more memorable moments.

"Hi, I'm Vanity, and this is Karoleen." Vanity, after making her introductions to the quiet couple, very candidly requests, "Tell us something about yourself." Vanity and Karoleen carefully manage to withhold their true feelings for each other.

"Well," he replies sarcastically, but with a seriously straight face, "I have a thing about expiration dates." He is quickly bored by these flighty women and is trying to figure out a way they can ditch them.

"I don't get it," Karoleen says, obviously confused by his response.

"If a food item is still in my fridge when it's past the expiration date, it's gone. Doesn't matter if it still looks good, smells good, whatever. It's gone. If it's April 3rd and the expiration date is April 2nd, it's gone."

"But isn't that the sell-by date?" Vanity asks. "Doesn't mean you have to eat it by then."

"Don't care. I live by those dates," he says with a pause. "It's a real phobia."

"That's interesting," Vanity notes, not quite sure what else to add. "My friend here has a strange quirk," she says, referring to Karoleen. "She likes to lean the back of her shoes up against a wall when she takes them off. Weird, huh?"

He looks down at Karoleen's feet and sees that she isn't wearing any shoes.

"Are they leaning against a wall somewhere in the house now?" he asks, wondering if this whole conversation is actually happening or is just some kind of psychological test to stir things up.

"I don't know." Karoleen giggles. "But I'm sure something *bad* must have happened." She laughs out loud, joined in the chorus by Vanity.

He watches the two sloshed women cackling like they've just been a part of the funniest inside joke ever. "I really can't pay any attention to stuff like that," he says as they continue chuckling. "I have a hard enough time paying attention to reality."

Karoleen stops laughing and studies him carefully. After brief reflection, she tells him, "You seem like you would be very clinical in bed—scientific and more into completing checklists than pursuing adventure and passion."

"Oh, have we slept together?" he asks lightheartedly. Her response is another immediate burst of laughter. He just watches her, searching for ways to extricate himself from these chatty drunks so he can spend some more alone time with his girl.

"Oh no, no." She laughs and then settles down. "I didn't mean it like that. It's just that I like to see if I can figure out what someone's like in bed by observing them. It's a challenge. If something clicks, then it's karma."

"I don't believe in karma as much as I believe that we all have the challenges of fate and coincidence. How we respond to fate and coincidence is entirely up to us."

"But it's true," Vanity adds. "You can tell a lot about a person's intimacy by the way they carry themselves, the way they walk, the way they act in social situations, and what they do when they're standing by themselves. Also by the way they dance."

"Yes, dancing is a big indicator," Karoleen agrees. "If a man's a great dancer, then watch out: he's going to be lighting it up in the bedroom."

Vanity and Karoleen hesitate for a second, and then both break out in uncontrollable laughter again. *He* looks over at *her* and rolls his eyes, frustrated that these women are taking up their precious time.

"Wanna hear about my worst night ever?" Karoleen offers.

"Your worst night?" *she* asks, entering the conversation. "Why would we want to hear about that?"

"Because it's interesting. Not many people are willing to approach total strangers and offer to open up their lives that much."

"That's true and probably for the best," he says. "Worst night I can remember is when my dad punished me by making me memorize everything in the dictionary from *tedious* to *unnecessary*."

Karoleen looks at him, a little bewildered, but thrusts ahead with her story. "So I guess my worst night was when I had to service a roomful of different men, their faces obscured by dark hoods, with a complete assortment of equipment, machinery, and devices. The men explored a whole series of fetishes and sick perversions, performing unspeakable acts on me. It was all done just because I felt the need to be punished—punished for my sins, punished for my pleasures, and punished because I love every second of it. After that I went home and found my roommate lying at the bottom of the stairs, dead. His head had cracked open at the bottom after he tumbled down. The paramedics came in and took the body away without even cleaning up the mess. It was awful. I had to clean up the blood and pick up little pieces of brain tissue."

They look at her with a horrified expression. She starts to laugh.

"Just kidding. There wasn't any actual brain tissue. It just kind of adds spark to the story when I say that."

"It's obvious to me that we have one thing in common," he tells the two women. "English is our second language. But unlike you, I have no first language." He pauses, takes his friend by the hand, and begs off. "We're gonna go grab one of those mini cheesecakes. Excuse us." Arm in arm, they slip away from Vanity and Karoleen and to find a space that is neatly tucked away, just out of sight of the more congested gathering spots. Within the giant confines of the mansion, this is a gem of a room.

"This place is like watching my old college textbook for Abnormal Psych come to life," he says jokingly to her as they walk into the place for solace.

Or so they think. Their privacy is only temporary.

Pat and Karen McLaren are first to turn the corner and happily enter *their* space, oblivious to the retreat, breaking the solitude, and bringing the couple abruptly back into the social arena. Walking in alongside Pat and Karen are the young couple Jack and Kristin—who now appear to be permanent fixtures of the McLarens'—Ned Symbol, the fashion designer, and Kip Balotta, the former child actor turned professional alcoholic and drug addict. Symbol and Balotta, two of Dr. Brooksby's prized patients, are used to appearing regularly on his weekly TV show. The briefly blinding glare from a handheld hefty-looking video camera being aimed around the room by a faceless, baseball-cap-wearing staffer gives away what now is obvious.

Dr. Brooksby is apparently filming some of this event to include on his television show. The producers thought it would be interesting for a show about sobriety to tape its Christmas special at an event that clearly sings the praises of decadence, with a knowing wink and obligatory nod to moderation.

As this small team of blasted party revelers invade our couple's privacy like a North Pole SWAT team, they huddle together to face the infiltration with smiles and glasses raised in the spirit. Their streak of ill-staged timing interrupting their plans continues.

"Hey, you two," Jack yells as he points at them. "Whaddya doin', trying to hide back here?" He looks around the elaborately decorated, quiet, just-off-the-main-drag room and, without bothering for a reply, asks, "Mind if we join you?" Pat and Karen just stand and wait.

The whole group steps in and settles around the room, quickly making this hidden quiet enclave their new clubhouse.

"Was I the only one, or were things getting a little exciting out there between the guests and the little Asian Lord guy?" Kip Balotta laughs, referring to some of the impassioned discussion between Zoo, McLaren, and Brooksby earlier. "And you were bein' a handful out there." He smiles, pointing at Pat. "I thought we were all gonna break out in a circle and start wagering … shouting and throwing handfuls of money down on the table."

"I don't know about that, but I love how they argue their points," Kristin says. "So he's *your* doctor, the one on the TV show?" she asks, directing her question to Kip and Symbol.

"Yep." Kip nods.

"Never watched," she mutters in Jack's ear.

"Yes he is," Symbol blurts as he grabs a bottle of vodka from one of the numerous stand-alone bar stands posted in every few rooms so guests can help themselves to a beverage at their leisure if the waiters aren't making their rounds quickly enough. He puts a long pour into his glass and waves the bottle toward the guests in the room. "Anyone need a refill?"

Jack and Kristin each eagerly ask for a shot. Symbol obliges.

"I think," Symbol says, addressing the room, "people do the wrong thing for the wrong reasons all the time. So doing the right thing for the wrong reasons is at least a step forward."

"It's not that deep," Balotta says. "It's just that life ends and death comes. But keep believing there's something waiting for us in some way if that's what gets you to sleep at night."

"There are attachments we make in life," Ned says, "even though it's all going to come to an end, that are worth so much. And we're so lucky to have been able to experience them." He walks over to a bookshelf and sees that all the books are holiday themed. "Life is short. Whether it ends here or some other time doesn't matter. What you have to hope is that in spite of how bad it might be, the end will be really worth it. So we choose to believe that something will be waiting for us."

"I'm starting to think a lot of that stuff is just bullshit, a part of the program," Kip counters. "Listening to all this makes me think that if you're reduced to quoting the mission of Emerson Brooksby, or Herman Zoo for that matter, then you're one step removed from quoting the homeless guy down the street who smells like piss and yells at clouds."

"Don't mind him," Ned says to the couple, referring to Kip. "It's not just that he's an egocentric curmudgeon. It's that he gets such a kick out of *being* an egocentric curmudgeon. He sort of makes being an asshole an art."

"It's like a blender full of psycho crap set to puree and then poured straight into a toilet," Kip adds.

"Sounds like they can argue both sides of an argument and have you believe both," Pat says, entering the discussion, "only to find out they don't really believe in either."

"Either that," Karen adds, "or it's just that we're all getting older and trying to make sense of it all. I know I'm confused most of the time."

"Yes." Pat laughs. "She's definitely that."

"Welcome to the club," Kip says with an enthusiastic clip. "Getting old. It sucks and there are no benefits. All that wisdom-with-age crap is nonsense. You begin to forget everything you learned that led to all that wisdom in the first place, and then you just sound dumb. You begin saying things like 'the good old days' or 'back in the day' far too often— two despised phrases, by the way. Then you start to think about the course of your life and how you're now on the back nine, probably closer to the fourteenth hole or so, maybe in a trap or lost in the trees. And while you're wandering around looking for your ball, you realize how really insignificant everything is. But then, just as you're about to get all depressed and drive your golf cart into the lake in front of the green, you start to get little flashbacks of the good times and the laughter and all those memorable moments in time that made the journey you've been on so far all the more vital to creating your chapter in this silly book of life. So you say "Fuck it" and drive the cart around that lake, strut up to the green, and sink the putt. Nope, you won't shoot your age, but you're still on the course, and that's what counts."

"Sounds like someone is following the program," Vanity blurts out as she and Karoleen enter the room like a couple of lit Roman candles.

"When does the key party start?" Karoleen laughs excitedly.

"Key party?" Jack asks, not familiar with the term.

"Oh, you know." Karoleen giddily explains, "Everyone throws their car keys into a bowl and starts pulling them out randomly. You go home with the key's owner."

"Really?" Jack says, intrigued. He looks over at Kristin. "That sounds pretty intriguing."

Kristin keeps the frozen smile as a cover for her face as she slowly sips a glass of wine while shaking her head no. "It really doesn't."

"I'm in." Kip adamantly voices his unsolicited vote. "But is it just limited to you people in this room?"

"We know what you look like." Vanity strolls across the room, continuing off camera the kind of sniping she does onscreen with her reality TV faux co-celeb. "Who are you afraid doesn't want to sleep with you? Is it straight women or gay men—or are you just afraid of anyone who dismisses fatties?"

Pat leans over and whispers to his wife with a chuckle, "Does this mean we're gonna have sex tonight … with somebody?"

"Look, there's no aphrodisiac in the world that has magical panty-eliminating properties when it comes to your tired ass," Kip barks back at Vanity. "If you can't deal with foreplay, then don't bother playing."

"Not for nothing," Vanity continues. "But no woman I personally know over the age of eighteen has a problem with heavy-set or even *fat* men, so don't worry. There is sexiness to hedonism. A big uncontrollable appetite with food can sometimes mean the same goes for sex and laughter and all other things. You know, 'food' for thought."

"Everything in this society is a glib advertisement for the immaculate sexiness that comes from being famous, wealthy, and accomplished," Symbol adds. "You two," he says, pointing toward Vanity and Karoleen with a testy finger, "you personify everything that's wrong with the world today. Instant *everything*. I think there is something so incredibly cool about being wise and hardworking and accomplished while not necessarily being loaded or exquisitely dressed."

"Hey, Virginia Slim," Vanity yells across to Ned, "mind grabbing me another drink while you're spouting off over there?"

"Screw you, sugar," he taunts back. "Stroll that unmade ass of yours over here and get one yourself. You just missed the free pours."

She gets up and makes a big production as she sashays across the room. "By the way, *Ned*," she says, exaggerating his name with disgust, "key parties have been around *forever*. It's not some big new thing that the latest and lamest generation thought up."

"That reminds me of a funny story." Pat nudges Karen, deciding to really check out the pulse of the room—cameras be damned. "I remember one morning years ago. This guy was in the basement of this clearly strange house. He woke up blurry-eyed and with a dry mouth." Pat studies the room, having easily locked in the attention of this dysfunctional group. "He was lying on his side, with the right side of his face to the ground." He animates some of the motions and poses as he describes the scene.

He looks at her and frowns. *She* locks arms with him and smiles. Their search for quiet is put on hold for just a little while longer. They look back over at Pat, listening to his "funny story."

"As he looked up through the sketchy haze," Pat continues, "he could see three very large men standing over him. He felt a tingle and pop as something hit his mouth. He forced open his left eye and was able to make out a fourth man putting golf balls near his opened mouth."

Karoleen takes a seat next to the spot where Vanity is standing. Jack and Kristin draw in to be closer to their party pals.

"'Do you know why Promised Lands are a major theme in most postapocalyptic stories?' the large putter guy asks him over and over as he putts another golf ball near the mouth of this guy. He lies there numb, but not paralyzed, although that's what it felt like. Still, he can't make himself move." The room is fixated. "The large putter guy keeps talking. 'If you're running away from zombies, there are always rumors about a cure.' Then he putts another, pops it right off the guy's teeth. 'If you're stumbling through a wasteland, there's always tales of a safe zone.' Then he putts again." Pat takes a prolonged drink from his glass.

"You see what I'm really getting at," Pat says. As he glances over at Karen, he notices a smirk on her face. "The big guy keeps talking to the poor bastard who is stuck on the ground, making random statements and asking unanswerable questions. If Big Brother is breathing down your throat, people whisper about an underground movement to escape. What do they all have in common? Cures? Safe zones? Escape plans?" He looks around at the waiting faces. "It's the destiny of dystopian stories. The morals won't work without them, because without them there isn't any hope. And hope is really the only thing we have that wakes us in the morning. So with hope comes reason. Then the golfer putts another ball at the other guy's mouth. After the ball hits the bridge of his nose, the guy on the floor tells the big guy that none of this makes any sense." Pat starts mocking his own story. The guests are locked in. "He tells him he doesn't know what he's talking about."

"Neither do I," *he* whispers in her ear. "I have no idea where this is going." *She* shrugs.

"When he died, all I wanted were his patio chairs," Pat says as he steps over to one of the chairs in the room, presently occupied by Karoleen. He looks toward the camera, which is following his slow snaking around the room, and stops to pat the back of the chair. "Just four little chairs. Nice, ornately designed with black wrought iron, shaped in the form of wild animals found in the South African safaris he used to love. They had soft handwoven cushions." He pauses.

"Why did I want the chairs? Just think of everyone who sat in those chairs throughout the years. I remember them all. The friends, relatives, loved ones. … If anything is haunted, it's those chairs." Pat stops walking as he returns to Karen's side. After an extended pause, he adds, "He was tragically disemboweled during one of his off-road *trips*."

"Are we still talking about the guy on the floor getting hit with the golf balls?" Jack asks Kristin, confused. The others have the same question.

"Yech, what a horrible way to die," Karoleen says, carefully following Pat's story.

Pat shakes his head. "No, strangely, it wasn't. That didn't kill him," he tells Karoleen and the group. "His initial injuries weren't fatal. Sure, most of his intestines were exposed and a lot of the internal organs were jumbled together, but that could have gotten sorted out at the hospital. On the way there, the ambulance ran off the road and swerved into a canal. It was submerged under water with everyone inside."

"Oh God." Vanity sighs. "Drowning has *got* to be the worst. So helpless, locked in, not being able to get out."

"No way," Kip says. "Burning to death … much worse than drowning." He looks around the room as if he feels an obligation to persuade the others. "It's a fact. Look it up."

"He didn't drown," Pat tells the group. "He was a tough son of a bitch. Hell, he survived a roomful of Sicilian wiseguys putting golf balls into his mouth." Some of the heads in the room nod, hearing that it *is* the same story of the guy on the floor. "No, he managed to work his way off the gurney while he was strapped into the back of the ambulance—as the water was filling the vehicle. Just as he made his way out through a window that he was able to break by using an oxygen tank, an alligator slashed into his neck and upper torso." He pauses for effect, trying hard to keep his smiling on the inside while maintaining a straight face for the guests. "Gruesome." He slaps his hands together loudly. "Ripped him apart."

The party guests who are standing in the room and have been circling to hear his story remain strangely quiet for what had up to now been a fairly loud group. They look exactly like what a group would look like after hearing such a peculiar tale.

"How is that funny?" Symbol finally asks what everyone else is thinking.

"This reminds me that I can be around people for only a few hours before I go nuts," Kip says. "No wonder I'm in therapy."

"And that is *exactly* my point," Pat shouts, pointing toward Kip. "It's the ridiculous nature of our conversations, telling stories to strangers, opening up our lives, playing hipster for the cameras. I've found that the people who deal almost exclusively in 'please' and 'thank you' are the ones destined to get you in *really* hot water. Manners are *so* fucking overrated.

"You know what?" Pat continues ranting. "I don't even know why I'm arguing, given the contempt I have for this nest of futility." He looks around. "And for this party. I don't care what you think while I'm talking, so why should I give a flying fuck about if you care? Laugh at whatever, feel offended at whatever. I don't care. I don't really know any of you, you don't know me, and we probably wouldn't get along anyway, so why bother circle jerking? We're just making small talk to pass the time. No one ever says, 'Huh, I've changed my mind on that issue because of the salient comment you just made.' If anyone ever quoted me as some sort of sage on any subject beyond my cat, I'd build an underground shelter and wait for a raging storm to carry the world away." He pauses. "Now I don't necessarily think that's all that healthy an outlook, frankly, but anything else would be disingenuous so I have to roll with it."

"I call bullshit. *No one* understands their cat," Vanity says.

"Maybe we should just stop being offended on behalf of other people," Pat says, ignoring her comment. "There's a tension between two ways of living—confrontational honesty and constant fabrication. You can be searching for the lost ark, the Holy Grail, a unicorn, or any number of other MacGuffins. The real quest is finding the true way to live a hard life—or any life, really—because all life is hard."

"So this is really about nothing," Jack says, looking at the heads nodding in unison around the room.

"It's never the arrow; it's always the archer," Pat says as he sees Kristin's face looking right at him.

"What the hell does that mean?" Jack asks, standing next to Kristin as Pat walks over to her and chuckles. "Your face has gone from aloof and vacant to detached and expressionless, and I can't *even* tell the difference."

Karen walks slowly over to her husband and puts a hand on his back. "I think that's enough for now," she says softly to him. "I think you've made your point. Not to mention all the potential future customers you probably scared away."

"Yeah," Pat agrees, stepping back. "You're probably right."

The convergence of the various party guests into this gilded vault of a party house brings some honest truths to the surface. It's hard for many kinds of people to meet and make new friends. When given the choice of hanging out with familiar faces or hanging out with a new group of people who could turn out to be great, most people choose the familiar. When you meet up with new people, there is so much you don't know. You don't have common memories of the past; you don't know what limits there are in their sense of humor or political convictions; you don't have inside jokes with each other that you reference. This is exactly why people want more of the same, nurturing the routine in their lives and never daring to try to expand beyond their limited and restrictive horizons. It's why they groan and cringe at having to step out of their comfort zone.

As the guests start milling about again, the drinks start flowing and the festive combination of Christmas music and twinkling lights brings the room back to life. It isn't long before a commotion coming from the main entrance area of the house causes a stir. The hostess is making another grand entrance for another wave of arriving guests.

Christina Marvel slowly descends one side of the curving double staircase in a manner reminiscent of a grand movie star, à la Elizabeth Taylor or Vivien Leigh, carefully taking each step with the hospitable grace befitting a Southern hostess. She is dressed head to toe in black for this portion of the evening—another outfit change—wearing a sharp, tightly curved dress fitted to her trim figure, with a string of pearls and shiny diamond accessories to complete her presentation. A red and green candy cane brooch encircled by a ring of glittering diamonds is pinned to her dress. This is certainly the most alluring of her wardrobe changes this evening.

When she reaches the foyer, she greets her guests again, kissing them on both cheeks, and says hello to the others outside kissing range. Everyone at the affair seems to be either some sort of a power player or a remora clinging on to suck the remains of the real deal makers. Her guest list is truly indicative of the frantically diverse nature of her prurient curiosities. She turns to a man she calls Ben. Whatever "Ben"'s official job title is around the house, apparently his actual name is *Bob*, and he corrects Christina repeatedly. She just smiles and obliviously continues her procession.

Herman Zoo follows her down the stairs, just a step behind. Considering he is the guest of honor, he probably had a private tour. It has already been a long night for Zoo. He is now just calming down after the hostile arguments from earlier, where he felt like he was promoting a religious special featuring a defense of his latest call to worship.

"It was fabulous," Christina says as she parades Zoo around. For Christina Marvel, everything about Zoo is fabulous or amazing or incredible or cute or epic or visionary. In reality, she is nightmarishly cultist in her devotion; her interest in everything even remotely associated with Zoo borders on possession.

Much of the room begins to empty, the people moving toward her audacious entrance, following the rush to see Marvel's and Zoo's reemergence while grabbing more food and drink. *He* turns as *she* stares out the window toward the back patio. A very thin, beautiful layer of freshly white snow is on the ground. It glistens in the sparkle of the Christmas lights glowing outside. There are several guests outside mingling and enjoying the wintry air.

"Looks like our crowd is dispersing," *he* says to her. "I hope it was something we said," he jokes.

"Is there anywhere we can go, I wonder?" *she* asks. "We should never have left the cottage. I don't suppose we can have any privacy at a spectacle like this."

"We already have," he tells her with a knowing smile. "But I can help a little, if you're interested."

"How?

He opens his coat jacket pocket a bit and pulls up a joint to show her. She spots it briefly. He winks at her, and she smiles.

"Hit me," she purrs.

They pull their coats tight around their bodies and step outside, slowly circulating around the handful of guests, navigating between them until they exit through the back patio gate. They find some bench chairs, where they take cold seats and share a couple of puffs of the fine weed. They sit together for a few minutes, enjoying the pleasantly chilly evening weather, sipping their drinks, and watching the star-draped skies.

They look at a thick cluster of woods that begins a few dozen feet past the grass lawn in front of them. There is a small rock pathway stretching out through the woods like a quiet nature trail.

"I think we should get high and go explore the woods," he says.

"We are high."

"Right," he says. After a pause, he says, "Then why are we still here? Let's go."

They get up and stroll hand in hand to the walking trail's entrance.

They explore the winding path, sometimes talking, other times just enjoying the cold evening breeze in silence. Each is thinking about the other and the next step along their way. They talk about their kids, marriages, careers, and life in general from all the years that have passed—anything to extend this short window of time together. They are bouncing from topic to topic in order to keep from losing each other.

"I guess everything with the family is okay," he says, continuing a long exchange they're having from the "life in general" category. "We're about as normal as there is these days. Time flies by. I can't remember half of what has happened over the years. Maybe that's a good thing. But the world is changing so fast that I'm finally trying to appreciate where I am in life. The world is not an easy place. Kids have to be able to adapt and change at a faster pace than we did or even our kids did. Our children will be the last bridge from any firsthand knowledge of our generation's history to the future. And even though they're grown up and finding their own ways, they are still so far behind where we were at the same age. Now for me, at this point, I'm just trying to keep the car from driving off the road."

She chuckles at his "off the road" comment. He loves to hear her laugh. He has heard it so infrequently that when she allows herself the joy, he takes it in like Communion. He watches her face as her laugh slowly turns into a pleasantly contented smile. She holds his arm tighter.

Although it is dark, their path illuminated only by the sharp moonlight and the abundance of glittering Christmas lights hanging in the trees that surround the backyard, he can clearly see her face. It is the color of a Savannah sunrise, her teeth as white and opaque as cotton skies. Her face is a masterpiece. Even her makeup is applied just right: perfectly blended foundation, precision-defined eyeliner, expertly contoured cheekbones with just a fringe added to highlight her absorbing eyes. Her hands are velvety and inviting, providing a charming contrast whenever she leans her chin on them. Her dark hair proudly highlights the shape of her face, swirling around it with a sense of style and madness that makes her all the more alluring.

She puts the perfect amount of air in her words, giving them a lightness that conflates optimism, amusement, and resignation. She's never seemed lovelier, more instinctive, or more present, even though he gets the sense that there used to be a lot more joy in her heart. That's one of the many things she has taught him to value more as he's aged: the daily laughter one finds and shares in a place that feels like home.

"Everybody I knew told me I just *had* to have kids. I heard that from more people than any other thing I can remember," she says as they reach a small creek that is slightly shielded by a cover of thin ice. "After I finally got around to having a few children of my own, I decided to stop being friends with all of those people." She blushes with a laugh.

"I think of raising kids the way engineers view the latest advancements in the AI models they create," he adds. "Each generation of people should, theoretically, be more advanced and *better* than the previous generation— the same way artificial intelligence is supposed to progress. They should be smarter, more adaptable, and more curious, learning from the mistakes of the past. As parents, I think it's part of our job to make sure that transition happens from generation to generation, the same way scientists and engineers try to evolve each new version of an AI being. The problem is that science and technology can keep evolving. I'm pretty sure *this* latest generation has reached the end of the evolutionary road." They share another laugh. "And don't let anyone who has more than one kid tell you they don't have a favorite. We all do."

"I guess that's human nature," she says. "I can't really say I love one of my children more than the other. The love is always there, and it's part of our humanity. But I guess there's some sense of favoritism, whether you think you're hiding it well or not."

"Humanity is a mess of certain confusion, accidental insight, and unknowable resolutions," he says. "It's easy to lose touch with real life when you don't have a sense of propriety and boundaries."

They take a seat on a bench near the place where the creek widens. The flow of water here is uninterrupted by small floating panes of ice, and the bubbling sound coming from the creek is a comforting and fitting atmosphere for their private moments.

Sitting quietly on the bench, he folds his arms together and leans into her. She puts her arm around him and squeezes.

"What's wrong?" she asks softly.

"I'm a guy who thinks way too much about *everything*."

"You need to be careful about the stories you tell yourself," she tells him in a soothing tone.

He turns his head to look her in the eyes. "We talk about the past. We tolerate the distance. We damn our timing. What happens when, after we've talked everything out and faced all the obstacles, we find out there's nothing left for us? I wonder that if after all of the time and energy we've

put into *finding* each other, we'll look around and realize we're nowhere."
He pauses. "If things were different between us, I might've walked away
from the whole thing and never looked back. But I *knew* this story wasn't
going to end that way." He gently brushes back her hair. "Maybe I'm just
being naïve."

"You're confusing optimism with naïveté," she tells him. "I work hard
to fuel my imagination at home, but we are quick to roll over and hide from
our realities. That's not what I expected from life. It's too convenient for
us to just ignore the harshness of having to deal with the world as it is. So
anytime someone comes along with that spark, the lightness of hope and
promise, we find it easy to dismiss it as excessive misplaced enthusiasm."

He sits back up and watches her carefully as she continues. "It's like we
look at a positive person and find ways to deconstruct their happiness. It's
a brutal outlook. I think our most valuable traits are the ones that drive
us forward with hope, desire, and a plan to improve our little space in the
world." She leans in, looking at him with a smile that means to reassure,
and speaks softly. This only raises his concerns. "I think that together we've
been able to improve those little spaces. We can only act on what we can
control—and there's so much out of our hands."

"I'm happy that I'm breathing the same air at the same time you are;
it makes the world feel like a better place," he says. "It's the same feeling
knowing that we may be looking at the same moon or watching the
sunset at the same time. It sounds like some old-fashioned romantic kind
of notion, but that only holds the place for so long before it's not enough
anymore. Those little spaces start drifting beyond our reach. That's what
scares me." He pauses. "I want to discover all those little secret places
with you."

She lowers her head, the look of joy replaced by a certain frightening
awareness that those discoveries will never happen. He sees the look and
smiles to reassure her, knowing his words are doing nothing to make her
feel any better. "When we're not together, every minute that ticks by is
another minute I'm farther away from you. You know, all we'll ever be able
to share are these moments. We lost our life together."

He thought that maybe, just maybe, this could turn out to be the
greatest love story ever told. He remembers that first night he found
her again. It was like a dream. Hearing the sound of her voice, carefully

listening as she spoke, he couldn't believe he was actually talking to her again after the years that had passed. He thought about when he called her for the first time after all those years, his heart pounding as the phone rang. He thought then that no matter what happened during the call, his life might be very different – the original formula from which all love stories are written.

He wonders if she has the same struggles and demons he battles. In the middle of the night, when it's darker than usual outside, maybe behind the backdrop of a thunderstorm and the constant sound of steady, soothing rain falling, he wonders who she is thinking about. Is she happy? If not, why can't she be happy? He knows the source of some of his own discontent. He wants his head full of memories of a life spent with her, but it's not. How terrible is wisdom when it brings no profit to the wise? He does a good job of getting to her doorstep. He just has a problem with coming inside. That doesn't diminish the fact that his sense of purpose was reawakened because of her.

That sudden display of wisdom and sadness finds a place where they are oddly at peace with each other—including his besieged self. He reminds himself to take a good look, thinking, *No matter how cleverly you sneak up on a mirror, your reflection always looks you straight in the eye. That's the person you have to deal with.* And he wants to be more than a person who's never at the center of anything more culturally important than a family portrait. He'd like to think he brings meaning to living and doesn't spend every day in the same boring rut and finish off every night with a scotch, falling asleep in his lounger in front of the blurry buzz of the television. He thinks about not being the safe choice for her. He is eager and adoring, but he is *that guy.* He couldn't be more than an afterthought, someone who could never live up to what she imagined she needed in her life. So she married a man because he was considerate, held a decent and respectable job, knew how to balance the checkbook, and already had a plan for a settled future. Sometimes he's either dull or cocky or both. But he is solid and stable and serious, all the stuff she said she wanted, when really what she *needed* had been there all along. She needed fun, she needed fulfillment and bliss, and she needed to dance with the exuberance of life as her loving partner. What she *needs* is him, but she has a life and there is no place for him in it. He may have swept her off her feet, but now she's back on dry land. He is everywhere but where she is. Some guys get the world; other guys get the girl.

He has a sense of guilt for feeling this way; after all, their lives are settled. He knows it is wrong to even consider that anything other than what they have together now has a place in the big picture. Sometimes he thinks she resents him because he's the only one who really knows just how vulnerable she is. It's a strange unconscious despondence over all the accumulated wasted time in life. Where is the line between vitality and rust? But this is where his mind goes: to how priceless and precious time is, considering the unknowable zones of human consciousness and confirming that what goes on as we live is actually as impossible as truly knowing what happens after we die. What we think we know will never surpass our expectations.

"Okay," she begins after a few minutes of quiet, having gotten lost in the landscape. "Usually it seems like we are always hitting the right notes, but suddenly something feels wrong. You need to tell me a story."

"What kind of a story?"

"I don't care," she says, flashing her embracing smile once again. "Tell me something fun."

"We would be so deliciously dangerous for each other," he tells her wickedly.

"No, no," she teases with a giggle and slap on his arm. "Not that. That could be bad."

"I know."

He sits quietly as she speaks, although he is recoiling inside, driven by that sweet spot of fear and possibility—the wild back pages of the human mind that are never fully realized.

"So I guess we're too old to fall in love again," is all he can muster.

"Love's not the question," she says. "That's not why this isn't easy." She pauses. "I guess I don't know the answer."

"I can still pray." He laughs.

"You don't need to pray," she says, almost whispering. "We are here … together. That's as much as we can ever pray for."

"No," he replies. "I don't believe that's all. My prayers are always answered because I dare to pray. I *never* thought you'd hear me say this, but I've seen it."

She looks at him cautiously, waiting for the punch line, knowing his sense of humor and sarcasm. "Really?" She sits up, carefully examining his words and expressions. "Example?"

"Okay," he begins. "A couple of nights ago this giant flying insect flew into the house when I was outside smoking. I had left the patio door open. I mean *huge*. It looked like some kind of snake-faced rodent-like flying moth with a circular mouth like one of those Australian lizards, and it flew around like a hybrid hummingbird monster. Anyway, I tried to kill it, but it kept flying around until it finally fluttered into a room somewhere and I couldn't find it. My wife slept through the whole thing. Like I said, it was really late, so I went to bed and forgot about it.

"A couple of days later she and I got into a fight, one of those where it looks like it is going to be very quiet or worse for a long time. I went to bed after the fight and tried to just crash. I felt terrible about us fighting and prayed that we'd be able to work things out and stop being mad at each other. About an hour later she came into the bedroom very calmly, but she was clearly very shook up about something. She looked over at me lying in bed and said, 'I think you're going to have to get up now.' She was dead serious. I looked up and asked what was wrong. She said she thought she had just been attacked by a giant bat in the other bedroom. I got up and rushed over to the bedroom, looked in, and sure enough, it was that little monster moth flying like a banshee around the room. I grabbed a broom, closed myself in so I could be alone with the beast—with my terrified wife outside the door listening—and proceeded to have a full-blown heavyweight fight with this thing. It was the hardest thing I've ever battled. Just wouldn't die. I must have smacked that bug into the walls and on the floor half a dozen times. When I finally got the money shot on it, its body actually separated from its head and back wings. The wings were still fluttering. It was trying to fly—half a freaking body cut off and it's still battling. I have a lot of respect for that moth."

"And then?"

"So she comes in after the death match and can't believe the size and gumption of this thing that is still flopping around on the floor. She drowns it in Raid. After we cleaned it up, we had great makeup sex. Imagine that, at our age." He laughs. "So that's an answered prayer. I asked that we'd work things out; I didn't know how it would happen, but

I prayed that we'd just get over the anger and opposition. Little did I know that when that moth flew into the house a few days before, it would be the answer to my prayer. And I challenge anyone who would say different, like it was a coincidence or that one thing has nothing to do with the other. I say, what are answered prayers supposed to look like? It looks exactly like what happened to me. Sure, it sounds strange, but it happened, so I like to think that's what it was. If there's something you want, something you pray for, and then that thing happens, then whatever led to that point must have been a part of the equation." He pauses. "In this case, it was an answered prayer in the form of an undeterred sphinx moth."

"All shapes and sizes," she says. "I can't say I've ever had that happen to me."

"You never have your prayers answered?"

"I don't know. I suppose. Nothing ever that obvious."

"I don't think *that* was obvious."

She shakes her head before making a bleak comment.

"Whether or not prayers are answered isn't what's important. What's a prayer good for anyway? You ask God for something you want. Maybe it happens, maybe it doesn't. But I do know that what's going to happen will happen. We can help along the way, but there's an awful lot we can't change." She looks over at him; he is carefully capturing each word as she speaks it. "If it was easy, it would have happened by now."

He studies her, carefully taking in every subtle nuance in the way she purses her lips, tosses her hair, and allows for a brief forced smile.

"You've never known what hurt really feels like because you don't know what it's like not to be wanted by someone you love." He brushes her hair back from her forehead. She looks dispirited, like some of her energy has evaporated.

I'm finished, he thinks to himself. He broke the first rule of having her. He fell in love with her all over again. It's never left. It's a part of his history. And now he can feel his overreaching solace. *What is history? What is a legacy? All we have is today.*

She remains uncomfortably silent. She looks at him, unable to think of anything to say.

He sighs and takes a deep breath. "I can't keep on missing you. It's taking too much out of me."

"Do you know what I miss?" she says, now with a soothing tone that reminds him of her playful voice. "I miss that slightly woozy feeling we'd get after sundown on a hot summer night when we got too much sun that day. Your skin was red and hot and maybe just starting to peel, but in a certain way it felt wonderful with the aroma of suntan lotion and sunburn spray." She fades her eyes away from his and looks to the night sky. "I loved those days."

"I remember holding your hand in the car while we were driving home and singing together to the radio."

He turns, leans back, and joins her in stargazing. "You know," he says, "if a bomb hits tonight and this house and everything around it comes crumbling down, after the dust settles you and I will still be here." He pauses and then looks back at her. She meets his eyes as he arrives at her doorstep once again.

"So let's work this out."

Until just a few nights earlier, he didn't even know that he'd be at this party. A last-minute invitation arrived at his graphic arts studio in Buckhead requesting his presence at the event. It was a welcome surprise. He knew the Marvels from his art gallery, as Christina was a frequent patron. He also knew they each had a friend in common. That opened the likelihood that if he attended the party, then she and her husband would be there. This was a drawing card far too compelling to pass up.

There are those who do not believe that a single soul born and nurtured can split into twin spirits and shoot like falling stars to earth, where, over oceans and across continents, their magnetic forces will finally unite them back into one. For a time this couple were convinced that there was no other life beneath the sky but theirs and that what they had would never go away.

But, of course, it did.

And after pushing away all of the romantic notions of forever, they knew there was no way they would have made it. But he always thought of all the fun they would have had finding out they weren't right for each other.

Earlier in the evening, he had found her standing and idly talking to another party guest, looking bored out of her mind as she swirled her finger around in the ice of her drink. Her eyes were wandering around the room, desperate to find anyone or anything that could save her from the interminable conversation. Before he could sneak up, excited for her to break out in a burst of surprise from his covert greeting, she spotted him over at the side of the room, foiling his plot. Her face immediately transformed from tired and weary into an effervescent spark of recognition and delight.

Approaching her now in a much more conventional way than the sneak attack, he put his arms around her, giving her an extended warm hug. She reciprocated, and added a kiss to his cheek. They immediately began talking and quickly made their way from the main house to the chilly outdoors, away from the enormous estate, away from the crowds. They exchanged stories they'd neglected to share before, and rapidly bonded into the impossibly difficult transition of finding each other again, lost in the feelings of the past. All pretense of vanity was stripped away, leaving them with familiarity, vulnerability, and passion.

He was overjoyed at finding her, and she was just as thrilled to be found. She had come to the party alone, her husband either not able to attend or not interested in attending. They spent a good while walking and discovering new things about each other while each knew in the back of their minds that the undeniable chemistry between them was at a pressure-filled bursting point.

Slowly, eventually, they found their way to one of the smartly decorated cottages, where they entered into their own world—if only for a few glorious moments together, away from the glare and the gossip and the gaudiness. They'd earned this.

She couldn't remember the last time someone's fingertips brought to the surface a level of apprehensive excitement she so rarely shared freely and intimately with another. His gentle caresses danced on the light of her skin, making it crackle and spark with rapturous pleasure and delight.

She reached around to the back of his head and took his hair in her grasp, guiding his mouth toward hers. With a swift, intense pull, she passionately kissed him, sliding her lithe body closer to his. She fully embraced him. He complied by enveloping her in his arms, moving with her in a mutual dance. Their bodies left nothing to imagination as they fully realized the subtleties and contours of each other. The tension continued to build as their passion threatened to swallow them together in emotional explosive bursts of pleasure and release.

He lay her body back on the bed, surveying the splendor that glowed from her natural beauty. Her body, tight and yielding, jerked with ticklishness as he teasingly kissed her softly and tenderly. Each encounter quickened his breath as he touched his lips to her skin. Her reactions ranged from silly, nervous giggles to voluptuous groans of satisfaction. She closed her eyes and turned her head to the side, burying it in the soft comfort of the pillow as she allowed him to explore and engage her in playful bliss. He found himself increasingly aroused as he watched the effect his actions were having on her.

"I want you to roll over on top of me," he whispered in her ear.

He carefully, almost surgically, worked his tongue and lips up from her thighs, stomach, sides, and chest, back to her neck and to the top of her shoulders. He took his time before reaching her mouth, where she waited agonizingly for his kiss. He teased her mouth with his lips before falling into another long, glorious exchange. The dark sky just outside their room covered them in a blanket of cozy security as they found each other's needs and longings waiting to be fulfilled. Their yearning screamed silently, breaking the quiet of the night and ushering them to a new realm of discovery they never dared question.

Alone now, as the quiet corners of their worlds finally united together, slowly they made love to the songs of their desire.

"I can't imagine how great my marriage proposal would have been," he said while nudging her, laughing with a wink.

She stopped to hold his face, to look into his eyes. "What we have between us, what we've learned," she said, determined and defiant, "it can't mean *nothing*."

He nodded and lowered his head. "We can never be what we could have been."

Chapter 17

The Least of These

While the poor people are sleeping with the shades on the lights, while the poor people are sleeping all the stars come out at night.

Leo and Maggie quickly formed an alliance based on like-minded thinking, an indifferent concern for their futures, moral apathy, and mutual misery. They shared a rage against the entitled and arrogant. After a few hours of talking with Maggie, since they first met outside earlier in the evening, Leo begins to rethink his mission. Not too long ago he was planning to escalate the scale of the attack; now he's thinking about aborting the plan altogether. He still plans on going forward, but he thinks it is certainly nice to have a partner now to share the glory with. He doesn't mind that he'll now be a cobilled act.

Together they slide quietly into the back of the large reception hall. It's hard to go unnoticed when you're dressed like Santa Claus and one of his elves, but they are where they need to be for the next move in their coordinated attack—a front-row seat to the lowlife oafs who are wandering around stupefied in their own oozing, pompous arrogance—waiting to unleash their redemption upon the haughty, mind-numbing guests. They watch as their victims provide no reason for mercy, engaged in their self-absorbed conversations.

Leo and Maggie have already laid out the plan and completed the coordinated arrangements with another newly found associate at the gala, a mysterious man with the plan behind a forthcoming special holiday surprise. This third man was brought on to work the party directly by the host, John Marvel himself. Apparently Marvel had developed a relationship with this thug and had him come on board tonight to act as muscle if he needed him to. Marvel wasn't specific, but he said he wanted the man there to keep an eye on things and to do whatever was necessary, if requested. The third man knew that some things might go down and the host might need some juice. Basically, he is the hired gun, the tough guy.

They mingle with guests in the main reception hall, enjoying the festive atmosphere while embedding themselves into the crowd. The glad-handing and boring chitchat lingers on as they wait for the appropriate moment to unleash their Christmas spirit. Leo and Maggie walk together around the room, passing on holiday greetings while sampling, without context, the various conversations happening between different people and groups. They are the proverbial flies on the wall, picking up on the crumbs around the room.

They are immediately drawn to the main event, the area of space occupied by the still-arguing Herman Zoo and Emerson Brooksby, along with their backers, who don't seem to be able to leave their differences alone long enough to enjoy the festivities.

"Jesus once said his good works were for the least of these," Zoo says as he waves his hands toward the people in the room, hinting that these aren't the chosen ones. "He wasn't looking to bestow the glory of God's kingdom on the people who don't recognize or appreciate it. The dangling carrot of everlasting life is the lure, and the temptation, for people who *need* it the most. We might get the world we deserve, but we can always keep dreaming. It's better than just giving up."

"These people don't want your help, Herman," Brooksby counters. "The people you appeal to are happy being losers since it absolves them of all responsibility in life. You can't save anyone. Some of us can't even save ourselves."

"I was called on to help explain to those who are hungry for knowledge what we feel and why we feel it. I try to answer why they have the rage that burns inside them."

"Wrong answer," Brooksby blurts out. "But that's a good way to trivialize it and the people who might benefit from it. What you need to preach is truth and the maturity of adulthood unburdened by the primal impulses that seem to control the majority of the adult population. People need the truth to live well. They need the truth as a map to guide them. You don't provide any truths; you look at the people whom you say are hungry for answers and give them your prepackaged spiel for a fee. Then you tell them you have the answers they're looking for. That's not truth. That's larceny." Brooksby, beyond exasperated, is ready to throw in the towel. He's growing tired of the same argument, and he's smart enough to know that nothing can be gained or changed by their words. "The important thing is to do what you love and then live with the rewards of that, whatever they may be."

Zoo hesitates, clearly frustrated and exhausted by the extended series of battles he's been having with his adversaries all evening. Throughout the duration of being repeatedly attacked, he remains as cool and composed as he was when he entered the house. Zoo doesn't get flustered; he's been through too much hatred pursuing his craft and won't let another heretic crack his poise.

"Just keep searching," he tells Brooksby. "Eventually you may find that our Lord has your answers. You just need to believe in something."

"I believe in God," Brooksby snaps back. "I know because he once answered my prayer. Thirty or so years ago my wife was in the hospital after a car accident. We all thought we were going to lose her. On the most difficult night when she seemed to be slipping away, I prayed to God to keep her safe and not take her. I prayed that if he saved her, I'd never ask for anything again. Well, she pulled through. After that, nothing good *ever* happened to me again. My business at the time failed. My youngest kid became a dropout and took up with a cult that ended her life. Eventually, my wife—yes, *that wife*—left me. But she lived. God saved her. He answered my prayer. And it taught me something very important—and I learned from it. I realized that there is a God and he does answer prayers. Just make sure it's really what you want, because when you make that deal with him, he holds you to it. You only get one shot. Don't blow it."

Brooksby's impression of Zoo—like Jim Bakker, Pat Robertson, Jimmy Swaggart, the Crouches, and even Billy Graham before him, all of the salvation-breathing, fire-and-brimstone-spouting brethren—was that he was a clown masturbating to the sound of his own voice. *These people are getting drunk off sanctimony and the wealth that comes with it,* Brooksby thinks. *It's all just stupid people in suits preaching at stupid people who live and breathe the fertilizer the former spout.*

Brooksby is predisposed to hound brain-shrinking parasites like Zoo and his ilk. He can't stand the deception and the financial basket of ruin they leave behind after blinding their faithful. Brooksby carries himself with a confidence, and an arrogance, that provides him with the nerve to unconditionally attack on all fronts. Losing his daughter fired his passion but left him emotionally incapable of figuring out who was really to blame and how to confront the pain. Every interaction with Zoo fueled many conflicted feelings within him.

In terms of classic Old World cool—in which a person is so talented, charismatic, and dysfunctional that no amount of PR could ever sand off his or her rough human edges—Brooksby stands alone among those who share his profession. His belligerence and outrage is so absolute that it almost seems to stem from some slight he suffered as a small boy—the kind of traumatic incident that can shape a mind from a young age, like he was baptized in some underground river of blood. He considers his pit bull approach to mercenaries like Zoo to be more of a public service than anything else. And it's nothing if not personal. Brooksby has dealt with this type of sociopath before and knows those streets. After his daughter succumbed to the cult of personality, he knew his addiction practice would eventually have to lead to his retribution. Zoo shows Brooksby a chilly, dangerous universe, one that has no interest or feeling about humankind's fate. He has no empathy for his fallen flock. If they leave or are taken back—part of a recovery/kidnapping network to bring them home—then it serves to strengthen his resolve. What happens in his world only exists to serve his inflated ego. The fact that there are so many people with a direct financial interest in the others and that the cash flow can vary significantly depending on the others' success or failure makes the antagonism all the more intriguing.

Returning from a photo shoot she had arranged outside the mansion with a local magazine's society section spotlighting the annual event, Christina Marvel drapes an oversized red sweater over her new sleek black dress and opts to go barefoot, kicking her heels into a corner. There's something really powerful and refreshing about a woman who is unapologetic. She doesn't care if she's fitting in or not. It's her party, and she'll play like she wants to.

"If you're gonna throw a big, festive party, this is the way to go about it," Karen whispers to her husband as Christina enters the room. "She's made a few grand entrances already this evening."

"Yes, and if you're gonna eat shit, these are the spices I recommend adding," Pat replies with a laugh.

As Christina walks by, Karoleen Young sidles up to Pat and Karen, who are now standing next to Kip Balotta and Ned Symbol. Karoleen jokingly mimics a Russian accent she overhears, saying a few sentences with the accent.

"Ooh, that's sexy," Kip says. "Keep talking that way."

"I don't know what to say," she confesses.

"Just say anything, but when you do, use the accent."

"But I don't—"

Kip interrupts her midsentence. "That's it. Just say anything."

"Be quiet," Ned admonishes, half joking.

"Just say what you hear other people saying; only say it with the accent," Kip pleads.

"Will you please shush?" Karoleen says.

"Good, say it in Russian."

"I'm leaving now." She starts to walk away. As she does so, Kip tells her to say it in Russian. She laughs as she walks away, not sure whether to be flattered or disgusted. She turns and gives him a killer look as she leaves. Kip calls out to her one last time in vain.

"This is what happens when the babysitter takes a vacation," he says.

An exuberant voice booms from the center of the room.

"Does anybody have any Christmas wishes?" The shouting comes from Christina, who manages a half twirl as she asks.

There's some chuckling and kidding in the room, several naughty glances filled with sexual agendas, and off-color, scandalous whispers. After a few moments, John Marvel lifts his glass and shouts out, "I have one."

He stands toward the center of the room and faces his wife while still maintaining a safe distance. Most of the guests are now surrounding the hosts, watching and wondering.

"I wish that you'd figure out what you want to do with all that crap you've got stuffed into our four-car garage and the barn so I can finally convert them back into their respective intended uses—to shelter automobiles and horses. But please don't promise me that you're planning on taking care of it. And don't give me a deadline or commit to a target date, because there's no point. Because of how often you've failed to deliver on your commitments, I won't even be upset or disappointed when the expected happens and you miss the target date."

There's a momentary hush in the room.

"What an oddly specific wish," Pat whispers, leaning on his wife.

Christina laughs wildly, runs over to her husband, and hugs him. "I will, honey," she shouts. She hugs him again, kissing his cheek. "I will." She laughs and turns toward the guests. In her most sarcastic and cocky tone, she announces, "And *now* I don't even have to worry about a deadline." She laughs again as the crowd joins in.

✳✳✳

Leo and Maggie edge their way around the rooms and stop when they happen upon another interesting conversation. It comes from a larger circle of guests, a combination of Brooksby's clients, Marvel's friends, and general strollers who were mingling around the house, in much the same way Leo and Maggie are strolling.

"It was all high-pressure execs—real power-driven players in the business world. One guy wanted me to completely wrap him in Saran Wrap. First, he had to dress up as a woman, and I wrapped him—except with holes over his nose and mouth so he could breathe. Then he wanted to be driven around town lying in the back of a pickup." They overhear the woman telling her story.

"Jesus, and he got off on that?" asks a startled guest.

"Well, he *was*." She pauses. "Until the incident."

"The incident?"

"Yeah. He wanted me to drip hot candle wax on him. I didn't think to unwrap the Saran Wrap, so he caught on fire." She pauses with a sigh. "It got messy."

"So you're a porn star?"

"No, I have a tendency to exploit sexuality in an aggressive and adventurously frequent manner."

"Huh?"

"I'm a nymphomaniac."

"Oh." The man pauses, flustered and struggling with his words. "I don't want to put you in any kind of position."

"I've been in every position possible, and I've always gotten out of it."

Yes, Karoleen and Vanity were now shocking all the guests with their gonzo brand of inhibition. If they can find an audience, no matter how small, they are ready for showtime.

Leo and Maggie watch as their mysterious new partner engages Karoleen in her conversation.

"I'd just be wasting my time anyway," he says with a laugh. "I'm an old, out-of-shape guy. You wouldn't have any interest in me."

"Is that why you're hitting on me?" Karoleen asks.

He laughs again, only this time failing to conceal his embarrassment. She can see the discomfort in his face.

"Let me tell you something," she begins. "Those of us who have had men on top of us or behind us or underneath us will say with a fair amount of certainty that some of the best lovers we've ever had were not in great shape. That's been true as long as I've been out there fucking guys. You simply cannot equate looks or body shape with being great in bed. In fact, the dirty secret most of us women know is this: the better-looking the guy, the worse he'll be in bed."

"Well, that's a fairly definitive opinion. It's nice to speak with someone so open about sensitive topics."

"What's sensitive about it?"

He pauses to think about her question and decides, at least in the context of inebriated partygoers, that she's probably right. Talking about sex with a nymphomaniac is like talking about bait with a fisherman. He figures that there's probably no topic that is inappropriate enough to cause her to blush or tiptoe around. Besides, he's just biding his time until he decides to change the course of their history. He loves knowing he has a power that no one else in the house knows he commands.

"Are you going to make any New Year's resolutions?"

"Nah," Karoleen replies. "It's been a whole year since my last resolution and I'm still waiting to become a better person." She chuckles. "How about you?" she asks, not so much because she really cares, but more just to be polite.

"I'm going to try to be a better father. I don't think my kids understand how difficult they can be. I have to do a better job dealing with them."

"Kids can be cruel."

He thinks and then responds. "Actually, I found the opposite to be true. The older I get, the more I find grown-ups pointing out my flaws."

He is intrigued by her charming laugh, which catches him a bit off guard. It's got the lilt of a child, surprisingly innocent and pure.

"So what do you make of all this arguing about God and religion?" he asks. "Personally, I think it's making this party a *lot* more interesting. I get infuriated with all the bullshit and just can't figure out whom I want to kill first." He laughs. "But I must say, you don't get to attend many high-profile hoity-toity functions where some of the guests are going at it the whole time. Sort of an explosive way to ring in the holidays." He grins with a goofy, punch-drunk, forced conversational smile smeared across his face. He knows better than to let a guest get to him. He needs to remained focused.

"That's the way it goes," she tells him. "You know, years ago there was this restaurant that I always used to go to. Once a week … like church. I loved their lasagna. Got it every single time. It was just the absolute best. But eventually, I started noticing little things around the restaurant that caught my eye, little things other diners wouldn't notice—but I did. A little decline in service here, a rip on the wallpaper there. And soon, the lasagna just wasn't as tasty or special as I remembered it. So I stopped going there and found a new place to fall in love with. I've been a patient of Dr. Brooksby for a while, and although I'm not in total agreement with everything the TV group does … I hate saying this, but I think that's where he is now. He's had too much lasagna. Almost everyone remembers something in the past as always being much better than what we have now, especially when it comes to going to something on a frequent basis, like a restaurant. Of course the first few times will be more exciting than the eighth or ninth time you experience it. It's a real challenge to factor the emotion out of this. The trick is not to resent the people who are still enjoying themselves. Who are we to tell them that they're not having as much fun as they think they are because things were better years ago?" She pauses as he tries to figure out her point. "It would be wrong to describe these as people with nothing left to lose; instead, they simply don't care anymore if they lose or win."

He doesn't even blink. He wasn't expecting such a specific response. All he allows is a change in his mouth, gradually collapsing from a grin to a forced smile to a pursed frown, which he holds, as stony as a sphinx. He's thinking he should start alternating booze and water.

"I know you have more insight into the doctor," he says, "but I think I have to side with him. I don't buy what those preachers try to force down people's throats. And all the money they take from their followers just doesn't seem right. It's outrageous."

"It's all part of their jobs," she says. "Zoo is no different than Brooksby. They both use motivational speeches as tools to take our money. There's barely a difference between the two." She sighs. "I find myself waffling all the time about why I continue going to him."

"Yes," he agrees, nodding his head. "But Zoo isn't giving a motivational speech; he's giving a motivational performance. He knows that his act is artificial. His smooth moves have the practiced look of a performer who's done them hundreds of times in a hundred different hotel convention centers. Zoo is a self-made spiritual concept that comes to life only under the spotlight when he's striding and swaggering around with his arms flying, acutely illustrating his points through fist pumps and heavenly shout-outs. He works on your guilt, something I bet your doctor doesn't exploit. I would hope Brooksby's goals are more noble and attainable. I hope I'm not being presumptuous, but I'm guessing he's only trying to get you to a point where someday you'll realize that opening yourself up won't necessarily leave you vulnerable or full of regret."

"It's mostly about learning to forgive yourself so you can begin to forgive others."

"When people can't forgive someone, my question always is, 'What have you done in your life that you can't forgive this other person?' I would think that the things you've got to take responsibility for in your life make forgiveness easier." He stops to watch her reaction. To his surprise, she seems genuinely engaged in what he's saying. He continues. "All we really know about anything is what other people tell us. Sure, we can watch for clues, make observational judgments, and look for behaviors to serve our prejudices, but in the end, all we know is what we're told. And sometimes that's a lie."

"No," she counters. "It's about the illusion of choice and the way some people are doomed by circumstance before they're even conceived. Dr. Brooksby views ignorance as further evidence that his patients are only searching for someone else to follow. I think that's why the preacher gets under his skin so much. He's *exactly* the type of charlatan the doctor warns us to avoid. The doc blames so many of our problems today on people like Zoo. You can see it in the passion of his arguments."

Maybe Brooksby's clients really are shocked that he might have slipped off the tightrope they'd asked him to walk. Or maybe they know that only a guy willing to fall would have gotten up on that high wire in the first place. He welcomes humiliation in a way that betrays his fearless devotion to and understanding of the business. This is a man who, through his own hard work, has found a level of success and is now staring down his superstardom and trying to understand why it doesn't necessarily fulfill him. His nemesis Zoo, when he is in the weeds, can preach every night for recognition, for acceptance. Zoo is able to disappear into a role. Brooksby, on the other hand, is taking a step back and seeing what he has become. Maybe he is too human for merely playing a role.

✳✳✳

The party has been going on for hours now; the time is slowly winding toward midnight. Many of the guests are still on the ascent libation-wise, but all are beginning to fall into that twilight sense of imbalance—a result of a combination of too much drink, too much food, and too much socializing. The atmosphere is still lively, but one can tell that the real *punch* is starting to disappear from the festivities. The gathering is simply that—people wandering around, having finished eating and drinking and talking, and either waiting for something to happen to liven things up or waiting to find the right time to excuse themselves and go home.

"Gimme another drink," Pat says to one of the servers. "I think I need another to hear anymore."

"I think we should probably get ready to leave," Karen tells him. "I'm tired. And listening to those two discuss grand illusions is getting to me. You ready to go?"

"I don't want to miss anything if some serious shit is about to go down."

"Really? I think we've heard enough."

"Doesn't matter to me," Pat says. "I'm planning on this being the only part of the day I'll remember anyway."

"I just can't figure out why so many of these people are so enamored with those two. They're both nothing more than glorified con men."

Pat laughs. "Yeah, they're the kind of guys everybody likes and then sort of resents, because why does everybody have to like these guys so much?"

Karen considers his confusing statement and shakes her head. "Yes, I think we should be leaving."

"You're slowly ruining this party," Pat says, smiling at his wife.

"You want me to stop?" She moans.

"No, I want you to pick up the pace."

As soon as Pat completes his sentence, a small parade of brightly dressed clowns walk into the room, completely changing the sense of place. Pat and Karen, along with the other guests gathered in the main hall, straighten up at seeing the clowns enter. It certainly brings a new dynamic to the atmosphere.

"Can't believe they brought in clowns for this party," Pat says. "What the hell do clowns have to do with Christmas?"

"They're not doing anything but adding to the atmosphere," Karen says, trying to settle him. "Just relax. I know you hate clowns, but they're fun. Look at them; they're just doing tricks and giving out prizes."

"Yes, clowns are clever like that. Just when they seem reasonable, they go psychotic and kill someone."

Leo and Maggie make their way toward the back of the room, where they perch on the steps of the staircase that provides a seamless entry into the further reaches of the huge reception area. They catch others' conversations as they stand and review the flock.

"Young people are the only ones who ever talk about growing old gracefully," they overhear an older, white-haired, elegantly dressed gentleman say. He is speaking to a frisky-looking young bottle blonde whose vapid eyes betray how much she actually comprehends. "For those actually in the thick of it, the romance of that notion burns off pretty quickly, and the wrinkles and creaky joints are the least of it. Growing old, gracefully or otherwise, means becoming the person you were always meant to be, only more so. After the years of gradual transformation, you wake up one day to find that you're 100 percent you. Your good qualities are entwined so thoroughly with the bad that it's hard to distinguish which are which. By the time you feel wholly comfortable in your own skin, everyone around you may find you unbearable."

The white-haired man takes a sip of his drink with a look that shows that he's not sure if he should continue with his train of thought or pause for a moment to let the young lady respond. He wonders if she even has a response to his comment. Stupid or untalented people lack the ability to understand their limitations. *One needs a certain amount of intelligence and experience to assess things accurately,* he thinks. That sounds fairly shallow and elitist, he fears, but in his mind that is the key to young people today.

"Life is not necessarily a peaceful proposition." She surprises him with her comeback. "The conflicts and desires never stop. If you want to live in Shangri-la, go ahead … but this is where the action is, right here, right now. That's why youth is vibrancy and why age is stagnated in nostalgia."

He's pleasantly surprised at her apparent awareness, whether or not they're in agreement. He chastises himself for being sexist enough to think she wouldn't be able return with a logical comment.

Before he can speak, she continues. "But I can see your point. Our generation can sometimes be flippant about the way we approach the same things older people have already experienced." He's impressed. She goes on. "For example, I have this friend. She can't even put together clothes to wear to work. She buys her outfits from what she sees on mannequins. And she shops at J. C. Penney. I've seen their mannequins, and I see how she dresses. What a mess. And don't get me started on her makeup."

Pop—the bubble of respectability is now dissolving into the air. She takes a big slurp on her straw that's inside the frothy daiquiri or piña colada she's holding. As she sucks on the straw, she takes a moment to look around the room. The elderly gentleman isn't sure what, if anything, to say next.

"I think it's sad that the only Hispanics you ever see at parties around here are the service people working for white elites," she unexpectedly adds.

"Would you rather see white service workers?" he snaps back. "They're working. They've got jobs."

She makes some kind of grunting sound. He's not sure if it's meant as a form of agreement or disapproval.

"You know," she continues, "I once dated a guy who got tattoos of the names of all the cities where he slept with girls but couldn't remember their names."

"I feel like an old rock and roller. I've been on too many tours for too many years, and I'm starting to get bored with the material," he says quietly, almost as if he means that his comment shouldn't be heard.

"He refused to work long hours, because what was the point of that, he figured," she rambles on, "other than to engage in some sort of reckless masochism that didn't apply to someone with his natural gifts. Why should a genius labor as hard as everyone else if they don't have to?" She smiles and takes another slurp. "And I have to say, I don't disagree with him."

Their conversation is a teasing, fire-stoking combination where both he and she use flirtation as a tool. He wants to charm her and her preconceived alerts; she wants to coo and smile until he drops his guard. Their dynamic is the distillation of every stereotype in the battle of the sexes—men using blunt chemistry to exert their power and women pretending to be impressed until either they're not or they decide to take control. He knows he's the underdog.

He doesn't even blink at her comment. All he'll allow is a change in his mouth, that same stony-as-a-sphinx expression his face held earlier.

She jumps back into the conversation as if she is completely ignorant of their previous talk. She is now clearly not paying attention to what he's doing. He can see that she's eyeballing an attractive young man standing alone a few feet away in the center of the room.

"Everything okay?" he asks.

"Yeah," she says, nodding toward the guy she's been eyeing. "See him?"

"Yes."

"A few minutes ago he asked me if I'd get him a bottle of water."

He stops to take a more careful look at the guy and then playfully jokes with her. "I wouldn't get anywhere near that guy," he says. "He's bad news. A common criminal, nothing more."

"You know him?"

"No," he continues to tease. "But just look at him. Not trustworthy at all. I can tell by the way he's standing there. He probably asked you to get him a water because he needs to put your fingerprints on something for him."

She makes the strange grunting sound again.

"He also asked me if I was tired, saying I look drawn and pale."

He raises his eyebrows, thinking of what an unusual thing that is to tell someone at a Christmas party—especially coming from what he presumed is a stranger to her. "I'll never tire of a guy who looks like a wallet with eyes and has the confidence to judge other people's looks."

The deadpan vibe between them breaks when she giggles at his observation.

"So did you get him the water?" he asks, following up his smart-ass remark.

"I told him no. I thought it was rude of him to ask. Who does he think I am, one of the helpers?"

"Can't imagine," he says. "You don't look Hispanic at all." He smirks. "Besides, you should know that being told no by a woman is the worst thing that can ever happen to a man, aside from a really bad thing actually happening to him. I mean, 'no' isn't the worst that could happen, but maybe sometimes it is. So it's natural to react poorly to it."

She was actively listening to him this time, only she replied with the last comment he needed to hear. "You remind me of my dad."

He felt his face drop. "Really?" he says with mock appreciation.

"Yes," she says. "He died in his sleep."

"At least he went peacefully."

"I hope. He passed out in his car while on a railroad track and was hit by a train."

"Lightning, meet bottle," he says to himself and then sighs.

A few quiet moments pass. Before he senses she's ready to duck out, he decides to try to engage her one last time. As fascinating as he finds her physically, he can feel the message of disinterest she's sending. She's playing along with the niceties and the friendly conversation, but she's only pretending and ready to move on.

"You've been refreshing to talk to," he tells her, trying to muster all seriousness with a preemptive strike. "All these disingenuous people talking on and on about hedge fund managers who are mostly assholes, and always obscenely rich. They love to rant about the occasional gaze into the affluent lifestyle of someone who knows so-and-so. Hedge fund managers aren't the most compelling of souls. You listen to them talk about their money and belongings and immediately understand that the usual interruptions of life rarely burden them. And these weasels are constantly—I mean constantly—fighting with their neighbors over stupid things like dock space at their Lake Lanier waterfront estates. But after all the stories about Wharton business school and Emory doctors and Georgia Tech engineers, these guys still need to have someone tie their ties. So they accumulate their millions and go to a retreat to learn to work through their second divorce and then go back to the job of relieving honest people of their money. They have their coup de grâce. They're nothing more real than Mr. Monopoly whining about his lawsuit because the dock he built for his garish yacht pissed off half of Forsyth County."

"Oh yes, absolutely," she practically shouts. "Couldn't agree more. So many of these people are total *bores*." She laughs. "And all this religious talk. I know it's Christmas, but can't they give it a rest and let the rest of us enjoy the holiday?"

"I don't want to leave any decisions in the hands of anyone who believes in angels but not gravity," he says, knowing that every word he utters is falling on deaf ears.

"I believe in God," she says, "but I don't need these people telling me what's what. Everyone here seems like they have some special insight into life, death, and the way we're *supposed* to live. I can't be bothered by all the preaching. I listen, I process, and then I make up my own mind. Besides, I already know what I'm doing when I die. Have it all planned out. I'm going to be buried next to my husband. We already have our plots paid for."

He is shocked at her admission of being married and does a quick side glance. "You're married? I didn't realize. Is your husband with you this evening?"

"No, we're separated. We don't get along. I'm not happy anymore. He does his own thing; I do mine. Separate lives. We probably should never have gotten married to begin with."

"So you're gonna be buried for eternity next to a guy you don't love?"

"I think it's the right thing to do."

He shakes his head, but then, not wanting to insult her, he becomes inquisitive. "How does that work in heaven, I wonder? Do you have to hang out with your 'loved' ones, or can you go find the person you really loved? Or is that person spending eternity trying to avoid you?" He pauses, and then adds, "Of course, that sounds too much like real life, so what's the point?"

"I'm just trying to keep it simple," she replies. "There are so many other things to worry about. I just wanted that to be one thing off my list. But it's also possible to go too far in the other direction, I guess. You can't refuse to notice there's a forest because you're too busy insisting that every tree is a special case. But that's a problem if you feel like you have to explore every little thing to death. I prefer to take things at face value and just move on—try not to have too much noise in my life. It keeps everything a little easier to take. I like to avoid messy."

"Sometimes messy can be a good thing. Someday you'll realize that opening yourself up won't necessarily leave you vulnerable or full of regret," he mentions.

"Regret?" she says, confused. "I don't *ever* feel that way."

He realizes that the conversation has crested and it's time to move on. There is no endgame to this interaction, he observes. Suddenly his time is becoming too valuable to spend by listening to anything else this woman has to say. They aren't hitting on any level.

"It's been nice meeting you," he says in closing, awkwardly starting to slide away to another part of the crowd. She seems disturbed that he's making the effort to leave her, almost disgruntled, thinking that she should be the only one entitled to end the conversation and part ways.

"So that's it then?" she asks suddenly, her demeanor turning chilly and indifferent.

Before walking away, he pauses to face her one more time. "Don't ever get confused with who you really are, sweetheart," he tells her. "I know how you like to present yourself to everyone, but let me tell you something.

Don't brag that you're the defending National League champion when really all you are is the World Series loser."

She stands for a second dumbfounded, trying to make sense of his analogy. She can feel she's just been slighted, but she isn't completely sure exactly how. Neither is she sure how to respond. She knows she'll have to flash some dismissive attitude though.

"Sorry, I didn't mean to be a thorn in your ass," she says with a nasty flip as he is slowly walking away. He stops and turns.

"For starters, it's a thorn in my *side*. And I didn't mean anything by that. I'm just concerned that the inflated opinion you have of yourself might end up biting you one of these days. Nothing personal."

"Hey," she says flippantly, throwing her hand in the air. "You didn't say anything I haven't heard before, usually by guys who finally figure out they're outta my league. I'm afraid if you were going for something outrageous, you've failed."

He looks at her carefully with a certain condescending sympathy. "You're probably a great consolation prize, but we've officially cried wolf as a species," he tells her. "So outrage means nothing anymore."

He finally breaks away and reenters the congestion.

Next to one of the temporary bar setups, which are conveniently arranged around the house to ensure that guests are being promptly served, stands what looks like a company team meeting for Elite Lawn and Landscaping. Pat and Karen look cornered as they are holding court and discussing business with a few of their employees, including Creep, Sherry Turnquest, and Pat's ever-loving, room-hopping sidekick Lord Biznez. Pat thought it was nice that John and Christina Marvel reached out to invite not just their friends and the owners of their lawn service company, but also some of the key employees who are responsible for making sure the Marvel mansion is always immaculately presented. Of course, diversity isn't a consideration for, and is not a component of, the invitation list, so the actual *workers* who sweat out the job are never represented at these events.

Karen is mocking Pat, kidding him about the way he handles the office staff. She enjoys ribbing him in front of his team. She mimics the way he talks, the way he saunters when he walks, and the way he speaks with his employees. The team all laugh out loud when Karen tells her stories, understanding that this is one of the few moments of sanctuary when they get to mess with their boss without possible recrimination or becoming victimized by pranks.

"He walks through the office smiling and glad-handing the workers who are sitting behind their desks at their little cubicles." Karen acts out the scene as she speaks. "He smiles and points, and walks around like he's running for office. He gets to Sherry's desk and says, 'Did I tell you what a great job you did yesterday?'" She laughs as she recalls, using a high-pitched voice to mimic.

"Yes!" Sherry yells enthusiastically, nodding her head in agreement. "I remember that."

"Then one of the guys looks up at him and says, 'Didn't tell me,' after he tells Sherry," Karen continues. "Pat tells him, 'Wasn't going to,' and then he walks on past, ignoring him."

"What's wrong with that?" Pat tries to defend himself, injecting himself into the parody. "I try to nurture and reinforce my team when I can, so I recognize their hard work."

They all laugh.

"Laugh all you want," Pat says. "And while we're discussing this, don't expect me to just arbitrarily tell you what a great job you're doing if it's not true or if I have to say it just to be saying something *nice*." He looks right at Creep and smiles, busting him in front of the group. "It is like a war zone out there."

"Have you ever been in a war zone?" Lord Biz asks.

"No."

"Then shut up." Biz exaggerates a grin and closes the door on that argument.

"You ever get a wicked buzz on then go check out the indoor butterfly exhibit at the zoo?" Creep asks, smiling mischievously.

"No, why?" Biz asks.

"It looks like a war zone."

They all laugh again.

"Ha, ha," Pat says slowly and sarcastically. "The guy who argues that Bigfoot exists is telling us about what's what. It's come to this."

"I told you," Creep reminds him, "there's a TV show where they search for Bigfoot using all kinds of scientific equipment. I'm telling you, they're going to find one."

"I've seen the show," Pat argues. "They *never* once show a single scene that has any proof. Not one time. You see the guys running around in the dark with the camera lights shining and flaring in the back. You see them react to sounds in the night. You see them acting scared and concerned. But you know what?" He lets the pause hang a moment. "You *never* see the beast. Hmm."

"You should watch online," Creep tells him. "They have behind-the-scenes footage."

"Behind the scenes?" Karen asks. "Is that when you see the guy putting on the costume?" The group laughs.

"You're just a cynic," Creep says.

"No, I'm a skeptic," she replies. "Big difference."

"There are things in nature that happen around us all the time and we just deal with them. Some of the things we can explain; some we can't. It's just stuff that happens. You can't close your mind to things just because you can't explain them."

"How is it you're arguing for the existence of Bigfoot and we sound like the crazy ones?" Pat mutters.

It's an interesting little circle, one of those whose members will leave the party closer than they were before, regardless of how close they are at work. Colleagues seem to warm up to each other at these little get-togethers in ways, not always alcohol-endorsed, that tend to settle the foundations of relationships. Humor is the thing that keeps the doors open.

"You know what, Captain Dickbag?" Pat looks at Creep. "You should just stick with NASCAR. It suits you better. It's the perfect blend of action sports and gonorrhea."

"And there he is," says Lord Biz, laughing, "the Patrick we all know and love. He goes immediately to crude and inappropriate."

"Okay, all right," Pat interrupts, moving toward the center of the group. "Before you all pile on, let me give you an example of what my morning is like—something, by the way," he says, pointing at Creep and Sherry, "you should have diverted and kept off my desk. But anyway. The Kensington neighborhood is being vandalized again. Somebody's breaking the heads off sprinklers at some of our customers' houses again. We're gonna have to work something out with them, because they still blame our mowers for the problem."

He takes a sip from his drink and continues. "So I've got this guy on the phone, Anderson"—he jerks forward, emphasizing the name—"the guy we call 'my favorite Martian.' Anyway, he's yelling about how he saw one of our guys clip the sprinkler heads and how I need to reimburse him and how our guy was an asshole when he asked him about it." He sighs. "So I'm trying to calm him down and ask him if he has our guy's name or knows who it is."

Creep has his head facing down. He's smiling because he knows he avoided this call and that it wound up with Pat.

"He was a sturdy black or Hispanic dude. Kind of balding, used really bad English, he tells me," Pat explains. "I hear this from *all* our customers *all* the time whenever there's a complaint. Every day. So I give him the same reply I give every customer who says that to me. 'I run a lawn service. That narrows it down to everyone,' I tell him." Pat sounds exasperated. "Dear God, we're dealing with people who have no life."

Creep raises his hand in confession. "Yep, sorry about that one, boss. I let it through."

"I know that," Pat says in mock disappointment. "And after I went out on a limb to save your job," he jokes.

"But you're the guy who put me out on the limb to begin with." He grins.

❋❋❋

Lady DeSanto is surrounded by a group of curious guests who are interested in hearing more about her psychic abilities. DeSanto is a local psychic and fortune teller—though she *hates* the latter term—who originally hails from Lily Dale, New York. Lily Dale is a kind of sanctuary for mediums and clairvoyants, DeSanto's preferred professional title, and home to psychics of all renown. DeSanto's first name is actually Marilyn, but she felt that using the more formal and gracious "Lady" added a more elegant touch. Besides, she thought that using "Madame" or "Mistress" would sound too whorish and sleazy.

Leo and Maggie take a spot near Lady DeSanto and are listening to the mind-numbing chitchat back and forth between the clairvoyant and those gathered around her. Included with the group, and listening to an entirely different take on the sweet hereafter, is Matt, the Georgia Bureau of Investigations agent, cynical as ever; John Marvel; and Karoleen, who seems like she's been setting some kind of room-hopping record for striking up conversations and generally taking in every aspect of this glorious function.

"I find all this talk about religion, the afterlife, and psychological mind games, and all the different arguments, to be both enlightening and frightening," DeSanto observes. "There is a lot of good information and some intriguing things to consider, but it all comes down to fairy tales and misplaced sci-fi rambling. Serves no other purpose than simply to create argumentative contests that neither side can win or compromise on."

"And being a fortune teller is above all that," Matt snidely remarks.

"That's a very uninformed opinion," she counters. "Religious beliefs and faith aren't the problem. It's forced conversion and intolerance. Those are the things that tip the scales. My profession is much more transparent. I'm not trying to convert anyone. I'm just trying to use the energy of the person to read their proclivities and see what they might expect down the road."

"This place is full of characters and personalities and the usual eccentricities and foibles," John says. "It's not just a recitation of occurrences or statistics or widely held beliefs. The more I listen to everyone, the more I realize it's about the heartbreak of time, about the cost of loss, and about how it all falls away sooner or later. And the losses stay with you. It should be about, 'What happened to the fun?' It just seems like we've gotten away from the more enjoyable aspects of our lives so we can just keep treading water, keeping our heads above the fear and despair the world would have us believe control the endgame."

"It's perfectly natural," DeSanto tells him, "however regrettable and stupid it may be, to look fondly back on totally ordinary things and value them way higher because they were around during your more innocent formative years. Once you start seeing the flaws in those once cherished memories, you find yourself turning to otherworldly explanations."

"And you are *right there* to swoop in and tell them everything will be all right," Matt says, still digging into her with sarcasm. "Read their palms, throw around a handful of tarot cards, and tell them they'll live long and happy lives, settle down with the love of their life, and make more money than they can spend. Sounds perfectly reasonable."

"I don't understand why everyone is so contentious about these topics tonight. I know you're not supposed to talk about money, politics, or religion, but this party is working those themes pretty hard," Karoleen says to the group.

"It's not all that complicated. And I'm really not as cynical as you might think," Matt adds. "Swear to God."

"You don't believe in a God," DeSanto says, half asking and half noting.

"Yeah, but you all seem to, so that must count for something."

As the Matt and DeSanto finish their verbal sparring, Dr. Brooksby approaches the group. He can tell they've picked up what seems to be the evening's universal mantel of finding discordant themes and driving them into the ground, squabbling over their disputed points of view.

When DeSanto sees the doctor approach, she reaches out her hand, introducing herself to Brooksby. He is standing with two of his patients, Karoleen—who joined him when he walked into the room—and Vanity. Emerson, who is now showing signs that the excessive imbibing and verbal hostilities have animated his actions, extends his hand and says, "And it's very nice to meet you, Ms. DeSanto." Gesturing toward the two women who are now with him and hanging on either arm, Brooksby says to DeSanto, "And I'd like you to meet Karoleen and ..." There is a toxic pause; Brooksby has clearly forgotten Vanity's name. He recovers by grinning and saying with a certain flourish, "Well, these are the girls!" After he blanked on Vanity's name, she made sure to make eye contact with him while wearing her best death-ray look. She is clearly annoyed with him and begins to walk away.

"Just give me a sign if you want me to come over," Brooksby jokes with her as she turns away, perhaps breaking every patient–client confidentiality clause there is, not to mention professional ethics and standards.

"Okay," she replies. "Feel free to join me when I jump into the air and don't come down." She struts back into the heart of the crowd.

"Don't bother with her," Matt whispers to Brooksby. "She has the face of a rhesus monkey."

"Well, to be fair," Brooksby notes, "those are one of the better-looking of the monkey species."

"A woman insulted is more dangerous than a woman scorned," Matt adds.

"Maybe we should alert security." Brooksby laughs.

"We can give my staff a heads-up," John says with a laugh. "My security guards may not be the most intelligent creatures in the world, but at least they're not dickweeds." As he makes this offhanded comment, two of his paid plainclothes security guards, who happen to be standing by, overhear him.

"That's the best he can say about us?" one of the security officers mutters incredulously to the other, who is shaking his head, repelled by the remark. "Pompous rich fuck."

✳✳✳

Leo and Maggie are tired of observing all the lecturing, the glaring level of non-self-aware inadequacies, and the buckets of hypocrisy. Leo wants to make his spree-kill statement, but watching these plastic phonies almost has him thinking that, whatever happens after the dust clears, all he'll really have accomplished is ridding the room of entitled, pampered pricks. It's not so much a statement for the disenfranchised as it is an extermination of unwanted vermin.

"What do you think?" Maggie asks him.

"I'm burning it all down," Leo says calmly. "Consider this a kind of invoice from the universe. Time to atone for their sins, and they're past due."

Chapter 18

Nobody Knows Them Like That

Brooksby is fascinated with the ongoing dynamic between the Marvels and the Zoos, especially the Marvels' adulation of Herman Zoo and his horror-show wife, Bev. The Marvels are reaching to impress at every opportunity—the very definition of classic brownnosing disgust. It is an embarrassment that they seem completely oblivious to. Brooksby does consider the thought that John is somewhat disingenuous about his level of commitment and is just playing along to placate his wife. The doctor can sense an underlying discomfort in the way John approaches all the hero worship. Or perhaps Brooksby alone finds the Marvels to be an embarrassment and the other party guests are either used to it or turning a blind eye. Some guests are so lost in their own games of one-upmanship to capture Zoo's attention that their blindness is the result of their own tunnel vision.

"I know what you're thinking," John says with scorn aimed toward Christina. He is clearly gearing up to speak. "Here he goes with another one of those boring stories from his childhood."

"I wasn't thinking that," she says defensively. "Was anyone thinking that?" She looks around the group. Everyone either shakes their head or stands with a glazed, jaded look in their eyes, waiting for the inevitable anecdote he's about to spill. Most down another healthy sip of their drink in anticipation.

"No?" She looks at John. "Please proceed."

"When I was a kid," he starts, "I was able to take charge of my group, the friends I hung with. I guess I had a way with people even back then. They'd look to me for leadership, you see." John looks to Zoo for affirmation, aiming his explanation, his self-aggrandizement, toward "His Holiness."

"It began when we were very young, maybe eleven or twelve. All of my friends would buy me the records that their parents wouldn't let them have at home: Iron Butterfly, Steppenwolf, Zeppelin, Stones, Zappa, Hendrix, Pink Floyd, and the Doors—the 'subversive' stuff. That way they could listen to them at my house and not get in trouble with their folks. We tried to make sure that our parents would only hear us listening to Three Dog Night or the Mamas and the Papas—or Dylan, Neil Young, or the Beatles—not fully realizing how subversive *they* were also. It just *sounded* safer to them."

"Personal growth and comfort can never coexist," Zoo says after listening to Marvel's little *Lord of the Flies* tale. "Sanity cannot exist in a vacuum."

Christina lets out an audible noise, blushing with breathlessness after absorbing Zoo's highly estimated valuation of her husband's description of youthful dominance. Brooksby just shakes his head, trying to decipher the meaning behind Zoo's gibberish throwaway line—repulsed while at the same time admiring the preachy old-school-style one-liners.

"When you start caring about what other people think of you, you risk starting to give yourself away," Brooksby says. He turns to Zoo. "You do realize that the only reason any of your bullshit works is because people are afraid of going to hell. Religious fundamentalists count on their flock feeling pressured to conform to teachings, whether they truly believe in them or not, because of the threat that lies in not believing."

"It has nothing to do with pressure," Zoo explains. "Do people feel pressure to get out of bed in the morning? No. You get out of bed because you're all slept out, because you're hungry for the day to begin, or because you need to get ready for work—whatever the reason. Did I feel pressure when I worked as a waiter back in the seventies at some sleazy lounge? I guess so, but who cares? Do people feel pressure to hit the gas when the light turns yellow? Do hikers, when walking across the Golden Gate Bridge for exercise, feel pressure not to jump off and commit suicide? I suppose you could say that there are different degrees of pressure and expectation that go with almost any activity, but it's a banal way of looking at it. It provides nothing constructive. It's not the pressure that causes people to believe; it's their inherent goodness and need to forgive that brings people closer to the spiritual freedom they seek."

"People are always saying you need to forgive others to achieve personal peace," Brooksby complains. "I don't get it. If someone hurts you and continues to hurt you even when they're no longer in your life, how does forgiving help? If you don't interact with them anymore, then how does forgiveness work? The painful reminders are still there." He takes a deep breath and continues.

"Sometimes the hurt is so deep, you can't find a way to forgive. The rage builds inside until it needs to find a release. I guess that's why they say to forgive but never to forget. But forgiving is a path to closure. You may pay the price repeatedly by bringing that bitterness into each new relationship or experience. But you risk becoming so wrapped up in the negative that you can't find a way to enjoy the present. Just imagine that your past is an ever-growing hedge that keeps getting higher and wider. It separates you, where you are now, from what's happened before. But that hurt is all on the other side of that hedge. There is no other time for you than now. And the time you waste praying for resolution or giving money to preachers, fortune tellers, psychics, the church—whatever entity is looking for you to pay your way out—can be better spent if you just address the issue face-to-face. Confront the issue and settle it."

Brooksby pauses, and then finishes his thought. "You've turned what has always been an entirely individual pursuit, thought whimsical by some, into a collective *need*. You're bringing the abstract into the realm of mainstream comprehension in such a way that it can be used for everybody in society. Religion isn't meant to appeal as a one-size-fits-all sales pitch."

Matt looks around the room and then at the two audible combatants. "Which one of you guys is gonna finish second?" he says, laughing.

Zoo's brand of spirituality has no roots in metaphysical reality or tenets. He maintains long-held notions about life, but his take on spirituality does not ignore common sense. His organization and its members are firmly rooted in a world of reality, but they respond to real-world crises with fantastical steps. His practices and teachings are simple and give a person no direct experience beyond a reliance on faith. You don't need any special spiritual abilities to feel the difference in your state of mind while singing in a choir or to realize that when you help somebody, you yourself feel uplifted. Zoo wants you to capture that feeling and find a way to spread it through every aspect of your life.

As a spiritual master, Zoo shatters all clichés that are part and parcel of the stereotype. He goes to the people; he does not wait for them to come to him. He does not reject commerce because it's "worldly." In fact, financial profit motivates him in the same way that seeking redemption through prayer motivates his followers. He is not afraid to comment or participate in political developments, but he only does so when he can stay on point. His programs have reached places that have nothing to do with spirituality, from prisons to pubs. In the end, if you take his message away with you in your heart, that's great. If not, just don't forget to leave a donation.

"Where there is honey, the bees will buzz," Brooksby says dismissively. "Where there is sugar, ants will gather." His slight of Zoo is apparent. The audience of onlookers grows larger. "Likewise, where there is Herman, all manner of devotees arrive and express their love. There is confusion, frenzy, and bliss."

"I used to wonder what I ever did to deserve all this grace," Bev Zoo tells Brooksby, defending her husband. "Now I say that I deserve every bit of it, as it's only love—and Herman Zoo is love."

"So true, and so right on target," Christina agrees with Bev. Then she turns to the group. "Herman Zoo is a mystery himself." She nods in his direction as she speaks. "He is as deep as your own soul, and with such an infinitely lively consciousness. Depending on what they need, he can be different colors to different people. And the way he lives with his all-inclusive love is transforming the world, from the roots up. I have known Herman now for quite a few years, and he has not changed a bit. He has the same quiet reserve, the same intention, and the same impeccable integrity. There is simply no one like him. It is a mind-boggling achievement in this world of tangled stress and complications that Herman's message can move unscathed without opposing, but just being supportive and expansive."

"We are breathing in a media space that is filled with stories of fraud, scams, corruption, deceits, and abuse," Bev agrees. "Seldom do we have stories that bring smiles, that touch our hearts and make us believe the worth of living itself. It's time to start fresh."

If hypocrisy could manifest as a physical form or entity, then this room would be smothered. With all of the illegal and immoral activity being perpetuated by most of the people here tonight, karma will see to it that the walls will start to crumble down.

"Ignoring a problem and waiting for it to just go away only works if the problem is just going to go away," Pat adds, seemingly subscribing more to Brooksby's take on the Herman Zoo phenomenon. "It won't."

"That's a fairly cynical approach to the problems in this world," Christina says, chastising him. "With crime out of control, school shootings, cops killing citizens, racial divides, national rage, and threats of terrorism hanging over us—and at the same time we're surrounded by a failing economy—people are justifiably outraged. These things may not go away, but at least we should try to make the world livable."

"You hanging around guys like me is the reason guys like you go to church." Matt laughs.

Zoo listens to the group argue for and against his ministry as they discuss the different opinions voiced this evening. He looks around and seizes the group's attention with the clearing of his throat.

"Consider the case of a classical singer giving a live performance," Zoo explains. "When he starts his program, he believes the audience should appreciate him. He is aware of himself, aware of the audience, aware of his singing. As time goes by, he is so immersed in his singing that he forgets himself, forgets the audience, and becomes his song. At that moment, something new happens. Creation takes place. He gets huge applause from the audience. So creation happens when the creator has forgotten himself. Creation happens when the creator is not aware of himself. Creation happens when the mind is totally in the present moment."

"Did you have to go to some kind of evangelistic retreat to learn that metaphor?" Brooksby asks. He continues, now speaking to the group, "You see, for those of you unfamiliar with a retreat, let me explain. It's a way for people who are already somewhat removed from the day-to-day interaction with reality to add the element of physical distancing from their workplace to get even further away from it. And that's *exactly* the kind of brainstorming bullshit story one would take away from a retreat."

John leans over and voices his thoughts about Brooksby and Zoo to his friend Pat. "One is detached from reality, and the other understands reality but just doesn't want to live by its rules."

Pat smiles, and then addresses Zoo. "If we do what you want us to do, then none of us will be around later to tell you that you were wrong."

Karen nudges Pat to quiet him. "Stay out of this."

"The reason I would never think to take sides in such a philosophical sparring match is because it takes a certain vulnerability to be a part of it. It's the gamble you take by being courageously ambitious," Pat adds.

"No need to go full-on crazy, people," Brooksby says, quickly thinking to himself that he shouldn't be throwing words like *crazy* around as a pejorative. He is, after all, a professional therapist. "It might sound hip, but the world is not flat. If the sun sets in the west, then it's bound to come up in the east.

"There are many secrets in us, in the depths of our souls, that we don't want anyone to know about," he explains. "There's terror and repulsion in us, the terrible rage that we don't talk about. That place is one that no one knows about—where we keep horrifying things secret. We need to find a release for that. And too many people these days find that release in carrying out spree killings. There is increased violence in the schools and a rise in the racial war in America. And thanks to our instant-lottery media, the broadcast glorification of these events gets 24/7 coverage and the designation of breaking news. And since 'breaking news' happens every day now, we barely even look up at the TV when they report it."

Zoo takes his arm from around Bev and steps toward Brooksby. "God isn't responsible for these reprehensible tragedies we see in the world. Evil owns it. Evil is why it happened. Evil just can't be wished away or explained away on a couch or in a counseling session or even in a church. It finds you and it feeds on fear because it is so spontaneous and hard to stop. I know that all the words I deliver might not make a difference. But maybe it gives us pause when we consider how compassionate we are to each other on a day-to-day basis. Negativity is a virus, and unfortunately too many people in this world allow it to take root in their minds unhindered. We shouldn't be arguing about our differences. Instead we should see that the more separated we become, the more illusion takes precedence over having actual communication with and empathy for each other. I agree, the triumph of spectacle in our country has made it that much easier for people who act out to believe they are heroes." Zoo pauses. "Or villains."

"What's wrong with America is you," Leo, now among the group as just another party guest, suddenly shouts out toward Zoo and Brooksby, who are standing next to each other. "Both of you, and people like you, turn tragedies into religious and political opportunities or moneymaking businesses. And rather than spending one fucking moment mourning the dead and injured, you immediately have to play the blame game. And that just doesn't apply to you left-wing liberal doctors and elitist shrinks," he says, pointing at Emerson. "You're on the same trip with the right-wing nutbag religious fanatics like him. During times of tragedy, can you at least pretend that you give a fuck about people's lives? The more each of you claims to be some kind of fucked-up answer to all our problems, the more I realize how stupid the rest of us are for even standing around and paying attention."

The group that is gathered together, uniformly uncomfortable with this outburst, try to maintain, to a certain degree, civility. This outlier to the group, Leo, who erupted onto the scene—now free from his party costume and wearing white underclothes beneath red painter-pant overalls—has had enough of the verbal wasteland and its already *done* subject matter and repetitive arguments. Leo glances over at Maggie, who winks, trying to keep her calm in the face of his entering the fray. He doesn't want to make a move against anyone or set his spree into motion just yet. He had the sudden adrenaline rush that comes with the sense of taking control and beginning to feel the presence of his will guiding his words and actions. He wants to toy with his prey a while and find his own role in this game while waiting for pulses to quicken or a sense of dread to come alive in the eyes of his victims. He loves the rush of intimidation.

"Bad shit like this happening all around us, every day," Leo continues, now with the somewhat stunned, but intrigued, attention of the group, "makes me think about how insignificant we all are in the grand scheme of things. And then I see the greed and the pure wanton that some people have. They're willing to take advantage of horrible disasters and to sacrifice others. I never will understand how nature justifies taking so much life so trivially." He sighs. "And I will *never* understand how each of you so easily lets that part of our world stay outside your walls."

"You," Leo says to Zoo, loving having this forum to air the grievances that are behind his plan, "your work just keeps praying at the same old well, when you should be teaching people about the continuing cycle of rebirth that individuals can break out of by performing good deeds. In fact, nobody ever imagines they are going to escape that cycle until everybody else does. That's why we have Holy Rollers—modern-day bodhisattvas—whom God speaks through to come back and save the rest of us. Zoo is the bodhisattva." Leo, drink in hand, points at Zoo. "He is not going to abandon the world. On the contrary, he is released back into the world to save us."

Zoo and the rest of the group remain oddly silent as Leo continues his discourse. Maggie, who has been getting her share of attention from the others who noticed the two of them together during the evening, moves quietly closer to the inner circle, better to watch the entertainment roundup.

Leo slides toward Brooksby, who looks to be standing with a more defiant, aggressive posture while listening. "I know you," he tells the doctor. He then looks at the circle of people around them, now becoming much larger and drawing interest from all over the house.

"He's used to keeping everything inside because he believes he's in control. Now, tonight, he has let everything go because he knows for certain he's not. Just watch the defensiveness and the posturing. He's more scared of his patients losing faith in him than the preacher here is worried about saving souls. Now they have that preoccupied glaze—one you'll never see when they're *performing* for you in the office or from the pulpit. This glaze never looks you in the eye."

The guests mutter among themselves for a moment before Brooksby steps forward to address the unkempt stranger, who looks exactly like what a dressed-up Santa would look like after decostuming.

"And who exactly are you?" Emerson asks politely.

"I'm just here to try and find the intersection of a few wise men. It's Christmas after all, and what's Christmas without wise men, huh? This seems to be where the avenues of popular entertainment and art, spiritual experience and metaphor, fact and fiction, comedy and tragedy, meet. I'm not debating *if* differing views can coexist. I mean, they obviously do. Every day we live with differing views all around us. They govern our actions.

Instead I am asking if different views *should* coexist. All the arguments, regardless of what side you're on, don't change minds. They only promote all the rage that is building inside—and this leads to retaliation."

"But who *are* you?" he repeats.

"I'm like Santa Claus," Leo snaps back. "You've seen me here all night making the rounds, entertaining the guests. I can walk around here and tell you who's been naughty"—he looks over at Maggie—"and who's been nice. Tonight would be the perfect evening to bring a sense of yuletide justice to the festivities. Everybody here hurts people in some way or another, but you two are the worst." He turns to Zoo and Brooksby. "You destroy people from the inside."

"And your girlfriend over there?" Brooksby motions toward Maggie, who beams at the exchange.

Leo walks over and waves her to come forward. She takes a few steps closer to the center. "She's a rich kid who had connections through her parents her whole life, so she never had to work a day in her life, never had to lift a finger a day in her life, and never had to struggle a day in her life. But she didn't want that, because what value is there in life made only by the rich? If you never had to struggle in life, you are not a real person, you are a poseur—and in her case, a beautiful, independently wealthy, hipster poseur, possibly the worst kind." He smiles, motions her closer, and puts an arm around her.

"I see you both when you talk to your friends here," Maggie says, addressing Zoo and Brooksby. "You tell them that they're so special, and you ask them to never change. Then you need to 'heal' them if they haven't conformed to your psychology or your religion. Well, which is it? Is change good, or should you stay the same? You're sending mixed messages. Unless you're willing to overlook human flaws and allow for the fact that real people are going to act like *real* people, you'll see that there are no more heroes." She looks at Leo. "So we have to become the healers in our own journey. We promise ourselves to lead a meaningful life."

"What are you doing about it?" Bev Zoo snarls loudly to the couple, taking the rest of the group by surprise.

"I never said a thing about any answers," Leo responds. "I am counter to anyone who believes they have answers, or callings or pathways or explanations. I've only been an observer of life, participating enough to justify having an opinion. I just ask questions, not to learn any profound mystery, but to show just how ugly and fraudulent the defenders are. I'm just afraid our efforts may be wasted here."

"I would caution you to be tolerant and consider your words more carefully if you want to stay involved in our conversation," Zoo admonishes Leo. "You stormed in here interrupting a conversation. Remember, we are not the bad guys."

Before Leo can respond, Bev Zoo interjects defensively on behalf of her husband. "Everything that man's done from the day he was born has been done in service, to prepare for his revelation that provides the foundation for this ministry. Everything has led up to this, from his first service over twenty-five years ago to his outreach today. His compassion was the lightning strike that forged the foundation for this ministry. He doesn't have anything to prove."

"Everyone knows it's over for both of them. That's why they campaign so loudly for their causes," Leo says. "And don't be fooled, it's for their *causes*, not for what they truly believe. The only cause they have left to prove is that they can keep the machine running."

"You seem to be active and robust," Brooksby says, trying to rebut Leo, "but I can't help but feel how unfortunate it is to see people with untapped potential wasting talent and peaking many years too soon. I'm afraid it's going to be a very difficult and downhill path ahead for you," Brooksby laments.

"Somebody who is truly tuned in, as you claim to be, Doctor, would understand that the journey doesn't end at a specific point during a lifetime." Leo kisses Maggie on her cheek as he squeezes her tighter. "Look," he tells Zoo and the doctor, "I'm not saying that there is a clearly insane person living inside your head and making decisions for you. I'm just saying you can't argue there's *not* a clearly insane person living inside your head making decisions for you."

Leo is beginning to rethink his plan and wants a few minutes alone with Maggie to talk it over with her. He is emboldened by the chemistry that has so quickly developed between him and Maggie this evening. He feels secure in knowing that she has his back and is there to support him in whatever he decides to do. And he's beginning to enjoy his role as spoiler at the party, wondering how long he can keep it going without getting called out on it. He seems to relish this new character he's become in front of the very group he vowed to take down this evening. It's as though sampling the caramel crème sauce on the peach cobbler is almost as satisfying as devouring the entire dessert. Playing with them is almost as much fun as imagining his final, haunting vision.

But now he needs to speak with Maggie. As the vibe in the room settles a bit, they try to move over to one of the sidewalls. Before they settle on a place, they overhear Karoleen shouting in excitement a few feet away.

"Oh my, they have cotton candy," Karoleen says excitedly as she spies the swirling machine spinning the sweet, sticky shreds of sugar. "I love cotton candy. What flavor do they have?"

"Pink," Pat deadpans with conviction.

❄ ❄ ❄

Leo and Maggie find a relatively quiet spot and begin to strategize. Leo's visualization of what he imagined has begun to change. After observing this disparate group of people fumbling with their thoughts, drinks, food, conversation, and revelry, he feels more contempt for them, collectively, than before he started planning his little Christmas surprise for the congregation. But now it isn't a question of whom to kill and when to proceed; it is a question of whether or not to proceed at all.

"It's like I had this dream and it went away, but now here a little glimpse of it comes back and I want to start doing everything I can to reach out and save a little piece of it," he tries to explain to Maggie. "Like all of a sudden the opportunity has arrived and my moment is finally here, but it's taunting me to see if I have what it takes." He looks around the room and at the flow of guests. "Something has changed. It doesn't seem like the correct response to all this." He flippantly waves toward the people. "This may sound crazier than the plan, but I'm not sure these people even *deserve* what I planned for this place."

Maggie sighs with a nervous humming sound, considering his comment. "So now what?"

"When your opponent's got all the aces, all you can do is kick over the table." He smiles at her.

The Christmas season always makes people try too hard to teach a lesson, usually that our material wealth and status-conscious climbing aren't important in the big scheme of things. We are told that what really is important are the bonds—family, health, friendship, togetherness … the usual stuff. But those days disappeared when we bowed to the religion of fame and fortune. Leo and Maggie, in an effort to ring in the holidays, had been hoping to combat the perversion that the Christmas holiday has become. They wanted to bring it all down, not just because of the extremist religious tropes, but also because of the crassness and the greed, the intolerance and loss of faith, the double standards and inequality. Religion, faith, spirituality—and by extension, Christmas—all needed a kick in the ass, they thought. And this party and these people, in Leo's mind, were the perfect subjects.

Leo has a gaze like some of those disturbing street people who watch the world with this intelligence, with a weary genius, but he just can't break back into the world, no matter how much he tries.

As Leo and Maggie consider their next move, they see Lord Biznez, John and Christina Marvel, Pat and Karen McLaren, the psychic Lady DeSanto, Matt, and Karoleen drift toward them. John has a particularly crooked smile on his face.

"That was quite the little sermon," John says to Leo as he extends his hand to shake. "I don't believe we've met."

"Actually," Leo says calmly, "I'm here working for you tonight. I just happened to walk into something there and felt compelled to comment. I'm sorry for the outburst. It's not my place."

John shakes his head. "Oh no, no," he replies. "No need to apologize. It's refreshing to see unabashed hostility toward my guests." He pauses long enough to allow his stern face to settle on the group. He looks upset, but he quickly cools and offers a modest smile. Before he can add to his comment, one of the party's waitresses passes by with a tray of appetizers, offering it to the group.

"What's on here?" John quickly pivots and addresses the young woman.

"We have some of our more eccentric choices coming out now," the waitress tells him. "From Chef Bemnati, our special guest chef from South Africa. He's created some bizarre delicacies. Here we have sautéed crickets, deep-fried black ants, and crispy beetles."

John turns to Karen, who is now standing next to him looking cautiously at the tray of peculiar eats. "Do you want to eat insects? I don't want to eat insects."

She looks at John and shakes her head frantically, passing on the offering.

"No, thanks," John says to the server. "We don't want to eat insects."

"Oh, John," Christina says is a joking tone meant to admonish him for turning down the odd selections, "we said we wanted to try something different and exotic. You have to at least *try* one." She reaches down and takes a sautéed cricket. The cricket is crispy on the outside but softer on the inside. It is sautéed in a garlic and shallot butter sauce, similar to the way escargot is sometimes served. She puts the cricket in her mouth and breaks into a wide grin. "Oh, these are delicious."

"Glad you like them, honey. There should be plenty for you to enjoy."

Pat tries a beetle, reaching across Karen to grab one from the tray as she continues to object. He pops it in his mouth and raises an eyebrow. "That's not too bad at all," he announces. "I'm not used to eating my bugs cooked."

Christina tilts her head, giving him a strange look, and then blows it off. She moves on.

"Don't fill up on all the appetizers if you haven't been to the main dining hall yet," Christina reminds the guests. "We've got quite a late-night spread set up there for everyone. Biggest midnight buffet you'll ever see. Ham, turkey, stone crabs, and all the fixins. And of course it wouldn't be Christmas without my famous roast!" She beams.

"Yes it would," John whispers to Karen, who giggles. He excuses himself from Karen and steps over to Leo.

"So you are my Santa this year?" John asks him.

Leo shakes his head. "More like one of his helpers, not the main guy. I'm just doing what they tell me, and tonight it was the Santa getup."

"Well, I hope you're enjoying the party," John says sarcastically. "I guess you must be on break or something."

Leo just looks back at John, not sure if he should say something that might antagonize his host and employer.

"You're better off not playing Santa," John adds. "You're too thin and fit anyway. Besides, the gig sucks. The guy we had playing Santa last year got hurt carrying a toy bag downstairs. You know how bags bounce around when you walk? His toy bag was filled and swung hard, slamming into his back. The corner of a Star Wars action figure box sticking through the sack hit his spine and partially paralyzed him."

"Then I'm glad I passed," Leo says. John considers him for a moment, not sure what to make of one of his contract service workers transparently dropping his job duties to join in and mingle with the rest of his party. He isn't sure if he should admire his pluck or kick his ass out of his house.

"Being upfront about your superficiality doesn't make it right," John tells him as the others stand by silently watching, waiting to see how he's going to resolve this interesting turn of events. "Enjoy the party." He pats Leo on the shoulder and walks back into the congested atmosphere.

Leo nods. The others seem to loosen up when it appears that their interaction won't become confrontational or testy. Matt takes this opportunity to chime in with a story he's been dying to tell somebody—anybody—in the house.

"So I was with this whack-job chick a few weeks ago," he begins in a decidedly unpromising, misogynistic way. "She's a firefighter, tall, blonde, thick." He pulls his fists down to demonstrate thickness. "We met on the patio bar at a restaurant. She invited me back to her place. Half hour later, she's being arrested and I've got a gunshot wound in the ear."

"What?" Lord Biznez says when he realizes what he's just heard.

"Yeah, can you believe that?" Matt says "Just because I wouldn't have sex with her."

"Huh?" Pat groans.

"We met at the bar. We had been drinking when she asked me to give her a ride home because she'd had too much to drink. When we got to her house, we started kissing, and then she insisted I have another drink. Instead of getting me a drink, she walked up to me and pulled my hands onto her chest and then around her neck. She was telling me that she got off on being choked during sex." For some reason he put *sex* in air quotes. "So I decided to get out of there, because things were getting weird. When I told her to go to sleep because she'd had too much to drink, she immediately did a one-eighty. She opened a kitchen drawer, and I saw there was a gun inside. I turned to leave, and she took the gun out and pointed it at me. I just about made it to the door when she took a shot at me that whizzed by my face. The shot stopped me in my tracks. I wasn't sure what was really happening. My ears were blasting with the ringing sound. I was able to run out of the house, but she was right behind me shooting, so I knelt down, held my hands up, and told her, 'Okay, okay.' She fired again at the asphalt, and fragments hit my arm. I fell over, and that's when the cops arrived and told her to drop the gun."

"But I thought *you* were a cop," Biz says, confused. "Couldn't you just arrest her?" He pauses. "Or shoot her?"

Matt fumbles with his answer. "Yes, I am a cop. But I'm currently suspended, pending the result of an internal investigation. I can't carry or present myself as a law enforcement agent." He takes a deep breath. "This wasn't good for me."

"Holy shit. So what did she tell the cops?" Lord Biz is really captivated by the story, having had his own share of creepy encounters through the years.

"She told the deputies that she couldn't recall most of the incident, except me 'choking' her and her grabbing the gun to protect herself. Fortunately for me, she had no marks on her neck and stunk like a brewery. So they took me to the hospital, where a doctor removed the fragments from my arm and bandaged up my ear."

"Jesus."

"Yeah, it was a helluva night." Matt smiles. "All better now though."

"Whoa," Lord Biz says after hearing Matt's story. "I've had my share of crazies. After some of my dealings with the ladies, I realized that love is not a victory march. Women with that kind of baggage who bring a scorecard to the dance generally have some scars and are bad news, so at the first sign of this nonsense I'm done with them."

"Wait, wait ..." Pat holds his hand up. He looks at Matt and squints through his alcohol filter. "I still don't understand. You are a state detective. I don't get it."

"That's what I said. I've been suspended. And being an agent in the GBI, I can't afford to let something like this spin too much out of control. It's something I need to be discreet about."

Pat closes his eyes and shakes his head while rubbing his temples.

"Like telling us the whole story in front of TV cameras and dozens of strangers?" he asks. "I'm gonna guess that your definition of *discreet* differs from mine."

Matt just looks at him with a half-smiling mentally challenged grin and grunts.

The group takes this opportunity to either freshen their drinks or sample the bugs and arachnids being offered on the appetizer trays. John walks over to Leo and Maggie as Pat, Karen, and Christina all stand by chatting, sipping, and chewing.

John puts his arm around Leo's neck and grins. "Why don't we all head outside for a little bit? The weather's perfect right now. It's just the right mix of frigid cold and a big, bright moon."

Leo and Maggie are hesitant, but they know they can't decline Marvel's invitation to join him. John turns and begins leading them outside through the back glass doors and across the patio, past the covered pool, and down into a large lawn area, which is perfectly manicured and lit up with a myriad of crossing Christmas lights. Some Norfolk Island pines planted in the back are decorated like Christmas trees.

John walks over to an aluminum shed covered with faux wood to make it look like a cabin. He's only in for a minute before returning with an armful of compressed-air pistols.

"What are those for?" Leo asks.

"Squirrels. We're gonna shoot some squirrels."

They walk down a few more feet to the end of the lawn, where the grass begins transitioning to the woods behind the mansion. Lawn chairs are set up on the grass. John, Leo, Lord Biz, Pat, Karen, Christina, Karoleen, and Maggie all find a seat. John, Leo, Lord Biz, and Pat all take a pistol and start looking out at the dark woods for signs of movement—any movement at all—to shoot at. John sees a rustling in the woods and fires a couple of shots toward it.

"That's not a squirrel," Pat says.

"Whatever it is, I got it." John laughs.

"Think you just killed a leaf," Lord Biz observes.

"So do you think it's a good idea to sit around drunk in the backyard shooting at squirrels in the dark?" Karen asks.

"I agree this is dangerous," Christina adds.

"Sure is," says Marvel. He adds, "More people die each year in compressed-air pistol shootings than are killed in felony aggravated assault cases."

"There's no way that's true," Lord Biz says. "You can't compare shooting air guns to felony assault cases. How does that even make any sense?"

"Think about it," John says. "We wouldn't come outside during a Christmas party to shoot squirrels if we thought we'd become assault victims." He pauses, and then in a childish tone adds, "Duh."

The rest of the group look at John, who is clearly enjoying himself as he continues shooting into the woods. Now the others have joined in the firefight. Christina shakes her head, upset partly because her husband has pulled a crowd of guests out of the party to shoot air guns at leaves and wildlife, and partly as a nod to the big kid that comes out in John he's had after a few drinks. She delights in seeing him this way.

"Ah." She sighs. "My husband's vanity and his little toys."

"So, you're vain?" Pat jokes with John.

"No," he replies in a firm but relaxed tone.

"Hah," Christina interrupts. "Not vain?"

"Example?" John looks at her for a response.

"Okay," she counters while addressing the group. "He won't ask for help if he doesn't know something. He hates the thought that someone might think he doesn't know everything about everything."

"Yes, but those occasions are rare because I know most everything about everything." He pauses. "I dream big in a timid world."

"I don't want to live on this planet anymore," Pat jokes.

"You guys must be a bad influence." John laughs back.

"You shouldn't be out here killing God's creatures anyway," Christina laments.

"Yeah," Pat adds, winking, "you brought us out here to kill things." He mutters, loud enough for the group to hear, "You bastard."

"Where do you think most of the *fabulous* buffet selections came from?" John says, mocking his wife's dramatics. "Where else can you get fresh food this late at night?"

Christina tries to catch his eye to give him a "fuck off" look.

Karen walks up to Pat and purposely bumps his arm. She leans over and tells him she wants to go back in the house.

"You always seem so bored," he says. "It's nice out here."

"I'm going back inside. I'm freezing."

"I'm always asking you to do things with me," he says. "I've suggested different things for us to do, but you never want to do anything I suggest. You always say no."

"I want to do all those things," Karen snaps back, grinning. "I just don't want to do them with you."

"Go inside."

Karen laughs, kisses Pat on the cheek, and asks if anyone wants to join her and return to the party inside. Christina takes her up on the offer, and the two of them walk back up to the main house.

After they walk away, Pat looks at the remaining group and begins to talk.

"There are two ways you can dwell on your life. There's self-reflection, when you analyze your thoughts, feelings, and actions; and self-rumination, when you focus on all the ways you suck." Pat pauses. "Karen is always there to help me with my self-rumination exercises."

"It's all about reducing stress in our lives," Lord Biz offers, diving into the conversation. "You're more likely to have more stress when your favorite restaurant closes than when you lose a finger. Your brain has coping mechanisms that help you deal with physical tragedy, but you're on your own trying to find a new place to eat—one that always makes your food exactly the way you like it, has a familiar staff, knows how to make your drink, and always has a table for you. Psychologically, that's a lot more stressful loss than losing a finger. Same theory applies to pain. You can handle losing your finger better than you can handle stubbing your toe. The doctor will give you painkillers for the lost finger, but you're not so lucky with a stubbed toe. It's gonna hurt no matter what you do. Therefore, the stress of stubbing your toe is much worse than the stress of losing the finger."

"What's that got to do with reflecting on your life?" John asks.

"Because no matter how you look at where you're at in life, how the tough times play out always comes down to how you handle stress." Lord Biz had a larger point, but he lost it somewhere during his rambling speech. "Or not."

"I just have passing moments when I fall into a dark place," John admits. "When I think about the general holiday thing, I like the jingle vibe as much as the next guy, but I always feel relieved when it's all over on January second." John pops the empty clip from his pistol and slowly reloads as he continues talking. "I've always found that the line between despair and ecstasy is negligible at best. Most people don't even know what they're looking for, but they're all looking. They may pretend they're not, but it's just an act. Our life is a movie and we're the stars. That's where we're most comfortable."

Matt, who is clinging onto these guys like mold spores, shakes his head and walks over to Karoleen, who is standing off to the side. She is chilling by herself, sipping on her drink.

"Too much humorless talk tonight," he says to her. "I thought we all came outside to get away from all the serious shit."

"It's interesting," she says.

Matt pauses before trying again to strike up a conversation with Karoleen, who has been very cool to his advances.

"So do you enjoy exotic dancing?" he asks, the question sounding harsher than he intended.

"I'm not a stripper or a hooker or anything like that. I'm a flight attendant," she says bluntly.

"Stewardess, hooker, stripper, or porn star—whatever you wanna answer to, sweetheart," Matt counters, sounding irritated. "God forbid. I wouldn't want to minimize your profession."

Lord Biz overhears his comment and interrupts. "Now that's uncalled for," he says. "Don't worry about him," Biz reassures Karoleen. "He's like that cow from the Chick-fil-A TV commercials."

Lord Biz then looks at Matt and says calmly, "You realize this is your 'I'm fucked' moment, right?"

Matt stares at Lord Biz, shrugs his shoulders, and snorts, upset with this takedown.

"You know who I am, what I do. I will be back on the job eventually," Matt says.

"Yeah," Biz says, "we all know who you are. Be sure to let us know how the internal investigation turns out. And if you're ever lookin' for me, I'm in the phone book."

Karoleen hears this and turns to Maggie, stumped. "The *what*?"

Maggie looks at her and grins. "Don't bother, they're old."

Matt acts like a little kid who has lost his lunch money or who wants to take his ball and go home because he doesn't want to play anymore. "This is a great party," Matt says politely. "Nice house, nice food, nice decorations." He starts to walk back toward the house. "Nice breasts."

"Thanks," Karoleen tells Lord Biz after Matt leaves. Biz nods. They and Maggie walk over to where John, Pat, and Leo are sitting. The firing range has stopped. They're all just talking now. Lord Biz, Maggie, and Karoleen rejoin the group.

Lord Biz pulls a joint out from his jacket pocket and looks at the group sitting in front of him. "Anyone mind?"

John smiles and nods. "Please, by all means."

Lord Biz lights up and hands the joint to John, who takes a hit and offers it to Leo, who declines. John coughs and chokes some when he exhales.

"Whew," he mutters through his congestion, clearing his throat to say to himself, "Way to hold your shit, Marvel." After he settles, he looks over at Leo.

"It sucks that coffee never tastes as good as it smells," he says, making a random observation with no apparent thought or reasoning.

Pat takes the joint from John's fingers and takes a puff himself. He offers it around for the rest of the group, but they wave him off. He hands it to Karoleen. She takes a puff and returns it to Lord Biz. As he takes another hit, a loud voice breaks through the dark, yelling across the thin air to startle the group.

"Do I smell pot?"

The group sit up and look toward the house, where the shouting is coming from. Walking quickly toward them is Emerson Brooksby. He has a big smile on his face.

"Jesus Christ, I had to get outta there," he says. He walks up to Lord Biz, nods, takes the joint out of his hand, and has a drag. "*That* was brutal." He takes another hit and hands the joint back to Lord Biz. He looks around at the group.

"Sorry, hope you didn't mind," he belatedly apologizes for grabbing the pot. "Did I miss anything?" he asks. "I hope you all didn't leave because of me and all that yapping back in there."

The others buzz, murmuring and muttering that they just came out with John and assuring Brooksby that it had nothing to do with him. Brooksby grins and takes a seat. As he does, John, Leo, and Maggie notice that he's wearing sandals instead of the dress shoes from earlier in the evening. It is very cold out; the light footwear has to be chilly. Not to mention the fact that he is now wearing sandals with his suit.

"Why are you wearing socks with sandals?" Maggie asks frankly.

Brooksby looks down at his feet. "Just lazy."

"What's lazy got to do with it?"

"I wasn't in the mood to tie my shoes when I was getting ready to leave the house to come out here."

"Then why the socks?" Maggie presses.

"When I decided that I was too lazy to tie the shoes, I had already put on the socks."

"Wait." John is confused. "You were walking around my house barefoot?"

"Sure," Brooksby calmly answers. His frankness silences Marvel.

"So you weren't too lazy for the socks," Maggie proceeds, "but you reached your threshold when it came to the shoes?"

He looks down again and wiggles his toes. "I guess."

"So you changed your mind in the middle of the process?"

"You are so annoyingly specific. No offense, but you really should have been my ex-wife," Brooksby says. Then he turns to address Lord Biz. "I don't know what I saw in her to begin with. And we got together so well—had so much in common and shared the same interests." He looks back at Maggie and exhales deeply. "You and I would have made a great divorced couple."

"Where did you get those sandals?" John asks.

"Christina gave me these. I don't know where she got them."

John purses his lips and looks at him. "Really?" He groans and sits back in his chair. Brooksby tilts his head and looks at the others. "Okay, I'll bite." John sighs and asks what everyone else is thinking. "So why did you feel the need to take off your shoes and put on sandals anyway?"

"I went to use the bathroom. When I got there, I had to move some guy's head away from the toilet so I could pee while he was vomiting," Brooksby explains, his words beginning to slur. "He missed a few times."

John slowly shakes his head and says quietly, "What a strange story."

"I just want to say," Emerson—who is clearly drunk or stoned—says, addressing the group and rising from his seat, "that if I said or did anything that may have offended you—" He pauses.

John jumps in. "No need to apologize, Doctor," he tells him.

"Not that, no," Brooksby corrects him. "I'm not apologizing. I wanted to say that I teach, coach if you will, all of my patients to be open and honest about their feelings and to speak their minds when they want to voice their opinions or defend their beliefs. Never apologize if you think you are in the right."

He leans over to Lord Biz and gestures for him to pass the joint. Biz hands it to him, and he takes a long drag. As he holds his breath, keeping the smoke in, he hands the joint back to Biz.

"Did you ever play organized sports? Ever been on a school team? Ever play ball?" John asks Brooksby. He holds a finger up, asking to be given a second, and then exhales a large plume of smoke.

"I was on my college golf team," Brooksby answers.

"Okay, good. That works. Myself, I played football. University of Georgia football. *Bulldog* football." Marvel chooses his words carefully. "Now you say you teach … you coach. And that's good. You're a doctor who treats certain special kinds of disorders and addictions. Me personally, I'm addicted to *everything*. I can't believe I'm not addicted to toothpaste, that's how bad it is." He ponders for a second. "Actually, maybe I am addicted to toothpaste. I use it several times a day." He refocuses on his previous train of thought, addressing Brooksby. "Part of your job is coaching. You use coaching to help improve your patients' health and well-being. That's what our college coaches tried to do for us. They were there to teach us more than just what our jobs were on the field. They were gonna give us life lessons. Teach us about humanity. Make us learn that it was more than just a game."

He looks at Lord Biz, who obligingly hands him the joint. Marvel hits it and hands it back.

"I remember," he continues as he slowly releases the smoke from his mouth while speaking, "it was halftime during the Kentucky game. Now we hadn't lost to Kentucky in about fifteen straight years. And here we were at home, losing, needing a win to keep our SEC title hopes alive 'cause we were down a couple of scores."

The temperature outside has dropped about ten degrees since the group had come out from the house.

"Our coaches stood before us in the locker room," Marvel continues. "They told us that we played like shit and were getting our asses kicked because we were worthless and weak. And worst of all, they told us they each had wives and families and that our shitty performance could impact their livelihood. They told us their jobs were on the line because the team was playing like crap. They said, 'That can't happen.' They said that if we didn't get our shit together and get our heads out of our asses and win this game, then we'd live to regret it." He pauses. "That was our lesson. That was our halftime 'pep' talk. Make sure we play harder and win so the coaches don't lose their jobs, ruin their careers, and beat the shit out of us. Yeah, that was inspiring as fuck."

John looks at Brooksby. "See what I'm saying?" he asks him.

Brooksby just gazes back with a blank stare. He looks completely spent from a night of argument, confrontation, alcohol, and marijuana. His film crew is nowhere to be found.

"Your kind of coaching and therapy," John says, "I think, is based on your own selfishness. It's not really what you can do *for* them; it's what you're doing for them that translates into getting more of what *you* want. I'm not saying there's necessarily anything wrong with that approach, but I don't think that's how effective coaching is supposed to work."

Brooksby looks at Marvel sternly and responds, "Before the final round of our conference championship, our team was one stroke up. It was going to be a real fight. We were under a lot of pressure because our school never won a golf championship. Coach gathered the team together and told us one thing. He said that whatever we did out on the course that day, 'Just don't think about pussy or jerking off.' That was all he said." Brooksby looks around the group, who are either chuckling or appearing as if they don't know what to think.

"Not long after that I quit golf," Brooksby says, finishing his story, "And now that's all I *ever* think about." He breaks out into a hefty laugh. "Best advice I ever had: 'Don't think about pussy or jerking off.' Because once you hear that, there's not a goddamn thing that you can do to get it outta your head. It's like going to Disney World and getting stuck with 'It's a Small World' eating at your brain all vacation."

John quietly studies Emerson's face. The stoned, drunk doctor has ditched his crew. Now everyone outside gets to see the real Emerson Brooksby. He is loose, relaxed, nonconfrontational, and frankly, not a bad guy. He is not at all like the stuffy, professorial, fake TV whore Marvel had to deal with when his wife, Christina, wanted the high-profile shrink to attend her party.

"So when do I get to review the footage your crew filmed tonight? I have a tight schedule, and you'll need any approvals from me before I leave town next week." John sits back in his chair, picks up his cup from the ground, and takes a drink.

"I'll let you know."

"You know," John says carefully, "you look like you've already had plenty of wake-up calls and slept through them all."

"I'm taking a break," Emerson tells him. "Been working nonstop for years, so I'm going on a vacation I have planned with my wife next month, no matter what. We've had to postpone the last two trips. It's the only time she fucks me."

"I think a nice vacation would be good for you," Marvel says somewhat cryptically. The mystery in his voice continues when he adds, "It's always nice to get away and spend some time out from beneath the spotlight."

"You have grandchildren?" Maggie disrupts their impromptu one-on-one.

"Oh, God no." Brooksby laughs. "If our children procreate, then it means we've failed as parents." He pauses after a momentary melancholy flash bolts through his head about the daughter he lost because of this madness. This is why he harbors some of the rage against Zoo and all his lethal flash and reward.

"Just be thankful for the little things," John says. "Like when the furniture-delivery guy shows up at eight in the morning after the place called the day before to tell you they'd be there between eight and noon."

"Life is a movie," Brooksby says. "You wake up every morning on set, unrehearsed and ready to play your next scene."

Leo has been listening to Brooksby ramble on outside, continuing telling his stories and working his way around the guests, the divisiveness, and the arguments. Finally Leo looks at the shrink, studies his face, puts his hand on Emerson's shoulder, and touts one of the more meaningful messages he's learned from his own therapy. "Let's be honest, Doctor. You don't come here just for the hunting, do you?"

John gets up and claps his hands together once loudly. "Okay, everybody out." He begins to shoo the others toward the house. "I want to talk to my new friends for a minute." He looks at Leo and Maggie and winks. He whispers to them to hang back. He turns to the group and says, "Refresh your drinks. Grab some food. I'll be back in just a bit."

The rest of the group trail back to the house. As they disappear into the home, John turns to face his "new friends."

"There's life after death, even if it's not the one you had planned," Marvel tells Leo and Maggie, who are sitting uncomfortably now as the chill is coming more from the menace in John's voice than from the temperature. "We learn about death and mortality and the responsibility that the living have to respect the dead, whom they once loved. If death is the most inevitable and life-changing event of human existence, then the anguish for those the dead leave behind is perhaps the thing that most powerfully surpasses it."

Leo looks a Maggie. Both of them are puzzled with the direction of his chatter.

"I don't think I understand," Leo says.

"I'm just going to say this," Marvel says quietly to Leo, his agenda lurking. "I think it would be very good for both of us if we could find a way to spend this night together. You see, I'm pretty sure I've figured out how you and I can help each other."

"Does this have anything to do with your friend?" Leo asks. "We met up with him earlier."

"Oh, a surprise twist." John smiles and nods knowingly. "Just as I expected." He laughs. "Life is whimsical today."

Chapter 19

God Has Left the Building

Shev Woodhull is the mystery man whom John Marvel originally contracted for the intimidation muscle job he had in mind to pressure Zoo into accepting a more favorable business partnership. Shev met up with John earlier in the evening and joined together with Leo and Maggie, hooking into their larger vision—one that Marvel was obviously unaware of, never suspecting he was funding an operation of a much grander scale. Marvel was somewhat street smart, but he was still naïve or oblivious, or both, to the fact that most street perps have big mouths and talk to everyone about their plans. It usually doesn't take more than about a dozen beers, a few shots of hard stuff, maybe a little coke or meth, some weed, or whatever may be on hand or available for every redneck domestic patriot terrorist wannabe to spill his plot to anyone who is willing to listen.

Shev's story involves another of your typically miserable upbringings—a difficult, dime-a-dozen juvenile horror-filled roller coaster of tragedies, changing homes, and generally bad things. His mom ran away to become an actress in Los Angeles when he was just five years old. That was forty years ago. He found out a few years back that she overdosed sometime back in the nineties on the Las Vegas Strip. When she ran away to LA, Shev's dad agreed to raise the boy. They lived in a trailer park outside Valdosta. It wasn't too bad, not the greatest accommodation, but the place and his dad treated him well. His dad tried to be a good person, at least for the sake of his son. He often used to tell Shev, "Do what you think is right and then hope that God agrees with you."

When Shev was about twelve years old, he lost his father in a freak attack. Apparently Shev's dad was sitting outside the trailer on a lawn chair under his awning, just enjoying the evening. His dog started getting into the neighbor's garbage. Shev's dad caught the dog, who turned around with her head stuck in a can. His dad started yelling out at his dog, "I saw that," laughing like he had caught a kid with her hand in the cookie jar. "I saw that," he kept saying to his dog. Well, at the same time, an intruder was in the next trailer and had just robbed and murdered the residents. When he heard the dad keep yelling, "I saw that," the assailant thought it was some guy who witnessed the crimes and was shouting about it. So he went outside and saw the dad out there smiling and holding his dog, a little surprised to see this stranger emerge from the dark. Before Shev's dad could say anything, the intruder shot him once through the head and once through the throat. As he dropped his dog, she cried out. When she hit the ground, the assailant shot her too.

The intruder looked up at the dad's trailer and caught a glimpse of Shev, who was peeking out the window and watching the whole event. The intruder was hesitant at first about going into the trailer where Shev was, now no longer at the window, but when police sirens suddenly surrounded the intruder and the crime scene outside, he made a quick dash to Shev's family trailer, busting through the door and looking to grab the kid as a hostage. As soon he entered the trailer, he turned to rush toward Shev, who pulled a large kitchen knife from behind his back and thrust it squarely into the heart of the intruder.

Shev struggled through the next few decades, having problems with addictions, unemployment, failed relationships, money woes—the usual checklist. After finally straightening himself out, finding a woman, having a child of his own, and finding his way along the "right" path, he encountered another horrific family event. Shev squarely put the blame for it on Emerson Brooksby and Herman Zoo. He holds both of them, and their aggressive influence, accountable for his latest tragedy. So here he is tonight, defiant, pumped and ready to make a little more history. He is ready to confront the target of his latest grief, this time with a couple of eager new accomplices. It is time to begin the unwelcome party barrage. The shock and awe they had planned is no longer just in the imagination.

✳ ✳ ✳

John, along with his two new friends Leo and Maggie, finish their woodsy huddle and come back into the house. John grabs a glass of champagne from a passing tray. He leads his duo through the guests, who are still milling around and taking full advantage of all remaining food and booze.

"I don't know how long everyone expects this party to last," John moans to Leo and Maggie.

"I've heard the parties here don't have a time limit," Leo says. John stops walking and looks at them with a grin.

"This isn't one of *those* parties."

He pats him on the chest. They keep walking, turning a corner and entering one of the more casually friendly rooms, the library. A small walkway connects the library to the cigar room, where the humidor stores Marvel's favorite smokes, many classic labels. An outdoor patio loft overlooking part of the winding backyard creek is just beyond a stained glass door near the back of the room.

They walk into the library, where Herman and Bev Zoo, Christina, the McLarens, Lord Biz, Karoleen, Vanity, Jack, and Kristin are all standing around chitchatting. It's that early morning hour when everyone seems to be waiting for someone else to begin the party exit strategy and to make a move to start leaving.

Lord Biz perks up when he sees John enter the room. He looks across the room trying to catch Pat's attention. When he does, he waves him over. John and Pat both walk over to him.

"Hey, man," Biz says, greeting John, "when you get a chance, we need to talk."

John nods at Lord Biz and Pat. "If it's about His Worshipness over there," Marvel says, motioning toward Zoo, "don't worry. We haven't had that talk yet, but I started thinking about the problem. Maybe there's a better way to do this. I just want a few days." He pauses, and extends his arm to Leo and Maggie, inviting them into the conversation. "I want to make sure I'm looking at all the possibilities. After all, I'm married to the head *Zookeeper*, for Christ's sake." He laughs. The others follow. "I just think we can all really benefit, so let's explore our options."

Pat and Lord Biz are always open to new sources of income and are eager to hear about the latest business venture. And they certainly advocate a more reasonable way to reconcile their differences with Zoo. John introduces Leo and Maggie, whom the two men obviously recognize from seeing them around the house during the evening—and from Leo's fiery speeches.

"I'm not so sure about some of the players who you still have hanging out here," Biz tells the group. "What time do you want them to start clearing out? Shit, man, there's still a goddamn TV crew filming. People are wasted and are talking openly about all kinds of shit."

"Crap." Marvel grunts, pissed off. "Well, hell … at least most of these people don't know anything. Let me get these cameras turned off." He looks around the room. "Where the hell's Brooksby?"

"When you find him, see if that dude is also one of his patients," Lord Biz says, shaking his head apprehensively toward Shev. "Spooky-looking guy. Stay away from him."

"Who are you talking about?" John asks, concerned that there's another dangerous unaccounted-for stranger in his house.

"I'm talking about Mad Max over there," Biz says, motioning toward Shev, who is across the room. "What is he, some wiseguy wannabe? Started telling me shit like, 'If they give you a choice, you should have your leg cut off instead of having your kneecaps broken.' Then he tells me to always remember one thing: 'If you ever get pistol-whipped, it's usually personal.' What kind of person talks like this? At a Christmas party? Am I wrong? Overreacting?"

When John sees that Biz is referring to Shev, he realizes that it's his guy on the inside and realizes he needs to diffuse the situation. He excuses himself from the group and heads over to intercept Shev.

"I know why you're here," he tells him.

"Yeah," Shev scolds him, "and I've changed the plan. So just back off and let me and my friends take care of everything." He looks over at Leo and Maggie. Leo gives him the "cut" sign motioning with his hand slashing across his throat. Shev is confused by the mixed message. He looks at John. John nods.

"We talked about everything outside," John tries to explain. "We reached an agreement. We help each other, and the benefits for both of us can last a long, long time." He smiles. Shev looks over angrily at Leo and Maggie.

"It's not their right," he yells. "They don't have the right to stop anything. It's not their call."

"No, of course not," John says calmly. He hesitates a moment before exploding for a split second in reply. "It's mine," he shouts, and then immediately returns to his calm, engaging hosting demeanor, though he is now smiling with menace. He pats Shev on the shoulder and says, "I want you to stand there with a stupid, moronic look on your face, if you understand me." He looks again at Shev closely. "Good."

As John turns to walk away, Emerson Brooksby enters the room with a bang. He is uproariously drunk, having continued to build on his steadily increasing inebriation throughout the evening. He is completely oblivious to the cameras as they are rolling away. It is going to be an interesting day in the screening room when they review the footage. This footage will immediately be vetoed by Brooksby as unwatchable material. It will be edited out and then destroyed. However, as good cameramen and shaky producers are prone to leaking footage, somehow these scenes will find their way to TMZ and the related henchman living among the social media sewer toads that infest the contemporary culture with "gotcha" videos showing behind-the-scenes footage of the decadent homes of the rich and famous. The cultural debate rages between those who feel that the reporting of these types of celebrity "news" stories isn't real journalism and violates the subjects' personal privacy, which should be kept private, and those who feel that these activities, however immoral and debauched, actually happen among the rich and famous alongside community *leaders*, and so the public has a right to know. Representatives from both sides of the argument dismiss the viewing of such stories and agree they have no value whatsoever, but both sides also won't turn away from watching.

The bottom line is that it is in everybody's interest to get the TV crew to stop filming and to find a way recover the already shot video. The footage being digital, however, probably means that it will be out there forever, so it may be an expensive deal to bury it. These things always have a way of showing up on TV or the Internet. And with the number of community power players in attendance side by side with some of the wealthiest shadow people—who usually live with the highest levels of secrecy, with the exception of parties like this one—showing up, some of the conversations, topics, language, and, certainly, behavior could prove very embarrassing at best and criminal at worst.

It was Brooksby's camera crew. He had contracted them to attend and record the party without prior consent. Marvel didn't think he would have a problem talking Brooksby into shutting down the whole production and ensuring the disappearance of the video. The doctor technically owns the rights to any film, although it was shot under shaky legal circumstances. The fact of the matter remains that the film exists and will continue to exist in perpetuity. The best Marvel can hope for is a reasonable assurance that it will never see the light of day.

As Brooksby approaches John, Shev cuts him off, stopping him in his tracks. Brooksby abruptly stops and straightens up, facing Shev, who is directly in front of him. Brooksby recognizes a familiarity in his face.

"Good evening, Doctor," Shev addresses Brooksby. "It's been a few years."

Brooksby examines his face carefully and remembers the connection. "Nuthall, right?" he asks Shev.

"Woodhull," Shev replies. "My wife was a patient of yours."

"Oh," Brooksby says nervously. The people in the room have now surrounded the two, elbowing and nudging for a better spot to see and hear the latest confrontation of the night. Several of the overstuffed rooms at the Marvel mansion seem to have doubled as gladiator coliseums this evening.

"I'm sorry," the doctor apologizes. "I remember you." He pauses and looks down. "Her name was Nancy."

"That's right, Dr. Brooksby. Her name was Nancy. It's nice that you remember some of the little people who die while under your care."

Brooksby looks back up at Shev. He musters all the seriousness he can, and then he lectures the newcomer on the scene. "When you think about it at night, whose face do you see when you think of your wife? What became of her, and what finally drove her to take her own life?" He pauses. "You know it's not me."

Shev looks over at Zoo, who is quietly huddled among a group of onlookers, uncomfortable and sensing that it's time to exit.

"I'm not here just for you," Shev says as he looks back at Brooksby. "I haven't forgotten about him. You can be happy knowing that whatever happens to you will be a thousand times worse for him."

"I was only trying to help her," the doctor pleads. "I did everything I could. He had completely poisoned her mind. I wanted her to try a different program, but she was too paralyzed with fear to move. There was nothing I could do to help her."

"So you kept her in there, charged us fees that should be illegal, and then buried the story so you and the preacher could settle up and keep going about your businesses without interruption or bad press. No matter what kind of show you put on about what a phony he is, you are right there on board. You couldn't even put my wife's story up at the end of one of your shows as a cautionary tale. But neither of you can avoid running into all the dollars that are lying in the road and blocking your way to televising the real truth. That's too risky for the bottom line. What would your other customers think?"

"So let's get to the bottom line, Woodhull." Brooksby stiffens up and counters Shev's threat with a backbone. "You never seemed like the kind of man who beat around the bush when I was treating your wife. I can't help you with what you want with him," he says, referring to Zoo, "but what is it that you want from me? I'm sure you didn't come here just to admonish us."

"You know what, Doctor, I thought the exact same thing about you two." Shev points at the doctor and Zoo. Zoo is still standing near a possible exit door, and Shev notices. "By the way, Reverend Zoo, why don't you come join us center stage? You're a big part of this show too." Zoo looks around at the dozens of faces that are staring at him now, waiting to see what he is going to do next. Zoo feels more confined and overwhelmed by this group than when he is stepping out into an auditorium filled with five thousand of his followers.

"I'm here," Zoo yells out from the back, where he was standing in the shadows. He now makes his way through the gathering to where the two men are standing. "What can you possibly want?" Zoo is incensed, exasperated with this new situation that is dragging him back into battle again. And he is in no mood to engage in any game with Shev or any other contender. He's been on the receiving end of several battles already tonight. He's tired and just wants to leave like everyone else.

"When I never heard from either one of you after my wife's funeral, I thought to myself, *Now why would they do that? They gotta know I'll come after them.* That's when I realized: *Yeah, they* gotta *know I'll come after them.* So here I am."

Zoo stands next to Brooksby, who is facing Shev. Leo walks through the group and reaches them. Christina joins John and stands at his side.

"What do you want?" Zoo continues. "You want us to apologize that your wife took her own life? That she was searching for something that was missing from her day-to-day existence? She couldn't find anything that fulfilled her, so she found my ministry and saw that faith was her answer. And because you couldn't deal with her newfound faith, because it threatened you, you took her away from the only thing she had left in her life that she loved."

Zoo looks carefully at Shev and then at Brooksby. When he sees Christina, he notices she is crying with his wife, Bev. He continues explaining his side to Shev and the assemblage.

"So you turned her over to this *doctor*," Zoo says dismissively of Brooksby, "and hoped you could reprogram her and change her mind. Think about that. You wanted to take away the one thing in your wife's life that was bringing her happiness. Why? *Because* it made her happy. That's all it took to kill her. No other reason. You gave her over to a man the way a child slave trader deals with a sex trafficker. Turned her over to take away her mind." Zoo now looks at directly at Shev. "You trusted this man to brutalize your wife and return her as an empty shell. I'm sorry, Mr. Woodhull, but I guess you didn't know that your wife was a strong, independent, beautiful woman who gave all she had to everyone in her life. She was too smart to let you take that away from her. Unfortunately she wasn't strong enough to find another way to break away from you."

This entire episode is sobering up Brooksby. He doesn't know whether to dig in or walk away. He speaks up.

"When you brought your wife to me for consultation, she was in a very fragile, vulnerable state," Brooksby begins. "It was going to take a long time before we would see any real progress." He looks as sincerely as he can at Shev. "She was a religious extremist. That's not something you bounce back from over a long weekend of soft music and group sharing. These people are willing to die for their faith. And in the end," Brooksby says, sighing, "that's what she did."

Shev looks at Zoo. "You promised her freedom from her daily sorrow." He then turns and looks at Brooksby. "You promised to take her back to the time before she found freedom from her daily sorrow. Both of your promises had one thing in common: they came at a price. For a price, both of you were willing to overlook the person and keep alive the symptoms."

Shev pauses, takes a full breath, and exhales deeply. "No, gentlemen, I don't want an apology. I just want to make sure you understand that the rules and penalties of the real world apply to the people who made them." Zoo can sense that Shev is looking to destroy his parallel monster and stay centered on the parallel medium. The irony of watching his prophecy in action and the twisted interpretation of it is not lost on him.

Leo interrupts the quickly escalating standoff and gets Shev's attention. But before he can speak, Shev pulls out a 9-mm semiautomatic pistol and aims it in the general direction of Zoo and Brooksby. "You can stay out of it," Shev tells Leo. "I understand. You and her," he says, motioning toward Maggie, "have different ideas. I'll leave it to you. But these two are mine." He refocuses his attention on his two enemies. The rest of the group have already spilled out of the room, running for the doors in typical panicked fashion—completely contrary to what experts have tried to teach people since the time they were kids: *Remain calm. Exit in an orderly manner. Do not run or push others.* All form of civility has now flown out the doors, along with most of the guests. Within a few seconds after Shev's firearm makes an appearance, the only ones left standing in the room are John and Christina, Pat and Karen, Herman and Bev, Leo and Maggie, Lord Biz, Brooksby, and Shev. Karoleen and Vanity have also stayed behind, but they've snuck around the temporary bar, trying to be inconspicuous while taking some cover. They aren't about to miss how this is all going to end.

"Well, it looks like everyone left us here for a good old-fashioned showdown," Pat says, trying to cut into the tension. "Isn't this the time when one of us is supposed to pull out our own gun and take this guy down? I mean, we all have conceal-carry permits, right? We can probably get our story published in the next NRA newsletter." He pauses and looks around at the others. "So is somebody gonna shoot this guy, or what?"

"Nobody's killing anybody," Leo announces. He looks at Shev. "Put the gun away, man. It's not gonna happen."

"But this was our one chance," Shev says.

"No, just stop," Leo tells him. "It never had a chance. We can work out a better arrangement that now buys *you* for a price they have to pay, but for all the right reasons. Consider it reimbursement for a customer service dispute. You won your complaint." He nods. "I'm not kidding. Everyone walks away a winner. There's no point in doing anything else. If you think it'll make you feel better, then know that it won't make a difference." Leo smiles. "Hey, this is coming from a guy who woke up this morning knowing that his life and a lot of other people's worlds were coming to an end tonight. I know because I had it all planned and ready to go. But that's not going to work. What's gonna work is that we are all going to walk out of here like whatever happened here tonight was nothing more heated than a bunch of friends who had too much to drink at a bar and a couple of them had to fight over a chick." He lets his words rest for a moment before adding, "We can be heroes just for one night."

After a few seconds of everyone looking around at everyone else, all of the people present in the room realized that what Leo just explained seemed to make sense—with a sort of warped rationale. Shev slowly holsters his gun. John ensures that this isn't the last time they'll all be meeting. The next time will be at a business conference to sort out the details from the evening's lessons. All pertinent parties will be invited and in attendance. No one will be sending regrets.

From their hiding place behind the bar, Karoleen and Vanity look at each other, still puzzled by what they just witnessed.

"So nothing's gonna happen?" Karoleen mutters. "No one's getting shot or anything? That's it, no action?" She seems genuinely baffled.

"I guess not," Vanity says, a little disappointed herself that nothing more exiting came from the standoff.

"Huh, that's a surprise." Karoleen grunts. "Did not see that coming."

❀ ❀ ❀

As the guests finally start getting around to gathering their stuff to leave, John and Christina stand off to the side of the kitchen. He can see the disappointment in her eyes.

"It's all right, honey," he says, trying to reassure her. "What was said out there tonight … you still need to decide what you want for you. I'll support whatever the things are that make you happy."

She sighs. "I'm getting tired of the failures in everything I turn to for comfort and faith. I think I'm done for a while. I am going to start listening to myself again. That's always when I have the most fun."

They walk back to the main room, where there is still some small talk going on. As much as it seems it should be winding down, the party somehow seems to be surviving. Marvel, who has never been comfortable with his wife's association with Zoo, has never liked the abominable Beverly, and has nothing but contempt for Herman, is conflicted about his business dealings with the man. He is equally weary of his smarmy foil, Emerson Brooksby, but is learning to understand that he can separate his business from his personal life. He never had an issue with that in the past, but somehow between all the religious talk and psychological babble— both shortcuts for double-talk—he let his guard down. Not anymore.

Marvel sees Zoo laughing and joking with a handful of guests who are standing by one of the warmly lit fireplaces. Marvel slowly strolls over to where Zoo is entertaining. Pat, Biz, Christina, and a few of the others notice and follow him over.

"Hey, listen. After all this, I just wanted to ask you something," John says to Herman as he looks at the remaining guests gathered around the room. "Are we still friends?"

Zoo looks at him funnily, surprised by the question. "Of course we are." He nervously notes the increasingly strange tone in Marvel's voice. "Why do you ask?"

"So it won't upset you when I ask you to leave," John informs him firmly and cordially, but with finality.

"What?" Zoo replies, obviously flustered. He looks first at John and then to Christina for support, but she's only firing back the I-can't-believe-how-much-you-disappointed-me look, which is usually reserved for her husband and which is now hitting Herman like an Apache attack copter assault.

John turns around to walk back into the house to begin the mental process of putting this all into some kind of context and trying to figure out just what the fuck happened.

"John," Zoo calls out. "Wait a minute. I want to talk to you."

John turns, and walks straight back to Herman Zoo, getting right into his face. "You're leaving."

Zoo takes a step back, looks up, and waves Bev over. He takes her hand, and they excuse themselves from the party. He watches as John turns and then goes back inside the house.

✳ ✳ ✳

Marvel closes the door behind him. Once John is inside, Leo pulls him aside to a place where they have some privacy to talk. Most of the guests have left or are leaving now, and the activity is winding down.

"Hey, just want to say I appreciate what you did for us tonight and everything we discussed," Leo tells him. "Maybe it's the chance I need."

"Just take care of that girl. She looks like a keeper. I'll be in touch. We'll figure out how to work you in and get you a share of this deal."

"That sounds good. We appreciate what you're trying to do," Leo says, and then he turns to leave the party for the night with Maggie. Outside, before they get too far away from the door, Leo remembers something he forgot to tell John. They stop. He returns to the house to tell him one more thing.

"I'll be back tomorrow morning to take out all the bombs and IEDs I placed around the house and outside in the yard," Leo says calmly, without a hint of alarm. "They are only set to go off on my detonation, so we should be fine. Just don't mess with anything unusual you find lying around. Wait until I get back. Thanks again. Have a great evening."

John looks at Christina and shakes his head. He closes the door after Leo and Maggie leave.

"I think I'll probably be up all night. I'll be awake and sitting on the couch if you need me," John jokes with Christina, who is clearly anxious about Leo's claim. "I don't think he's the kind of person who would have booby-trapped the sofa."

Christina can barely smile. She looks and feels exhausted, but nevertheless she maintains her stunning, albeit tired, appearance.

"I'm going to take my chances with the bedroom," she says, beginning to walk slowly up the stairs. She won't have to start planning for next year's gala Christmas event for at least a few more months. Now she can lay herself down to get some sleep.

Between all the wine and all the confusing talk, however, she isn't sure when she prays just whose soul should be kept.

Chapter 20

Harmony

Maggie watches as Leo picks up the bag of dog food from the pantry and carries it over to the kitchen counter. As he sets it down and rips open the top, she offers her observation.

"Have you noticed it looks like she's put on a few pounds?" she asks, referring to Flagler, Leo's—and now her—dog. "Pick her up. She's heavier. There's no way she's still only fourteen pounds."

Leo looks at Maggie and then down at Flagler. "She looks fine to me," he then adds in his sweetly hushed, kiddie-voice tone. "Don't ya, my little girl? You're not fat, are you? You tell Maggie that. You just look *healthy.*" He reaches down and rubs her head behind the ears.

Maggie shakes her head and smiles. "Okay," she says, grabbing her purse off the counter. "Gotta run. See you tonight, honey."

She walks over, kisses him on the cheek, turns, and bounces down the foyer and out the door.

❋ ❋ ❋

Something happened when they stood together by that door at the Marvel mansion that evening. As they walked back inside from the cold outdoors, where they'd met, neither of them was expecting what happened between them. When they finally summoned the nerve to face each other, he softly stroked her face and they were overcome. It was a terrifying moment, to be sure, when the sexuality, seduction, and intimacy were all crashing down, happening all around them. And that was the great thing about it.

There were so many things happening, so many ideas and actions they had in common, the same thoughts and fears—that it made their chance encounter, and subsequent partnership, all sort of confusing and exciting and scary. But they were both game to give it a shot.

After what they'd already dodged, and now living with the choices they never dreamed they would make, Leo and Maggie knew they could only keep removing themselves from the realities of life just so many times before the rage would finally engulf their better selves. Leo, just a few short months ago, would never have believed he'd be where he is today. Sure, it's nothing fancy, but having a nice place to call home, a great, supportive woman at his side, and a great dog following his every move is a whole lot more than he ever dreamed of. And he thinks hard and often about so many of the innocent lives he might have taken, including his own, if it hadn't been for the very strange convergence of personalities at the Marvel Christmas party. With the envoys from the worlds of religion, science, spirituality, paranormal clairvoyance, evangelistic fawning, hero worship, cynicism, resentment, betrayal, mass murder, and revenge all drinking together and pretending to enjoy each other's company, it was certainly a moment of clarity for Leo, and for Maggie too.

The house is quiet except for the background noise of the television steadily humming away. Leo takes a bottle of water out of the refrigerator and plops down on the couch in front of the TV. Flagler jumps up next to him.

Leo watches a cable news show. The anchor is barking about breaking news somewhere in another town in America. Is the next story going to be about people killed in a theater shooting or about a school in lockdown because of a bomb or shooting threat? Is it another white cop shooting another black teenager? Is it a slow-speed chase that lasts for hours on a somehow easily navigable Southern California highway? Has ISIS or a lone-wolf terrorist committed another unspeakable act?

Does it really matter? Leo looks blankly at the program and wonders to himself: if he had carried out his plan, would he be the breaking news story of the day? Whom would reporters dig up to interview? What secrets from his past would they find and report on? How fairly and accurately would they tell *his* story? Would anyone ever know or even care about who the real Leonardo Rickenbacker was?

Leo laughs out loud to himself and pets Flagler on the back, thereafter rubbing her head. He watches the rubbish for a few more seconds and then clicks the station over to something much more appropriate and far less likely to stir his rage, which is now securely capped and immune to the types of television and media reports that once served as his fuel.

"Look at that, Flagler." He points Flagler toward a chef on the Travel Channel who is making a quick version of a croque monsieur—the delicious ham and Gruyère cheese sandwich fried in butter on a crusty, thin-sliced, brioche-like bread.

"You see this," Leo says to no one in particular, but especially to his dog, while watching the show. "Had I known this sandwich existed out there in the world"—he smiles broadly and sits back comfortably in his sofa—"I would *never* have gotten so angry and worked up over all that other stuff. Just look at that thing. It's amazing."

The chef plates and completes the presentation of the croque monsieur, arranging it on the table. He cuts a beautifully toasted piece of the delectable treat with his knife and puts the food in his mouth, his eyes closed in blissful absorption. When he opens his eyes, he looks right into the camera. Paraphrasing a well-timed Thoreau quote, he soulfully tells his viewers, "Dare to live the life you've imagined. In so doing, you will meet with success unexpected in the common hours."

Leo gives the quote some thought and smiles, nodding as he looks at Flagler, who is sitting next to him, just thrilled to be there. He takes a sip from his water bottle and eases back to enjoy something he hasn't in a long, long time—a lazy, relaxing afternoon at home without a worry on his mind.

Success unexpected in the common hours, he thinks, sighing. "I think I get it."

Feeling pretty good wasn't such a bad thing after all.

Acknowledgments

Scripture quotations are taken from the English Revised Version of the Bible. Copyright © 2001 by Bible League International. All rights reserved.